To my parents, Jaseup and Young Il Kim,
who always told me stories.

To Rob, who makes real life better than fiction,
even for a dreamer like me.

EVERYTHING
BELONGS TO US

EVERYTHING BELONGS TO US

A Novel

YOOJIN GRACE WUERTZ

RANDOM HOUSE

NEW YORK

Copyright © 2017 by Yoojin Grace Wuertz

All rights reserved.

Published in the United States by Random House, an imprint and division of Penguin Random House LLC, New York.

RANDOM HOUSE and the HOUSE colophon are registered trademarks of Penguin Random House LLC.

Library of Congress Cataloging-in-Publication Data
Names: Wuertz, Yoojin Grace, author.
Title: Everything belongs to us : a novel / Yoojin Grace Wuertz.
Description: First edition. | New York : Random House, 2016.
Identifiers: LCCN 2016012226 | ISBN 9780812998542 |
ISBN 9780812998559 (ebook)
Subjects: LCSH: College students—Fiction. | Nineteen seventies—Fiction. | Friendship—Fiction. | Ambition—Fiction. | Motivation (Psychology)—Fiction. | Sæoul Taehakkyo—Fiction. | Seoul (Korea)—Fiction. | Psychological fiction.
Classification: LCC PS3623.U37 E95 2016 | DDC 813/.6—dc23
LC record available at https://lccn.loc.gov/2016012226

Printed in the United States of America on acid-free paper

randomhousebooks.com

2 4 6 8 9 7 5 3 1

First Edition

Title page image: copyright © iStock.com / © SUN-A

Book design by Victoria Wong

I

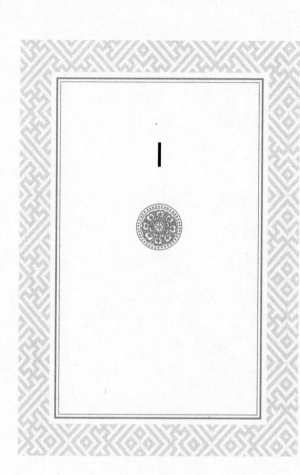

1

Seoul, 1978

They had come to the roof for three days to watch the strike at the Mun-A textile factory. It was April, the early mornings still damp and gray, the sky a ragged blanket thrown over the city. In the pre-dawn, the women gathered like ghosts around the factory yard and formed rows as if on lines etched into the concrete. They sat shoulder to shoulder, close enough to link arms and share warmth. The drumming began with the sun. At first the rhythm was simple, almost laconic. *Pum-pum-pum-pum.* The pulse rolled over the street like slow thunder, beckoning. By seven thirty, the strike had mustered full force. Three hundred women in khaki uniforms overflowed the narrow yard onto the sidewalk, fists in the air, chanting, shouting, singing. Neighborhood workers watched from behind windows, as if still under curfew. Pedestrians hurried to cross the street.

Dull tan slacks, matching blouse, and navy kerchief: They were an industrial army trained to sew buttonholes and block seams with military precision and discipline. Throughout the city each morning, the public loudspeakers broadcast the president's slogans: *Work cheerfully, courageously, for a more prosperous nation! Let's be industrial soldiers for a brighter future!* If the thrust of the rallying cry was somewhat diminished by the staticky sound quality, more warbling than exalting, no one was surprised. As with most aspects of President Park Chung Hee's administration, the objective—and the means—called for force, not finesse. The industrial army did not need a special sound system. It needed earlier mornings, later nights, unity, focus. Sacrifice. Sacrifice. Sacrifice.

So these were the soldiers. Skinny, pale-faced girls and women built like furniture, all limbs and angles. Even in protest, they maintained orderly ranks, churning out dissent with the same single-minded efficiency with which they had created cheap exports for Western markets. They marched in unison, danced in unison. They shouted in antiphonal ecstasy, two megaphones leading the call-and-response that never flagged. When individual voices grew ragged and hoarse, fresh voices took up the amplifiers, rejuvenating the whole. And the drums beat on like a sonic spine.

From a distance, their rigid organization made them appear simultaneously mighty and destructible. They were a focused defiance, conspicuous and easy to stomp.

Guarantee basic labor rights!

We are not machines!

Throw out the illegal union election!

Union revote!

On the roof across the street, Sunam and his new *sunbae*, Juno, stood watch. Juno Yoon was a year above Sunam at Seoul National University, the most prestigious college in the country, and Sunam vigilantly took cues from the older boy. Just getting to SNU was an accomplishment, requiring a grueling entrance exam that demanded years of around-the-clock preparation. Succeeding there put you in a different category altogether—it was a chance to become part of the professional elite. The best students transformed from pimply, stressed-out nineteen-year-olds to national assemblymen, judges, doctors, *chaebol* business leaders, and famous scientists. And the fastest ticket to success was gaining entry to a special group known only as the Circle—a kind of social club, founded by the heir to an enormous shipping fortune. Juno was already a member. As Sunam's *sunbae*, Juno was meant to be his elder, mentor, initiator. Sunam might squirm under the older boy's brash shows of authority, but as the younger, or *hubae*, he had a lot to gain from being considered Juno's protégé.

"Look alive, Sunam," barked Juno. Sunam snapped his eyes open as wide as he could. In the previous days, the chanting had grown so embedded in his consciousness that he lay awake at night frantic with exhaustion while the echoes of slogans cycled relentlessly through his mind. After years of rigorous exam preparations, he was no stranger to painful mornings, to burning eyelids and limbs that felt waterlogged with sleep, but dragging himself here for this third day had taken more willpower than any other morning of his life. *You are lucky,* he told himself in the sternest mental voice he could muster. *You have an opportunity ten thousand young men would gladly snatch from your hands. You made it. Now climb.*

It was 1978, only a generation after the end of the Korean War, which had flattened Seoul to a pile of rubble. Almost every family had been touched by recent memories of poverty. Sunam's family had been relatively well-off, but even he could call to mind the lean years of his childhood. While he had never been forced to skip any meals, he remembered the gnawing preoccupation with food, always hungry for more. At school, his first- and second-grade teachers served gruel, ladling out extra portions for the skinnier, clearly malnourished kids with their eyes huge in their heads, their skin white and flaky with a kind of fungal infection that seemed rampant in those days. He often wondered what had become of those classmates, if their families had managed to pull themselves up.

So a university degree might not have meant the difference between life and death, but for Sunam it meant a job in an office rather than a factory or steel mill. It meant the ability to buy an apartment in a new, high-rise development equipped with indoor plumbing, a kitchen installed with a washing machine, a TV in the living room, and—one day, perhaps—a car. And Juno was not just any *sunbae,* but a personal friend of Min Ahn, founder of the Circle. All of the Circle's members were hand-selected by Min and his cronies. The bullying, the twenty-four-hour demands, the nonsense ritual humiliations—it was all part of the process. A survival game. If he made it, Sunam would gain entry into a rarefied world of status and privilege. If he failed, he'd be a nobody. No connections, no tribe. He would stay in that middle heap of life—better off than most, perhaps—while his lucky peers broke away into unimaginable echelons.

To survive, there was just one rule: obedience. Blind. Unflinching. Total.

THIRTEEN HOURS THE first day. The second, fourteen and a half. The predawn mornings, the thunderous drumming, the eye-watering monotony of watching three hundred women in the throes of misplaced democracy—it was all terrible and life draining, uncomfortable, boring, tedious. What were they doing here? Why this place, this strike? Sometimes hours would pass in stultifying silence. *Watch,* Juno would say, but nothing more. Watch for what? Sunam knew better than to ask, but the boundless uncertainties filled him with panic. Surely he was missing something of critical importance. Something crucial to his future, which he would learn only in retrospect and regret for the rest of his life. From the moment he greeted Juno in the morning, bowing ninety degrees from the waist, to the final moments of shadowing him an exact half step behind to his bus stop home at night, Sunam wrung his mind for clues. There was nothing.

Eight o'clock. Juno observed the scene below with a hand shielding his eyes against the glare of the sun. Built like a judo wrestler, Juno was thick and short, with biceps that strained against the fabric of his windbreaker. He had a soft, murmuring voice, which could sound deceptively contemplative even as he cut to the bone. "This is the third day, Sunam," he said in his way, the octogenarian to a toddler. "I hope you've gathered some conclusions."

Sunam cleared his throat. "About the strike?"

"Yes, Sunam. About the strike."

"It seems nothing has changed."

"Does it. What else?"

"They seem well organized."

"Well organized to strike in front of their place of work, you mean."

"Yes."

"Sunam, I know you're a smart guy. When I ask you what conclusions you've reached, it's because I assume you've considered the various possible outcomes. Now. I'm tired of this two-word baby nonsense. What conclusions have you reached? And be smart about it."

So this is what he should have prepared for—an analysis of the strike. Sociopolitical ramifications. Labor. Leadership. Democracy. He had been so busy thinking about himself that he had not bothered to consider those angles. Strikes were what you walked past every day in Seoul. Small, big, the same one, a different one. For most people trying to live their lives and stay out of trouble, strikes were simply obstacles to avoid. Some people might feel a perverse desire to stand by and gawk, but reasonable folks didn't want to risk getting mixed up with the crowd and possibly taken for a sympathizer or fellow activist. Same for the campus demonstrations at SNU and other universities, called "demos" for short. The campus demos were more political and less practical in nature than the labor strikes—protesting the president's repressive Yushin Constitution and demanding transparent, democratic elections. Sunam considered these issues the domain of hippies destined for lives on the fringe, not for him. What conclusions had he reached? Sunam had less than a second to think, and he blurted out the only thing that came to mind.

"I don't care about the strike, really. My conclusions were possibly that you were a labor sympathizer or had some interest in factory girls. They're not too bad to look at, I guess. Some of them are kind of pretty."

Juno's expression did not change, which Sunam took to be an auspicious sign under the circumstances. "Some of them? Tell me which."

"Well, I didn't exactly make a list."

"And this is your serious answer?"

Sunam chewed his lip, regretting his moment of flippancy. "No."

"Then try again. Tell me what you see."

"I see factory workers demanding better conditions. I see that if they don't get back to work, they'll probably lose their jobs and have to go back to their families in the country."

"And?"

"The factory will easily replace them."

Juno looked at him closely. "We've been here three days. Do you really not know?"

Sunam froze. A bad idea to bluff. Slowly he shook his head.

"Activists, Sunam. Some of those girls are college students. Some are even from SNU. They go underground and work in the factories, pretending they're like anyone else, but they organize strikes and union votes."

"Is that legal?"

"No, of course not."

"But even so, what does that have to do with us?" Sunam asked. "You're not a labor sympathizer, are you? What difference does it make if some of the workers are students?"

"I happen to have an interest in one of the students," Juno said enigmatically. "I like to keep an eye on her."

"An interest? Are you . . . in love with one of them?"

Suddenly Juno let out a booming laugh, which stung Sunam as much as being slapped in the face. "You really are a baby, aren't you? Love? Is that so important to you?"

"I know someone like you doesn't just take 'an interest' in a girl for no reason," Sunam said, attempting to flatter Juno's ego. "Who is it? Will you tell me?"

"I intend to marry this girl," Juno said matter-of-factly. "You'll laugh if I say it's fate, but she and I are fated to be together. I've known it since I was a ten-year-old boy. It's the perfect partnership and I intend to see it happen."

"This sounds like love to me, *sunbae*," said Sunam.

Juno shook his head. "You haven't heard me," he said. "Not love, Sunam. Just good planning."

THE HOURS OF the morning passed in the same monotony he had endured over the past two days. The women yelled. The drums clattered and crashed. Pedestrians streamed by. Juno barely spoke a word, giving no further indication of what they might be looking for.

It was uncomfortable on the roof with nowhere to sit except the hard, dirty floor. Sunam felt his eyes burning with boredom. The ceaseless noise settled into the recesses of his eyes and temples, stirring a fierce headache that made his vision hazy with pain. Juno seemed impervious to the ruckus, as if he were enclosed in a soundproof capsule. Sunam tried to imagine what sort of girl would inspire such stoic concentration. He assumed she must be very beautiful for Juno to overlook the fact that she was an activist.

At lunchtime, Juno sent him to bring up noodles from the restaurant downstairs. "Hot noodles in soup. Don't spill." The idea was to bring it back up as quickly as possible so that it was still steaming when he arrived. There were four flights and a roof exit, no elevator. The restaurant *ajummas,* wary of customers' complaints about stinginess, filled the enormous steel bowls to the brim. It was impossible not to spill.

Sunam was ascending the final flight with the heavily laden tray, sweating from the effort of simultaneously rushing and holding still, when he heard the drums kick up as if someone had suddenly removed a sound barrier. The bass hit him in the chest like a fist. Scalding soup splayed over his hands and shirt. Cursing, he abandoned the tray and ran the rest of the way, taking the steps two at a time. On the roof, noise overtook everything. The drumming was ramped to a frenetic tempo, reverberating against his rib cage, bouncing beneath his feet. The chanting rose like a groundswell, an intensity so fierce that it could only be described as a roar.

He ran to Juno, who was leaning on the roof to take in the full scope of the street. "What's happening?" he asked. His voice was immediately swallowed by the noise.

"Cops," Juno shouted.

They strained over the edge of the roof to catch the line of gray police vans pushing through the street. Red lights whirled over the sidewalk. The eagle police insignia multiplied over every surface as cops rushed out of vehicles. Traffic was stopped and metal barricades erected. Already clots of bystanders, who evidently had nowhere better to go and did not mind risking their own skins for the sake of witnessing a spectacle, were jostling for position.

The protest drums beat on louder, faster, against the encroaching line. Banners rippled and bobbed like a platoon of sails.

Guarantee basic labor rights!

We are not machines!

Throw out the illegal union election!

Union revote!

"Watch," Juno said in a low voice.

Men in riot gear streamed out of the vans with a terrible clatter of body-length metal shields and helmets. They moved like automatons, pre-choreographed and bulky in their thick leg and arm padding. In minutes they had flanked the gate, six deep. Dark blue uniforms showed up flat and rich against the faded factory khaki. Light glinted off their visors and helmets. With silent precision they planted their shields at their boots, resting white padded gloves over the edge in a posture of casual aggression. The movement unfolded in increments, suggesting the next step, building fear. The effect was of a slow, calculated escalation.

Below, a male voice boomed from a bullhorn. It was the factory foreman in shiny black pants and company jacket, his large bald spot creeping out from beneath the bottom of his cap. "Ladies, you know this is an illegal protest. Let's just get up and go home, shall we? Take the day off. We'll get back to work tomorrow. Better yet, get to work now. We'll get in a half day at least. You know what happens next. These men would rather not work up a sweat. Let's not tire ourselves out for no reason. . . ."

Across the yard, the drums took on the slow, predawn beat. *Pum. Pum. Pum. Pum.*

The foreman's voice warbled from the bullhorn. "This is your last warning."

The riot police stood ready, shields raised. A line of cops in regular uniform moved in, batons in hand. In the front row of the strike there was a sudden flash of movement. A young woman stepped away from the line, pulling the khaki blouse from her body and dropping it at her feet. Her white bra stood out for a speechless moment before it too was unclasped and thrown to the ground. For that instant, all there was was her body. Flesh. Pale breasts. Heaving rib cage. Her black hair was wild against her skin. Raising her fist, she resumed the chant.

The effect on the ground was immediate. Cops froze mid-movement. The crowd seemed to lurch toward the topless woman, the collective attention shifting violently to her body. Sunam let out a gasp, stunned by the unfolding scandal.

All around the first topless woman, her colleagues were following suit. Garments fell like discarded skin to the ground. Young, old, thin, heavy, pale, dark, taut, women stood with their breasts bared, united in defiance. The chanting hushed. Drums fell silent. No one moved. The sirens continued to spin, splashing red lights over the scene, but for an extended moment the women were captured in perfect stillness. They had become inviolable, their determination stronger than any army. A young voice screamed, "You call yourself men, attacking unarmed women? Touch us now if you dare."

The first man out was powerfully built, with short arms and thick, muscular legs. He moved in with firm, measured steps as if to say, *Look, I'm coming. You've had your fun, now it's over.* When he grabbed the young woman by the arm, low near her wrist—a small mitigation toward her exposure—his manner was brisk, almost paternal. Sunam sensed the danger brewing under the surface, the kind of final-warning patience he recognized from his own father before a total explosion.

It happened so quickly, he could process it only in retrospect. Wresting out of the officer's grip, raising her fist against him, the young woman spit in his face. Sunam saw the unmistakable jerk of her head, the split-second delay. Then the response. The officer tackled her to the ground, folding her body under his as easily as if she were a reed. He had her under his knees, her face and chest pushed against the ground. His fists came down between her shoulder blades—three sharp blasts—until she went limp.

The rest of the force rushed in. With only their bodies for weapons, the women threw themselves on the ground in an attempt to make themselves heavy. They clung to anything stationary and entangled themselves around each other's waists like lovers. The men pried them apart with boots and batons and dragged them across the street into the waiting vans, two men to each girl, hoisting her by the wrists and ankles. Others who ran were herded back. The youngest workers hid their faces from the staring crowd and sobbed against each other's slumped shoulders. One woman fainted and was laid out on the asphalt, her face strangely composed in the midst of the blood and havoc.

There were girls who fought every step, who struggled and clawed and kicked to hold ground. One woman twisted like a trout on the line, her body a heaving muscle in protest. She was nearly naked, dark nipples flashing and the waistband of her pale pink underwear pulled low over her hips. Finally the men swung her down and kicked her until she curled up tight, arms wrapped overhead, exposing the pale contours of her ribs.

There was no more center. Each was fighting for herself, running for herself. After so much noise, individual shrieks evaporated like weak echoes. There were hands everywhere, grabbing the easiest circumference: shoulders, necks, ankles, thighs. Clothed or naked, it made no difference. Everywhere, bloodied women were being pushed into vans. Behind the barricades, the mob grew rowdy.

Sunam felt simultaneously paralyzed and hypercharged, as if his muscles would jump out of his skin and plunge into the mob below. The memory of those women, statuesque and strong, standing their ground against uniformed police, already seemed like a dream.

"The cars are full," he said to Juno. He was surprised to realize his voice was steady and unchanged, as if nothing had happened. "They can't take all of them."

"They'll grab enough."

"Enough—for what?"

"To make an example. Enough to get names on a blacklist. Those women will never work again in Seoul. Effective, I'd say." Juno glanced at him. "Shocked? Get used to it, Sunam. Power always wins. That's life."

"So this is what you wanted me to see? Girls being beat up?"

Juno made a strange sound, sucking his teeth and releasing air in an explosive click as if closing a lid on the whole pathetic situation. "Don't be melodramatic. I didn't know this was going to happen. But it's a good lesson for you, anyway. You see how it is when people make stupid decisions. They were in enough trouble as it is and now they've only made things worse for themselves. Bad gamble. They should have been smarter."

"But that girl you're interested in—"

"Is none of your concern at the moment."

"Did you see her? Was she . . ." It seemed too personal to ask if she was one of the women who had taken off her clothes. Surely Juno would not like to answer that question. Instead Sunam stuttered, "I mean, what if she got hurt? Were you able to see . . . ?"

"She'll be fine," Juno answered curtly. "I told you, don't worry about it."

"But I could help you," said Sunam. "If you needed me to do something. I could go down there. I could deliver a message or—whatever you needed."

Juno stared at him with unconcealed puzzlement. "Sunam, I can't decide if you're incredibly idiotic or some kind of savant. You must be a genius to be this dense. Do you actually think I want her to *know* I'm watching her? You think I'm going to send you down there to deliver a message? Tell me, what kind of note did you have in mind? 'I know you're in the middle of a police raid and all, but I just want you to know I have my eye on you'? Use your brain, man." For a second, Sunam thought Juno would reach over and slap him as if he were a delinquent fifth grader who had failed to do his homework. Juno sighed. "Anyway, even if I wanted to send a message, what makes you think I would trust you with something so important? You haven't even managed to deliver a bowl of soup correctly—" Sunam suddenly remembered the lunch he had abandoned on the stairs. It had slipped his mind completely.

Sunam knew his face must have turned deeply crimson. The burn spread over his cheeks and blazed down his neck. Hot tendrils of shame wrapped around his throat. Of course Juno wouldn't want to reveal his position to the girl. He, unlike Sunam, conducted his life with calculated, measured calm. He would never rush into impetuous action with some puerile idea of rescue. Just thinking about what he had suggested flushed Sunam with a new wave of mortification. "I'm sorry, *sunbae*. You're right, I wasn't thinking. But give me another chance. I know I can do better. Let me do something to prove it to you. Anything."

Juno peered down at the mob below, apparently considering his proposal. Sunam braced himself for whatever difficult task would be required of him. This time, he would not let his *sunbae* down. No matter what was asked of him, he would approach it with the utmost care and seriousness.

"Doesn't seem to be clearing up anytime soon," Juno murmured. "It'll be a mess for a while."

"Are you going somewhere? Would you like me to hail you a cab?"

"Me? No, *I'm* fine where I am," said Juno with an exaggerated drawl. He grinned. Whatever he had in mind, he was enjoying himself. "But you seem eager to get places. Bet you've never seen a naked girl up close, eh? Go ahead, Sunam. Enjoy yourself. Grab yourself a souvenir while you're at it. I'll wait."

"A souvenir?"

"Sure. I see a bunch of ladies' underwear lying about. Of course, it's nothing fancy, but you're not picky, are you?" He had never seen his *sunbae* look so happy; it was a task that had no purpose other than to humiliate Sunam. "I don't want you saying I never taught you anything."

"You want me to bring up . . . underwear?" he asked incredulously.

"And be quick about it," Juno said in his normal voice. "After that you're going to get me another bowl of soup."

2

. . . .

Four flights had seemed an interminable distance just a short while ago, but now Sunam wished it were much longer to save him from the humiliation of this fool's errand. He paused on the step where the now congealed noodles remained where he'd left them. Yellow gray floes of fat clung to the bloated dough. Slimy onions lay slick and sweaty on the thickened broth. Only recently this had been a delicious meal. Now it was an inedible wreck. Somehow the awful state of the noodles seemed to mirror the mess he was always making of his own life. What should have been a pleasure turned grotesque. So much wasted potential.

He had no choice but to go forward. *Let me prove myself,* sunbae. *Ask me anything. Let me, let me!* Downstairs in the lobby the door was crowded with onlookers, all the building's employees and customers smashed up against the windows to catch a glimpse of the action. More police vehicles were arriving, sirens flashing. The first vans must be packed by now, but uniformed men were still herding the workers into custody and fighting back the crowd, which was growing thicker and more unruly. Sunam shoved his way to the building's exit, still hoping to get out. The closer he got, the more unwilling people became to give up their spot, pushing him back with dirty looks as if to say they had paid good money to get these seats.

"I need the door. I'm leaving." Sunam jabbed desperately at the air above his head, illustrating how quickly he intended to disappear. "The door," he shouted again. The folks guarding their positions finally relented, letting him pass.

Immediately the crowd swallowed him up and swept him toward the barricades, the crush as powerful as a dragging riptide. Sunam threw his weight against it, but it was no use. There were moments when he felt his feet lifting off the ground, a sickening lurching sensation he had never experienced even during the worst commuting times. This was not a simple matter of too many people in a limited space. This was havoc fueled by the dark electric buzz of violence, the giddy tinge of sex.

People he could smell but not see were shouting in his ears. Boots connected sharply with his ankle. His feet were trampled. A throaty voice yelled, "Move it!" and someone else laughed, a high, hysterical pitch. There were long minutes when nothing moved, every shoulder and elbow jammed in gridlock, followed by sudden slides when the crowd heaved in a collective stumble. These were the times to maneuver if he could anticipate them and move quickly. He tried to identify a path out, but the street was narrow and his only recourse was to push against the flow of the mob, back toward what must be its end. From the roof he had seen where it started, where it thickened and became a throng, but once he had stepped out onto the street, there was no sense of dispersing or ending. He was stuck in the middle, unable either to escape or to get what he'd come for.

Sunam saw a wedge of space opening up in front of him and prepared himself. Maybe he could still make it to the barricades. And maybe once he got there the crowd, in view of the cops and contained by the metal gates, would be more manageable. With a huge effort, he twisted away from the shoulder lodged against him and hurled his weight into that tiny opening.

Brown mottled teeth sneered in his face. "Relax, college boy— enjoy the show. What, scared?"

Another voice. "Look at him, he's never seen a woman."

Sunam caught a flash of oily stubble. The second man had on a blue jacket identical to his friend's, same filthy sleeves. There were three of them, probably unemployed millworkers. The smell of their grease stung his nostrils.

"College boy, time to become a man!" Two stubby fingers jabbed at

Sunam's groin. A gurgle of a laugh, like a cough bringing up phlegm, sprayed in his face. The fingers jabbed him again, harder. "Wake up! Come back when you grow something."

With the pretext of being shoved themselves, they slammed their bodies into him, laughing. They hit him repeatedly, slapping his face and grabbing his crotch with exaggerated, fake apologies. He knew these types, workers who hated college students for their educated privilege, who believed their own working-class backgrounds earned them the right to harass anyone they wanted, to assuage their sense of inferiority. Sunam shoved back, trying to put bodies between them. But the crowd shrank away, leaving a halo of space around them.

Sunam was outnumbered three to one. The first guy was built like a ram, with a bulging brow bone and shoulders that seemed to round in with the weight of his muscles. "Get him a better view," he taunted. "Let him get his first eyeful, at least. Help him, boys. There are things you don't learn in college." They poked and prodded, delighted with their new toy. "A day off from school today, a field trip? No girlies at school want to show you any of this?" He mimed squeezing a pair of nipples. "No fun in the library?"

The others were smaller, barely any weight on them. If it weren't for their bullnosed leader, Sunam might have considered fighting. But pinned in with no exit and outnumbered, he knew it was useless. The big one was squinting at him with an appraising eye. He flicked his flat bovine nose, releasing a wet-sounding sniff. "Now. Let's have your jacket," he said.

Sunam wore a calfskin leather jacket, a graduation present from his parents. *Our proud firstborn. Wear it well.* The jacket fit him perfectly, the tan color creamy against his skin, the long sleeves and waist hitting his tall frame at just the right length. He felt like a young heir in that jacket, cosmopolitan and undeniably first-rate. The thought of losing it, and to these guys, made his jaws clench. "Funny," he said. "I think your jackets suit you perfectly."

"A sense of humor on this one," said Bullnose. "We won't kill you because you're funny. Now hand it over."

"Can't do it," Sunam said.

A blow landed between his shoulder blades. A jab, not hard enough to take him down but serious. When he turned around, there was a switchblade in his face.

"We won't ask you again."

Slowly Sunam shed the precious garment and handed it to the sidekick, the one with the knife. Bullnose grinned with his bad teeth. "Come on, fellas, we're done here." Now the crowd parted. They split to let the gang pass as if for a presidential motorcade, huge margins opening up like a sea parting. Then they were gone and the mob swallowed Sunam up again.

He didn't know how long it took for him to get beyond the crowd. It was like wriggling through a tunnel blind. He did it person by person, pushing past one set of shoulders, then another and another. Their scents seemed to rub off on him, smells that lingered in his nose long after he had left them behind. Drenched in sweat and shivering, he stumbled his way out. The sound of the police sirens, people hooting and shouting, receded so gradually that he couldn't pinpoint the exact moment it went away. Even after he faded into normal pedestrian traffic, he still sensed the roil of the horde as if they were pushed close behind him.

At the first empty alley, Sunam sat down and fumbled for a cigarette. He lit it with shaking hands and inhaled deeply, feeling the hot smoke travel down his chest. He finished it and lit a second, hoping that the fire and nicotine would spur him to go back and fulfill Juno's ridiculous task. He smoked it down to the last bit, his fingers pinched tight against his lips, but it was the same. No epiphanies, no new courage.

Slowly he got to his feet. Juno would be waiting. Going back empty-handed was like delivering a resignation letter when he desperately wanted the job. But not to show up at all—that was the ultimate cowardly act. To explain about the jacket would be just an excuse and make him look weak besides. He had failed. It didn't matter that it wasn't his fault, that it might have been impossible to do what Juno had asked. He already knew his *sunbae* was interested only in sending him on impossible errands, apparently to see how he coped with the humiliation of failure. There was no need to demean himself further with sad stories.

Sunam flicked the cigarette into the gutter and tucked in his shirt.

"Wait," a voice hissed from deep in the alley. *"Don't go."* Sunam looked behind him but saw nothing. He felt a queasy flicker of doubt—was he hearing things?

Then he saw her.

A young woman crouched behind a battered wooden pallet. She was barefoot and her khaki pants were shredded at the knees. Sunam saw a smear of blood on her bare shoulder. No shirt. He realized she must be one of the factory girls, escaped from the riot. She had somehow made it all the way out here in the initial chaos but could go no farther without attracting dangerous attention.

"Please help me." She was as small as a child, her body narrow enough to hide behind a box. She had the uncanny look of a hungry cat. Wide, unblinking eyes, as fierce as they were frightened. Warily he watched her, as if she might spring. She was as light as air. She could cover the distance between them in a single leap, disappear like a mirage. She said, her hands fluttering over the sharp ridge of her collarbones, "Please. If you could give me—I mean, I need—"

"How did you even get here?" he interrupted. They were at least five blocks from the factory.

"I ran." She had a gulping way of speaking that made her words sound swallowed rather than spoken. Glancing at him, she gave her head a slight shake as if he had asked her a confusing question. "Are they looking for me?"

"You should go home," he said. It seemed crazy that she should be lingering around here where anyone could see her. He remembered what Juno had said about the blacklist. "You should go home and say you weren't here at all."

"But—you see, I can't." She seemed emboldened by his mention of home. "I think there's a market around the corner. I can't give you any money now, but I'll send it to you, I swear."

He realized she was unwilling to say the word *shirt,* calling attention to her nudity, but that's what she needed. She could not come out of the alley and go home without it. A shirt.

He backed away. "I'm sorry—I can't," he mumbled.

He turned and ran, knowing she wouldn't—or couldn't—call after him. He told himself that someone else would come along to help her. A nice older *ajumma.* The girl was one of the lucky ones, after all. She had gotten away. All she needed was a shirt.

"I'm sorry!" He yelled it this time, buoyed by sudden inspiration. A shirt.

He ran around the corner to the market she'd mentioned. It was a small hole-in-the-wall store, the owner a grandmother who sat cross-legged on a low stool, eating an apple with big cracking bites.

"A lady's shirt," he said. He motioned toward his own chest as if that would clarify what he wanted. "An undershirt." He couldn't bring himself to say the word *bra.* An undershirt was good enough. It would do. He could rough it up and make it just right.

The grandmother motioned to the corner where she had them piled up, rubber-banded by size. Sunam picked the smallest one, sleeveless and stiff, a bit of lace at the neck. The new cotton was thick and glaringly white, but he already had a plan. He would soak it in the puddle outside, make a few tears. He would drag it along the curb and trample it until it was dingy and gray. He wondered if there was any way he could simulate blood.

He had the golden ticket. Finally he could proudly say to Juno, *Look,* sunbae, *I did as you asked.* He had completed the impossible task. And it had cost him less than a pack of cigarettes.

3
. . . .

After the arrests, the women said they had not planned to remove their shirts. That it had happened spontaneously: an act of last-resort defiance. When it began, Jisun was far from the center. She didn't know the woman who started it, but she felt the ground tilting as woman after woman threw off her shirt and linked arms with her neighbor, anchoring one another against the attack. She joined them, flinging off her shirt and bra, trampling the garments underfoot. Fused in a human chain of resistance.

In the vans, the police reprimanded them like children. *Is this how you girls were taught to behave? What*—ajumma, *you're too old for these shenanigans. Are you a mother, behaving like this?*

It was warm in the van with so many bodies pressed together, but some girls hugged themselves, shivering, their lips nearly white with the effort of holding back tears. Those who still had shirts or kerchiefs removed them and passed them on to the undressed women, leaving just a bra or undershirt for themselves. Jisun untied the kerchief from her hair and covered herself with it. It was almost sheer with sweat and useless. Remembering how terrified she had been at her first arrest, she wished she had something to offer the younger girls—if only just a smile or reassuring word—but they had withdrawn into themselves and would not meet her eyes. Someone started to sing. An older woman with a good folk voice, now hoarse from shouting. *Saeya, saeya palang saeya.* They had been singing it since the first day of the strike, a simple peasants' song asking the bird not to devour the crops. A minor-key lullaby, cyclical and easy on an empty stomach. But here in tight quarters, interpreted by this strong, rough voice, Jisun could see the sky and fields. She heard the farmer counting his plants, fearing a lean winter.

> *Hey, bird, don't sit in my field.*
> *If the green pea flower drops—*
> *The merchant will go crying.*

"Why do we sing this song?" Jisun asked. "It's not the bird's fault for eating."

The singing woman had started again— *"Saeya, saeya . . ."*—but stopped at Jisun's question. "It's not the farmer's fault for hating the bird either."

"All the more reason," Jisun said. "We need a different song."

If they were going to sing such a song, she wanted to hear herself in the story.

The woman picked up again and sang it through to the end. She hummed a few bars of the beginning. It was a song that could not end at the end. A song that demanded repetition.

"Bird and farmer, natural enemies. Old, old song."

"But you see, we need to have a *different* cycle, because it's not natural for *us*—"

Jisun couldn't finish because of the way the woman was looking at her.

"That's the difference between you students and us," the *ajumma* said quietly. "You students think everything is an argument. We have to work to eat, we can't just quibble with words all the time. Old songs are for comfort, not ideology."

"But I agree with you, *ajumma*," Jisun protested. "I'm critical of these attitudes just as much as you are. I only meant we have an opportunity to represent a different message. Something stronger that might go further in clarifying our demands. . . ."

A smile played across the older woman's lips. "Do you want to debate me, then, right here and now? Wait, we better organize a meeting and take a vote," she said. Despite the clear sarcasm, there was a calm and gentle quality to her voice, as if she were simply explaining a fairy tale to a child. "But first we must collect everyone's suggestions for better songs. This could take a while. We should also make sure to elect a proper leader of this committee."

Without raising her voice or even letting the harsh edge of bitterness creep into her words, the woman had perfectly won her point. Jisun felt her heart slamming against her chest, her face prickling with shame. She wanted to say so many things: about how she was not just a student playing activist for fun. Or the kind of student activist who spouted philosophy and argued theories all day long. Protests quivered on the tip of her tongue: *I've given up everything to be here. I share your position exactly.* But it was not true—they were not in the same position, nor would they ever be. And Jisun had committed the cardinal error: lecturing without permission or proper experience. Forcing amends now would not help.

Jisun bowed in apology. Her father had taught her this. To condemn her mistakes with the strongest possible conviction. To never let anyone defeat her with shame.

"You're right, *ajumma*. We call people like me *mongmul*."

Mongmul, diluted ink. People who pretended intellectual superiority in activism but barely lifted a finger to work.

Patting her arm, the *ajumma* picked up the refrain where she'd left off. "*Saeya, saeya* . . ." Little bird, little bird . . . Singing, rocking, she held on to Jisun's arm for a long time—an intimate gesture, maternal and possessive—as if to say, *This one I claim, I accept.*

The air inside the van grew heavy. Sweat dripped and pooled between Jisun's breasts. But the hand stayed on her arm, firm and dry.

Jisun's father, Ahn Kiyu, owned the largest shipping conglomerate in South Korea. Three years younger than the president, he would proudly point out that, like Park, he was a self-made man from a humble family. To Jisun's father, Park Chung Hee was half brother, half deity. Never an affectionate or expressive man, he loved Park with a nearly boyish infatuation. Jisun was just a toddler in 1961 when Park—

then general, not president—staged his military coup, but she had been raised on stories of Park the way other children were plied with fables and nursery rhymes.

"Think what it meant to be among the poorest countries in the world," Jisun's father would say. "Wondering how long we'd be trapped in this fate when all our politicians and so-called leaders could do was kowtow to foreign governments, begging for aid. Licking their boots as if we were starving dogs with no plans of our own. But President Park had the vision to say, *No, we will be modern and autonomous. We will have a national economy using our own resources, our own power.* What do you think it meant for us to hear that? He gave this country back to the people."

Even as a young girl, she found it strange to hear her father describe their country as among the poorest in the world. Jisun was not blind—she saw the beggars in the street and the children, younger than she was, who fought one another to be allowed to polish a passerby's shoes for a couple of pennies. Skinny, bedraggled boys darted around traffic all day, hoping to sell bits of stolen candy and gum to pedestrians and drivers at intersections. But even before the Ahn family moved to the big mansion on the cliffs overlooking central Seoul, Jisun and her brother, Min, had never known a single moment of feeling poor. They had always had more than enough, more than she was comfortable admitting to her classmates at school, who seemed to envy her and treat her differently because she had better clothes, a telephone and TV at home, and even a private family car.

But it was not until Jisun started middle school and met Namin Kang, who had to bus an hour every morning and afternoon from a poor, working-class neighborhood of Seoul called Miari, who seemed to know things that she, Jisun, had never thought about, that she began to feel differently about President Park. Their neighborhoods were only about ten miles apart, but Jisun lived in an estate amid lush gardens, whereas Namin lived without indoor plumbing or hot water. Jisun's father owned a huge company with so many employees that Jisun didn't know whether they numbered in the hundreds or thousands. Namin's parents ran a *pojangmacha*, a tented food cart that served cheap liquor and fried, spicy food from early morning to near midnight. Her older sister, Kyungmin, worked at a shoe factory.

Namin didn't like to talk about her family or living situation, but Jisun was nosy and persistent. She knew Namin sometimes lied to other schoolmates about where she lived or why she didn't have the things most girls at their school took for granted. Maybe it was because Jisun was so shamelessly curious about her friend's life, or maybe it was Namin's way of standing up for herself, of facing down some private, inward challenge, but she never seemed to lie to Jisun. It was a different kind of education. A powerful counterpoint against her father's narrative of the new South Korea led by President Park and supported by a hardworking and patriotic labor force, happy to toil away their days for the sake of national prosperity.

That year, President Park declared a state of national emergency, banning public demonstrations and enacting martial law. Jisun began to understand that the president beloved by her father was a tyrant. He had not "restored the country back to the Korean people," as her father claimed, but had taken it from them with threats of tanks and summary execution.

Over the next three years, there would be nine emergency decrees added to the constitution, the last of which prohibited any kind of antigovernment activity.

By 1975, Jisun was supposed to be preparing for her college exams, expecting to follow in her older brother's footsteps to Seoul National University. While pretending to show an interest in the campus, Jisun secretly soaked up the invisible thrum of collegiate activism. The demo groups had been driven underground, but she knew they were still active and present by the continual whiff of tear gas in the air and the riot soldiers stationed at the gate. Tattered remains of protest placards that had been torn down blew over the quad. Sometimes she

splatters of vomit and what they hoped was not blood, but there were too many of them to spare the space. Someone had to stand in the mess. Jisun, without meaning to, stopped short and let someone else be pushed into the worst of it.

She counted fifty-seven women in her cell and the adjoining ones, as far as she could see. They were standing nearly hip to hip. Sitting down was out of the question, unless they made a group effort to allow certain women to do so. Using the toilet would also require an announcement—unless you were unlucky enough to be standing near it already. How would they possibly spend the night like this, pressed together like caged livestock? At least the chickens in the market could breathe fresh air.

Of course, Jisun never found out.

It took less than an hour for the authorities to realize who she was and hurry her out of the cell into the office to wait. When the guard called her name, she already knew what to expect: she had been identified and would be released, as she had the other times. If she resisted, they would haul her out bodily. A punch line: Dragged in, dragged out. She would not let that happen. She would walk out on her own two feet, denying the cops that satisfaction, at least.

"Hurry up. Move it, princess."

In the long seconds it took to squeeze through the mass of bodies and through the unlocked cell gate, Jisun felt more exposed than if she were completely naked. The eyes of her fellow inmates bored into the back of her skull. The guard slammed the gate behind her, then checked the lock with an unnecessary jangle of keys. He shoved a stiff inmate's T-shirt in her hands and waited, leering, while she put it on.

Somebody yelled, "Hey! Where're you taking her! Guard, what'd *she* do?" A few other women took up the cry, shaking the bars and reaching for her hand.

The tears seemed to burn as they rushed down Jisun's cheeks. She had never cried at the police station, not even at her first arrest when she was certain they would treat her more harshly to make an example of her. How wrong she had been. It was true that the police hated student protesters, whom they viewed as overprivileged troublemakers. But contrary to her fears, Jisun's status as her father's daughter had set her apart in a different way. It made the authorities afraid to touch her, afraid to do anything that might incite Ahn Kiyu's displeasure and rain down inconvenient consequences on themselves.

The police had discovered who she was, but her fellow activists did not know, nor did they understand that she was being released. Whoever it was that had spoken up, a stranger, had thought Jisun was being singled out for something worse. By raising the alarm, the brave woman had risked being next.

"Sister!" the woman continued shouting after her. "Tell us your name so we can tell your people where you are. We will not let you be forgotten!"

Jisun wanted to beg the woman's forgiveness, to thank her for her courage and tell her not to worry. But she was too ashamed to attract further attention to herself, nor could she explain where she was really going. It was best to remain silent and hope the woman would soon forget about her.

She followed the guard through the holding area to the front of the station, an open area arranged with gray metal desks. There, another officer was waiting to collect her, a baby-faced young man who appeared flustered by her tears. Awkwardly he tried to pat her elbow as if she would be grateful, like a child separated from her parents at an amusement park. Undoubtedly this junior officer had been sent by his superiors to save face, told to do or say whatever was necessary to smooth out the "misunderstanding." The captains would hide behind their big desks and closed doors until Jisun was safely collected and kowtow to her father or whoever had made the call, promising that it would never happen again.

Never. Always. Jisun's father had a way of pulling those words out of people's mouths.

The young officer was trying to offer her a tissue. Jisun said,

"Do you think it's right, jailing honest women for exercising their rights?"

His expression hardened, aging him suddenly. "I know who you are and who your father is," he said roughly. "You made a fool of us— what right do you have? Not everything is your plaything. Not everything belongs to you."

4

Her father had sent his driver, Ko, a former dock employee who had gotten his left foot crushed in an accident six years ago. All the way to her father's house, Ko filled the rearview mirror with sour, disapproving looks. Jisun rolled down the window to let wind gust through the vehicle, disturbing his carefully oiled hair. Since his promotion, Ko had taken to affecting a "gentlemanly" appearance, which to him meant a 1930s Shanghai hairdo slicked to match the polish of his patent-leather shoes. In his early tenure he had also tried to grow a mustache, but Jisun's father forbade it. *I am a businessman, not a Mafia don.*

"Kindly give me advance notice of your next little spree," Ko said now, one hand tamped over his rebellious part. "I'm missing a visit to my mother."

"You should have gone to see her. I would have preferred that."

"I would have preferred that also. *Unfortunately—*"

"I know, Ko. I didn't choose this, either."

"Didn't you? Now close that window."

It was a strange thing, obeying the orders of her father's staff. Ko's loyalty to her father was absolute, and he seemed to take particular pleasure in thwarting her desires, as if each instance of shoving her back in line proved the strength of his devotion to the boss.

When they arrived at the house, he stopped the car in front of the first gate and waited while the heavy iron bars slid open. The machinery made a rumbling sound that always triggered a sense of panic in Jisun, a tightening in her chest that forced her to search for air. It had been three months since she'd left home to live in factory housing and work with the Urban Industrial Mission—a lifetime in some ways, but not long enough to override the years of feeling caged. There was beauty here, which she could plainly see and sometimes even admire: rare indigenous trees, a sunken garden with a duo of resident peacocks, and a pond glazed with lotus leaves as wide as circus rings. But after the months she'd stayed away, the carefully tended grounds no longer touched her. She had felt more life in words printed on cheap yellow paper, pages circulated and handled so often that they became translucent and tattered like lace. She read and reread the diaries of jailed workers, whose yearning for the education she took for granted shamed her to the core. She memorized poems by the dissident poets Kim Chi-ha and Ko Un, satirical lines so true they made her laugh aloud. These experiences—not the peacocks or the iron gates—had made her rich for the first time.

Pulling into the driveway, Ko said, "From this point forward you are to speak to me before leaving the grounds. Outside the house, he wants you to be accompanied at all times. There will be no exceptions."

But Jisun was only half listening. She was staring at the topiary in the front garden, which had been recently shaped so that the branches appeared to be balancing heavy plates. In her absence, even the shrubs had become servants. "I see the gardeners have developed a sense of humor," she said. "Very nice."

Ko loudly snapped his fingers inches from her face. "Did you hear what I said? You're to tell me before you go anywhere. I suggest you give me plenty of notice. I have no intention of being at your beck and call."

This time Jisun heard him. "But that's ridiculous," she protested. "How can I do that? I'd never go anywhere that way."

"I'm sure that would be my preference also."

"That's fine," she said. "I'll be out of here in a day or two, anyway."

Now it was Ko's turn to laugh, a sly, nasty sound that foreshadowed exactly how unpleasant his next words would be. "And live where? On the street? You might find arranging shelter a little more difficult in the future," he said. "Your factory housing has been notified. If they choose to take you back, there will be consequences for them, which I'm sure they will be very eager to avoid. Any other dorm or boarding-house will face the same unfavorable options—your father has made certain of that. And another thing, you will resume classes at the uni-versity immediately since you seem to have neglected them of late. Your father has arranged for that also."

Finally Jisun understood. He would not let her go back to her free-dom so easily. She had been locked in these tactical battles with the man all her life and there was no need to be surprised. In a way, she was grateful to Ko for having given her a head start. Now she had time to prepare.

"Do me a favor, Ko," she said. "The next time he sends you to get me, just tell him I was shot dead in the street. Save us both the trouble."

Ko switched off the engine and carefully fixed his disheveled part in the rearview mirror. "Doesn't save *me* any trouble," he said. "I believe I would still have to collect the body."

SHE HAD EXPECTED her father to be sitting in his chair in the living room, his favorite seat outside his study where he could observe visi-tors as they entered without being seen himself. He would be waiting with the crease in his pants leg aligned over his knees, a finger of Chi-vas Regal in his cut glass. His only casual allowance would be the lack of a tie, the top button of his shirt open to a perfect V.

When Jisun did not see him she headed toward the study, asking the housekeeper *ajumma*, "Is he there?" No use putting it off. She was still her father's daughter; she never liked to draw out an unpleasant en-counter.

Even though her brother was home—she had noticed Min's wallet and car keys, his impeccably shined Ferragamo shoes by the door—she knew *ajumma* would know whom she meant by "he." She and Min had never been close and had not spoken since he'd left to study in Germany after graduation last year. *Ajumma* had mentioned he was home for the time being. Something about having blown through too much money too quickly. Min's profligate tendencies were no secret, but their father usually tolerated it with silent judgment. He must have achieved a truly impressive level of recklessness—even for him—to warrant being called home.

"Wait." *Ajumma* pulled her into the hallway, the two of them uncomfortably close in that confined space. Forced to look at her, Jisun realized these past months had been their longest separation since she had been hired when Jisun was four years old. She suddenly saw how *ajumma* had grown old. Not just in her absence, but in the unknown length of time in which she had stopped noticing. The roots of her dyed hair were coming in gray and white, that thick, translucent white that would not hold dye for long. The skin around her eyes drooped like mismatched hoods. Underneath her cheap beige makeup, Jisun could see dark shields of pigmentation across both cheeks. They appeared almost shiny, like an artificial application of dirt or fine soot.

It frightened Jisun to see this familiar face so altered. It had happened right in front of her, day by day, but she hadn't noticed. Now here it was all at once. Fifteen years in a glance.

"Well, what is it?" she said, harsher than she'd intended.

"He won't see you." *Ajumma*'s eyebrows pinched at the true arch, not the one she had penciled in. "Go ahead to your room."

"He knows I'm here?"

"He does."

A new game, then. New game, new rules.

She turned to go.

"When you're ready, lunch is on the table."

Jisun knew better than to argue or to claim she was not hungry. *Ajumma* had been in her father's employ long enough to know that she should mimic his tactics, using quiet, persistent moves that battered people into submission. If Jisun did not come down for lunch, the tray would appear outside her door as if she were a prisoner. If she ignored that, a larger spread—lunch suitable for four—would appear on her vanity in the morning. Freshly prepared food that would get tossed into the trash without a second glance. Any waste or consequence, her fault.

Fifteen years. Jisun had known the housekeeper longer than her own mother. On the hall table outside her bedroom door was a framed portrait of her mother sitting stiffly in a photographer's chair, wearing a black skirt suit. At her throat was an oversize silk bow, the center of the knot jabbed with a brooch, a diamond-studded lily. The photo had been taken before Jisun could remember, years before her mother died. Her face still had a touch of roundness, the wariness in her eyes not yet dulled to apathy.

Jisun flipped the frame facedown on the table. She had long ago given up trying to replace the studio photos with better ones, the photos that showed her mother wearing clothes she was comfortable in, her eyes settled on something off frame, never exactly smiling but reposed. The good photos disappeared as soon as her father noticed them. Sometimes the photo would be returned to her, surreptitiously tucked into her underwear drawer where only she would see it. Jisun knew this was *ajumma*'s doing. But most of the time the photos never reappeared, and Jisun was forced to give up. Her father would never relent and she could not afford to gamble with rare memories.

She picked up the frame and set it right on the table. After a moment, she opened the back and removed the photo. An empty frame suited both mother and daughter much better.

5

. . . .

The next morning, Jisun asked Ko to drive her to the bathhouse.

"You have your own bathroom. Use it," he said curtly. "Anyway, I'm busy."

"Your job is to be my chaperone, not my jailer," Jisun said. "And I know it's not up to you to decide where I practice my hygiene. I'll meet you in the garage in five minutes." She didn't stick around to see his reaction. They both knew his only recourse was to bring it up with her father. On her first day back, even Ko would not dare to disturb the boss over such a petty thing.

There was no bathhouse in their immediate neighborhood, which was too secluded to require one. She made Ko drive twenty-five minutes into the city, claiming she had a favorite location where the steam was scented with mountain herbs. Ko rolled his eyes but did as she asked, stopping the car in front of the dark gray building indicated with the usual red neon bathhouse sign—tendrils of steam rising like a flame. "One hour," he said. "I'll be right here."

"Three," she countered quickly. "It's been a long time since I've been here. Go ahead, you don't have to stay here and wait."

"Absolutely not," he said. "Ninety minutes and that's final."

It was more time than she had expected. Jisun quickly agreed. She ran into the building and was grateful to see there was a back exit—she would not have to wait for Ko to pull away. After exiting the building from the other side, she hailed the first taxicab she saw. She had never taken a taxi to the UIM office and would have been mortified if anyone saw her, but even in a car, it would take at least another twenty minutes to cross the river and make it to the office. She didn't have time to wait for a bus.

In the cab, she tried to compose her thoughts on what she would say to Peter. She had been so focused on getting there that she hadn't planned how to explain everything she needed to say. She would have to improvise and hope that the strength of her feelings made her eloquent and convincing, to defend herself against any judgment Peter might have made about what had happened at the police station the day before.

She and Peter Lowell had spent every day of the last three months together at the Urban Industrial Mission, meeting with workers, union leaders, and church groups. Peter had arrived from a church in Oregon via his orientation in Incheon last fall with only a handful of Korean words and seemingly boundless plans. By necessity, they had been inseparable. Every morning he showed up with a new sheaf of unlined pages written closely from margin to margin, front and back—pages he wanted translated on the spot, as if he believed she were some kind of machine. Flattered by his confidence and determined to exceed his expectations, Jisun had worked harder than she'd ever worked in her life. After more than a dozen years of private tutors, she knew her English was fluent. But her fancy lessons had never included vocabulary about labor laws, nor did she know anything about Christianity. She could sense that Peter was being careful to keep religious references to a minimum until he could earn the workers' respect, but she knew his faith was deeply important to him. Every morning at dawn, he attended a local church service, praying silently in the back pew while other worshippers made loud petitions to God. He invited Jisun to join him and she had accepted once out of curiosity, but she never felt comfortable returning. It was the one aspect of Peter's life that felt completely closed to her.

For long hours each day, Jisun carried out the painstaking double process of first translating his talks from English to Korean, then transliterating each Korean syllable so he would know how to pronounce them. In the early weeks when his grasp of Hangul was unreliable, this was the only way he could produce recognizable Korean words. She wondered if he ever slept. To keep up with him, she barely slept four or five hours a night herself. Yet he arrived each morning having written more work, memorized more speeches. He recited them swaying slightly on the balls of his feet, as if giving a musical performance.

Jisun had fallen for him with the headlong absorption and obsessive hope of first love. She marveled at how they'd been tumbled together from opposite sides of the world, only to find that they were more effective, more powerful, as a team than either could hope to be alone. As partners, they were seamless. And although Peter had never said anything directly, she was certain he shared her feelings. She knew this by the way he skirted around her in their narrow space, careful not to brush against her, as if even an inadvertent touch would reveal too much. She noticed how his posture changed whenever she entered the room, stiffening and then going slack, as if he were willing himself to relax. He was as physically aware of her as she was of him. With so many words traded between them, words that required constant debate and fine-tuning, there had been something precious to her about leaving the larger emotions of the heart unspoken. These were things they knew perfectly well without doubt or translation, without even having to say them aloud.

She didn't have time to waste in sentimental meditation, but she stood on the street gazing at the familiar building, taking in its unremarkable brick facade and dirty windows. She wanted to file away each detail in her mind. This was where she had spent the happiest months of her life, where she had discovered a world-expanding purpose beyond the narrow confines of her former life. She ached to be in there today, working as if it were any other day. She could close her eyes and see the exact pages they'd been translating last. Her fingers itched to feel the paper Peter used to draft his notes, a cheap newsprint that was simultaneously soft and rough like felt.

This was her home. After working with him in such proximity, Jisun felt she knew Peter intimately, from his tight, angular handwriting to the shape of his mouth as he struggled to form Korean words, to the way he smiled, a mixture of warmth and natural reserve. She knew the tea stains that would not wash out of his cherished dove gray sweater, among the few items he had brought from home. *Fisherman's sweater,* he called it, though his family did not fish.

Because he repeated the same garments over and over and lived in a shabby boardinghouse near the steel mill where he focused the majority of his work, Jisun had assumed he must have been chased out of his own country, penniless and without prospects. They had worked together nearly a month before she heard about his family's lumber fortune. *A famous name, his family,* people whispered. Jisun dismissed the talk as idle gossip, but the workers insisted that they had heard it from the previous UIM emissary, who had returned to the States after he found living in Korea too difficult an adjustment. When Jisun finally asked Peter about it, she admired the way he dispassionately confirmed the information, as if they were discussing some minor news item that did not pertain to him. But he refused to elaborate, irritated by her questions about his past and likewise disinclined to ask about hers. Knowing who her father was, Peter seemed to think the less said on the topic of their families, the better. Jisun had been as confounded as she was grateful. It was the first time in her life she felt acknowledged for her own merits.

But now Jisun knew they could not ignore the facts. She wondered if Peter would maintain his usual policy of avoiding the issue—or would he blame her as everyone else did, holding her accountable for her father's decisions? She hoped he would know her better than that, that he of all people would understand. Taking a deep breath, Jisun crossed the street, hoping the right words would come when she needed them.

PETER MUST HAVE heard her climbing the old creaky steps and entering the office, but he stayed seated even when she crossed the threshold. His back was to the door, his shoulders bunched around his neck. His silence and that subtle slight of pretending he hadn't heard her communicated everything she had feared.

"Hello, Peter," she said, trying to quell the panic in her voice. When he finally turned to face her, she knew he had not moved from his desk all night. His light brown hair spiked in pieces around his crown where he must have pulled it away from his head as he grew tired, a gesture she knew well. His eyes, normally a luminous amber tone like the eyes of an owl, were sunken and flat.

"I came as soon as I could," she said. "Yesterday was—"

"Didn't think I'd see you here," he cut in briskly. He laid an old notebook over the pages he'd been working on, as if she could not be trusted to glimpse what might be written there.

"I can't stay long," she stammered. "I only came to tell you I won't be able to come back for a while. I'm so sorry. You'll have to find another translator." There was so much more she wanted to say—not just that she was sorry to have inconvenienced the work or that she would dearly miss coming to this office every day. She needed to tell him how devastated she was at the thought of not seeing him. That the idea of another translator taking her place filled her with such childish jealousy and despair, she could not imagine overcoming it. Before coming here, Jisun had hoped that Peter would at least acknowledge the work they'd accomplished together, the connection they'd shared as partners and colleagues. But much more than that, she had hoped Peter would finally reveal his affection for her. Jisun needed to know that losing her hurt him, too.

She took a step toward him, but there was nothing in his eyes to say that he felt anything other than resentment. Again he turned his back. "After what you did yesterday, I don't know why you bothered coming at all," he said.

She had never known Peter to be cruel, even to people he disliked, yet he was treating her as if they were enemies. She might have been prepared for disappointment or even indignation, but she did not deserve this scorn. "After what *I* did?" She could not control the higher octave of her voice. "Do you actually believe I had any control over what happened yesterday? I didn't ask to be released, Peter. You of all people should know that. It would have been the same for you as a foreigner. And what would you have done differently?"

"I would have stayed."

"You wouldn't have had a choice," she said.

"There are always choices." His eyes flashed with conviction. "That's the difference between you and me, Jisun. You're still stuck on your family, blaming them for everything that happens. But that's ancient history for me. I'm out here on my own. I'm not looking for an almighty hand to save me if I get in trouble."

It was a stunning accusation, drawing a line as thick as the world between them. Jisun fought back as if for her life. "Don't be stupid," she said. "You know as well as I do what would have happened." Peter might be far from home, but his American passport and white skin meant he would always have the privilege of representing his powerful government. No amount of pious denial would change that. "You, Peter—*you* wouldn't even have made it into the police van. You think they'd touch you out there and risk the press? 'American Aid Worker Arrested for Peaceful Protest.' That doesn't sound like ancient history, Peter. This is current history. This is now.

"And you want to know the real difference between you and me?" she said. "I wouldn't blame you for that, because you didn't make this history. You're here trying to change it, just like I was. Do you truly think I *wanted* to be released, do you think that was my plan? And if we're pointing fingers, at least I got involved," she said. "I was out there, Peter, while you were here, hiding behind a stack of papers."

To say he was hiding was just as unfair as his implying she had run away, but Jisun was past caring. His self-righteousness felt like hands closing around her throat. Later she would regret the words, remembering the way he hunched into himself as if shuttering his heart against her. But now it was all she could do to fight for breath.

"If it's a contest, then you win," Peter said bitterly. "You're the real saint. Topless and all. Congratulations, Jisun. Now excuse me, I have work to do."

Dumbfounded, Jisun repeated the word. "Did you say *topless?*"

"You didn't think I'd hear about that? I heard it was quite a spectacle."

"Is that what you think it was, a spectacle? Do you think that's why we did it?"

"Then why?" he said furiously. The question seemed to explode from his body, as if it had been compressed under enormous pressure. Jisun had never heard Peter raise his voice. She could not believe what he was saying, but it was a relief—at last—to know that the mask had dropped. Finally, this was Peter without calculation and control. Jisun felt as if she were seeing him for the first time, stripped of all the attributes—American, aid worker, Christian—that had made him seem so different from everyone else. In that moment, she felt surprising tenderness toward him. He had always seemed so stoic and strong, but now she saw that he was as fragile as a little boy, confused and frightened by events he could not understand. If she were not careful, he would shatter like a vase thrown against the wall.

"The riot police were there and they were threatening us," Jisun explained in a quiet, steady voice. "They were coming and it was a spontaneous response. I don't know how it happened, but I know for sure—it was never meant to be a spectacle. *Never.* They were trying to protect themselves. *We,*" she corrected herself quickly. "We were trying to protect ourselves."

Peter took a long inhale and let it out slowly. "But you should have known better, Jisun," he said. "I expected more from you."

"But we did nothing wrong," she said. "What should I have known? How could I have been better?"

"I thought we had a future together," he said. "But I see now that I was wrong. I misjudged the situation. Forgive me."

"Because I tried to protect myself, you misjudged the situation?" Jisun said. "I don't follow, Peter. Explain this to me."

"My work is everything, Jisun," he said. "And you and I—I thought we would continue as we have, working together. We had—at least I thought so—a unique connection."

Despite everything, her heart leapt at the words. She wanted to hold on to this last sentiment and discard the rest, which didn't make any sense at all. "But I agree," she said. "We do—"

"Please, Jisun. Let me finish." Peter refused to meet her eyes. "But you see, going forward I need a partner who shares my values. Who understands the expectations of—of a missionary's wife."

And now Jisun understood.

Peter had let her believe she had betrayed the cause by allowing herself to be released while others still remained in jeopardy. But now she saw the real reason for his rejection. Peter was offended—no, scandalized—because she had bared her breasts in solidarity with a workers' protest. And what did a missionary's wife do in such a situation? she wondered. Did a proper woman, in Peter's imagination, run around a police raid imploring battered women to remember their chastity? Did she fall to her knees and pray for police clemency?

"You pretended it was my father that was the problem. You acted like I was some kind of traitor." She was so angry that it was an effort to speak at all, to find the proper words to contain her fury. "But it was this all along, wasn't it? Is your God so squeamish that he hasn't seen uncovered breasts? Does he begrudge women the right to protect themselves?"

For a long moment, neither of them spoke. She thought it was possible he would apologize. He would apologize and she would forgive him, she knew she would. If only he would say the words, they would make it right between them.

"I'm sorry. I didn't mean to hurt you," Peter said finally. But it was not the apology she expected. He was not sorry for what he had implied, only that she did not agree with him. And he was not sorry she would not return. It was an apology that was more a goodbye, a gesture to end an awkward conversation.

She started to answer, but Peter was not finished.

"And I never pretended about your father," he said. "I can't take back what I said because it's what I believe, but I should have spoken differently. I was angry. Forgive me."

With this, he eliminated every shred of friendship, any shadow of affection, between them.

Jisun wished she had the conviction to walk out and never look back. But even now, after everything he'd said, she could not bear to destroy it all as if there were nothing worth saving.

"How can you leave it like this?" she said. "Is this truly how you want to end it?"

"How *I'm* ending it?" Peter said. "It was your choice, Jisun. You did this."

He sounded genuinely sad, as if she were the one who had broken his heart, not the other way around. He gave her a final glance and picked up his pen, clearly dismissing her.

ALL THE WAY back to the bathhouse, Jisun's ears pounded with his words, which heaped every blame, every possible failing, on her. She felt as disoriented as if she'd been flung into a new body, a new country where she did not understand the language or know a soul. And in a way, she realized it was not far from the truth. In one day, everything had changed. All her work, all her passion, had amounted to nothing. To less than nothing. She had lost not only her job and her freedom, she had lost her respect for the person she'd most admired.

The city flashed by in grays and browns outside the window. Inside the cab, the driver was listening to the new song by Shim Soo-Bong, which was playing endlessly on all the stations since her debut. The driver tapped the wheel in time with the mellow beat. "Great song," he said. "Talent like that, bet she'll have a long career. You know she won the College Talent Search with this song? Wrote it herself." He kept looking in the rearview mirror at Jisun as he talked. She nodded and cranked open the window, pretending she needed some air. Of course she knew about the contest. Everyone knew everything that was public in Korea. The media let them know only what the government allowed, the same few things that kept the country in a tight loop of sanctioned influence and safe, useless information. It was why she and her fellow activists were so desperate to know and experience what was not normally permitted. Now all that would be cut off for her.

The driver, failing to catch the hint, kept up his casual chatter. "You a college student too, eh?" he said. "You don't sing, do you? Maybe next year we'll be hearing you on the radio."

"Why do you think I'm a college student?" Jisun asked.

He shrugged, and even that was in time with the beat. "Just a hunch," he said. "You get a sense for these things when you meet as many people as I do."

"Well, you're wrong," she said. "I work."

"Oh yeah? What kind of office?"

To be contrary, Jisun considered telling him that she worked at a factory, that she had nothing to do with an office at all. It was not completely untrue—she had lived in factory housing for three months, and she often met with the workers during their meal breaks on the factory floor. But Jisun knew better. Sharing living conditions and having periodic meetings was not nearly the same as being a true worker, and she would never forgive herself for claiming it just to satisfy a fleeting antagonistic impulse.

"Never mind," she said instead. "You can drop me here."

Ko WAS PARKED exactly where she had left him. She was a block away when the car sprang to life, taillights flashing, exhaust pumping the curl of smoke that signaled he had seen her. Jisun went into the bathhouse anyway, and came straight back out through the same double doors she'd just entered. Not that her story would prevail, but it would be his word against hers.

"You forgetting something?" Ko asked when she slumped into the backseat.

"What? I don't know."

"You had a bag," Ko said.

She had stashed her bag of toiletries in the alley behind the bathhouse and forgotten to go back for it. "I'll get it next time."

"If there's a next time, I'd be surprised."

If she were a stronger person, someone who valued her own dignity, then she would have let him take her home, locked the door to her bedroom, and wept in the privacy of her own lavish misery. Perhaps she would have done so many things differently if she were that person.

Instead Jisun told Ko to turn the car around. "Take me to Miari."

6

. . . .

The car inched through the narrow alleys of Miari, crowded on both sides by street vendors selling vegetables and underwear, fly-swatters, pots of every size and shape, live chickens, and fish stacked on graying Styrofoam beds laid thinly with ice. It was like being squeezed through a tunnel of human curiosity, a wall of eyes following the slow movement of the car. Jisun knew they couldn't see her through the darkened windows, but it was something she would never get used to, being simultaneously conspicuous and invisible. Whether they considered the intrusion merely interesting or ominous, the neighborhood would keep its collective mind on the black car until it moved on. Every detail was monitored and saved for future retelling. When it arrived, when it left. Where it had stopped and who had gotten out. Nothing was left unexamined in Miari. Everyone had time, and gossip was its primary trade.

Ko stopped the car at Namin's house.

"Do you have to stay?" Jisun asked.

"We can leave right now, anytime you're ready. Well?"

Jisun let herself out, slammed the door. Ko turned off the engine and cranked the window, a slit barely wide enough for a ribbon of smoke to escape. It made the car look like a steaming animal, a mechanical projection of the driver inside. Before she had even approached the gate, Jisun heard Namin's next-door neighbor, whom everyone called "Busan Mother," call over the wall, "Namin—your fancy friend is here!"

Jisun rapped on the gate, swinging the tiny, anvil-shaped knocker.

Nearby, a little boy clutched a rubber ball in his fist. The ball was dull pink, no larger than a peach pit. Together they waited for Namin to come to the door. When no one came, he threw the ball at Jisun's feet, letting it bounce off her shoe. He watched expectantly for her reaction, and when Jisun hopped on the foot, pretending to be hurt, he cracked a smile and went chasing after his ball.

She knocked again, louder this time. Namin was in there and they both knew it. But the door stayed shut.

The Kang family lived in three rooms facing an open courtyard. The courtyard was a bare rectangular patch of concrete and thin dirt that housed the family's single cold-water faucet used for washing and cooking, outsize jars of food that could not be stored in the tiny kitchen refrigerator, and all manner of half-useful junk that did not fit indoors. During the warm summer months, the courtyard could be made to look almost attractive, with clay pots overflowing with bright red and green peppers, purple pole beans, eggplants, and cucumber vines, all of which created a lush cover for the less appealing odds and ends. It was too early in the season for all that now, but Namin noticed there were a few pots of lettuce her mother had recently put out. The tiny green frills were barely taller than her pinky finger, but they still added a bit of cheer.

Namin's parents slept in the first room, nearest the main door and the kitchen. The second room, what they called the "parlor," featured cast-off furniture that Namin's mother had rescued from neighbors or the trash. There was a gray tweed love seat, the back of which had been slashed and peeled open as if someone were expecting it to contain hidden treasures, an enormous octagonal glass-topped table, a radio with one of the speakers blown out, and a record player that had once been smashed and reconstructed with translucent brown packing tape. The sofa was put up against a wall and looked fine as long as you didn't pull it out to look at its backside, and the radio and record player were more or less functional except during periods of heavy rain. But the giant geometric table—which pinned people to the room's

perimeter and made moving around a puzzle of knees and ankles—
was an ongoing joke, humiliating to Namin and amusing to Kyungmin,
Namin's older sister, who had long ago detached herself from their
mother's schemes to appear better off than they were. Because it was
too grotesquely conspicuous not to mention in some way, guests fell
to praising the table. It was "unique," "majestic," "structurally interesting," "European." Its size and scale seemed to imply that the Kang
family was accustomed to grander circumstances and that this cramped,
humid abode was just a temporary downsizing, soon to be redressed.
At least this was what Namin's mother hoped they might think.

Namin and her sister shared the third room. This was the room
nearest the toilet, an indoor latrine that required periodic emptying by
a sanitation worker. Twice a month, they had to search the neighborhood for the latrine man, Mr. Hong, and beg him to come service their
house. Somehow he was always working in a different part of town
when they needed him, besieged by others willing to exaggerate their
situation, claiming their latrine would overflow outright if he would
not agree to come immediately. Everyone always seemed to wait until
the last minute to call Mr. Hong, as if living in perpetual denial of their
shit.

Normally it was Kyungmin's job to find him, as it was her responsibility to do many of the physical chores around the house. In the
Kang household, everyone's roles were strictly defined according to
greatest utility. It was Namin's job to study, which was something only
she could do. Laundry, cooking the rice, fetching the latrine man—all
of this was general work that anyone could do, and therefore Kyungmin would be tasked to do it on her time off from working at the factory. If she complained, it was pointed out that Namin spent as many
hours studying as Kyungmin put in at the factory and at home—
perhaps even more. Namin secretly agreed with her sister—it *was* unfair that she was always stuck with the grunt work, whereas studying
was something Namin actually enjoyed, most of the time. But since
Kyungmin's sharp tongue never let her forget how hard she worked at
her miserable job so Namin could go to college, there was no use say-

ing anything nice. And in the end, they both knew their parents were right. Namin needed to be left alone to study, since a college degree—and the salary she could earn as the physician she hoped to become after graduation—could lift them out of their situation for good. No amount of time at the factory could do that.

But lately Kyungmin had been letting the level in the latrine rise dangerously high before finding the latrine man. The chain of begging now started with Namin imploring her sister to find Mr. Hong. The longer Kyungmin put her off, the more unreasonable Namin's panic became. She knew it was absurd not to be able to perform this simple chore that any child in their neighborhood could do. She was nineteen years old and studying to be a doctor; she could hardly afford to be so squeamish about the most basic by-product of human existence. But everything about it—the smell of the full latrine, the humiliating wooing of Mr. Hong, the thought of him slopping what must be oceans of shit in a month, not to mention in a year, a *lifetime*—overwhelmed Namin with misery. As much as she might berate herself for this embarrassing streak of prissiness, she could not make herself overcome it.

This morning, she had tried again. "Please, Kyungmin. Couldn't you do it on the way to work? It'll take you no time at all. You won't even be late."

"Would it kill you to get him yourself for once?" Kyungmin had said. Her face had been pale and bloated from having worked three consecutive overtime shifts at the factory. The butterfly embroidery of her pillow had been imprinted on her cheek as if she had collapsed on it and not moved all night. Namin had felt guilty for nagging, for not owning the courage to do it herself, but the situation in her mind was dire. It looked as though it might rain, which would significantly compound the problem. Humidity never helped. At least in the winter a good hard freeze acted as a kind of antiseptic against the odor, but it was April now and showing signs of spring. With each rising degree, the smell seemed to fester inside the house.

"Next time I'll do it. I promise." Even this false promise had made Namin's palms clammy, but she'd pressed on, desperate. Maybe next time Kyungmin would be in a better mood, more generous. Maybe in a couple of weeks, things would be different. It was important that she make herself believe this, even though the opposite was likely true. In a few weeks it would be warmer. Her sister would be more exhausted, made testier by the sweaty commute and growing airlessness on the factory floor. And lately Kyungmin rarely made it home before curfew even when she wasn't working.

There was always some flat, dubious reason why she was out so late. A new friend in a distant neighborhood. A blown tire on the bus. A long movie. Excuses that might have seemed credible once, but not night after night.

No one—not her mother, not her father, certainly not Namin—was prepared to discuss where Kyungmin might be, if not the places she claimed. But it was on their minds all the time, a snaking fear that made them even more terse with one another than usual. Like everyone else, they were familiar with the rumors of girls who slipped from factory life into the Itaewon nightlife, working at bars and brothels frequented by the American soldiers stationed in Seoul. Girls who were tempted by the promise of money—more money in one night than in a week at the factory—or, more naively, lured by the prospect of romance. An American boyfriend might become an American husband, a ticket out to a new life. Never mind that any Korean girl seen with a GI in Seoul would be viewed as a prostitute. Even if they were a legitimate couple, married or in love, their children would be shunned. It was one thing to be politically grateful to the United States for coming to their aid during the war and continuing to protect their northern border these past two decades. But friend or not, it was humiliating to be so firmly indebted to a foreign army and a seemingly omnipotent government against which they had no balancing power. And no one was willing to see their daughters and sisters become an American soldier's plaything, easily exploited and left behind, the rest of their lives ruined in the aftermath.

Perhaps these were girls who had no reputation to lose, no families to disown them. Perhaps for women like that, the slim chance of gaining an American visa was worth the risk. But Kyungmin had a family who worried about her. Namin hoped that she had met someone else, a secret boyfriend—a respectable Korean man, not a GI—who was keeping her out late at night. In the past her sister had nurtured a romantic streak, favoring scarlet lipsticks in winter to make her pale skin stand out against the snow. She liked to save her money to purchase lush fabrics that she fashioned into skirts that hugged her hips and tapered at the calves like the couture of a 1940s Hollywood star. Three years ago, Kyungmin had almost married a furniture salesman who took college classes at night, inching his way toward a degree. But he had ended up throwing her over for another girl who was a few years older, a university student majoring in home economics.

If there were any other boyfriends since then, Kyungmin had kept quiet about it. And try as Namin might to imagine it, her sister did not seem like a girl in love. Her face was dark and shuttered, her moods as brittle as February ice. Kyungmin no longer sewed the beautiful garments that made her walk taller, her back straight to show off her figure. Instead she dressed recklessly in increasingly revealing, unflattering clothing that cut into her slender frame and showed the seams of her undergarments. Namin had the sense that her sister would no longer settle for any night degree or pockmarked salesman; she had waited long enough and would not make the same mistake again. But looking like that—if Kyungmin had been any other girl on the street, Namin and her parents would have a word for what she was.

"Please, Kyungmin. Just this once," Namin had begged again.

"What are you, the royal princess around here? If it bothers you so much, take care of it."

It *would* kill her. But she'd realized her sister was serious this time. If she wanted it done, she'd have to do it herself. And the longer she put it off, the worse it got.

There was a knock at the gate and Busan Mother called over the barrier separating their courtyards: "Namin—your fancy friend is here!"

Jisun always used the knocker, sending that hollow, formal sound through their narrow courtyard. Everyone else just yelled over the gate or simply let themselves in, since the door was locked only if no one was home. Namin closed her eyes, fighting an irrational instinct to hide. Of course, she was already hidden behind her bedroom door and the walls of the house, but Jisun had a way of making her feel exposed.

Since Jisun had gotten involved with the activist groups, they barely knew anything about each other's lives. Namin accepted the distance they had drifted apart, but Jisun seemed to take for granted the fact that *her* life was always in flux while other people stayed put— preferably in the spot where she'd left them. When she'd found out that Namin planned to go for the Circle, her brother Min's pet project that had become SNU's foremost status symbol, Jisun had thrown a fit. That was months ago, and they hadn't spoken since.

"You *can't*," she'd said. As if Namin had asked her permission. "Namin, have you thought this through? This can't really be what you want."

"It's exactly what I want."

"But it's so elitist. You know the Circle is just a bunch of phony social climbers. You'll get in and become just like them. Another stupid bourgeois sheep. Namin, no! You're better than that."

Namin had laughed. "'Bourgeois sheep'? They must be brainwashing you in those demo groups of yours. Just because I don't think like you doesn't make me a dumb animal. Don't worry about me, I'll be fine. Anyway, I could use a little elitism in my life."

"How can you joke about this?"

"Jisun, obviously you don't need things like the Circle. You can afford not to be such a 'sheep.' So go ahead, spend your life marching and shouting slogans," Namin had said. "But I can't. I need this. People rely on me, you know."

"And you think no one relies on me?"

"Who, Jisun?" she'd said. "Who relies on you? You have no responsibilities! Everything's always been given to you."

Jisun had actually stamped her foot like a child throwing a tantrum, raising a low cloud of dust over the courtyard. "No responsibilities?"

she'd shouted. "Who do you think I'm doing this for? Why should I work so hard when people like you don't even appreciate it?"

" 'People like me'?" Namin had shouted, too, forgetting to keep her voice down. The neighbors could repeat this argument word for word in the market for all she cared. " 'People like me,' you mean, who are helpless, who need big, powerful champions like you to fight their battles? Is that what you think you're doing? Let me get this straight. Do you actually expect me to be *grateful*?" She'd been so angry, she'd wanted to smash Jisun across her smug, patronizing face. She'd wanted to knock her down and pummel her until they were both senseless. But tears were already quivering in Jisun's eyes.

It had made her furious that Jisun was crying. As if this were about *her* sad feelings, *her* disappointment in the shortcomings of their friendship.

"I thought we relied on each other, Namin."

"People like me can't rely on people like you," Namin had spit out. "We just call that charity."

She'd left Jisun standing in the yard. She couldn't bear to hear or say another word, not even *Get out,* which she knew Jisun wouldn't obey anyway. That's what happened when you let someone get too comfortable in your life. You couldn't even kick them out of your house when you needed to.

That day, Namin had stayed away for hours in case Jisun decided to wait her out. Coming back, she'd expected some melodramatic communication taped to her desk, impassioned pages purporting to explain or apologize that would just yank the knots of their conflict tighter. When she found nothing, Namin saw for the first time how they could begin to let each other go. Slowly nudging closed, not slamming, the door to their childhood.

It was just the quiet she needed.

8

· · · · · · · · · · · ·

Namin could not remember the first time she and Jisun noticed each other. All the girls were new to one another at the time, nervous to be starting at Kyungki Girls Middle School and anxious to prove they belonged there. They had all passed difficult exams in order to be admitted, but most of the girls were daughters of government officials and top businessmen. Girls who were used to enjoying elite privileges, unlike Namin, whose parents had barely been able to afford the black-and-white sailor uniform and matching coat that Kyungki required.

Far from scrambling to make friends like the other girls, Namin had kept to herself, unwilling to expose her poverty by getting close to anyone. She knew she could outperform the other girls academically, but no amount of hard work would make the things she needed to fit in materialize. Everyone else had new leather satchels and a wardrobe of expensive-looking shoes, compared with her dingy canvas bag and the scuffed black loafers she wore every day. Many of the girls were dropped off by their family's chauffeurs each morning, while she had to take a bus that snaked through north and central Seoul, across the Han River, before it finally let her out in Gangnam. It was a ride that took more than fifty minutes and sometimes felt like a battle even before the day had begun. In bad weather, Namin wore triple layers of socks and stockings and arrived at school drenched while other girls barely had a drop on their heads from being ferried under umbrellas to the building's threshold. During the warmer months, her desk mate made nasty comments about *washing once in a while*. Namin bit her tongue because she washed every day, twice a day; but not everyone on her bus did, and they were packed in like sardines by the bus attendants whose job it was to forcefully shove as many bodies as they could into the bus at every stop.

There were things the other girls at Kyungki seemed to know intuitively about one another's families—what it meant to live in a certain neighborhood or own a particular make of car—that Namin could not grasp. But even she knew about Jisun, whose father was one of the most powerful *chaebol* leaders in the country. For that reason alone, Namin kept a wide berth, wanting nothing to do with her. But Jisun had pursued her friendship, drawn to her for reasons that were entirely unclear.

Namin remembered one day, a few weeks into the new school year. It was after lunch and she found herself standing alone with Jisun. A short distance away, the other girls were crowded around a classmate who was showing off a box of Swiss chocolates, a gift from her diplomat father. Namin had pretended not to care but mentally recorded every detail of the tiny chocolates, dark little bites drizzled with a slightly lighter shade of chocolate. They were shaped like hearts, each nestled in its own perfect compartment. The other girls, chattering and cooing in appreciation, reminded her of a well-groomed flock of birds.

"Don't be fooled by all that," Jisun said in a low voice. "You aren't, are you?"

"Of course not. What's there to be fooled by?" Namin said, pretending she understood what Jisun was talking about. In reality, she had no idea.

"That girl's making a big deal out of those candies when they're just cheap little things. You know, they sell them at the airport next to the aspirin and the chewing gum. No real Swiss person would think to make such a fuss. It would be like us singing hymns to a common steam bun. Actually I love steam buns, so forget that. It would be like us going crazy over any old plate of kimchi."

"Well, maybe in Switzerland they would go crazy over kimchi," Namin said doubtfully. The chocolates looked pretty special to her.

She wouldn't mind trying one, even if it turned out to be as common-place as kimchi—or airport chewing gum. Considering she'd never been on an airplane or even seen the airport in her own country, airport chewing gum sounded like a fantastic concept, like buying Juicy Fruit on the moon.

"The point is, she's showing off like it's a big deal," Jisun said. "She just wants everyone to envy her. That's why I can't stand those girls, all they want is for people to follow them." She looked at Namin. "And that's why I like you. You don't care what anyone thinks, do you?"

Namin thought about how ashamed she felt of her shoes and how she often wished some mysterious rich relative would show up with expensive gifts so she could be like the other girls at school. Despite what Jisun said, she envied those girls and wondered what it would be like to own something they would admire for once. But she would never admit such feelings to Jisun.

"But aren't you just as bad," Namin said, "bragging about how you know all about those chocolates? I suppose you have even better ones at home."

Jisun glared at her. "The only reason I know about those stupid chocolates at all is because my father shoved us away to Switzerland so he could kick my mother out of the house while we were gone. She died last year, you know. Probably just to spite him. I would try the same if I thought he was worth the trouble."

The revelation shocked Namin. Immediately she felt the need to lock down her own secrets, as if somehow Jisun could read her mind and discover what she was hiding.

"I don't believe you," Namin said.

"Well, it's true," Jisun said. "And I don't care if you don't believe me."

They were eleven years old. Together, Jisun and Namin practiced the art of being unfazed. Each pretended not to be shocked by the other's household, by the huge gap in their social and financial realities, which was so obvious that they could neither deny nor discuss them beyond the most superficial levels. Already, they knew much more about life than most girls their age, but they pretended to know even more than they did—about money, about families and death, friendship and betrayal. About love and lies.

Or perhaps only Namin was pretending and Jisun truly was as detached as she appeared.

The following year, when Jisun started receiving love notes from an older boy named Juno, a friend of her brother's, Namin was stupefied. But Jisun barely glanced at the carefully folded stationery before tossing the sheets in the trash.

"Don't you even want to know what it says?" Namin asked, fighting the impulse to fish them out. Jisun's garbage was so clean that it wouldn't have been a big deal, but her pride kept her in check. "At least see who it's from."

Receiving a love note seemed as marvelous and exotic as finding an uncut diamond in the gutter. Namin was appalled by Jisun's carelessness. Boys and girls rarely mingled in middle or high school. They attended separate single-sex schools and socialized strictly within their gender. The only time they could even catch a glimpse of any boys was on the street or on Sunday afternoons. Under such circumstances, when would anyone even have the opportunity to develop any kind of serious crush or love interest? Of course, people still made eyes at each other, but it rarely went beyond that first nameless stage.

If anyone ever wrote *her* a love letter, she would certainly read it. Even if she decided she didn't like the boy, she would save his letters as a memento, as evidence of having been admired.

"I know who it's from," Jisun said grimly. "This kid Juno. Family friend. He's been sucking up to us since we were babies. He already follows my brother around like an orphan duck, and now I guess he's using me as insurance."

"How are you *insurance?*"

"He probably has this stupid idea that if we get married one day, then he can get a part of my father's company." Jisun looked askance at her. "My father says people don't get rich by accident. He says it takes 'long-term planning.'"

It was a stunning piece of information, and Namin packed it away to think about later. In the following years, she would return to this bit of inadvertent counsel again and again—it would become a kind of touchstone—but for now she had other questions and more pressing concerns. At their age, the idea of marriage seemed as impossible as it did inevitable, but she had never heard any girl discuss it so matter-of-factly. As if her future were already engraved in granite.

"Isn't it possible that he actually just likes you?" Namin asked.

"Isn't it more possible that I'm just right?" Jisun said. "Whose side are you on, anyway?"

"Yours, I guess," said Namin. But sometimes it seemed Jisun went out of her way to make it hard to be on her side.

Jisun was as unimpressed with love letters as she was with Swiss chocolates, the grandeur of her family's home, her wardrobe, which appeared magically stocked with new clothes each season, her driver, her housekeeper—her effortless life in general. She had everything, yet she refused to understand why someone else—someone like Namin, for example—might want a taste of that fantasy for herself.

"Trust me, you wouldn't want this either," Jisun said now, about the letters. She heaved a sigh, as if being admired were the heaviest burden in the world.

She always seemed to know what Namin was thinking yet still arrived at the wrong conclusion.

"You're probably right," Namin said.

LATER, WHEN JISUN left her alone to use the bathroom, Namin poured out a bottle of Jisun's red nail polish into the wastepaper basket, dripping the bright scarlet color over the pages. It was a childish, spiteful impulse, satisfying her need to waste something precious that they both enjoyed. The nail polish was not allowed at school, and they'd be scolded by any adult who saw them wearing it on the street.

But they spent painstaking hours coloring their nails anyway, changing their minds, rubbing or peeling it off, choosing another color, and starting all over again. All the while knowing they could wear it only in Jisun's bedroom and would have to remove all trace of it before they went out. Jisun owned three colors: red, pale pink, and clear. The cap of the nail polish was made of smooth black plastic and stamped with a logo of white interlocking Cs facing opposite directions. Jisun had once explained that the Cs stood for Chanel. From France.

Drizzling the polish in wide, lazy swoops over the ruined love notes, Namin inhaled the sharp fumes of the chemicals until her eyes started to water. She was careful not to get any drops on the white carpeting, which would have been a far more serious transgression—way beyond what she wanted to achieve. She wanted only to know what it was like to destroy something simply because she wanted to. The way Jisun did all the time, without considering the cost or consequences.

9
. . . .

The anvil dropped again on the gate, louder and more insistently this time. Knowing Jisun, Namin was sure she would stay out there knocking for hours until she was let in.

Namin stood on the other side of the door and considered her options. She was surprised to discover she no longer felt angry about their argument. She had been furious at Jisun's claim that her activism was somehow meant to benefit her, as if Namin were helpless to fight her own battles. But she had covered so much new ground in the past months, worrying about her sister, launching her bid for Circle membership. Her emotions about Jisun seemed like a point on a map, far away. Already their lives had shot out in such different directions.

She opened the door.

Jisun had a way of looking disarranged and wild that was not simply a matter of what she wore or how she combed her hair. Her features—eyes, skin, mouth—readily betrayed the color and heat that stayed hidden in other people. Her posture and the angular cast of her arms made her look perpetually poised for action, restless. Even in the coldest winter, she could never be bothered to button her coat or wrap a scarf over her throat, a vision of layers that did not lie still. Everything was on her face—so Namin saw the apology, whether or not Jisun spoke the actual words. Apologies were never difficult for her anyway, because she had no fear of diminishment.

"I'm surprised you had time out from your busy savior schedule to come here," Namin said. Their old routine. A way to come back. "Is someone else keeping an eye on the world for you?"

"Truce," Jisun said.

Namin saw the car and Ko's telltale cigarette smoke. "I seem to re-member someone accusing *me* of elitism last time," she said. "What did you do, donate your bus tokens to your factory sisters? Are you protesting the treatment of transportation workers? What is it this time?"

"So I guess you haven't heard yet."

Namin laughed. Typical Jisun, thinking the world revolved around her latest skirmishes. "If it's about you, no, I haven't heard. Was there a news flash? I'm not exactly tuned in to the underground circuit."

"Let me come in."

"What about him?" She nodded at the car. "Isn't he leaving?"

"He'll have to stay. I'm not allowed to go anywhere without him."

Namin thought quickly. She knew Jisun probably wanted her to ask, but she didn't need to be a detective to figure out that if Jisun was being chaperoned, she must have crossed the line with her father some-how. The car was here and Namin had a better idea than letting Ko idle on the corner. She stepped over the threshold and shut the door behind her with a resolute bang. "Tell me later," she said. "As long as he's here, we might as well make him useful."

THEY SPENT AN unproductive hour combing the neighborhood for Mr. Hong. Namin kept thinking he must be on the next block, just out of sight. It was a strange experience to drive around the neighborhood she knew so well, ignoring everything for the exception of one man. She had thought the car would make it easier, but it was like navigating a tank around a rice field. She wished she could lift all the buildings off their foundations to get a clear view of the streets. Or fly up like a bird and get the hawk's-eye view. She shook her head, realizing Kyungmin would have found him by now. She knew whom to ask—the shop clerks and street vendors who kept track of such things as instinctively as they did the weather. The car was useless.

Ko dropped them back in front of her gate.

"Giving up?" Jisun said. She had been quiet in the car, obediently looking for the sewage tank Namin described but otherwise saying nothing.

"Of course not."

Having Jisun there made her more determined to get the task done before her parents returned for the evening. It was one thing for her sister to call her a princess and imply she shirked the dirty work, but she couldn't have Jisun knowing she felt squeamish about her own toilet.

"Doesn't Kyungmin usually do this?" Jisun asked.

"She's busy."

"Shouldn't we split up? We'll cover more ground that way."

Times like this, Namin wondered if she was the terrible one, bitter and proud. If the situation were reversed, if *she* were the daughter of a *chaebol* leader and Jisun were the one in Miari with the overflowing latrine and the sister who might be off where she shouldn't be—would she have made the same offer to wander around looking for the poop man? The question barely had to be asked.

When Jisun repeated the question, Namin pretended she hadn't heard. She headed for the corner store, where the owner, a mother of triplets whose husband had a sporadic definition of responsibility, knew things: when to expect rain even when it wasn't cloudy; which brand of cigarettes a new customer would want before he asked. She would know where to find Mr. Hong.

The *ajumma* was rolling a large brown egg on her forearm. She showed Namin a small semicircle of teeth marks halfway between her elbow and her wrist. Around it the skin was broken and swollen. The bruise, a huge spread of blue and purple, was as wide as her open palm. "Now the little devils are biting," she said, scowling. "Hand me a fresh egg."

Namin went to the cooler and removed another egg. She knew the *ajumma* would sell these eggs, even though she was using them to massage her bruise. The smooth, cold surface was better than any poultice. It would reduce the spread of the bruise and make it heal faster. Namin had always thought there must be some kind of magic to the treatment, but now she knew the cold massage probably took down the inflammation and improved circulation. Maybe there was some mineral in the eggshell that also helped.

"Are these eggs still good to sell?" she asked innocently.

"The yolk doesn't break, however you try," *ajumma* said. "I tried shaking it as hard as I could. Open it up and it's still a perfect round thing."

Nodding, Namin put the used egg back in place in the cooler. She noted the spot so she wouldn't inadvertently buy it later. "Have you seen Mr. Hong . . . ?"

"Hong? Haven't seen him yet. His wife's got the morning sickness." She said "morning sickness" with the same tone she'd said "biting" earlier.

Namin tried not to think about what it would be like to share a bed with a man who scooped other people's latrines for a living. And if the woman woke up nauseated, how could *he* possibly help? She supposed their bathroom was pristine. Or what was that about the cobbler's children going barefoot?

A group of teenage boys, six of them, rushed in, crowding the tiny store. The spiky smell of oily scalps and pubescent undershirts filled the air. The boys were picking up candy bars, putting them down, opening the freezer to examine the Popsicles, slamming it shut. Tiny bouncing balls jumped from one hand to another.

Namin spoke loudly over them. "When does Mr. Hong usually pass my street? Do you think—"

"Just listen for the bell," *ajumma* said. "I'm sure he'll be by anytime now."

Of course. The bell. Every traveling vendor had his trademark signal, and that was his—a copper bell. Namin thanked her and quickly got out of the way. If the store *ajumma* said he would be on his way, then he would be here. Today, she would get it done.

She and Jisun walked the short block back to the house, the black car trailing them like an unwanted younger sibling.

Jisun said finally, her voice low with hurt, "Don't you want to hear what happened?"

Namin shook her head. "We probably shouldn't even talk about it, it'll only make us fight again."

"What if it's important—you still don't want to know?"

Namin said, "Whatever happened, you're here now. So."

"So it must not be important, you mean?"

"So you must be okay."

"That's how it works now? If I'm dead in a ditch somewhere, then you want to know. Otherwise I'm fine and we talk like strangers?"

"Look. We're fighting already. See what happens? You'll tell me and then we'll fight some more."

Jisun stopped walking and stood in the road, eyes flashing. Her cheeks were ablaze and her hands were balled into fists. Namin wondered what would happen if Jisun actually swung at her. Would she hit back? Would they actually do this in the middle of the road? The thought perversely appealed to her, the possibility that they would drop all the words they had thrown at each other all these years and just batter each other like rams.

"Go ahead," she said to Jisun. She wasn't sure if she was goading her to tell or fight.

"You are so heartless," Jisun said. "All this time I thought it was just an act to seem tough, but this is you, isn't it?" Her voice was steady, as if she had landed in a moment of perfect understanding and composure. But just as quickly her expression switched to fury. "Or you must think I am. You must think I have no heart at all."

"Why does it have to be either of us?" Namin said. "Neither of us is heartless, neither of us has to be."

"But you are," Jisun said. "All you care about is yourself. That's all you've ever cared about."

They knew each other better than anyone else in the world, yet it seemed they barely knew the first thing.

Namin wished they had just hit each other. She wished she had never opened the door in the first place, letting that anvil knock and knock until the iron ground down to dust.

"Because I don't care about every detail of your life, I don't care about anyone? If it's not you, then it's no one—Jisun, are you the whole world? And you think *I'm* the selfish one?"

"You win, Namin." Jisun was already walking away, but she turned back to say, "But you know what? I hope you never need a friend. Because I would hate for you to feel how I'm feeling right now."

Then she walked the few steps to the waiting car, where Namin realized Ko had been watching their exchange with unconcealed interest.

It was difficult to feel sorry when Jisun's dramatic exit involved speeding off in a shiny black car while she had to go back to her own shit-stinking house. But closing the heavy gate behind her, Namin couldn't shake Jisun's final words and the hard knot of guilt tightening in her gut. Jisun was right. She had won—but she'd gone too far. She sighed. There would have to be another buried apology, another chilly restoration period. How many times could they circle the same track before one of them stopped running?

10
....

The copper bell was long, like a pipe. Mr. Hong struck it with a syncopated staccato: *Tak! tak-Tak-tak!* A sonorous, jaunty march. With a beat like that, you expected a candy seller or a prelude to a festival.

In the silence after Jisun left, Namin listened as if feeling for vibrations, as if the room around her had turned liquid and would swallow any normal noises if she did not focus hard.

Tak! tak-Tak-tak!

Tak! tak-Tak-tak!

Barefoot, she rushed to the door and flung it open. There he was. Broad and straight, with a surprisingly placid face that she had never really taken the time to notice. He was no older than thirty, clean shaven, with prominent ears and the kind of lobes that curled forward slightly and showed a halo of down in full light.

"I was wondering what was happening with your house. It's been a long time," he said easily. He was wearing a thick rubber apron, black rubber boots. Behind him was the sewage tank, an enormous drum labeled WASTE. The letters, painted white, were badly chipped. "Usually the *unni* comes to find me, but it's been a while." He used the word *unni*, older sister, as if Kyungmin were his sister, too, and they were all one family. "You must be the brilliant student I've heard so much about." He said this over his shoulder, striding past her toward the bathroom. It occurred to her that he must know the exact location of every latrine in this neighborhood, the toilet habits of every family.

He pulled out two long plastic sleeves, which he rolled over his shirtsleeves. Namin thought, *I don't even know how much to pay him.* Somehow the idea of asking how much the service cost was more than she could bear. He stepped into the bathroom, ducking around the doorway to find the light. His apron was tied smartly behind him, the two sides of the bow perfectly symmetrical. The knot was tight against his back, and he was squatting to examine something. Namin tried to rehearse what she would say when he came out. Would they make small talk? Would she ask how his wife—who was nauseated not by him, but by the new creation of their child—was faring this morning? And this last plagued her worst of all: Should she *apologize* for the mess? Or was the right answer to pretend there was nothing to be ashamed of, nothing *he* should feel ashamed of?

Namin took a book and waited outside, leaning against the outer wall of her house. She pretended to read, even turning the pages at proper intervals, but the text was just lines on a page, nothing she could form into meaningful words. When a neighbor came by and asked what she was doing, she avoided answering but managed to ask how much she should pay Mr. Hong.

"You mean you really don't know? I guess even a college student like you has to have something to learn."

It was irritating to have her flaws pointed out so baldly, but Namin understood the neighbor meant this in a friendly way. This was the way of Miari—opinions were free and abundant. Namin would always be measured against her status as a Seoul University student, an ongoing honor that still earned her a measure of local celebrity. But the attention cut both ways, as even the most casual acquaintances felt free to dissect her shortcomings as if she were a member of their extended family.

Namin sighed. "It's just that usually my sister takes care of—"

"I understand, dear. We all have our jobs."

The cleaning took less time than she thought. In her mind it was a drawn-out process that required hours of waiting, as if Mr. Hong were a surgeon performing a difficult operation. But he was out just as she was thanking the helpful neighbor for the information. She paid Hong as if she had done it a thousand times.

Mr. Hong's fingers brushed her palm as he handed back her change. "See you in a couple of weeks, then." His hands were rough but dry, the leather of frequently scrubbed skin.

In her room, she stacked the coins on her desk and lay down on the floor. She closed her eyes. Inhaled a long deep breath: letting air shoot directly up her nostrils, straight to the brain.

Nothing. She smelled absolutely, blissfully, nothing.

AT ELEVEN THIRTY, Namin's parents staggered through the gate, smelling of grease and boiled pork, the day's cooking from their *pojangmacha,* the food cart they operated from dawn to curfew. Kyungmin was late again. The last bus that stopped at their neighborhood had passed and she had not been on it.

"What happened—Kyungmin didn't say anything?" Her mother sat on the lip of the courtyard and pummeled her swollen calves with her fist. She'd recently dyed her hair, and the black pigment—reddish gray now—still shadowed her hairline. Namin thought how her customers must have noticed it all day, wondering why no one at home had cared enough to tell her. Her father was already inside, reading the last of the paper. He prided himself on being the sort of man who never skipped a word, not even the advertisements crowding the margins. Long ago, Namin had realized he busied himself with these abstract goals to save himself the trouble of becoming too involved in the concrete complexities of his own family and business. Tonight she was grateful for his vacancy. It saved her from lying to him, too.

"She told me this morning. She's staying in the dorms," Namin said quickly. It felt necessary to continue the charade, even if she did not expect her mother to believe it. Kyungmin had never bothered to ask Namin to make any excuses for her, but with minutes left before curfew, it was clear she would not make it back tonight. Lying was a reflex, like putting out her hands to stop a blow. Even now, it wasn't clear whom she was trying to protect, Kyungmin or her mother. Perhaps she was only protecting herself.

Her mother stopped pounding and looked at her sharply. Kyungmin never stayed overnight at the factory. Even if she wanted to, the dorm mothers patrolled the place as if they were running a fancy hotel, not a basement labyrinth. Besides that, her sister hated to associate herself with the dorm girls, who had rough rural accents and never spent a penny on decent clothes or a night out, sending everything home to their families in the country. The city girls might work the same job, but they considered themselves a different class. Kyungmin and her friends never wore their factory uniforms outside of work. Instead they changed into street clothes just to ride the bus home. To try to pass as college students, they carried backpacks and read important-looking books in public. Namin had even heard them refer to the dorm girls as *gongsooni,* "factory girlies," using the belittling term as if it didn't apply equally to them.

"Tell me what she said exactly," her mother demanded.

"She said she might stay if she was too tired—and not to worry if we didn't see her tonight." Immediately Namin regretted the *might,* which opened the door to other possibilities. The point of the lie was to establish Kyungmin's whereabouts as a firm fact. *Might* made it a question.

"She must have been joking."

"Maybe. I thought she sounded serious."

"What else did she say?"

"Just that she's been tired and might get more rest if she didn't commute."

Her mother's expression revealed everything they were thinking but dared not say. With her heels planted in front of her, she yanked back the toes, cracking all the knuckles at once. Each night she applied the same brutal pragmatism to her feet that she did to her aching calves, her shoulders, her two brooding daughters. It was always her strategy to meet force with force. Pain with pain.

"Go ahead and wash up," she said finally. "I'll listen for the door."

In her room, Namin lay down and stared at the milky white bowl covering the dim ceiling bulb. Over the years, insect carcasses had collected inside it, forming a kind of pattern in the glass. She thought of the generations of bugs that must be mixed up in there. Whole family trees. She wondered if they considered it any consolation. *At least we're here together.* Or if, like her family, they barely knew one another at all. A random leg here, a nameless antenna there. Her mother was now smashing her shoulders with her fist. Right fist crossed over the chest, smashing left shoulder. Left fist over the chest, smashing right shoulder. The rhythmic thumping of her exhausted flesh reverberated across the yard.

The gate hinges screeched and Namin sat up, listening for Kyungmin. She heard her mother's voice instead—"Just me"—and lay back down. Her mother continued to speak, her disembodied voice carrying through Namin's closed door. It seemed they were always speaking through walls.

"You got Mr. Hong, I see."

"I did."

"Aren't you washing up?"

"Coming."

Namin hauled herself off the floor and went back out to the courtyard to wash. The curved neck of the faucet glinted dully in the moonlight. She filled the basin halfway, rolling up her sleeves and cuffing her pants, pulling them as far up her shins as they would go. The water was bracingly cold, but she didn't mind. She splashed her arms and legs, scrubbing hard between each toe, getting a fingernail under each toenail. She threw water in cupped handfuls behind her neck and washed until her earlobes squeaked clean. Water dripped down her neck and into her bra, trailing icy fingers. She flicked her head impatiently, shaking off the shivers. Her shirt would dry overnight and be fine in the morning, cleaner for having been partially doused.

When everything else she could reach was clean, she washed her face and brushed her teeth, the now damp towel hung around her neck.

She bade her parents good night and slid her bedroom door closed. When she lay down under the quilts, her face was still half-numb, almost sterilized with cold. Her teeth tingled with the taste of toothpaste.

She heard her parents wash up. She heard her father's newspaper being carefully closed. She heard their light click off, the sound instantly corroborated by a deeper settling in her own room. They were all listening for the squeal of the door. The absence of it had its own sound, a kind of hollow echoing. It badgered her, making her doubt her senses.

If Kyungmin came home, nothing would change. The Kang family would continue as before in their unequal division of labor. Parents running the food tent, Kyungmin at the factory. Namin at the top of the pyramid with her books and exam scores and degrees, buffered from the worst of her family's poverty by the expectation that one day her great success would rescue them all. Everyone understood their respective roles, and Namin for her part did not resent the burden of carrying her family's future. It was only the past that truly haunted her, particularly on a night like this when it was impossible not to remember and take stock.

In mentally listing the members of her family, she had left out her younger brother, Hyun. Five years younger, he had been born with physical disabilities that she now knew represented a form of cerebral palsy. As a child, Namin was told nothing to explain why he appeared different from other babies, why she was not to speak of him to friends or neighbors, or why he was never to be taken outside of the house. She was too young to understand the shame his condition caused her parents, the belief that outsiders would see him as a curse on the family, a sign of some deserved misfortune. After his second birthday, Hyun was taken to live with their grandparents in their rural village. Afterward, their parents never spoke of him and—as far as she knew— never saw him again.

If success meant rescuing her family, then Namin was determined to include her brother, who mattered more to her than anyone else.

Years ago, against her parents' wishes, Namin had begun to visit him in the countryside. She made the trip whenever she could get away for a weekend. They had been raised apart, but there was a bond between them that Namin had never felt with any other member of her family. Each of the five Kangs was tough, resourceful, resilient; but her parents' and Kyungmin's inner lives were locked within armored exteriors that rarely showed a crack. Only Hyun, with his slow, careful speech and affectionate manner, was truly accessible to her. She planned for their future together as assiduously as if she were his sole guardian. Their grandparents had taken faithful care of him, but they were getting old and would not live forever. She hated to think what would happen if they fell ill or died, leaving Hyun without a caretaker. When that time came, Namin was determined that he would not be abandoned a second time. He would come to Seoul and live with her.

And so it was critical for everything to remain on course. Kyungmin had to come home. Namin had to graduate and secure a good job. All this so she could afford to take care of Hyun when the time came. She would not let herself—or him—down.

Namin traced the contours of the silence, feeling the dark, inky night. In his room, her father coughed three times. She strained to check the stillness of the door over the coughing. But it was the same. Silence.

When she finally fell asleep around dawn and her sister still had not returned—her first overnight absence—it was with the knowledge that Kyungmin had as good as declared war on their family, wiping out their future and replacing it with a new script that no one wanted.

In the morning, the three of them went about their usual business, refusing to acknowledge the advent of their new reality. Her parents left at the usual time, wearing their usual clothes. Everyone said and did the usual things. "Lock the door," Namin's mother said, the last thing she always said before leaving. Namin nodded and did as she was told, though she wondered what was worth safeguarding now within their family's gate.

11

....

n the following weeks, Kyungmin's overnight absences became more frequent. The first few times, her mother dragged Kyungmin into her room and slapped her hard across the face and demanded to know where she'd been. Each time, her sister said nothing. She did not cry or beg forgiveness. She did not try to explain. It was this total lack of fear that terrified Namin more than anything: it signaled that her sister had already made irreversible choices. That the force of their disappointment no longer carried enough weight to matter.

On the nights she did return, Kyungmin slunk through the gate minutes before midnight and went straight to the room she shared with Namin. Around her eyes and lips were lurid traces of makeup. The skin around her lips was stained and swollen pink. Not bothering to wash up or even greet anyone, she simply lay down and went to sleep. Finally, Namin would call over the courtyard, "She's home!"—which her parents knew, but acknowledging it temporarily defused the alarm. For another night, the family settled into an uneasy détente.

"I gave you girls everything I could—and this is how she repays me," her mother said bitterly. "Everyone told me it was useless to put too much stock in a daughter. Why bother worrying over someone else's daughter-in-law, why waste your heart, but I said no. I said girl or not, they're mine. Haven't I always treated you as I would a son?" Namin flinched at that, thinking how her mother had treated her only son. Her mother went on, seemingly oblivious to her mistake. "My only sin is being poor. I grant you that. But I'm not punished enough as it is being poor; my own daughter becomes a—" She always stopped short of saying the word. Taking a deep breath as if to reset herself.

The final time began as usual. Seventeen minutes before midnight, the family watching the clock. Waiting.

Eleven minutes before midnight, the gate shrieked on its hinge. Namin slid open her bedroom door and peered into the darkness.

Her mother and sister faced off in the courtyard. The light from the bedroom cast uneven shadows over their features and emphasized Kyungmin's dark eye makeup. Her hair was teased and swept back around her cheekbones. She looked beautiful and fierce, like a woman onstage.

Her mother's voice was cramped with the effort of controlling herself. "Come in and talk to me."

"I'm tired. Another time."

"Then we'll talk here. We don't need to be long. I want to give you the chance to tell me the truth. Have you been staying in the dorms? Are you too tired to come home?"

Silently, Namin begged her sister to agree. It wasn't the truth her mother was after, but a way for them to live together in peace for a little while longer. Whatever the real story, here was a pardon, a truce. *Say yes,* she pleaded into the darkness. Perhaps it was even true, and perhaps they would believe her. *Say yes.*

Namin strained to hear her sister's response. But there was nothing. No acceptance, no rebuttal. Silence.

"Did you hear me—" her mother said. Her voice caught, and Namin knew she was crying. "I asked you a question."

Kyungmin said, "Do you think I'm in the dorms?"

"That's where I hope you are."

"Then that's where I am."

Her mother recoiled as if Kyungmin had struck her. Her chest heaved as her sobs became wails.

Kyungmin started speaking in a low voice. Calmly, as if she'd rehearsed the speech for years. "I'm twenty-seven years old. Three more years to get her to graduation and I'm thirty. Namin will have her degree and what will I have? Nothing."

"Namin having her degree is not nothing," her mother shouted. "It's for all of us."

"But I don't need her to help me! I can help myself. And I don't have to wait until I'm halfway dead. I can help myself *now*."

"Looking like that? By being a *whore*?"

The word she'd refused to say all these weeks uncoiled and snapped like a snake from its nest. Namin trembled, not because of what it would do to her sister or even the shock she felt herself, but what it had meant for her mother. To finally release the word that had been stuck in her throat.

Kyungmin shrugged. Her eyes stayed hooded, unalarmed. "Namin has people to impress and so do I."

Namin sensed it before she truly saw it—her mother's hands around Kyungmin's throat. Her sister's face white against the dark gate. Her mother screaming.

Her father was already there, trying to break her grip. He pried at the fingers one by one, methodical as always. Working with all the concentration in his body, his fists bunched around her fingers so tightly, it looked as if Kyungmin were being doubly strangled.

Namin ran and grabbed her mother by the shoulders. She heaved with all her strength, but her mother's body was as rigid as a boulder and she would not let go.

They breathed as a family. They collapsed as a family. Her father had his arms wrapped around her mother like a human straitjacket, holding her tight. Her body looked so small, depleted. She lay in his arms crying and choking as if she had been the one near strangled.

Kyungmin, who had fallen a few paces away, was straining on all fours like a dog, heaving for air. With a huge gasp she vomited a clear, syrupy liquid, then lay down with her face in the dirt.

For several minutes the four of them stayed where each had fallen, listening to the ragged edges of one another's breath.

"Take her to bed," her father told Namin finally.

Her mother was still sobbing. He half carried, half dragged her away to their room. Namin heard the sounds of sleeping mats being taken out and arranged, of her father saying, "Lie down, Mother. You must rest." She heard her mother's fists pounding the floor, her cries becoming a kind of keening, more animal sounding than human. It was a rolling, high-pitched wail that frightened Namin more than the welts rising on Kyungmin's neck. In the neighborhood, two dogs began to howl. Namin wanted to clamp her hands over her ears and howl along with them. She wanted to curl up in the dirt next to her sister and discover that this had been a terrible nightmare and she'd soon wake up.

Instead she balanced on her haunches next to her sister, timidly stroking her back. She felt Kyungmin's shuddering breath vibrate under her fingertips. She was so skinny, the knobs of her spine clearly defined under her hands. They had shared the same bedroom her whole life, their bodies always in proximity, but she could not remember the last time they had touched each other out of affection.

When Kyungmin could sit up, Namin asked, "Can you stand?"

She nodded, wiping her chin with the dirty palms of her hands.

Namin helped her to her feet and to their room. She brought a wet towel to wipe her face and hands. Despite the intimacy of these gestures, it was like ministering to a stranger. Kyungmin accepted the help but did not thank her. She lay down under her quilt and turned her face to the wall.

For a long time Namin sat up, watching her sister sleep, blotting her sweating forehead with the towel, smoothing her hair. Even in sleep, Kyungmin's face never relaxed. Her complexion retained a pale gray cast like watered-down milk.

Finally she lay down next to her sister, sharing her quilt the way they used to as children. She slept with her head nestled near Kyungmin's bruised neck, careful not to hurt her but close enough to feel her sister's breath in her ear, the warm air on her cheek.

. . .

IN THE MORNING, she was gone. Namin combed their room for clues, looking for something her sister might have left behind as a message. She found nothing. The things she had taken were concise and pragmatic: underwear and bras. Her favorite cosmetics. Clothes. Anything they shared that Namin might miss—a red resin comb, hairpins, stockings, picture frames—were all left behind. Books, papers, pens. Untouched.

Something was nagging at Namin's subconscious. Something important was missing.

With a sinking feeling, Namin slid open the bottom drawer where she kept her only framed photo of the three of them. Kyungmin aged fourteen, Namin aged seven, and Hyun, two years old, sprawled over her lap like an oversize rag doll. Even before she felt the weightless slide of the drawer, she knew it was gone.

Kyungmin had taken it, and Namin knew that meant her sister was gone for good.

II

1

. . . .

Four thirty-five A.M. The predawn mornings still had the breath of winter, a soft-focus chill that seemed to move her destination farther away, as in the never-ending journeys of childhood. In Namin's memory, the long bus trips to her grandparents' village always seemed to be accompanied by extreme weather. Every New Year, they would pack up bundles of traditional food their mother had spent days preparing and squeeze onto the bus next to other similarly laden families, everyone wearing layers of their warmest thermal underwear and pressing the hot food bundles against their bodies to endure the hours of unheated travel. If it was snowing or sleeting, the bus driver would have to periodically pull off the road and hack at the dirty black ice encrusting the windshield wipers. But the freezing cold was preferable to the stifling heat and humidity of the summer trips. At least in the winter there was the comfort of eating freshly boiled potatoes, licking the melting salt off her fingers as steam wafted into her nose. Or the pleasure of peeling a roasted yam, bit by bit, as she nibbled at the sweet yellow flesh. During the hot months, there were no treats and no relief. The adults grew short-tempered and liberal with punishing slaps, easier to land on limbs bared in summer T-shirts and shorts. It was inevitable that some kid would become sick and need to throw up in a plastic bag, which his mother would tie up and toss out the window without looking where it might land in traffic. Trapped within the pressure-cooker environment, the vomit smell lingered in the bus, and Namin, fearful of suffering a similar outcome, would force herself to breathe through her mouth for the remainder of the trip.

After Hyun was born, there were no more trips to see her grand-parents. As if his disability had infected the whole family, as if they were all as paralyzed as he was. Namin recalled the heavy stillness, the sense that she must not bother her parents or talk to anyone in the neighborhood about the new baby.

"But why shouldn't we talk about the baby?" Namin remembered asking her sister one day. "People are always asking about him. What am I supposed to do?"

Her sister's eyes flashed contempt, letting Namin know how dumb she was to even ask such questions. "What's there to be so proud of that you want to chatter about him, anyway? A baby like that should never have been born. Better for all of us—including him." Her voice sounded strained and unfamiliar, and Namin understood she was only parroting what she had heard and what they were supposed to believe. Still, the harsh words stung. The baby was barely old enough to seem like a real person, but he was still her baby brother. *Their* brother. Her eyes welled with tears.

Kyungmin sighed in exasperation. "Just say you don't know any-thing. Better yet, say nothing. They'll stop asking soon enough."

"It seems rude," Namin said in a small voice.

"Well, princess. We're not exactly living at the royal palace, are we. Only well-off people get to worry about being rude."

This time it was her sister's real voice. Her own mocking words, which Namin had heard a hundred times before.

"I'm not a princess," she said.

Her sister rolled her eyes. "I *know*."

Hyun was sent away when Namin was seven, too young to under-stand, thinking she was merely getting an afternoon's break from her brother. Thinking it was about time her mother finally took him out of the house.

"Say goodbye," her mother had said, and Namin barely waved from the floor, where she was arranging her paper dolls in a parade. She remembered she'd felt glad to see them go. What luxury to have the place empty of him for a change. His rickety, smelly chair was always in the way, and he was never quiet, not babbling normally like other little brothers but squawking and hooting like some kind of human chicken. After they left, Namin had spent the afternoon drawing new dolls and outfits for her collection. She had been in such a good mood, she had drawn herself a brand-new house.

Two days passed. Saturday, Sunday. The house was so quiet, she could hear the suck of the filter each time her father inhaled on a cigarette. She could hear the slight rattle of the pot lid over boiling rice. At night, there was a rustling under the floor, sharp, scuttling sounds and a drone of persistent chewing. Namin stayed awake the entire first night listening to it, at first afraid she was imagining things, then afraid to ask what it was.

"Rats," her sister said the next morning. The light was painful to Namin's scratchy eyes. "Have you really never heard them before?"

Namin admitted she hadn't. She always fell asleep with the lights on while her sister stayed up poking at herself in a red plastic mirror, applying one or another potion to her face or hair. Namin had never in her life slept in a room by herself. She had never stayed awake long enough to see the lights turned out. The revelation of the rodents seemed to add another week to her mother's absence. Their arrival, new to her, seemed an ill omen.

When her mother finally returned, Namin, so intent on telling her about the rats, did not immediately realize Hyun wasn't with her. She had already begun the story of the sleepless night, the strange sounds that had concerned her, the speechless terror—when suddenly she noticed how quiet it still was.

"Where's Hyun?"

"Hyun?" Her mother repeated the name vacantly, and Namin suddenly saw what she should have noticed earlier. The mismatched buttons of her mother's blouse. Her collar pointing jaggedly at her throat. Her face looked gray and rumpled, like old newspapers.

"Didn't he come with you? Where is he?" Namin looked to her sister, but Kyungmin had turned her back. Her father, too, refused to meet her eyes.

Her mother murmured, "Hyun needs to stay in the country awhile. He has more room with your grandparents. He'll be more comfortable there."

Namin pictured the tiny farm hut where her grandparents lived. The thatch-roof structure struck her more like a freestanding cave than a house. Everything was small and dim and low. Even her mother had to duck through the doorways. The walls smelled like glue from the constantly peeling wallpaper, and there were no light switches, only strings hanging from the bare bulb in the ceiling that she could not reach. Worst of all, the bathroom was in an outhouse beyond an overgrown hedge. At night, the thorny bushes swayed and took on beastly shapes. Terrified, Namin limited food and water so she would never have to use it, which insulted her grandmother so much that she did not even pretend to like her.

The only good thing about the place was the nearby stream, where she looked for snails under the rocks. The water was cool and clean. In the rice fields, there were frogs the color of new clover and fat-bodied tadpoles. Namin tried to stay outside as much as possible. She would rather pee in the stream while pretending to swim than do it at home.

But Hyun would never be able to walk or swim in the stream, looking for snails. His chair wouldn't roll very well over the dirt roads.

"For how long?" she asked warily. "When's he coming back?"

"Try to understand," her mother said.

"But how long, *how long?*" Namin shrieked.

Kyungmin's shoulders jerked, and she kept wetting her lips as if she would speak. But instead of the grief or outrage Namin expected, her sister made only a thin gulping sound, a sound like crying without tears.

Only then did Namin realize her family already knew. They had planned it together and agreed to keep it from her.

Betrayal was a word she knew, but it was not sharp enough or big enough to express this event. Namin suddenly understood that families were not permanent. They could abandon you without explanation or warning. They could erase a member without so much as a tear.

Wasn't the world full of strict hierarchical words meant to tie everyone together? *Unni:* older sister of a girl. *Nuna:* older sister of a boy. *Nam-dongsaeng:* younger sibling, boy. *Yuh-dongsaeng:* younger sibling, girl. Aunts on your mother's side, a different word from aunts on your father's side. Your father's brothers, more honorific than your mother's brothers. So much careful specificity built into the language so no one could forget. And none of it mattered.

That day, Namin dropped them all as lies. She never again called Kyungmin by her expected title, Kyungmin *unni,* older sister. Scandalized, the neighbors criticized their parents for permitting such a breach of basic manners, but there was nothing anyone could do to change Namin's mind.

Hyun hadn't died, but he became a ghost. He followed Namin everywhere she went, making her see how things weren't always the way she thought. People said she had an uncanny air about her, what they called a *heavy presence.* Namin thought this only natural, since she was carrying two people in the space of one.

WAS SHE ASHAMED? Jisun asked her once. This was soon after she found out about Hyun. At home, Hyun was a taboo topic, strictly avoided. It had been so long since Namin had even said his name out loud that she had felt superstitious and fearful, as if she were somehow harming him by doing so.

Of course Namin was ashamed. But not the way Jisun thought. It was never that Namin was ashamed of Hyun. It was more complicated than that. To be ashamed of him because his body was twisted and weak or because he had been marked with an illness people considered a judgment on the family would have been a more straightforward thing, a reason she could explain to herself the way her parents had— neatly and permanently. Instead her feelings were a tangled confusion, gnarled around the shame of knowing her parents had abandoned him so easily. Of having accepted his disappearance as a child because she had been told to forget him.

Young as she was, shouldn't she have resisted letting him go?

Shouldn't she have known better? And since she had done nothing to stop it, didn't it make her just as bad as the rest of her family?

Shame was not just about secrets or covering up. Or about failure and not having the things other people casually had.

Shame was being afraid that she was from crippled, graceless stock, unworthy of the good things other people had. That the mistakes that would chart her life forever had already been made.

Maybe Kyungmin was right. Maybe it was only well-off people who had the luxury of behaving with dignity.

FOUR THIRTY-FIVE A.M. Namin boarded the bus and chose a seat on the right side, two-thirds of the way back. She tried to make this trip as often as she could. Monthly, she promised herself. That wasn't too hard, was it? Visiting her brother once a month? But time had never been on her side, and the visits stretched to once every other month, sometimes once a season. Each time, this journey stirred up her most vulnerable insecurities about the past and the future. How she would make it up to Hyun for all the years of his life she'd missed, denying his existence. And how she would ever repay Jisun for forcing her to finally acknowledge her brother when she might have allowed him to fade out of her life forever.

2

. . . .

It was toward the end of Namin and Jisun's first year of middle school when a girl named Minju jumped from the roof of their school, impaling herself on the wrought-iron fence below. A notoriously bad student and a jokester who flaunted not only her poor ranking but also the abuse she received from the teachers, Minju had seemed the last person who would do something so serious as killing herself. It seemed like one of her bad jokes. For days after her death, even the teachers went around with looks of puzzled suspicion, as if they believed they'd been pranked. Then the wisecracks started.

People said she'd jumped from that spot on purpose to cause the biggest headache. A mangled body on school property? What a nuisance! They also said it had been the smartest thing Minju had ever done—to correctly calculate the right distance and velocity to land on just that spot. It mustn't have been that easy, they said. Let's see the equations.

When rumors of a ghost sighting began to circulate the week after her burial, the faculty didn't pay much attention. It had been a grisly death. The students were at a vulnerable age, prone to imagination and hysteria. They were stretched too thin by their new academic responsibilities. The student who reported it was told to get more rest and to think before making up stories that would only upset the rest of her classmates.

But no one could blame it on nerves or adolescent hormones when Mr. Kwon saw Minju as he was locking up the faculty lounge at the end of the day. An eternal bachelor and scholarly expert in ancient Korean naval tactics, Mr. Kwon was the strictest teacher in school. Behind his back, the girls called him "Professor Ostrich" because of his long, protruding neck and the way his throat jumped each time he swallowed. No one thought him at all capable of imagination or hysteria. While he seemed unhappy to talk about it—he must have thought it diminished his authority—his ghost sighting actually made him popular for the first time in his tenure. The students flocked to hear details, then magnified them for their own retelling.

Namin never heard the original points, only the inevitable exaggerations. Considering ghosts a kind of personal specialty, she declined to muddy her experiences with secondhand tales.

To say she expected to see Minju next would seem facile in retrospect. But leading up to it, there had been that ticklish feeling. A kind of wriggle at the back of her knees and throat that felt half like sleepwalking and half like the moment before a sneeze, extended.

It had been several weeks since Mr. Kwon's sighting, the day before an important math exam. Namin and half a dozen others had stayed after school to study together. It was around eight o'clock and they had finally broken into their dinner boxes. On long study days like this, their mothers packed two meals—lunch and dinner. Some girls always ate their better meal earlier in the day and bartered for choice bits during dinner. The second group dealt with dinner as a kind of longer-term investment. They could either trade for favors from the first group or enjoy the simple satisfaction of being envied. Usually Namin had the most coveted meals since she had the pick of her parents' cart, but that day she'd overslept and had time only to grab the first thing at hand: cold rice and a few vegetable *banchans,* truly disappointing fare after a long day of studying. Having no patience for hunger, she'd managed to haggle a fried *bindaeduk* out of Jisun in exchange for the hated task of filling up the enormous water kettle downstairs.

The kettle, as round and wide as a ripe watermelon, was heavy and awkward to haul up three flights of stairs. A taller person could possibly hold it in one hand, throwing her weight the other way as a cantilever. But Namin, among the shortest girls in class, didn't have the height to leverage. She had to use both hands to lug the kettle in front of her. It knocked against her knees at every step, sloshing cold water over her feet. She stopped to rest at each landing.

Namin saw her first out of the corner of her eye. Thinking it was one of her study group friends coming to help, she said, "Hey, that *bindaeduk* is mine. No sharing—" And realized with a lurch that it was not her friend, but the recently dead girl, Minju. Namin had always heard of ghosts wearing white clothing, floating on air, but Minju appeared as solid and unghostlike as ever, only less rumpled. Her school uniform appeared crisply ironed, collar straight, shoes shiny. Actually, Namin had never seen the girl look so neat.

The ghost gave her a friendly smile.

"Do you need some help?" she asked. Her expression was so warm and open, Namin felt obliged to stay and talk. She shook her head. When she was alive, Namin had always taken great pains to stay away from her, if only to avoid the inevitable lecture they'd both endure if any teacher happened to notice them together. *Now look, Minju. Why can't you be more like Namin here? So nice and quiet, studies hard. You could learn a thing or two from her.* They might have thought they were motivating Minju, but the attention only heaped further humiliation on Namin. The other girl might gain a little sympathy from classmates who pitied her for always being in trouble. No one ever felt sorry for the teacher's pet.

"I know you think I can't do it, but I can," Minju was saying. "I can lift all sorts of things. I could carry that kettle with one hand." Her neat appearance had fooled Namin into thinking that perhaps in shedding her life, she had also managed to come free from her burdensome persona. But the petulant, boastful girl who was always arguing, always tilting the conversation in her favor, had not changed. "Everyone thought I couldn't do it, but I can. You wouldn't believe the things I can do now." The more she talked, the more her voice took on a menacing edge, as if she would not take no for an answer. Namin took a tiny step back, hoping the ghost girl wouldn't notice. She did not want to see what Minju could do now.

"No, it's really fine," she said. "I know you can do it, but I'm sure I can manage. It's only one more flight and—"

"You don't want to scare the others." Minju nodded sagely. "Of course. I understand."

And she did seem to understand. Her expression softened and she ran a hand through her hair as if embarrassed to find herself in this position. Namin held her breath, wondering if the ghost girl would simply vanish or if it was up to her to walk away. But she couldn't bring herself to turn her back. Perhaps if she said something comforting . . . "I hope you're not suffering now. It's terrible . . . what happened."

"Oh, it's not so bad," Minju said. "At least I don't have to worry about exams. I do whatever I want all day. I guess you'd better get back to your studying."

"Yes. Well. Good chatting with you."

"Likewise." Minju gave a stiff little wave, her fingers wiggling in an uncomfortable way as if they no longer bent at the knuckles. Flickering ever so slightly, the ghost girl turned and sauntered back into the corridor. "Oh, by the way—"

Namin looked up. "Yes?"

"Your brother's dead."

THE OTHERS IN the study group later said that Namin's screams were so loud, they searched the wrong floor, thinking she was closer. When they finally found her, she was slumped on the floor, the kettle completely overturned at her feet. They assumed she had slipped and kept asking where it hurt, but she could not stop sobbing long enough to answer.

Finally, Jisun told the others to leave her with Namin. "Let me talk to her. We're crowding her, she's obviously overwhelmed." The others retreated, promising to track down towels to dry her off. Walking away, they rolled their eyes. It seemed like a crazy display over nothing, too much for a simple fall. She didn't even seem hurt.

Jisun waited until they were completely alone.

"You saw her, didn't you. The ghost, I mean. What did she say?" she demanded. "Come on, tell me."

Namin shuddered. "I can't."

Jisun sat back on her heels. She looked right at the spot where the ghost girl had been. "Then I won't tell you what she told me."

So Namin told her everything.

The ghost, her brother, the disappearance. The story came out in a rush, like water over a shattered dam. When she was through, she felt the immediate panic of having released a secret she had never told anyone else. Now that Jisun knew, they would have to be friends forever. She could not bear to have her secrets walking around, unguarded. "Now you tell me what she told you," she said quickly, hoping to regain some balance between them. She hoped Jisun's secret was just as awful as hers, although Jisun was so careless about her family that she always told Namin everything without an ounce of shame.

Jisun made an innocent face. "Who? Told me what?"

"You said you saw her too." Namin couldn't dare say Minju's name in case she reappeared. "The ghost."

"I never said I saw anything," Jisun said. "I only *implied*. You filled in the rest."

"But you were looking right where she was standing."

"Was I?" Jisun smiled, unable to hide her delight. "Then it was just great luck."

Namin was stunned. She had told her worst secret to a liar. A liar and a cheat.

"Don't be mad," Jisun said. "I won't tell a soul. And listen, I'll help you."

"Help me with what?" Namin said. "I don't need your help."

"Well—we have to find out if what she said about your brother is true, don't we?" Jisun said. "I suppose you couldn't just ask your parents."

Namin shook her head. "Of course not. They're the ones who sent him away. Anyway, we never talk about him. They pretend he doesn't exist."

"Why? Because they feel guilty about leaving him?"

"Guilty? No—" Namin paused, confused. She'd never considered if her parents felt guilty. They'd always behaved as if they'd done absolutely the right thing, the thing anyone else would have done in their situation. And it was true—no one in the neighborhood had seemed shocked or troubled when he was sent away, as if they had expected it all along. "I guess they feel it's easier if we just forget him."

"That's stupid," Jisun said flatly. "He's your brother. Do you really think you should just forget him?"

It was the first time anyone had ever given Namin the option to say yes or no when it came to Hyun. It was the first time it seemed possible to think, *Everyone else was wrong about Hyun and I was right. I was right all along.* It was an exhilarating idea, like being allowed to breathe cold fresh air after being trapped all her life in an underground cave. She felt a surge of gratitude for Jisun, who just by saying the word *stupid* had given her something to feel wise about.

But Namin couldn't help remembering what her sister had said— that only wealthy people could afford to be nice. She could hear Kyungmin's voice in her head, saying, *You think she's so smart? So special? Of course she thinks that, the rich brat. They think they're so much better than us.*

So Namin buried her gratitude. She was just as good as Jisun and didn't need her to tell her what to think. "Of course I don't think I should just forget him," she said. "And I *haven't.*"

"So then you have to go find him," Jisun said.

"At my grandparents'? No way."

"Namin, how can you stand not knowing if your own brother is alive or dead? What if he died years ago and you didn't even know? If you can't ask, then you have to go. You have to find out."

It seemed foolhardy to even consider taking Jisun's advice now, the clever liar, but Namin knew she was right. She had to find out. And what was the alternative, really—continue as if nothing had happened? There was no way to undo what she'd seen and heard tonight. She would never sleep again if she didn't at least try.

· · ·

TOGETHER THEY DECIDED that Namin would take the bus the following Saturday and tell her parents she was staying overnight with
Jisun. Jisun would lend her the money for the fare.

But when the day came, Jisun was waiting at the station, heavy
backpack slung over her shoulder, a plastic bag laden with snacks dangling from her hand.

"I never go anywhere," she said defensively, as if she'd been arguing with Namin in her head all morning. "Anyway, it's safer if we go
together."

Steeped in anxiety for days, Namin was secretly relieved to see her
friend. She knew Jisun would get on that bus no matter what she said
to dissuade her, so she pretended to be annoyed to save face. "Who
said you could come? Anyway, I'm perfectly safe. It's just a bus ride,
not a trip around the world."

"You know, when my mother died I didn't find out for almost a
week. *He* probably wouldn't have told me at all if it wasn't for the funeral. He had to have me there for the ceremonies, you see. It wouldn't
have looked right otherwise. So it's good that you're doing this, taking
control of your own information. That's important." She was chewing
her lip. "I didn't tell anyone where I am. It's our secret—I mean, *your*
secret. You'll let me come, won't you?"

Namin nodded. She never knew what to say when Jisun talked
about her father. It was as if she were talking about God—and Namin
didn't believe in God.

"Just don't blame me if you get in trouble," she said. She wondered
what someone like Jisun's father would do when his only daughter
went missing overnight. Would he call the police? Have all of Seoul
searched, block by block? Namin imagined flashing lights and helicop-
ters descending over the city, loudspeakers blaring Jisun's name, offering rewards for any acts of bravery, and threatening maximum
punishment to those who might be responsible for her abduction.

But Jisun seemed completely untroubled by such considerations.
She was busy unwrapping one of the chocolate bars from her stash,

dividing the squares, and offering Namin the larger portion. Her smile was as bright as the shiny gold wrapping.

"Blame you? For what?" she said, and jumped on the bus ahead of Namin.

Namin had expected a long, somber trip, a journey of remorse that would give her the strength to confront what her family had done. To face her brother—if he was even alive—and let him know that she had not forgotten him and that she was sorry. She was terrified not just of what she might discover, but of the more mundane logistics of riding a long-haul bus hours away from Seoul, the only place she knew, and arriving unannounced at her grandparents' village. Would she even remember the way to their home? Lying awake the night before, Namin had tried to mentally trace the walk from the bus stop to their gate, but it was a jumble of disconnected landmarks. A dusty yellow road. A field lined with squash blossoms. A gray concrete wall topped with a bright blue roof advertising Fanta orange drinks and cheap perms. Her best hope was to rely on the tiny size of the village, where someone might remember her, or at least know her grandparents and give her directions.

But instead of the miles of silence she'd anticipated, there was Jisun chattering as if they were going on a holiday, offering her endless treats and pointing out evidence that they were approaching, now passing, now well beyond the city limit, as if Seoul were a prison they were leaving behind.

"Aren't you excited about finally seeing your brother again?" Jisun asked in an exasperated voice when she had finally run out of things to notice outside their window. "You look like you're going to your own execution or something. Cheer up, Namin. This is supposed to be an adventure."

"For you, maybe," Namin said. "I doubt you'd feel so cheerful if you had to face your brother after so many years. He probably thinks we're all evil monsters. I guess we are."

"But not you," Jisun said. "You were just a kid, like him. He can't blame you for that."

"If he's even alive," Namin muttered.

"I bet he is," Jisun said confidently. Her face was set with the kind of stalwart certainty Namin imagined came naturally to someone like her, whose life always unfolded in good, predictable ways. The urge to wipe that unearned assurance off Jisun's face overwhelmed her. Namin squeezed her hands between her thighs to keep herself still, but inwardly she fumed. Jisun had no right to be so sure, to make such easy wagers on other people's futures as if it were all just a game. A fun adventure.

Namin closed her eyes and pretended to sleep.

"Do you want to practice what you're going to say to your brother?" Jisun whispered.

Namin ignored her. She could hear Jisun holding her breath, which meant she was thinking of the next thing to say, debating if she should say it or leave her alone. Her breath caught in a half hiccup, then exhaled in a soft *whoosh*. "Okay, I'll wake you up later," she said in that same fake whisper, which amplified rather than lowered her voice. "We can practice then."

Namin opened her eyes and glared at Jisun. "Who do you think you are, my teacher?" she asked. "Did you have a script in mind? Are you planning to make me memorize it?"

"I only meant if you want," Jisun said quickly. "Anyway, it doesn't hurt to practice."

"Why don't you practice leaving me alone," Namin said. Immediately she regretted being so mean, but she didn't feel like apologizing.

Jisun opened another package of sweets—caramel puffed corn—and ate the whole bag without offering a single piece to Namin, even though they both knew it was her favorite. *Typical,* thought Namin. They rode the rest of the way without speaking.

But that weekend Jisun surprised her more than once, and she had to admit, if only to herself, that there were things to learn from her friend that she might not have previously surmised.

Where Namin was squeamish about rural discomforts—the outhouse latrine, her grandparents' cramped and musty hut, their humble food and faded, patched bedding—Jisun appeared completely at home. She ate everything they put in front of her without even asking what it was. She slurped the brown, slimy mystery soup, more grease than broth, and ate the bitter dandelion greens that stained the tongue and left a harsh aftertaste, and chewed the coarse barley rice, which Namin compared to small pebbles. Jisun drank the water poured from the kettle with the rusted handle without a moment's hesitation, and when the time came to use the bathroom, she marched herself out to the privy with toilet paper in hand and came back with a shrug toward Namin's questioning glance, as if to say, *So it's an outhouse, what's the big deal?*

But even more surprising was Jisun's attitude toward Hyun. Namin had forgotten the way to her grandparents' home after all and had to be directed by a neighbor, who led them out to the field where her grandparents were harvesting great fistfuls of spinach. Nearby, a boy sat in a wheeled cart, shaded by a giant blue umbrella.

All three members of Namin's family stopped what they were doing and stared as the girls approached.

"Is that you, Namin?" her grandmother called when they were within earshot. She did not sound happy to see them. "Is your mother with you?"

Tongue-tied, Namin shook her head.

"We came alone," Jisun said.

Namin's grandmother squinted at Jisun. "And who're you?"

"I'm Namin's friend. We came to meet her brother. This must be him," Jisun said, walking over to where the boy was sitting. "You're Hyun, aren't you? Do you remember your sister?"

Suddenly everyone was speaking at once.

"Of course he does, his own sister," said Namin's grandmother at the same time that she, Namin, said, "Of course he doesn't. He was too young." Maybe she hoped he wouldn't remember. All her own memories of him had grown so thin and threadbare that she was startled to see the real boy, seemingly all limbs tucked into his chair. He was slender like everyone else in the family, but less frail looking than she would have expected. He had a healthy tan like any other country kid. He held her gaze with bright, curious eyes.

"Let him answer," Jisun said firmly. "No one is letting him speak for himself." And somehow they all obeyed—turning with expectation to the young boy.

Hyun studied both girls, Namin and Jisun, carefully turning from one to the other as if comparing their features. Namin noticed he had the same jet black glossy hair that she and Kyungmin had. His was cut differently from either of theirs, of course, in the helmet style of a little boy, but it was his hair—so familiar that she knew exactly how it would feel if she touched it—that made her think, *I know you. We're blood, you and I.*

"So *you're* my sister?" Hyun asked Namin finally. A lump rose in her throat as she realized it was the first time she had heard her brother speak. When he had left as a toddler, he hadn't yet managed his first word, and her family must have assumed he would never speak, thinking his mind was as affected as his body. But Hyun's words, while slow, were clear and easily understood. She could see the intelligence shimmering in his eyes as he examined her face, searching for familiarity.

She nodded, not trusting her voice.

"Yes," he said. Dragging out the *yes*. "I remember."

3
· · · · · · · · · · · ·

Five fifty-one A.M. Beyond the city, Namin watched the sky erupt with ribbons of pink and orange like molten steel, illuminating fields and squat concrete buildings still wearing winter grime. The fields were studded with young shoots. The dark, rich water glistened like glass in the morning sun. Her mind groped at these images, searching for significance and clarity. The forward progress of the bus was, for the moment, soothing. She allowed her thoughts to rove over the landscape, subconsciously ticking down the minutes until she would force herself to work. The textbooks, which she could not leave at home even for the day and a half she would have with Hyun, were both ballast and security blanket. She needed them to remind herself who she was. Without them, she was just another girl. Poor family, poor prospects.

She pulled her chemistry book from her bag and opened to the last earmarked page. As a rule, she never left off studying at the end of a section or even the end of a page. She always left it in the middle. Concept, sentence, equation, it didn't matter. Just when she might be ready to understand, she shut the book, forcing herself to revisit it from the beginning next time. That way it was underlined twice in her brain. She allowed herself one last look out the window.

Hyun asked so many questions when he saw her now. He knew about SNU and about the Circle. He knew she wanted to study medicine and how badly she wanted to succeed as a physician. He knew about their parents and Kyungmin, too—though of course not the recent news about her leaving home. Namin had promised herself she would never lie to her brother. She owed him that, at least. But this was so unspeakable that telling anyone, even Hyun, was out of the question.

Hyun always asked about the family with a sense of polite distance, as if they were strictly *her* parents, *her* sister, not related to him at all. Namin ached to hear what her brother really thought of them, especially their parents, but whenever she brought it up, he acted as if all of it had happened centuries ago. In that way he was like their mother, who could make any decision seem inevitable. The past was the past and it could never be different.

That first time seven years ago, when Namin and Jisun had gone to discover if Hyun was alive, Namin's grandparents had called Jisun's house to notify both parents where the girls were. Namin's parents did not even bother to collect her at the bus station at the end of the weekend, waiting at home for her to arrive on her own. She was exhausted, not just from the long physical journey, but from the immense mental and emotional distance she had traveled to claim back what she'd lost. It had not occurred to her to feel guilty for what she had done.

That night, when she let herself into the house, her parents were in their bedroom with the door closed. It was late, and the light of their lamp shone two orange squares at the glass panels above their door. "Come in here," her mother commanded. When Namin went in, they were sitting side by side as if they had been waiting in that position for hours. Waiting to interrogate and condemn her.

What had possessed her to do such a thing? they asked, as if she'd been caught shoplifting jewels at a department store, not simply visiting her own brother at their grandparents' home. Perhaps they would have been less puzzled if, in fact, she had been caught stealing. They might have understood a young girl coveting bright, shiny goods she could never have. But digging up the useless past? Why had she done it? they asked. For what?

That night, Namin looked at her parents and knew they would never truly forgive each other. For leaving Hyun in the first place. For conjuring him back.

"I just wanted to see him," Namin said simply.

Her mother sighed. Her father looked away, apparently distracted by an invisible spot on the wall. Namin realized they had expected her to apologize and beg forgiveness, but she would never rescind the first good independent thing she'd done. "And I'll see him again," Namin said. "As often as I want." Her mother opened her mouth and shut it again without saying what she must have intended.

"Go to bed," she said finally. "Don't forget to wash your face."

They never brought up Hyun again.

The past was the past and it could never be different.

The last thirty minutes of the trip, the bus rattled over country roads so rough and pitted that it was a hazard to lean too close to the window. On an unexpected lurch—Namin had learned from experience—you could slam your face hard enough to bruise. On certain stretches she heard the crack of foreheads hitting glass, those who had fallen asleep and not roused themselves in time. It was around this part of the journey that people who had maintained a solid block of silence suddenly became chatty.

"Family here, eh?" said the fortyish man across the aisle. He had sat with his hat over his eyes the entire way, refusing to notice even when she dropped her pencil and it rolled under his foot.

"Grandparents," she said tersely, and immediately felt ashamed of herself. She forgot that she was allowed to mention her brother to strangers out here. Sometimes she forgot, even among people who knew and loved Hyun, that he was not a taboo topic.

"Must be a good student," he said, nodding at her books. "Sleep at all?"

She shook her head.

"Early trip," he said, as if giving advice. "Most people sleep."

"Thanks, I'm fine."

By nine thirty, she was walking past the tiny general store where her grandmother bought everything from soap to sewing needles. She ducked inside and picked out four different candy bars, cheap luxuries she had saved for. Impulsively, she added an aftershave. Hyun would turn fifteen next month and was proud of his new shaving regimen. Last visit, she'd watched their grandfather do it for him in the yard, a towel draped over his shoulder like in a real barbershop. He would be happy to receive the gift. She hoped it would make up for her long absence.

HYUN WAS SITTING in the yard, a flat brown stone wedged under the wheel of his chair. Their grandparents had put him in a patch of sun and tied a wide straw hat with a cord under his chin to protect his skin from burning. He despised the hat, but without it they could not let him sit so long outside. As the weather warmed, he would sit there for all the hours of daylight, long enough to shrivel a person like a dried persimmon.

When he saw her, Hyun's face broke into a wide grin. "You came."

He had an old caster wheel in his hand. The treads were peeling, but the metal parts had been recently polished. He loved moving parts, anything he could spin or turn or hinge. She spun the wheel as a hello, kissed his cheek. "Sorry it's been so long."

"It's been cold," he said. She knew he meant that it had been too cold for her to travel during the winter months, not that he himself had been cold—though that was probably true, too.

"Ready for a walk?"

He smiled.

She moved the rock out from under his wheel and pushed him toward the gate. They headed toward the stream.

Years ago, their grandfather had fitted his chair with wheels meant for an oxcart, better for these dirt roads. He had also devised a reversible handle so they could pull him like a rickshaw. They moved him less frequently now since they were weaker, but Namin knew that when he was younger and lighter, they had taken him everywhere with them. To the fields, where they worked all day. To the market. To visit neighbors. Out here, where everyone kept animals and killed calves and piglets born with deformities, Hyun's disability was no less accepted than it was in the city, but Namin's grandparents had raised Hyun with their own program of practical defiance. Because he could not be left alone, they took him with them, strapped in an A-frame or pulled in a rickshaw. They touched him and talked to him as they did their animals, their tools and pots and daily implements. All the things they loved, which over decades had become dearer to them than their closest neighbors.

In retrospect, Namin saw that a healthy child would have fared worse in their care. They would have fretted about how to raise him. How to navigate schooling when neither had completed high school. How to speak so their rural accents would not imprint and mark him as a provincial. They would have suffered doubts, believing themselves unequal to the task.

But Hyun existed firmly in their world now. He hadn't seen a city since leaving Seoul as a toddler. Did he remember tall buildings? He had never seen a traffic jam or a commuter crowd. He had hardly seen anything other than their grandparents' little home, their patch of farm, and these surrounding hills and streams.

Namin pushed hard over the uneven road, her body light and tense after the hours on the bus. Always, the speed of the chair seemed exhilarating and unreal on the first ride. The weeks—now months—of anticipating the visit, of worrying, flew away on the first ride when they were both so glad to see each other and neither had fully integrated the other's reality.

When they arrived at the stream, she slid her brother out of his chair and laid him carefully on the grass. She removed his shoes and socks, balled them up, and deposited them on his chair. Then she half carried, half dragged him to the water, to a spot where he could sit with his back against an embankment, his feet in the icy pool.

She left him for just a moment to take off her own shoes and socks. Then she ran back, the spring grass not yet soft under her feet. She walked into the cold stream, careful on the slippery rocks, wading back and forth in front of him, splashing him with her feet, raising up arcs of water in the sun.

She splashed Hyun until his wet pants clung to his thighs, until she could see his teeth chattering. "Time to roast awhile," she said. And this was the hardest part, bringing him back up the bank, moving against gravity. She would try not to drag him as if he were a too-big log, but she wasn't strong enough to lift him otherwise.

By degrees she pulled him out of the water, then brought the chair down to the pebbly mud. After wedging the chair between two boulders, she wrapped her arms around his chest, holding him from behind in a tight hug. In this way, she crab-walked the two of them to the chair, where she tried to side-launch him into the seat, slipping herself out from behind in the process. There was no graceful way to do it, and by the time he was finally situated, they were both smeared with mud and breathing hard. But he was laughing, teeth no longer chattering.

"Good job," he said.

"Don't congratulate me yet." She still had to roll him up the bank.

She sat on the stones next to him, piling a handful of pebbles in his lap. She threw them lazily into the water, barely watching where they landed. She began to talk.

She told him about the house they would live in together after she graduated and became a successful physician. Each visit, they designed another room or wing of their house. Today, she told him about the gardens. The wide paved paths that would be easy for his chair to roll on. The fruit trees that would bear cherries and pears and persimmons.

"We can build our own stream. We'll work out a design to make it easier to get in and out. Maybe an elevator. An open one, like a diving platform that goes up and down over the water." But that didn't seem right, it wouldn't be like wading in a stream if he was still sitting in the chair. "Maybe we should have a kind of float. You can ride it all the way around."

"We better have fish," he said.

Over the years, they had built an enormous house in their minds, with rooms for every function: for eating, for sleeping. For storing fishnets and cowbells, for listening to stories and music, for looking at pictures of birds. Rooms that smelled like roasting corn, rooms that eliminated stomachaches. Rooms lined with linen, with rubber, with grass. Anger rooms, with pictures of ancestors. A room that was a perfect sphere, built purely for novelty's sake.

Sometimes Namin lay awake in her bedroom calculating the number of years until she graduated and could earn enough money to take care of Hyun. Three more years of college. Then medical school? Seven more years until she could earn enough to bring him to Seoul. Could her grandparents keep him seven more years? And who would take care of him while she was at work? At night, these questions swung over her like a pendulum, marking the sleepless minutes. Time with their grandparents was running out for Hyun, yet she could not accelerate her progress to keep up. The minutes of her life marched on in slow, uncaring sequence, semester by semester, year by year.

"What do you think is the first thing you'll do when you come to Seoul?" she asked. This was a departure for them. Although they often spoke about the future, it was always tied to the fantasy house, which existed outside of geography in the realm of dreams. In the real world, he and Namin never existed in the same place at the same time, except for these brief visits she managed a handful of times a year. The question had surfaced without her thinking about it, but now that it was spoken, the image of Hyun in the city, navigating her narrow, hilly neighborhood, his chair parked in a sunny spot in their cramped and dusty courtyard, came to her like a physical shock, as thrilling as it was frightening.

He let his head fall back against his chair and looked at the sky without speaking. The muscles of his mouth and throat twitched under his skin, ferrying his thoughts. As she waited for his answer, her mind flooded with guesses. *Ride the bus. Visit your campus. Use an elevator. Look at the river.*

"Take a tour of our house, of course." His voice, low and warbling, conveyed affection more directly, more intensely, than that of anyone she had ever known. His smile made her feel invincible.

"You'd better see the city first. So we can decide where to have our house. You want it in just the right place, don't you?"

"I don't care about the city," he said.

"Just the house?"

"Just the house."

Even though they both knew it was a game, Namin ached to make it true.

It was only on the ride back to the city that Namin realized Hyun hadn't asked about their parents or Kyungmin this time. In the seven years she'd been visiting, he always asked. Of course she knew it was a matter of formality, like children who automatically greeted any adult they saw, but he had never forgotten before. Actually the omission was a relief, and she hoped it marked a new phase in their relationship. It was better if they considered themselves their own little family, just the two of them, separate from the others. She hoped he thought so, too, because that was their future, what she was working so hard to achieve.

It was late when she let herself in at home. Her mother, wearing nightclothes but clearly still awake, slid open her bedroom door to check which daughter it was. When she saw it was Namin, her face resolved from faint hope back to worry. "How are your grandparents?" she asked without interest. "Anything new?"

"Fine. Nothing new."

"Was the bus crowded?"

"Not too much."

"Get some rest, then, you'll be tired tomorrow."

Namin washed up quickly and prepared her quilts for bed. They had always avoided talking about Hyun, so that was no surprise, but now there was a second sibling they did not talk about. Wherever she was, whatever she was doing, Kyungmin was becoming someone they did not know. Another ghost.

1
. . . .

Sunam and his friends chose the northern exposure beside the elms lining the main university quad, the first of many strategic decisions. They could sit there playing cards all day—the record so far was nine and a half hours—and be sheltered from the sun, if not the condescending glances of passing professors. They could also keep an eye on the pretty coeds who swished by on the way to class, the long straps of a handbag carving that alluring valley between their breasts, the compact weight of a leather pouch thumping against a thigh. They could pretend, seeing as how they were within sight of lecture halls, that they might actually attend a class or two this time. After this game. Or that point. If not today, then certainly tomorrow. The vague obligation to heed responsibility at some point, to make some concessionary gesture—after all, they could not spend the entirety of their college careers playing Mighty—made the game that much more exciting, necessary, delicious. This seemed the primary pleasure of life: to sit in the soft shadow of these accommodating trees and call out bids, tossing cards on the wrinkled cotton of somebody's shirt, whoever had sacrificed it for the day as the makeshift playing surface.

They always played five to a game—not always the same five, but a predictable cohort. Kihun, Daesung, Chang: guys who played every day and understood one another's mannerisms, foibles, and strengths, like a tripartite brain. Wonu, a memory champion who played cards the way other people chewed gum, happily enough at first, but becoming bored and mechanical after a few minutes. Youngwoo, who was so taciturn that he spoke only the words associated with the game. Tae, clever at jokes and a willing scapegoat for mistakes.

Sunam might play every day for a week and not show up again for a month. As a result, he was always welcome and slightly overcelebrated, as if his presence each time were a fluke.

Tae was dealing when Sunam arrived, but he handed over the deck with an excessively dramatic bow. *"Hyung-nim,"* he said, proffering the cards with both hands. Tae called everyone *hyung-nim,* honorific older brother, whether or not they were actually his senior. He had failed the entrance exams twice, making him two years older than his class, and he enjoyed tripping people with this hierarchical quandary. If they accepted his calling them *hyung,* then he would act offended and demand to know how old they were. If—as they should—they gave him the proper respect due his age, he would enact an obsequious attitude of lowering himself ("No, *you're* the *hyung-nim.* No, you!"), taking perverse pleasure in embarrassing everyone. It all depended on his mood, which was slippery and mercurial.

They played smoothly for several rounds, with Wonu picking up the most points. It was early in the day and he was still interested.

13 with spades.

14 with no-trump.

Pass.

17 with hearts.

Full score with diamonds.

Friend: queen of diamonds.

During a lull, Tae lay on his back with an arm flung over his eyes. He wasn't saying a word, but there was a silent buzz coming off him, as if he were plugged into an electric outlet, gathering charge.

"You're quiet today," Sunam said. "Did you forget to take your vitamins or something?"

Tae changed positions, propping himself up on his side. His eyes were bright. "You guys ever go to Itaewon?"

There was a brief but significant pause in the game as everyone registered the question.

"Where in Itaewon?" Sunam said casually, as if the specific location would change his answer. People he knew didn't go to Itaewon, a neighborhood around the U.S. Army base infamous for prostitutes. These women worked in bars, nightclubs, and brothels, selling sex and overpriced liquor, which kept the soldiers' dollars circulating in the local economy. The minister of education had once praised the women as "dollar-earning patriots" owing to their role in attracting much-needed foreign currency.

On campus, the minister's inflammatory comments had caused an uproar among the coeds. Immediately, signs went up defaming the government as "the Gross National Pimp." They put out leaflets, too, exposing how city clinics forced mandatory health testing and tagged women like livestock to guarantee they were free of disease, whereas GIs and local men underwent no testing. It seemed half the city officials were busy regulating the illegal sex trade for their own profit while the other half gave lip service to the moral high ground, pushing for more arrests and police raids. Sunam had read these leaflets with interest, but the information seemed biased and too outrageous to be true.

"You know what you can get in Itaewon, don't you?" Tae asked.

"Play," Chang said. But everyone had closed up their cards. They watched as Tae flamboyantly unzipped his backpack to reveal the top few centimeters of a glossy magazine. Block lettering spelled out PLAYBOY. "Well, for starters—" Tae tossed the magazine into the circle. *"This."*

It was rare enough to get foreign magazines of any kind, but to get a *Playboy*, which Sunam had heard about but partly discounted as a Western myth, was genuinely shocking. The game was instantly forgotten as everyone zeroed in on the contraband in Tae's hands.

On the cover was a woman photographed in a hazy morning light as if she had just been pulled out of bed. She had soft brown hair, luscious pink lips, and enormous eyes that stared directly at the camera. There was an expression on her face Sunam could not quite name. Wistfulness? Longing? Boredom? Her lace top was loose and coming untied around her breasts. The crescent of a tawny nipple peeked over the edge of the white translucent fabric.

Tae picked up the magazine, ostentatiously flipping the shiny pages with his thumb. A gesture like fanning a roll of money. They could see foreign shades of flesh flick by. Bare breasts and yellow hair and bits of underwear like fancy gift-wrapping ribbon.

"Put it away," said Chang. "Do you want to get us expelled?"

"Over this?" Tae scoffed. "It's just a bunch of pictures."

"*Put it away.*" Chang was only twenty or twenty-one, but he looked like an old man. His face was square and puffy. His chest seemed to sink into his belly, which protruded like a cartoon drawing. He'd developed the unfortunate habit of yanking up his belt with a severe twisting motion, as if screwing his pants on over his abdomen. Despite these characteristics, no one dared ridicule him. He was so serious and steady, he could make you feel infantile for even considering it. Compared with Chang, Tae seemed like an overgrown child, even though he was actually older.

Tae put away the magazine. Under Chang's insistence they resumed the game, but the attention had irrevocably shifted. The closed bag was like a bomb or venomous reptile, something requiring high vigilance.

Wonu said finally, "Why are you hanging around Itaewon, anyway?"

Tae took his time answering, pretending he hadn't been waiting for someone to ask. "No sense getting an education if you don't learn anything really useful. This is the sort of thing a man *should* know."

Sunam stiffened at the words, which echoed the taunts of the men in the crowd from the Mun-A strike. He assumed most of the guys who had managed to land at SNU had been too busy studying, like him, to know anything about women or sex. Even if they had the time, dating before college was considered taboo, forbidden by both parents and school administrators, who made it their duty to rout out any inkling of romance. High school was strictly a time for books and equations, not hormones. The boys were required to wear their hair in military buzz cuts, the girls blunt bobs cut at the ear.

Everything changed in college. Boys and girls grew out their hair and became men and women. They experimented with individualized clothes, finally able to abandon the black-and-white military-style school uniforms they'd lived in for the six long years of middle and high school. For most people—if they were not die-hard bookworms—study loads were relatively light. The educational aspect of college was almost a formality, overshadowed by the general and long deferred enjoyment of leisure. Students were suddenly encouraged to date, not just for fun but for the purpose of finding a marriage partner. They were expected, as if overnight, to become full-fledged people. *Adults.*

With their newfound freedom, some of his classmates seemed to have rocketed forward in experience, while others—like Sunam—continued in their well-worn, precollegiate ways. As other guys bragged about bedding girls and becoming "real men," Sunam worried he was being left behind.

"Any of you boys have a girlfriend?" Tae said. "Of course not, you wouldn't know what to do with a girl even if you had one. Now—" He threw down his cards and brought the bag into his lap. "What do you think college is for? Men, we need to get some experience. We need to *live,* for a change. What are we waiting for? This is the time!" He looked at Sunam. "You ever see girls like this?"

Sunam thought of the women he'd seen at the factory protest. Of course, not close up and perfect like this cover model. Not dressed up with lace and makeup. But he had seen them, and he wanted to fling them like so many pictures in Tae's smug face. *I've seen them. You wouldn't believe the things I've seen.* If it had been Tae on the roof, Sunam knew he would have cataloged every detail. He would have filed, for future telling and retelling, every breast in size and shape. Every girl who threw herself, kicking, on the ground. Girls who had lost every bit of clothing, their heavy trousers sliding easily over their hips. Tae would have trotted out the image of those girls, stark naked and furious, to titillate anyone who would listen.

But Sunam felt squeamish about admitting that he'd thought of those workers sexually. That he had stared at their bodies, memorizing their shapes and sizes. Of course he'd thought of them in the days since. The shame of it was still clammy on his skin.

"Play," he said, picking up his cards. It was Wonu's turn to bid. "What do you bid?"

Wonu glanced at his cards. "Fifteen. Spades."

The bidding went around until it was Tae's turn. "Bid," said Sunam.

Tae hadn't even picked up his cards. He smiled. "Pass."

It was his right to pass if he wanted, but they knew he was intentionally throwing the round, dragging out his moment and forcing the others to wait on him.

"Call," Sunam said.

"I said pass."

"And I said call." He could sense the other guys backing him even if no one knew what would happen. He put down his cards with a decisive snap. "Here's an idea, tough guy. If you lose, you forfeit the magazine. If you win—"

"Forfeit it? To who, you?" Tae cut in with a laugh. "Why would I do that?"

"It's just some pictures, you said so yourself," Sunam said calmly. "You know plenty of real girls, don't you? What do you need pictures for? Go ahead, play."

There was a moment when Sunam thought Tae would pick up his cards and play. Instead he got to his feet in one fluid motion, not stiff or hurried with anger. A simple unfolding of legs and torso, coming up to full height. When his hands came to his fly, that too seemed a matter of posture. Sunam—and the others—didn't realize until it was too late, until Tae had unzipped his pants and started to urinate liberally on the cards they'd just played. A full stream at close angle, splattering warm piss in a wide, unpredictable radius. They scrambled, shouting, to their feet. Wonu, farthest away to begin with and almost certainly safe, kept brushing his pants and shaking off the hems as if he thought the stains would scatter off him like crumbs.

At their feet were the ruined cards, splashed and soaked through.

"Are you crazy?" Chang's old-man face was nearly purple. He kicked a batch of the cards near his feet. The soggy card stock stuck to the bottom of his shoe so that he had to scrape it forcefully on the grass, pawing like a goat.

Tae zipped himself up.

"Like I said, it was a shit deal. Anyway, I never make decisions on a full bladder."

The *Playboy* was in his hand. He let it drop open over the wettest part of the puddle.

"The best pictures are in the middle."

LATER, SUNAM TOLD Juno the story about the *Playboy*. Omitting the part about the urine, the inevitable aftermath in which the boys rescued the magazine and smuggled it into one of their homes in a soggy paper bag. Even Chang had come along, citing a curiosity of "foreign cultures." Once behind closed doors, they had argued over the best way to dry the pages, finally deciding to set sheets of newspaper between them. None of them had foreseen the disastrous effects of pressing wet newsprint to urine. They'd ended up with naked American girls superimposed with local headlines, a uniquely disorienting and disappointing experience.

Sunam had hoped to amuse or even impress Juno with the story, but he didn't seem to be paying any attention.

"You like that game?" he said suddenly. "Mighty—whatever it's called. You like it?" He had that pinched, appraising look Sunam was becoming familiar with, as if he were an investment turning sour. "How many hours a week you spend with them, you think? Playing that game."

"I barely played all week," Sunam said defensively. He knew his *sunbae* thought those guys were completely useless, losers without a future, but actually they were smart, decent guys who probably would do fine in life. Sure, they played a lot of cards, but that wasn't so unusual. They did the same things most guys did: cards, *baduk, soju,* and cigarettes, fall in love or chase some girls if they felt so inclined. What else was there to do around here, really? It wasn't as if they were constantly hanging around the comic-book stores, waiting for the new issues to show up. Or nailed to their seats at the library, primed to slit their wrists over a disappointing exam grade. The Mighty guys were not as upper echelon as Juno and his cohort, but they were far from scraping the bottom of the social barrel.

"But other weeks," Juno said. "What's the most you've ever played?"

Sunam thought back to that nine-and-a-half-hour marathon. Since then, far more extreme records had been set indoors. When it was too cold to sit outside on campus, the guys holed up in one of their bedrooms—*that* record was more than thirty-eight hours—and no one went home or to class or even slept. Thirty-eight hours of bleary-eyed gambling fueled by snacks and drinks delivered to their door by someone's mother, as if they were members of some national council conducting a vital symposium. Some of the mothers would have fed and coddled the boys for weeks. Not Sunam's, who barely tolerated the odors and disarray created by her own four sons. His mother, seemingly traumatized by the concentration of testosterone in her home, nurtured a general mistrust of males behind closed doors. It was her belief that the air in such a space would fester, attracting insects and grime.

"Let me say something to you as your *sunbae,*" Juno said. "What do you think those guys are going to do when this is over? After college, I mean. Those guys you play cards with."

"Probably do their military service."

Juno shook his head impatiently. "Everyone has to do that. I'm talking *after.* Real life. What do you think they're going to do?"

"Chang is an economics major. He wants to be a college professor. Wonu—I suppose he'll get a job somewhere. Maybe an electronics company. Tae's got such a big mouth, maybe he'll go into broadcasting—"

"So no plans," Juno cut in. "No one's going anywhere."

"I just told you—"

"Here's what you don't understand," Juno said. "Our country? Think about it. It's like a little pond. Everyone's swimming around, all together. Nowhere else to go. You know what happens in a little pond? You don't have to be a shark. You just have to be bigger than the tadpoles and the microscopic algae. You just have to be that much higher on the food chain. It's just a *little* pond, you see? And everyone seems happy enough to be a tadpole. Just getting a little bigger every day. You know what happens when a tadpole gets bigger? It becomes a frog. That's it, just a frog."

Sunam looked at him blankly. Not sure what to say, not even sure what Juno was really talking about. The idea of their country as a "little pond"—it seemed somewhat disloyal to speak in such diminutive terms. Of course their country was small, a tiny peninsula between giants. China, a land giant on the west. And Japan, a superpower that had almost succeeded in overcoming the West. But from their earliest childhood, Sunam and everyone else he knew had been taught a fierce pride in their country. The Republic of Korea was not just a political designation, but an extension of family, of self. It was *uri nara,* "our country"—the first-person plural, everyone speaking for everyone else. *Uri nara,* which was small, poor, and vulnerable—but which was unquestionably more valuable and more precious than any other country because it was theirs. Ours.

"I don't want to be a stupid frog," Juno said vehemently. "If we're going to live in a pond, I want to be the fish. Big fish with a big mouth. Eating whatever I want. You understand what I'm saying?"

Slowly Sunam nodded, but he didn't really.

"What you're doing—playing cards all day, hanging out with those losers. That's tadpole behavior. Frog track. Pretty soon, other people will catch on to the game. They'll start zooming ahead of you and you won't be able to get off that loser track even if you want to. Too many people. Small pond. It's wide-open now, but you don't even see that, do you? You're sitting around playing cards.

"To be great you have to follow your instincts." Juno's self-importance was total and completely unapologetic. "When I believe in something—well, I do it. Because, have you ever noticed, Sunam, how people *say* they believe in certain things? Sacrifice. Determination. Hard work. But when it comes time to act on it, to really do as they say, they don't seem to believe as hard as they claimed." He paused, the master waiting to see if the student understood. "So that's a sign of weakness, knowing something and not doing it. You may as well stay in the dark and not have known it at all."

"You mean like the girl at the Mun-A strike," Sunam said.

"Exactly. I've made my plan and it's only a matter of time. You should do the same—whether it's a girl or a job or—whatever it is. Set your goal. See it through. Who else will do it for you?"

"I only want the chance you had," Sunam said. He ducked his head, adding hastily, "If you think I deserve it."

"It's up to you, Sunam. You show me what you deserve." Juno clapped a hand on his shoulder and seemed to be arriving at some internal decision. "Lucky for you, you'll have your chance this weekend."

He slipped him an address scrawled on thick card stock like a business card, but blank. "This is Min *sunbae*'s address. Don't lose it. Eight o'clock this Saturday, don't be late." He didn't have to say anything else for Sunam to understand that this was a tremendous honor, to be invited to the house of Ahn Kiyu. There were probably men twice and triple his age, powerful men, who would tremble at such a rare opportunity.

"Is this the . . . final interview?" he asked.

"It's a party, Sunam. A party. We'll have fun."

2
. . . .

The card he was given did not say what he should do when he arrived at the designated house number and there was no house that he could see. Instead there was a massive iron gate flanked by stone columns. Soft footlights shimmered along a paved driveway that disappeared out of view. An artfully designed forest—or maybe it was a true forest, how did one tell?—made whatever lay at the end of the drive a mystery.

It should have been a quick twenty-minute bus ride from Sunam's house. He had set out with plenty of time to spare. But at the last minute—the bus was pulling up to his stop, brakes squealing, exhaust fumes backlit by the beams of following headlights—he had felt certain he had miscopied the address and could not convince himself otherwise. He'd have to go back to campus, where he had another copy, to check. It usually took a half hour or less to campus from his neighborhood, but it was past the commuter hour and the buses were running longer, less frequent routes. It would be a long wait. Still, Sunam waved that first bus along, knowing he would be monstrously late to the party. He rationalized that if he didn't have the correct address, he might not get there at all.

It had taken forty-five minutes to campus, only to confirm the address had been right after all. Another hour to double back across the river, transferring two buses to arrive at Min's neighborhood. Then another twenty minutes lost in the maze of private, unmarked streets, where he could not find a soul to ask for directions. Overheated and two hours late, Sunam had cursed himself for succumbing to doubt and wasting precious time. But now, staring at the high, forbidding gates, he wished the bus had taken even longer, or that he was still en route, or that he had not come at all.

The right-flanking column was fitted with what could only be an intercom. A silver call button was centered beneath the speaker. His only option seemed to be to press it. Instead, Sunam paced. The address matched the one on his card—he had checked it a hundred times—but still, he worried it was the wrong house. He had never stood at such a formidable gate. And what would he say to whoever answered the intercom? Of all the words he'd uttered in his life, he could not think of anything that might be appropriate in this case.

Hello . . .

I'm here for the party. . . .

May I be let in? . . .

All ridiculous. He would have felt better if he had a secret password, allowing him to bypass all the hapless, generic things one could say.

Without warning the gates started to rumble, sliding open on mechanized rollers. The intercom beeped once and a voice said, "Stop pacing. Come in already."

By the time Sunam thought to answer, the intercom had gone dead. He slipped through the gate, peering around for the camera, his back prickling with embarrassment and paranoia. Wherever it was, the lens was so well hidden that he could not find it even now.

Once inside the gate, the outside world fell away. Great trees loomed overhead, their heavy arms illuminated by spotlights aimed for maximum impact. Smaller gravel paths branched off the main drive into secret gardens. The call of night birds twittered with almost cartoonish clarity. Even the air took on new scents—the brisk fragrance of mountain trees and the earthy tang of freshly laid mulch. The familiar smells of the city—car exhaust, garbage, *yeontan* coal smoke— were completely absent, as if they had been denied entry at the gate.

When he rounded the bend in the drive, he finally saw the house. It was cut into the mountainside in protruding stacks of wood and glass, as if a giant child had devised it layer by layer. Haphazard and poetic. A thing of great beauty and striking ugliness.

A sound released from the back of his throat, a low hiss like steam escaping a boiling pot. It was the sound of fear and awe. Of disbelief.

This was it. Everything he had hoped the Circle would be.

INSIDE, THERE WERE fewer people than he had expected. *Sunbaes* in black turtlenecks lounged artistically on low leather furniture. Smoke curled from crystal ashtrays. People turned when he entered, then, seeing no one of importance, quickly resumed their nonchalant postures. Sunam wandered near an elegantly arching ficus, pretending to admire a watercolor. He thought he must have seen it in some museum or art book. It was a depiction of cranes in downward flight, melancholy and expensive looking.

"Bet you that's a fake."

Sunam jumped. A girl peered at him from under thick bangs. Her eyes, a little bloodshot, were lined with dark pencil, and he could smell the faint whiff of alcohol on her breath. She was wearing frayed but well-fitting blue jeans and a simple white T-shirt that had an ink stain on the hem. His immediate impression was that she did not belong in this house or with these people. Who had invited her? Was this some kind of joke, meant to test or harass him?

"That could have been done by a first grader. But you'd think it was a real masterpiece just because it's in this house." She leaned closer and whispered loudly, "Take those vases in the hall, for instance. If they're really so priceless, would they leave them out for anyone to knock into and break? It's the lighting," she said knowingly. "All for show."

"They looked nice to me," Sunam said cautiously.

He looked around, feeling as if they were caught in a spotlight. The girl made him feel hot and tight, as if he'd been shoehorned into his own skin. Later, if someone asked what she looked like, he would have recalled only the drama around her eyes. He would have conceded that she was pretty—in a wild, messy sort of way.

"So . . ." She eyed his outfit doubtfully. "What are you?"

Sunam looked down at his white-collared shirt and sweater. The carefully pressed slacks.

The correct uniform, in evidence throughout, would have been dark knit and corduroy. Black, gray, or brown. Sunam's sky blue sweater stood out like a beacon of error.

The girl didn't wait for an answer. "Ah, one of the *strivers*," she said, drawing out the word. "Don't worry. Hopefully all this"—she indicated his outfit—"is the worst that'll ever happen to you. If you get in. *If.*"

"Yeah, well . . . what are you?" Sunam hoped to mirror her tone, but the question came out mumbled and rushed.

"No one you need to worry about. I'm not one of the judges."

"There are no *judges*," he said.

"No? If that's what you think, you're in worse shape than I thought."

Finally, he saw Juno across the room, struggling to open a bottle of beer with a glistening silver hook. There was a small explosion, then foam sprayed with a loud hiss. Sunam waved overhead, huge, desperate waves begging for rescue. Juno smiled coolly, dried his hands and the dripping bottle with a clean white napkin, and started to make his way over.

The girl rolled her eyes when she saw who was coming. "Time for my exit." Slowly she sashayed across the room, sliding around the furniture as if she had the steps counted and could cross in the dark.

Juno thumped his shoulder. Close up, his skin had the dark purplish sheen of too many beers. "Where've you been? I expected you hours ago. Nice sweater."

"Who was that, anyway?"

"Her? Don't worry about it." He flashed a smile that could only be described as brightly unpleasant. "We have more *important* considerations tonight."

"What considerations?" Sunam tried to decipher how drunk Juno really was. Some people, like his uncle, would turn that color after half a beer. His father, on the other hand, could drink all night and each empty bottle would render his complexion increasingly pale and flat. Only the whites of his eyes would darken to a dank yellow, like the contents of a wet ashtray.

"Don't you want to be surprised?" Juno giggled. So he was quite drunk. "It's more fun when it's a surprise."

Sunam was relieved to discover himself on firmer footing with an inebriated Juno than a sober one. His whole life he had dealt with drunks and their idea of humor. He knew what to do. When to be firm, when to relent. "More fun for who?"

"Don't be such a wet blanket," Juno said. "Everyone else wanted their guy, but I got you in. So don't let me down. I didn't get you this far for nothing. You'll thank me later."

"Tell me. I'd rather thank you now," Sunam said.

"You know there's a girl in the mix this year. That gives us certain attractive opportunities," said Juno, giggling again. "Normally we have to bring in a coed or somebody to play this game, but no need for that this year. Convenient, right? Fifteen minutes in a luxury bedroom suite, right here in this house. A fun little diversion to make sure you're not bored. We call it 'Patriot Hostess Game.' You can figure out the rest."

"No way," said Sunam. "That's sick. I refuse."

"I haven't even told you about the girl—"

"Doesn't matter."

"I disagree. This one *will* matter. You're going to want to hear about this."

"*Hyung-nim,* you always speak to me in the future tense, like you can predict the future—"

Juno cocked his head. "Hey, you busy tomorrow?"

Sunam stared at him, trying to release the trick in the question. Unable to figure it out, he shook his head.

"That's right. Keep this up, you're not going to be busy the next day either," Juno said. Every word he spoke seemed to make him more sober. "See, that's one kind of future. I keep showing you how to get on the right track. And you keep wanting to stay on your nice, warmed-up loser track. You like it there? You want me to tell you why I always speak in the future tense—it's because of people like you making it easy for me. What did I tell you the other day?" he said. "You don't have to be a shark, you just have to be one little step ahead. And if everyone else is thinking *today,* all you have to do is think *tomorrow*."

It was watching this, this seemingly impossible transformation—the alcohol gone in seconds—that silenced Sunam.

"So the girl. You decide what you want to do. But you'll see what I mean. A very attractive opportunity."

Sunam stiffened. That future tense again.

It was the name that bothered Sunam the most—*Patriot Hostess*. He knew it referred to the minister of education's speech about prostitutes, euphemistically called "hostesses."

Fifteen minutes in a bedroom with a strange girl was meant to embarrass the couple and titillate the others, who would enjoy imagining what might be happening behind closed doors. It was a childish prank, but also genuinely nerve-racking since Sunam had never been alone with a girl.

And the name "Patriot Hostess" made it insidious, as if they expected the girl to somehow *service* him. It was a crude and savage joke, and Sunam hoped she didn't think he had come up with it. He was a victim as much as she was.

THE BEDROOM WAS not so much a suite as it was its own apartment. It had a sitting area with two round-backed chairs upholstered in an elaborately brocaded fabric, green and gold. There was a writing desk with a red carved lamp on either end. He could see an open door to a marbled bathroom. In the middle of the room was an enormous bed, made up with a gold-tasseled spread. There were flat, round pillows emblazoned with dragons and cranes and mountains and pines that jutted precipitously from the sides of cliffs. An enormous vase stuffed with white flowers emitted a heady, oppressive scent. There was nothing in the room Sunam felt comfortable touching or looking at.

The girl was sitting at the writing desk, her body turned to face the door. He had to cross in front of her and walk past the bed in order to sit in one of the chairs. Their eyes met immediately. He looked away. She was as striking as Juno had intimated, with sharp, upturned eyes and a wide mouth. She wore a printed blouse that made her skin appear creamy and flushed.

Beyond the door, someone shouted, "Fifteen minutes . . . starts now!"

It seemed important that he not speak first, which could be misinterpreted as an advance. He was prepared to spend fifteen minutes in complete silence, strenuously ignoring their mutual confinement. But the girl seemed completely at ease. She sat crisply in her seat, gazing at the objects surrounding them with steady, intelligent eyes. She looked as if she were capable of getting up at any moment to rearrange the furniture to her liking.

Her name was Namin Kang. First in her graduating class at Kyungki High School. An impressive feat, but not unheard of—that was the nature of ranking, someone had to be first. What was unprecedented was the perfect score on her college entrance exams. The provost himself had examined the results, searching for errors or some evidence of cheating. He found nothing. "The Machine," they called her. She must have some kind of photographic memory.

She was on the physician track, already involved in the premed circle. No doubt it was a useful association, connecting her to other future doctors. But the premed circle was a boring academic club compared with Min's flashy clique, and evidently Namin had pulled her nose out of a textbook long enough to realize that. According to Juno, she'd approached them with her bid for membership, asking, "Any of you score perfectly on the entrance exam?"

It was hard to argue that point, Juno said.

Anyway, no one was seriously opposed to her joining. They were fascinated and secretly wanted the proximity to check her out. Only, they had a reputation to uphold. To be regarded as her "second" circle was unacceptable. They had to make it difficult. They had to be able to say she had truly subjected herself to their demands.

Hence the Patriot Hostess Game, designed to mortify the female ego.

"We thought she would cry when we told her the plan," Juno said. "Storm out."

"But she agreed?" Sunam asked. "Just like that?"

"She said anyone could be a patriot for fifteen minutes." Juno grinned. "She said either we were misusing the word or else we needed to raise the challenge to something worth aspiring for."

Sunam shook his head in disbelief.

"Tough girl," Juno said. "Hope you're ready."

Now she looked at Sunam and said, "I suppose they told you what my name is. They told me yours."

He nodded, not trusting himself to speak. The pressure in his chest seemed to make a sound of its own.

"Are you scared of me or something? You seem terrified."

"No." His throat was so dry, it came out like a croak. He cleared his throat. "Just a little—uncomfortable," he said.

"It is rather barbaric, isn't it."

From outside, several fists were banging the walls. "Can't hear anything! Quiet as mice in there!"

Namin raised an eyebrow. "Clearly they've never had the misfortune. Mice are not at all quiet. You get a good-sized nest of them in your house and it sounds like someone's sawing trees over your head."

She got up and walked over to the bed. "Don't be alarmed," she said. "I'm lying down, but I don't mean anything by it. I've just never lain in such a fancy bed before. Better take the opportunity while I can." She arranged herself in the middle of the bed, legs straight out. Hands clasped across her belly. "Nice," she said. She spread her arms out to either side, her fingers outstretched as if to reach the edges of the bed. They were nowhere close. "You could sleep in this thing for a week and never touch the same spot twice." The banging continued outside, but she lay quietly. He could swear, despite the clamor, that she was actually *enjoying* the bed.

"Halfway there!" someone shouted, and the pounding on the walls took on a more frenetic rhythm, as if several more people had joined in. "Halfway, man! Better hurry up!"

He saw them on the other side of the wall. Drunk and excited, imagining what he was doing in here. Probably most of them knew or at least strongly suspected that nothing was happening. But not knowing—at least not knowing for *sure*—they could imagine whatever they wanted. They could make it custom-suited to their needs. And in that realization, Sunam suddenly became aware of himself from that distant point of view. He saw what they imagined. Undressing the girl on the bed. It was so easy, she was right there. Kissing her mouth, her neck, her breasts and stomach. Or perhaps she would be the one doing the kissing: his mouth, his neck, his stomach. In that stiff European chair that dictated how he sat, where he placed his arms, Sunam felt himself getting aroused. He saw what he would do. And what she would do. What she was wearing under her blouse and trousers. How it would look coming off. His pleasure expanded like a hot glow, a color in his brain. The real girl lay on the bed; she seemed as relaxed as if she were alone in the room. As if in *her* mind, she had erased him completely. But in his mind, she was straddling him. He was following the curve of her hip, squeezing her thigh.

"I can hear you," the girl said without rising from the bed. "You're breathing like a buffalo."

He caught his breath mid-inhale and started to choke. A terrible minute passed as he hacked and sputtered, trying to clear the blockage. There was no question of trying to salvage his composure. He was completely helpless. Eyes watering, throat burning. The ability to find air was always just a fraction of a second beyond him. She sat up on the edge of the bed, watching him with controlled concern.

"Are you all right?" she asked when he had finally resumed breathing normally.

He nodded. "Time's probably up soon." He didn't know why he said that, it was just something to say. The time had been irrelevant for her all along.

"Are you sorry about the way you've spent it?" Namin asked, amused. "Any regrets?"

He wanted to ask why this didn't bother her, why none of it seemed to register at all. But the question implied too much. It made her out to be the victim when she had already refused to play that role.

She was studying him. "They probably told you I'm some kind of freak. A machine," she said, echoing Juno's word. "But I'm not. I'm just not scared like everyone else."

"Scared?" It annoyed him that he was probably included in her "everyone else."

"Isn't that what this is about? We're supposed to feel harassed and intimidated. But I'm just not. Why should I be? Because they say so?"

The boys were banging on the door, shouting, "Finish up in there! Thirty seconds! . . . Fifteen seconds!"

"So you never feel any pressure—"

"Of course I do. But this isn't pressure, Sunam. This is a game."

"Ten . . . nine . . ."

"Games can be a lot of pressure," he said, forcing himself to level his voice against the increasing volume of the countdown. "And some have serious real-world consequences. . . ."

"I guess it depends on what kind of games you like to play."

"And what games do you like to play?" It was a genuine question that came out sarcastic sounding, as if he didn't believe her. In fact he was afraid it was too obvious how impressed he was.

She pursed her lips as if suppressing a smile. Or maybe she was annoyed. Sunam had never felt his ignorance of the opposite sex so acutely. "I think that's enough secret telling for our first time," she said lightly. ("Five! . . . Four! . . . *Three!* . . . ") "As lovely and romantic as this was."

"Too bad! Time's up!" The crew outside flung open the door as if to reveal an eye-popping scandal. They scanned the room drunkenly and groaned to find the two of them sitting on opposite sides of the room.

Namin looked at him and smiled for the first time. She had a crooked left incisor. The way it poked out of her smile, the irregularity of it, was like a wink given just for him. "Otherwise, where's the mystery?"

"So NOT BAD, right?" Juno said.

Sunam had never managed that eloquent shrug-off he envied in other guys, that cool deflection that spoke louder than any boast.

But he was achieving it now—and he could tell it was having the intended effect.

"What'd I tell you?" Juno said, but this was an unconvincing display. For once Sunam had the upper hand, and he felt a head taller for it. Stronger. Smarter. More handsome.

He thought about that crooked smile. *As romantic as this was.*

"Did she do anything?" Juno demanded. "Did you get her to—"

"We talked."

"You had her, alone, with that crazy bed—and you talked?"

"That's usually what people do when they don't know each other."

Juno was studying him. "You seem—different," he said suspiciously.

"Good."

"Good?"

"Isn't this what you wanted from me? For me to be different?" Sunam couldn't help smiling at the consternation on Juno's face. "You should see yourself," he said, laughing. "You look like a frog."

"Careful," Juno said—and he wasn't kidding. His face was etched with sharp irritation, quickly verging on violence. The laughter caught in Sunam's throat and stayed there, like a thumb pressed into his trachea.

"You celebrate too soon," Juno said. "You do one thing right and think you're on top. Let me tell you something, it takes more than one step to get to the top."

Sunam lowered his head in an outward gesture of humility. Inwardly he was roiling. Wasn't Juno always telling him how he was supposed to step out, move ahead of the pack? Now he was being reprimanded for stepping out too far.

As if reading his thoughts, Juno said, "I told you to think ahead of the crowd, but your superiors are still your superiors—and they always will be."

But not your *superiors,* Sunam thought. Juno loved to brag about how he had risen to a position of leadership in the Circle as a second-year, beating out the upperclassmen "who had four years to get where I got in one." Sunam had heard it so many times, he could recite the whole speech, top to bottom. But now he was being lectured about remembering his position, about the sacred order of hierarchy that must never be crossed. *Convenient,* he thought.

"You hear me, Sunam? I don't see you listening."

"I'm listening, *sunbae-nim.*"

"Well? Is anything getting through that thick skull of yours?"

"Everything," Sunam said.

Juno narrowed his eyes but let it go. "Go find me something to eat," he said. "And hurry back. We're just getting started."

3

On the low couch, the upperclassmen sat with their knees far apart like grown men, watching a *baduk* game that had advanced to fill the entire board. *Baduk* was a game of strategy, its objective to surround a larger total area of the board with your stones than your opponent's. The covered areas were considered "territories," and there was a meditative, warlike quality to the game, in which each player had to weigh the benefits of his possible advances versus potential losses with each move. It had been considered a scholarly art form in ancient China where it had originated, but contemporary players—especially those who played only sporadically—tended to think of *baduk* as a macho battle of wills.

In this particular game, the black and white territories were packed with only a few possible moves left. Each player took a long time to decide, fingering each stone in secret soothing patterns, then releasing it with a resounding clack. Sunam had never been personally introduced to Min, but he knew he was the player using the white stones. Anyone else with Min's physique might have been considered bulky or overweight, but with his meticulous grooming and sleekly tailored clothing, his size only contributed to the impression that he was not a young man to be trifled with. Ahn Kiyu's son had a reputation for quick violence, hard partying, and an indiscriminate taste for women. Even now, relaxed in his own house, every muscle in his large frame seemed flexed with an excess of energy, as if he might spring up and overturn the board if the outcome did not please him. There was no need for that now: Min was the obvious winner of this game. If black didn't surrender soon, he would be ridiculed.

"If you know anything about oil . . ." This from the guy on deck to play the winner. His voice was slippery and thin, unpleasant to listen to. But he kept up a steady lecture of self-important chatter, every other statement rising in an annoying rhetorical question. The others simply called him by his initials: H.G. "You know how to shift power, you know the little guys aren't so little anymore."

"But we don't *have* any oil," said someone else, humoring him.

"You don't have to *have* it," H.G. said. "Just follow it, be involved. First thing after graduation, I'm heading to Saudi Arabia. You know we're building a harbor? Place called Jubail? Ocean tanker terminal. You think they'll stop at just one? First the terminal, then more ships, more tankers. I'm gonna be the first one there, get friendly with all the execs out there, all the sheikhs. You guys should really think about this too, if you have the guts. Stick it out a few years, come back a real big shot. Don't come asking me for favors when you wake up late. I plan to be way too busy."

"Yeah, great, you become the emperor of Saudi Arabia. I'll come ride your camels."

"They have a *king*. And it's *hereditary*? You can't just go in there and crown yourself whatever you want."

The game ended with Min as the victor. Taking his seat, H.G. slid the black stones neatly into their bowl, creating a tiny avalanche of pebbles. Juno said, "Who's playing after this, nobody? Let's have the new guy play next. *Sunbae,* you know the new guy? He used to be a tournament player."

Sunam was convinced that the only reason Juno had taken him on as *sunbae* was his brief success as a ranked player in junior tournaments. Sunam had met plenty of people like Juno, who worshipped the game and considered a special talent to be something like a mark from heaven, a measure of excellence that other mere mortals could never reach. Juno's grandfather had been a master player who had moved to Japan to be trained at the Kitani dojo. Juno's father had also been highly ranked, even chairing the national association for three years in the 1960s. Juno refused to touch the game himself, claiming his own facility was so mediocre that even friendly play on his part was a dishonor to the family legacy. More and more, Juno seemed disappointed that Sunam did not show evidence of genius outside of the game. Sunam did not know how to explain that *baduk* talent was just that— a set of skills and training narrowly focused on the game, without any extra promises about winning in the real world.

Min ignored Juno's remark, keeping his eyes on the board, setting stones with a quiet precision that kept both players moving steadily over the grid. Ten minutes lapsed in silence, punctuated only by the clicking of stones and H.G.'s uneven, whistling breath as he struggled to keep up with the game. Juno fidgeted behind the couch with a look of intense concentration on his face, as if he were completely absorbed in the game and had not noticed being dismissed by Min earlier. Sunam could tell this was what Juno was doing because he had put on the same face after being snubbed by Juno.

"You, new guy," Min said, without looking up. "You any good?"

Sunam had assumed Min had forgotten about him and was caught off guard by the question. Managing to gather his composure, he said, "I've played a few games."

Min put down his stone with a decisive clack. "I'll play him. H.G., get up."

"What, already?" H.G. said. The game had barely covered a third of the board.

"You lost."

"How did I lose?"

"Just think about it. You'll see. Get up." Min cleared the board, separating white from black with flicks of his finger. The stones scuttled across the wooden surface, knocking into one another.

"We barely started," H.G. whined. "How can you possibly know you won?"

Sunam knew the most talented players could read ahead dozens of moves. The legendary Cho Hun Hyun had once claimed that he could read thirty-nine steps in advance. As a young player, Sunam had loved to deploy swift attack moves to intimidate his opponent and had never developed the patience to build up slow, effective formations. So he was not the best reader of future plays, but even if Min was exceptionally intuitive, it was impossible to foretell the rest of the game so early. No one doubted that Ahn's son would have won in the end—but how H.G. might lose was still up to him.

Sunam was ready to play, though. It was an opportunity to grab Min's attention, and he was not about to waste it.

The stronger player always took white. In light of Min's seniority, Sunam picked black, even though he knew he was the stronger player. Min was an intelligent, competent player with some clever moves— but he didn't have Sunam's experience or training. Still, at a time like this, when it was more about social hierarchy than about objective mastery of the game, it was the right gesture to yield the white stones. Min started in the upper-right corner, moving quickly the way he had with H.G. He seemed relaxed and focused, setting up territories without looking at Sunam, as if he were playing against an invisible opponent.

He was building a simple ladder, easy to break. Sunam knew it was probably a test, to gauge his skill level. If he crushed it, then Min might surge forward and quickly expose Sunam's weakness. It was better to head it off slowly. Break the ladder, but don't be flashy. Flashy got people's attention and gave away information. Then, while you were busy gloating, you'd be scooped in three different ways.

Sunam broke the ladder and played a new corner. He wondered how many moves Min had already predicted. Sunam didn't always know his own plan, but did his opponent? Was there something his game betrayed that he hadn't yet detected about himself?

They played steadily, building out from their corners, creating decoy territories to sacrifice later. Each time Sunam invaded one of Min's carefully crafted frameworks, the older boy gave a small grunt of recognition, as if the pain of losing ground were counterbalanced by the pleasure of a skillful attack. Sunam forgot his earlier resolve to stay back and try to read his opponent. He played his usual aggressive game, forcing Min on the run. The board filled up quickly. The sequence of stones hitting and sliding onto wood created a predictable rhythm with rare lapses. By the end of the game, Sunam had enclosed more area, but Min had displayed greater ingenuity, playing cool reduction tactics tailored to Sunam's style.

When Min stood up, Sunam did, too. The older boy smiled and stuck out his hand. "Excellent game. It was a pleasure."

"But you haven't lost yet," Sunam said. Realizing his gaffe, he tried to recover. He blurted, "The great Edward Lasker once said the rules of *baduk* are so elegant, if aliens exist, they probably play."

"Don't know about aliens, but you're good. Probably the best I've seen in a while." When Min laughed, his face opened. He laughed not just with his mouth, but with his eyes and shoulders, his whole body telegraphing warmth. In that moment, it was as if they were on the same level. It seemed possible they could become friends and, in due time, old friends. Sunam desperately wanted this. Not only to become Min's friend, but to be the kind of person who could merit his long-term approval. Suddenly he had a flash of intuition. This was the moment he could take control of his future. He had already earned Min's respect. All he had to do was show that he was more than just a good *baduk* player; he had to prove he was someone worth knowing. Clear-eyed, not intimidated—*not scared*—like the others.

"You could be really good too," Sunam said. He had been impressed by Min's tenacity and levelheadedness. There had been a few moves that had struck Sunam as genuinely original, surprising. "They say the best players aren't just born with the gift; they use what they have, they adapt. Some players can take a minor talent and really become huge. The secret is figuring out how to hide your weaknesses."

" 'Minor talent.' Like me, you mean," Min said pleasantly. Someone in the room snorted, but Sunam ignored it. Naturally, he couldn't reveal the highlights of his tournament history without seeming boastful—but he wanted to encourage Min. Let him know he had played well and could become even better if he tried.

"You have the talent," Sunam said generously. Of course it occurred to him that he might seem inappropriate and patronizing, praising a *sunbae* in this way as if he were the elder of the two. But surely someone of Min's stature wouldn't see it that way. He would know that Sunam was offering a genuine compliment. A guy like that who was on top of the world was probably allergic to flattery. If anything, Sunam should worry about laying it on too thick.

"Of course, in your case, you don't have any flaws to hide," said Min, crossing his arms. His pushed-up sleeves revealed thick forearm muscles threaded with veins.

"Sure I do! For example, I'm impetuous, I don't see my own gaps—" As he rattled off a complete litany of his flaws, Sunam privately congratulated himself for being so humble.

"But you see them now, right?" Min interrupted.

Juno was making sharp throat-slitting gestures, and everyone, even Min, had turned to look. With a sickening gut lurch, Sunam realized that the room had fallen unnaturally quiet and must have been for quite some time. He had allowed himself to go on, mistaking the hush for admiration, drunk with the surprise of his own success. But this wasn't a *baduk* tournament. This wasn't even a normal party where he was expected to enjoy himself as a guest. This was an event where his express function was to ingratiate himself, to be the butt of the joke. Juno had already made that clear, and he had foolishly ignored it, believing that he could prove his *sunbae* wrong and achieve what he had done by impressing Min and skipping up the ladder with one giant step.

Sunam had miscalculated completely. When he looked to Juno for help, he was as blank as a Buddha.

"But you see them now, right?" Min repeated. This simple question, repeated by someone who had moments ago seemed friendly, had a terrifying edge. Now he understood how powerful Min was, how he could command the full silence of the room and take down anyone mercilessly over a tiny misstep. Sunam was afraid to speak, afraid to take in more than the very minimum of air.

"Yes," he said.

"Yes what?"

"Yes, I see them now."

"The great lessons of *baduk* are for people who live in their heads," Min said in a cruel, sarcastic voice. "The rest of us prefer the real world. Far more rewarding, I find. Anyway, good game." After thumping Sunam heavily on his shoulder, he pushed through the narrow space between the couch and the table and walked out of the room.

Sunam tried to pretend it had been a natural exit, that the hand on his shoulder had been a friendly one, but it was impossible not to notice how the room reorganized after Min left. People who had been avidly watching drifted away in search of someone else to flatter—or bully. H.G., who had probably never let a silent minute pass in his life, maniacally chewed a red plastic straw and didn't say a word. Even Juno seemed ill at ease, nursing his drink with a grim expression. By the time Sunam had gathered himself and thought to ask for advice—should he find Min and apologize? should he laugh it off?—Juno was gone.

Finally, to give himself something to do, Sunam got up and poured a generous drink from the heavy decanter at the bar. The amber liquid sloshed nearly to the top of the gold-banded glass. He was unfamiliar with whiskey or whatever this was; he licked his fingers where it had spilled. His tongue burned in a way that was not entirely pleasant, but the heft of the glass calmed him. Sunam took a deep swallow and, trying not to choke, walked himself through a different door from the one he'd entered. He would try to acquire the taste.

AT THE END of the long driveway, he couldn't find the mechanism to unlock the gate. On the way in, there'd been an intercom, but whom did you call to let you out? There must be some kind of release key or dial pad, but Sunam could see only what the path lights illuminated. Shaded lanterns produced small golden circles and disorienting shadows. Fine gravel amplified every footstep. He kept picking up sounds—wind, probably—that made him jumpy, thinking someone was near. And he had managed that first whiskey, followed by a quick second.

Sunam shook the gate hard, rattling the lock. "How does this thing open," he muttered. He was just about to try climbing when he heard a female voice behind him.

"Give it a good kick, why don't you?"

Gears whirred softly, opening the gate. Spotlights clicked on, but he didn't need them to know who it was. It was the strange girl from the party. He recognized the dense timbre of her voice, that unmistakable mocking tone. She stood gloating at what he now saw was a camouflaged control box. She wasn't alone. There was Namin, black glove raised against the glare.

The strange girl zigzagged across the gravel, ostentatiously drunk, waving the arms of her huge sweater. She lurched into him and he had no choice but to catch her. "Hope you had a very, very good time. Name's Jisun. Did we do that earlier? Do I know your name?" Her *soju* breath was unbearable even in the brisk air. She briefly steadied herself, then sprawled giggling to the ground. She lay on her back kicking up stones, rolling over the gravel as if the tiny, cold shards were summer grass. "Namin here said I needed a bit of fresh air. She thinks I might be a little drunk," Jisun said in a raspy fake whisper. She sat up and looked at Sunam. "Then we heard you making such a ruckus—thought we were being invaded by North Korean spies! That would have been a bit of excitement, wouldn't it? Though I suppose real spies wouldn't be so clumsy. What were you doing, anyway?" She didn't wait for an answer. "Namin, this is the new guy. New Guy, he's so *impressed* with everything."

"Name's Sunam," he said, to save Namin the embarrassment of explaining how they'd already met. Not that she seemed to require any rescue. Of the three, he was the only one who appeared at all flustered.

"Shouldn't he be impressed?" Namin wore a red coat, and her hair was tucked into the collar, her silhouette as sleek as a marble statue. He could tell even in this darkness how shiny her hair was, how alive. Her breath rose in puffs as she looked back at the house. "Look at it, it looks just like a stack of mon—"

"Don't say it," Jisun warned. "You know how I hate it when you say that." She took hold of Namin's hand and pulled her to the ground. "Don't be such a grump," she said. "Lie down, it's fun. You can see all the stars. You can see the crown of Cassiopeia and the bear-y thing."

Sunam looked up through the trees, but he couldn't see anything.

"I worship this lady," Jisun declared. "This is a lady of true virtue and devotion. Do you know we've been friends twenty years? And I have worshipped her every single day."

"Twenty years?" Sunam asked. He had an early birthday and had just turned nineteen. Weren't they all the same age? He felt suddenly unsure of his own age, as if time had rapidly unspooled here in this dark driveway.

"She has trouble counting. That's why she thinks she's only had one drink," said Namin, not looking at him. It was awkward to be standing over them, Jisun spread-eagle on the ground and Namin crouched unwillingly at her feet. Unlike her earlier demeanor, which had seemed supernaturally relaxed, even playful, every move Namin now made seemed entirely utilitarian and hard. It seemed she would have liked to fold up the other girl, pack her up in a box, and haul her up to the house.

"This is a woman with exquisite scientific perception," Jisun said. "The great physician of our generation." She kicked up another toeful of gravel at Namin. "But not without the curse of malice."

Namin said to him, "Help me. Take her hand."

Together they yanked Jisun up. Namin took one side and he took the other, draping her arm around his waist to keep her steady. He had been careful to keep his distance while she was on the ground, but now he allowed himself to be used as a crutch. She was a girl and he was a piece of furniture. With each step, the warm arm around his waist flopped. He had to hold her hand clamped to his side.

"Tell me, I'm truly interested." Jisun dragged her feet and turned her face up to his. "Why are you here? To get rich? To buy a house like this?" She stopped short and clapped her hands, which were entombed in the enormous sweater. "Eureka, Namin! He wants to have a gate he can't open."

"At least he's allowed to leave if he wants," muttered Namin, pushing her hair out of her face. "Can we focus on getting back? This is another reason you shouldn't drink. You have no idea how much time you waste. I know you don't care, but I do."

"Malice," said Jisun. "A very destructive streak. But don't let that fool you, Sunam," she said. "This one has a tender heart, I think I saw it one time. Once? Maybe it was twice. . . .

"But this one—I think *he* may be in it for the glory," said Jisun. "He's a clever one, this guy. He's got the light, Namin. He's got the hungry eyes."

Sunam let go of her arm. She stumbled but didn't fall. "Why are *you* here?" he asked. Then, deciding he didn't care, he said, "Never mind. Thanks for getting the gate open. Your friend can help you from here."

"Why am *I* here?" Her lips were twitching as if she might cry, but instead she broke into a hooting laugh that rang out too loudly in the night. He winced, even though there was no one to hear. "A very, very, *very* good question requiring a proper answer. The very good answer is: It's my house. Well, it's my *father's* house. I don't really live here, except when I'm in jail. Then I live here, enjoying the full protection of a tyrant."

Her father's house?

Sunam laughed. "Right. You're Ahn Kiyu's daughter. That makes me the president's son. Pleasure to meet you."

"Go on, Namin. Tell him," Jisun said. "Tell him I'm not lying."

"I'm not your secretary," Namin said. "Tell him yourself."

"As my friend, Namin. Tell him as my friend. Anyway, I did tell him myself, but he doesn't seem to believe me."

"She's not lying," Namin said flatly. "Now can we go inside?"

This was Ahn's daughter? That made her Min's sister. . . .

"I would have gone to jail," Jisun insisted. "They didn't *let* me. You know what they said?"

"Jail? What jail?" he said. He felt as if he'd stumbled into a dream. Maybe he had fallen asleep. Maybe he was more drunk than he realized. Suddenly the whisper of the trees was a howl, dragging across his consciousness like a rasp. The call of the night birds seemed to erupt in piercing cacophony. He swayed slightly on the balls of his feet, his body testing the pull of gravity. But the ground was solid, nothing odd or unnatural about it, and the cold air felt bracingly real against his cheek. It was never cold in dreams, was it?

Jisun was oblivious to his astonishment. "Did you hear about the Mun-A strike? They took all of us away. But they threw me back like a bad fish."

"The Mun-A strike? You?" The facts were piling up too fast, and he needed time to understand. If Sunam could have asked for a pen and paper, he would have sat down then and there to work out what was becoming an inevitable equation. If Jisun was really Min's sister, and if she was at the Mun-A strike, where he had been with Juno— then wasn't it possible, wasn't it *likely*, that she was the girl they'd gone to watch? And yet, it just didn't add up. *This* was the girl Juno had his eye on? *Her?* He remembered how she'd made a pointed exit when she saw Juno coming—and how Juno had put off his questions. *Who? Her? Don't worry about it.*

"What were you doing there?" he asked.

"Striking, of course," Jisun said. "But listen! You're missing the point. I'm trying to say something, New Guy. They wouldn't let me stay, do you understand? Do you know how humiliating that is? When all your colleagues think you're abandoning the cause? Just like that, like it never mattered to you at all—"

"I don't understand. Who wouldn't let you stay?" Sunam looked over his shoulder. *The new guy who's so impressed with everything.* Was Juno here? Was Min? He was exhilarated by the information—and hopelessly confused. He wanted to lie down, close his eyes, and sleep. Right here, under the heavy boughs of the centuries-old trees.

"The cops!" Jisun said. "The cops. They took me in and kicked me out."

Sunam dragged a hand over his eyes. Namin said, "Just let her talk and don't ask questions. It takes longer if you ask."

"This is what they said. Didn't I have plenty of rights already? Couldn't I have some other hobby? It *embarrassed* them when they found out who I am. Made them look bad."

"But she was really there? At the Mun-A strike?" Sunam asked Namin.

"But they wouldn't keep me—"

"Of course they can't," Namin interrupted, her voice rising. "They can't just treat you like you're anybody else. Can't you understand that?"

"But I *am* anybody else!"

Namin looked at her. "You get away with most things, but you can't just make things up to suit you. Facts are facts."

Jisun grabbed his arm. "New Guy. Do you see? This is what I was talking about. *Malice.* This one, she could cut glass, diamonds, with her tongue. She never lets me win, not the tiniest point. Not once."

"But you just said you want to be treated like everyone else," he said.

"And *she* just said I couldn't be everyone else!"

"We'll be going around all night at this rate. If you're not lying, if this is serious—" Sunam felt the need to say this, to hedge himself from ridicule in case it was all a crazy joke. "I don't know why you bother."

"Bother arguing? Because I want to—"

"Bother *protesting*," he said. "Namin's right. Maybe it makes sense for real factory workers to do it. It doesn't make any sense for you."

"Barely makes sense for the workers either," Namin spit out. "They lose their jobs, they get blacklisted. It ruins them, their families—"

"And that's why it makes sense for me," Jisun shouted. "Because I don't have seven family members waiting for my measly paycheck. I don't have a reputation to lose!"

"But you're flaunting it!" he said. He realized he was shouting, too, but he didn't know why. What did he care what she did? The footlights bounced in his vision. The gravel was slippery under his feet. "You're shoving it in their face."

"Funny," Jisun said. "All my life people who've known me less than fifteen seconds decide I'm flaunting something. Money, lack of money. Power, lack of power. Whatever it is, surely I'm flaunting. So join the club, New Guy," she said. "You're just like everyone else."

"Fine. I apologize," he said grudgingly. "You're right. I don't know you."

"And even if you did, you would be wrong. Remember that." Jisun stumbled back toward the controls that closed the gate. "Now don't think I'm flaunting anything," she called from behind the pillar. "But it's past curfew and you're going to have to stay here tonight. Here's another fact, not flaunting—there's plenty of room." The rumbling machinery slightly muffled what she said next, but Sunam thought he heard it correctly. "Even for a no-name new guy like you."

Sunam thought about running through the open gate—there was time, he could slip out before it closed. Namin's hand touched his wrist. It was both intimate and authoritative, as if she had no doubt she could stop him with just three fingers on his pulse.

"Go ahead," she called out to Jisun, who was already on her way back to the house. "I'll meet you inside."

Jisun waved an arm overhead without looking back at them. She disappeared into the darkness around the bend. Silently they listened to her skidding footsteps on the gravel fade away. Just when they thought her out of earshot, Jisun's voice carried back to them, a shrill careening falsetto. *"A looooove connection?"*

Sunam was grateful for the night hiding his embarrassment. He cleared his throat to make a joke about it, but Namin silenced him with a finger to her lips. "Don't you dare say anything. Just let her go."

"You two seem very different," he ventured when he was sure Jisun was beyond earshot.

"There's no *seem*. And you don't know the half of it."

. . .

THEY WALKED BACK toward the house with a deliberate slowness that made Sunam understand that Namin wanted to be alone with him. This was a new experience, to have things happen—things he actually wanted to have happen—without any scheming or effort on his part.

As the eldest of four boys, Sunam didn't even have any female cousins close enough in age to have taught him anything about the opposite sex. It was all strange, all confusing, what they did and said and thought. Even his mother seemed to reinforce the notion that there was something unknowably separate about the genders. She was considered lucky by all to have borne four sons—tall, healthy boys with her light skin and their father's strong rural features. But she was forever lamenting the lack of a daughter. A daughter would understand the things her husband and sons could not, she complained. A woman could have ten sons and be the envy of the neighborhood while she was young, but a daughter was what you needed when you were old. You would die comfortably with a daughter tending your bed.

Girls, Sunam had always thought, must be so different from him that he could not possibly understand what they thought about or wanted. He had thought of them as a cross between exotic bird—infinitely fragile, whimsical, and skittish—and mystical pilgrim, capable of intuiting those elusive *female* things his mother could never expect to share with her sons.

And yet—there was something startlingly direct and corporeal about these girls, Namin and Jisun. Their motives, from what he could gather so far, appeared just as self-serving and sturdy as his.

He and Namin walked around the front gardens and settled on the stoop of a low wall, three stone steps leading down to a sunken alcove etched with moss. Down here, close to the ground, the scent of spring—that damp night scent that smelled like rain and dirt and something else indescribably alive—was as intoxicating as the liquor in his veins. Already the alcohol had eased the memory of his failure with Min, casting his humiliation into the distant past. The sky, now bright with stars, seemed both low enough to touch and endlessly expansive, redoubling his sense that everything was new and would get only bigger and better. Arriving here this evening, he had had no idea what the inside of Ahn Kiyu's house might look like or who his daughter was. He had never even heard of Namin—an omission that had disgusted Juno, and now he understood why. In just one night, he'd gotten all those connections clicked in together, all those crucial boxes checked. Imagine how things would progress with even more time. He would become more confident, more suave. He would be the king of the Circle.

"Have you and Jisun really been friends all your lives?" he asked Namin. He realized she'd been quiet as she led them around the house to this corner of the garden, speaking only to point out where they were going. It had been a comfortable silence, at least he thought so, but now he wondered if he should have acted differently. Had he missed an opportunity?

"I don't know why she always says that. It's not even close to the truth," Namin said. "I think she likes the idea because it makes her feel less guilty."

"Guilty?"

"Like if we were truly friends since birth, we'd have grown up in the same neighborhood and I'd have a rich dad too, right? Actually we met in middle school. If I hadn't tested into Kyungki, I'm sure we never would have crossed paths."

"Why, where did you grow up?" Sunam asked. He had never been to a house like this before, and he wondered if Namin thought not being this wealthy was something to be ashamed of. No one lived like this. No one he knew, anyway. His own family, for instance, was fairly well-off since his father was a director at a shipping company. They lived in a two-story house with two bathrooms with flush toilets. He remembered they were among the first families on their block to own a color television, the first to install a private telephone line. His mother had daily help—a girl who did the wash and cleaning and a woman who cooked and shopped. But he never thought of himself as *rich*, not really. Certainly not compared with this grandeur. He wondered if

Namin was jealous because Jisun's father was so successful and if she was dissatisfied with her own lesser circumstances, whatever they were. For all he knew, perhaps Namin's family was better off than his, just not as fabulously wealthy as Jisun's.

"Where did I grow up?" Namin echoed. She seemed to take a long time to consider the question, though it should have been a simple answer. He began to feel uncomfortable, as if he'd inadvertently made another mistake.

"Never mind," he said. "Sorry."

"Sorry for what? It's a simple question. It's just, usually I lie and say I'm from Jeongneung. But I was thinking I wouldn't lie for once—that's why I didn't answer right away. I live in Miari, actually. That's all. Bet you've never met anyone from Miari."

"It's true, you're the first," he said. He was too surprised to think of a different answer. He suddenly remembered her earlier comment, about mice not being quiet at all. It hadn't meant anything to him at the time, just a correction he'd ascribed to her being such a know-it-all: she knew about mice because she knew everything. He hadn't considered that she *really* knew about mice.

"So the Miari girl made it all the way to Seoul National University. Pretty wild, right? I should tell you I was the first kid in the history of our elementary school to get into Kyungki. They would have thrown me a party except the town forbids celebrations of any kind. Only misery and destitution allowed in Miari."

"That was a joke, right?" he said weakly.

"About the party? A bad one, but yes, of course it was a joke. Actually people acted like I was some kind of hero, they were so proud. For years they used to give me free things in the market whenever they saw me coming in my fancy school uniform. I still get free food from some of the shopkeepers. They have a long memory."

"So we'll have to hang out in your neighborhood, then," he said. "To take advantage of all that free food."

Namin smiled. "Maybe," she said. "But watch you don't get caught up in Miari gossip. It's not all free food and SNU fanfare. Everything you've heard is true."

"Some fortune-teller will put a hex on me if she doesn't like the looks of me?"

"Yup."

"And I'll start seeing the ghosts of POWs—or maybe fall in love with the spirit of a tragic heroine, lost too young?"

"Anything is possible," Namin said.

He felt the urge to take her hand. It was the perfect time. Here they were, in this garden under a spring moon. She had just shared something valuable and private, something she admitted she didn't tell just anyone. They were seated close enough that all he had to do was reach a tiny distance. Yet his hand felt leaden in his lap, as if the synapses that made his body move according to his bidding were irreparably snapped.

Instead of the romantic gesture he intended, he blurted, "Are you cold?" and without waiting for her answer took off his jacket and shoved it awkwardly around her shoulders. She looked absurd piled with the second unnecessary jacket. Her coat was already thicker than his and looked warm enough. But she let him settle it around her shoulders, even though he took too long to adjust the seams. He was too nervous to meet her eyes. "There," he said, arranging the collar under her chin. His fingers brushed her face. "I don't want you to be cold."

She was looking at him with that crooked smile. Already these aspects of her seemed familiar and close. That smile, which was half-mocking. Her intelligence, which gleamed in her eyes even when she said nothing. "Don't be so terrified, Sunam," she said softly, and brought her lips to his. Her lips were startlingly warm. He touched her face and kissed her in return. She was swaddled to the neck in layers, only her face floating above their jackets. He threaded his fingers through her hair, laying his palm along the curve of her neck. He could feel her pulse bouncing along the meridian of his lifeline.

"How come you decided to tell me?" he asked when they had pulled away.

"Because I wanted you to believe me. I said I wasn't scared, and I'm not. I don't want anyone saying, later—you or anyone—that I tried, you know. To trick you."

"Trick me?"

"People assume if you're poor that you're ashamed. That you're always trying to cheat, somehow, to get ahead. I don't want anyone saying that about me. Especially not you."

"I would never say that about you."

"How are you so sure? You don't even know me yet," she said. Although Sunam guessed it was meant flirtatiously, an invitation rather than a correction, he still felt wounded. It was technically true, but he was disappointed to hear it put so bluntly.

"I wish you would give me more credit."

"Look at us, look at this place," she said. He was sure she meant the garden, the ambience, the lights glowing through the drawn shades of the house. They were close enough that he could feel the heat of her breath as she talked. He had taken her hand in his, and it was as easy and as natural as he knew it could be. He rubbed the fleshy part of her thumb, tracing the invisible swirl of the fingerprint, memorizing each new part of her. She lowered her voice and began to speak very softly, as if she knew it would make sense to him only that way. "I'm at the bottom rung, the very lowest," she said. "I need to get to the top. I need to, for my family."

His fingers continued their automatic movement, tracing the loop of her fingerprints over and over, stuck. What she was saying was as familiar to him as his own mind—every day he thought about it, where he was and where he wanted to be, the distance between the two points. Their reasons were different, of course. His family did not need him the way she implied her family needed her. But the hope was the same. And to hear it from Namin, not only a girl but a girl who had not existed for him this morning, was a shock. He had not known he could find so much in common with someone so quickly.

But already there were the nagging questions pulling at the edges of his mind: Was she too ambitious? Too smart? Would he be able to keep up? Perhaps they were matched in drive and determination, but Sunam knew he would not be able to equal her achievements. Already he was far behind. Having made it to SNU, Sunam had assumed that he would be more accomplished than any woman he dated. The thought was so natural that it was jarring to have to examine it now as a fallible premise, like having to take a closer look at the sky and question what color it truly was. Come to think of it, the sky wasn't always so blue after all.

"I'm sure you think it's odd that I'm being so open with you when we've just met," Namin was saying. "But people seem to have opinions about me without knowing anything at all, and I want things to be different between us. I'm telling you everything so you can make up your own mind."

"But why?" he finally asked.

"Why what?"

"Why are you telling me all these things? Why me?"

Namin laughed. "Listen to yourself," she said. "Just now you were telling me to give you more credit. Now you're implying I've said too much. I never knew a guy could change his mind so quickly."

"I said give me more credit. I never said I earned it," he joked. "That's why no one calls me the Machine."

"But I'm not one either." She took the jacket off her shoulders and handed it back, squeezing his hand in the process. "Now don't be too sensitive, it's not that I don't want it," she said. "But I'm warm enough and you're shivering." He put it on because it was true, he was cold. "But thank you," she said. "It's nice to be treated like a human being."

AFTER A WHILE, it was too cold to stay outside. Namin knew the place so well, she took them to the back of the house, up a wide stone terrace that led into a solarium. Inside, huge skylights let in moonlight, and potted trees emitted a soft floral scent. A massive round table was centered under the peaked roof, loaded with orchids that bobbed gently with the breeze from the door. When they took off their shoes, Sunam noticed the tiles underfoot were heated.

"This is a good place to sleep if you're tired," Namin said. "No one will bother you here. This part of the house is private. Jisun's father doesn't like for anyone to disturb the plants. They look like regular plants, but trust me, some of them are really valuable." She walked to the longest couch and settled in one corner, her legs tucked under. She motioned for him to join her.

"So maybe we shouldn't be here?"

"Oh, I didn't mean us. He wouldn't like for other people to be here."

"So you're almost part of the family." He wondered if he should ask about Min, if she had any influence with him. She seemed so familiar with the place, the family—for all he knew, she and Min were as close as brother and sister. Perhaps she could talk to him and smooth things over.

"You make it sound like I'm an orphan," Namin said. "I have my own family, Sunam."

"Of course." Trying to understand her, her relationship with Jisun, was like walking a tightrope. It appeared simple enough on the surface—two friends, maybe one slightly jealous of the other. A thing like that seemed understandable. Wouldn't anyone be jealous of Jisun? He, in fact, was jealous of Jisun now that he knew who she was. He suspected he would be far more so if he knew as much about her as Namin seemed to. But what he didn't expect and did not know how to navigate were the slippery, shifting allegiances. He envied Namin's ease within this world, but his admiration seemed to offend her. "I just meant that you seem really close," he said.

"We aren't as close as she likes to think. Actually we've barely spoken in months. We're friends because I owe her for something she helped me with a long time ago, and I guess I always will."

They lapsed into a silence then. It was obvious he shouldn't ask what or why Namin owed Jisun. He assumed it must have something to do with money. Probing for details would only embarrass her.

He said, "If we get in—"

"*When* we get in."

He laughed. "*When* we get in, we'll make those new recruits do something crazy next year."

"Not me," Namin said. "Leave the torturing to the idiots. I plan to be busy."

"Not too busy for me, I hope."

She leaned her head on his shoulder and yawned loudly, without the least bit of self-consciousness, as if they were old friends. "Sure," she said. "If you think you can keep up."

He couldn't decide if she was flirting again or just too sleepy to lie.

THEY MUST HAVE fallen asleep because the next thing he knew, the glass room was flooded with morning light and Jisun was standing over him with a steaming cup.

He looked around and blurted, "Where's Namin?"

"Namin?" she said. "Shouldn't I be asking you that question?" Her eyes had that tight, glittering look of having drunk too much and stayed up too long the night before, but otherwise she seemed remarkably composed. "Sleep well? I can never sleep after drinking."

"Like a brick."

"Lucky you. Actually I never seem to sleep well even when I'm sober. Must be a bad conscience."

"I'm sure you have a much better conscience than the rest of us."

Immediately he regretted bringing that up again, the whole business with the strike, but she simply shrugged. "At least one of us is sure."

She perched herself on an iron garden chair and took slow sips from her cup, watching him. "She probably left because she knew I'd be here. This is where I drink my coffee."

Sunam was surprised to realize that Namin's voice was already embedded in his mind; he could easily imagine what she would have to say about Jisun's breakfast routine. *The empress takes her coffee each morning in the glass room.*

"I should go," he said. "I've stayed much longer than I meant to. Thank you for"——he gestured awkwardly at the room, the sofa that still bore the imprint of his body on the cushion, the view of the garden beyond the terrace—"everything."

She nodded and put down her cup. It made a precise clack on the glass tabletop. "If you see me on campus, you don't have to say hello. I won't."

"It's fine," he said. "It's not a problem."

"Isn't it? You'll see."

4

. . . .

When weeks passed and he didn't hear from Juno, Sunam understood that he had been dropped. He had performed poorly at the party, annoying Min and embarrassing Juno in the process. His Circle prospects, which had seemed so certain after his success at the Mun-A strike, were now surely dead. It should have devastated him. But while he wasn't happy about it, Sunam found himself feeling surprisingly calm. Perhaps he was not yet in full possession of what it meant to have been so close and unceremoniously shut out. Maybe he really was as dumb as Juno had often suggested, in which case he could look forward to a massively delayed reaction in a month or two. But for the moment, Sunam was preoccupied with the unexpected connection he had made with Namin Kang at the party. It formed a thick buffer against disappointment, buoying as it was mystifying, and effectively crowded out most thoughts of failure and defeat. The Circle had always represented the future—but Namin was part of the momentous now. Surely things could not be so bad when, for the first time in his life, there was a girl to think about.

The guys, Chang and the others, asked if he was coming to play cards, and Sunam said he would stop by. He was tired of worrying, of parsing past conversations he could not change and making plans for a future he could not steer. He missed having a group where he didn't have to worry so much about every move. With these guys, the game was the game. Cards, not life. Some of them knew he had been going for the Circle, but they rarely mentioned it. Whether the omission indicated true lack of interest or secret envy he didn't know, but it didn't matter and that was the point. These guys would probably be friends until the day they died, not because their bond was so great, but because they were content to stay on the given track. It was not a bad one, after all—they would probably get good jobs, marry, have children. Sunam had been taught to feel critical of people like this, guys who took the first decent option that came along rather than waiting for the best. But now he wondered if he had judged too soon. What he might have dismissed as complacency in the past seemed a useful talent now. Constancy. A tribe to call his own.

But when he arrived at their usual playing spot, he couldn't stop Juno's voice rattling in his brain. *Frog pond. What're you doing today? What are you doing tomorrow? Nothing.*

He hurriedly mumbled an excuse and left them under the trees.

"Hey, are you coming back or what?" someone called after him.

"Let him go," Chang said. "He knows what he's doing."

BUT SUNAM DIDN'T know what he was doing. For the first time in his life, he felt completely rudderless. No exam to study for, no Circle *sunbaes* to try to impress.

As for Namin, his mind tossed from possibility to possibility, one moment in pursuit of love, the next suspended in doubt. She had probably been invited to join the Circle already. If so, Sunam figured his chances with her were slim. They had probably been flimsy to begin with. She, more than anyone else, knew her worth. She must have calculated how he rated against her. What did he have to offer that she didn't already have in excess herself? His only consolation was that she had kissed him that night, though that worried him also. A girl like that, who decided to kiss someone she'd just met, would probably take away her affection as easily as she had given it.

So he was caught off guard when he ran into her the following afternoon a few blocks from campus. It was a clear spring day, buds on the trees. Birds in the sky. Nothing unusual to inspire a witty comment. There was the smell of cooked sugar floating from the molasses lady on the lawn. A slight breeze pulled at the hem of her skirt.

"Hi," he said.

NAMIN SAID SHE'D like a molasses candy.

All day the molasses *ajumma* sat in her vinyl tent and poured the sugary mixture on a hot flat griddle, creating a perfect caramelized disk, wafer thin and just wider than a child's palm. When the candy was almost set, she stamped a shape into it: a star, a hexagon, a heart. The next one was free if you could eat perfectly around the outline. This was not as easy as it seemed. The candy, as delicate as ice, would break in unpredictable angles. As a kid, Sunam had eaten himself silly trying to win the prize. But whenever he managed to succeed, the free ones never tasted as good. It was the meticulous task of gnawing around an arbitrary line, the hope of finally capturing that elusive victory, that made the candy delicious.

The molasses lady had skin the color of her candy and a missing front tooth. The gap in her mouth flashed as she talked, wishing her young customers good luck. Namin showed Sunam her disk stamped with an octagon. "Too easy," she said, snapping off a side. She was right; the short lines were easiest. The heart or circle was the most difficult, the extended curves nearly impossible to follow cleanly.

Sunam's stamp was a simple outline of a house—triangle over a square. He turned it around, considering the best plan of attack. He could start with the roof point and work his way down. Or tackle the long foundation, get the most difficult part out of the way. He could see how it would look if he managed it—an edible ornament like an image from a picture book.

Impulsively he bit into it, disregarding the shape. The smoky sugar dissolved in his mouth, satisfying and sweet. "It tastes as good as I remember," he marveled. The familiar ritual and reward of the candy eased the need to talk about anything else. Even Namin seemed softer today in her yellow skirt that matched the forsythia blazing around the quad.

"You sound just like an old man," she said. "Surely it hasn't been so long."

"No, it's been years," he said. "Can't even remember the last time I had one of these. I don't know why I stopped."

"I can't go a week without it. I'll probably eat these until I'm an old lady with no teeth. Do you know"—she smiled, the edge of the disk in between her teeth—"it's a secret talent of mine, breaking out these shapes."

Sunam had noticed how quickly and precisely she worked. In seconds she had the perfect octagon lying flat on her palm like a jewel. The lines appeared as clean as if she'd chopped them with a knife. "I have a record, the most I've ever done in a row," she confided. "Want to hear it?"

"Let me guess. Four?"

She shook her head.

"Seven? Eight?" He wasn't sure if he could actually believe someone could do more than eight in a row. "Come on, more than eight?"

"Twenty-seven," Namin said proudly. "I was nine. I'm way out of practice now, but I'm sure I can still do at least ten or fifteen."

Sunam had always assumed there was just one freebie, one reward. You ate it. The end. He'd never even tried for more. "You were a greedy child," he said, and it struck him that maybe she was still greedy. He remembered the stories Juno had told him about Namin, how she had pushed into the Circle with that self-assured comment about her perfect exam scores. In many ways, she and Juno were alike. Not content to swim around the tadpole section of the little pond. Shark track. Unafraid to demand the best from any situation. Only Namin seemed to hide her ambition better than Juno. Or maybe it just seemed that way because she was a girl.

"I told the neighborhood kids if they bought me the first one, I'd give them all the free ones after—the shapes, anyway. Of course I had to eat the outline. Finally the *ajummas* said I could only do the ones I ate myself. I guess it was only fair."

Sunam went with Namin to collect her prize. The molasses *ajumma* pretended not to see them, taking her time with the other customers, stalling them with honeyed small talk. Hoping Namin would give up and go away. Finally, when there were no new customers remaining, she scowled at the crisp lines of the octagon in Namin's hand. She clucked her tongue, two sharp clicks indicating what she thought of them. SNU students demanding freebies from a poor candy vendor.

"You said good luck," Namin reminded her.

"Who said I didn't?" grumbled the *ajumma*, handing over the free candy. Sunam wondered if the *ajumma* would feel differently about Namin if she knew her true situation. Surely she wouldn't mind treating a Miari girl, especially one who had come so far.

He watched Namin nibble its circumference, running the melted edge along the length of her tongue. The dark sugar coated the pink inside of her lips.

"You said something at the party I've been wondering about," he said. "About everyone being scared? You've really never been scared?"

"'Course I have," she said. "Just not of a silly college party. Or silly college people."

Silly, twice in one breath. "Why bother being in the Circle, then?" he asked. He was hoping she would mention if she had been accepted or not.

"You know better than that. You wouldn't have been there if you didn't." When she spoke like this, assuming his intelligence but exasperated at his failure to demonstrate it, he didn't know whether to feel insulted or flattered. "Everyone knows what these things are for," she said. "Why does anyone make groups? It makes people feel important. When people feel important, they go up together. You've seen it. The same kids who were bossy in grade school are bossy now. They'll be bossy thirty years from now, only they'll have fancy titles and big offices.

"Me, I don't have a rich dad like Jisun. My family can only pay for one of us to go to college—that's me—so I can't afford to be scared and lose what they've worked for." She showed Sunam the shape she'd pulled out of the candy. She'd done it again, this time without him noticing, slowly licking the sugar away. It was a four-point star, and she had just one short edge left to cut.

"So you're the eldest, then," he said casually, as if people talked like this all the time. Revealing their private troubles as frankly as if they were telling the year they were born or how many siblings they had.

"I have an older sister," Namin said. "Seven years older."

"Didn't she want to . . . ?"

"Maybe she did. Now she works at a factory. Running shoes."

"Seven years older. Makes her twenty-six. Not married?"

Namin looked at him with an expression he couldn't quite grasp—amused, but not entirely pleasant. "Look at you, calculating her age like a worried auntie. You have any proposals for a match? She's twenty-seven, actually," she said. "Born in the year of the tiger. Very charming when she's happy. We won't discuss the other side, of course." She laughed with the candy in her mouth, a laugh with bared teeth. "You can tell them she's a very *old* tiger."

"Now I can tell you're the youngest."

"Beware the younger sister of a tiger—" she said, but the joke fell strangely flat. He gathered they did not get along, Namin and her sister. It must be awkward for them, the shoe factory and SNU under the same roof.

After that, Sunam didn't know what to say. Of course, he knew of other students who had come to college with their family's expectations heavy on their shoulders. He knew of it hypothetically but had never met anyone in that situation, at least not anyone who admitted it so readily from the start. He felt a mixture of admiration for Namin and dread for himself—it would not be easy to date someone like this. Even if she consented to be his girlfriend, he would have to tread lightly introducing her to his family. He was certain his father would not approve. Since it had been so difficult for him to establish himself, alone in this city with no relations or family resources to help, Sunam's father was devoted to the principle of prosperous families producing prosperous offspring. With Namin's family background—the sister in the factory, the parents in Miari—even the perfect exams and every-thing the scores represented for her future might not be enough to win him over. Sunam knew the smart thing would be to give it up before things became too complicated. But he couldn't bear the idea of some-one else having the courage he didn't if he gave her up without even trying.

"You don't have to warn me, I already know what I'm up against," he said. "If I hang around with you, for sure no one will ever notice *me* again. I'll become totally invisible. Only a fool would erase himself like that, right?

"I guess I've always been a fool, though," he said. "Hey, check me out." He waved his arms overhead as if she were on a mountaintop, searching for him at the bottom. He mimed shouting, cupping his hands around his mouth, his voice projecting across vast distances. "Can you see me? Am I invisible yet?"

Namin looked at him as if she didn't know whether to laugh or cry.

"Am I invisible yet?" he said again, this time whispering conspicu-ously.

She took his hand. She laid her hand on top of his and slowly smoothed the flat of his palm, stroking it from heel to fingertips as if it were a piece of velvet. She gave him the star, the candy edges still damp from her mouth. He held his palm perfectly flat, so as not to dull a single crystal of that sugar.

"I should say something romantic," she said with a smile. "I should make a speech. What do you think?"

"Like 'With this star I give you my heart, my undying devotion'?" he said.

"More like 'With this star I give you a portal to future cavities, per-haps the early loss of an important front tooth.'"

"Finally! Something you're not good at," he said. "Don't ever be-come a poet."

"You didn't like it? I thought it showed a bracing commitment to realism."

"In that case, it's a masterpiece. What do I know? All this time I thought this was just candy. Never knew it was such an art form. Anyway, I'll treasure it always."

Laughing, she broke off one of the points and popped it into her mouth. She broke off another and nudged it at his lips. "We may as well eat it. That *ajumma* will kill me if I go back for another."

He opened his mouth and took the candy between his teeth. He knew he had done the right thing by not bringing up any business about the Circle, pretending that nothing had changed or would change between them. Surely it would only embarrass her and make her feel sorry for him—the last thing he wanted. From the first, Namin had been clear she would not tolerate pity. In his arrogance, Sunam had assumed it was only pity directed at her that she hated. Now he understood that it went both ways. Just as she rejected it herself, Namin would never indulge in pitying him, no matter what happened.

"Hey, put in a good word for me, would you?" he said.

He could tell she knew instantly what he meant. She plucked the remaining candy from his hand and broke it in half, but she didn't meet his eyes and she didn't answer his question.

"Will you?" he asked.

The candy had broken unevenly, so that one side was significantly larger than the other. She handed him the bigger piece and popped the smaller shard in her mouth.

"You don't need them, anyway," she said with a sudden fierceness that seemed to clash with the melting sweet in her mouth. "You have me, remember?"

So it was true. She was in—and Sunam was out.

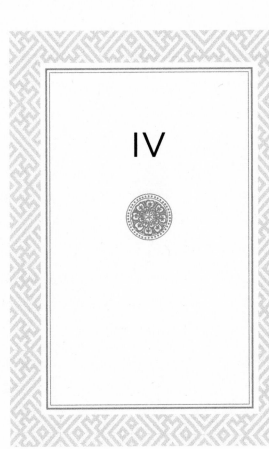

IV

1

....

In the beginning, Jisun had felt brave. She had felt that there was something noble about her being so angry, when people thought she should be content.

Rich girl, daddy's girl, throw me a pearl, the neighborhood children chanted when the chauffeur dropped her at school. They waited, of course, for the car to pull away before throwing dirt clods aimed at her head. Though it was softer, they preferred dirt to rocks, which left marks and could get them in trouble. Anyway, seeing dirt on her was just as satisfying as seeing her bleed. They could watch it worry her all day. Lodged into her part and crammed into a thousand hiding places. Dribbling onto her paper when she bent over her desk. Dusting the white shoulders of her uniform, making her look *dirty*. It was fun to watch her scratch under her ponytail, poking with a pencil. They faked concern: *Oh, teacher, should Jisun be checked for lice?*

Jisun never cried and she never ratted. "Complaining is the vice of the lower classes," her father always said. The gold rims of his glasses glinted as he peered over them. "If you want to waste time bellyaching, go talk to the mailman."

Jisun would never understand her father's disdain for ordinary folks when he had come from humble roots himself. Ahn Kiyu was born and raised in Janghowon, a farming village southeast of Seoul, the second son and fourth of five children. Against his father's wishes, he set out for the capital at age sixteen and apprenticed himself at a bicycle repair shop, where the owner promised room and board in addition to a small stipend. By the time he was eighteen, he had bought the shop. At twenty-five, he married Jisun's mother, a girl from his hometown two years his senior whom he had always admired. Once the town beauty, she had refused so many suitors that no one believed she would ever marry. In their wedding photo, Jisun's mother looked surprised herself.

Perhaps in those early years when they lived above the bicycle shop, Jisun's parents had been happy. In time the business expanded to include automobile repair, then dropped bicycles altogether. There were photos of a new garage, four mechanics standing proudly with tools in hand, caps at jaunty angles. A new house with a persimmon tree in the courtyard. A car, which her dad polished himself every Sunday.

By the time Jisun could form memories of her own, they had moved to the house on the hill overlooking the city. Each year the lights below grew brighter and the house seemed to expand with the accumulating weight of precious objects. Furniture. Paintings. Rugs. Crystal. Things her father collected but barely looked at before he acquired something else even more priceless and rare.

But the intangible things proved heaviest in the Ahn household. The eroding glare of her father's ceaseless scrutiny. His disapproving silences, punctuated by ferocious outbursts that reverberated long after the noise died down. These confrontations usually coincided with important business or social events where Jisun's mother was also required to attend. Inevitably, her dress would appear too cheap or it would be a repeat of an outfit she had worn too often. She would have been too quiet, like a sullen shadow, or laughed too loudly, like an ignorant peasant woman. She would have slighted someone Jisun's father was trying to impress or been too friendly with an inferior associate who did not merit such attention. Day by day he whittled her down, mocking the way she ate her food, spoke to the servants—even the way she stroked the children's faces. "Like an alley cat," he said. "Like a bitch licking her young." Each morning, he dressed Jisun's mother as if she were a doll. Shoving her limbs into clothes too constricting, too fine, which she wore with an expression of mute outrage.

Jisun's father had adjusted to wealth—there would never be so much that he could not adjust to it—but his wife had been happiest on the farm, where her family grew snow white turnips and radishes and made a summer kimchi famous many towns over. As for adjusting, she proved ultimately unable. By the time Jisun was in elementary school, her mother had already attempted to abandon the family twice. Once with her older brother and the second time alone. Never with Jisun, who was younger and arguably needed her mother more. She was the girl her mother should have favored—but her mother believed in the value of sons. Or perhaps she knew, even then, that Jisun was her father's daughter, unwilling to run when she could stay and fight.

Jisun's father did not wait for her third attempt before cutting his losses. For years, he had claimed poor health to excuse his wife's absence at social functions. It was a simple matter to remove her altogether, explaining that she was better off in the countryside, where the air was cleaner and the pollution would not bother her lungs.

The week their mother was banished, Jisun and Min were taken to Switzerland to learn how to ski. They did not ask why their mother was not coming, assuming she had refused to make the trip. By this time she rarely left her bedroom, tucked away at the back of the house separated by a narrow staircase from the main wings, where the architect might have imagined the maid to live. Though she remained secluded, *ajumma* never failed to leave her meals by the door, no matter how many of them went uneaten. The dishes grew smaller and smaller—*ajumma* hated to see her cooking go to waste—but she never skipped the offering. Jisun knew because she always checked.

Her mother died in her hometown under her parents' roof, apparently having starved herself to death. Jisun's father had her body brought up and buried in a fancy grave far from her ancestors. He arranged a funeral grand enough for a first lady. With four hundred wreaths of white chrysanthemums and a catered dinner that fed more than twelve hundred people, mostly business associates who got drunk and squeezed out alligator tears to impress the boss. A top-to-bottom production that would have made his wife howl with rage.

Jisun never forgot that her mother's first choice, when she was strong enough to flee on her own two feet, had been to leave with Min. At the funeral, she did not cry. That night she drank her first bottle of *soju,* filched from the kitchen. She had stolen two. The first she drank. The second she poured out for her mother, who was finally free.

BY THE TIME Jisun arrived at the lauded gates of Seoul National University, she wanted to burn the whole place down. Not just for democracy or the repeal of the repressive constitution or anything else that the student activists shouted about every day. These were heady concepts that were still only symbolic to her, as they were for many of the young activists. They joined the cause not quite understanding what to expect, not knowing what could be done or even what they hoped to achieve. It was the same for Jisun. She was fueled by personal vengeance, a blurry sense of vendetta on behalf of her mother, who had been lifted out of rural contentment and made to parody a false, totalitarian notion of prosperity. Later, she might come to label and disown these feelings as childish outposts of delayed adolescence, but in those early days, Jisun was poised for any blunt rebellion. She wanted blood. She wanted fire.

Of the underground network called "undercircles," it took one semester to develop a usable mental map of hierarchies, rivalries, alliances. Groups sketched out like neighborhoods connected by subterranean threads, like the new subway system that had recently been installed in Seoul.

Each group, like a family, had its own particular identity. A face it showed to friends and a secret face it tried to hide.

Apple was an agro-sociopolitical study group, known for its obsessive newshounds who prided themselves on originality, humor, and radical criticism. The members of Apple fanatically published original content not just about agricultural issues and the impact of government manufacturing regulations on small farms—their pet topics—but also on broader social issues. Every Tuesday morning, huge broadsheets appeared in campus lavatories and filtered out to public places as supporters pasted them to windows and tacked them to trees. For these publications, the members of Apple favored provocative topics such as government surveillance, media censorship, and Park's maneuverings for international—particularly U.S.—aid. Since she didn't know any of the individual members, Jisun developed a crush on Apple as a group, stalking the bulletins the way other girls sought out news of singers or film stars. Finding them was just a matter of determination and endurance. It was—she was her father's daughter—a matter of forming a plan.

Jisun chose the first-floor women's lavatory in the political science building on a Monday night. She had watched this bathroom for weeks and knew there would be a bulletin posted by morning. All she had to do was wait. She packed a hot thermos and wrapped herself in an enormous hooded overcoat, prepared to huddle on the cold tile until morning. When the door creaked open at half-past twelve, she was relieved to be saved from enduring a long, cold night, but also disappointed—had it been too easy?

"What are you doing here?" said the startled boy.

"Waiting for you, actually." Jisun scrambled to her feet, knocking over the thermos in the process. The metal canister clattered horribly on the tile. "You're from Apple, right? I want to join your group."

"You can't. We're full."

She noticed he didn't even deny whom he was working for, which he must have been trained to do. He was probably the lowliest peon, someone she could easily manipulate. "How can you be full? Couldn't you always use more members to get the word out?"

"No."

"I've read every one of your bulletins since I've gotten here. I even saved some of them—"

"It's not getting the word out if you *take* them for yourself. Now get out of my way."

After dumping his things on the ground, he took out a roll of tape and unfurled the bulletin. The thin newsprint flapped and folded against itself. Reaching for the tape, he struggled to keep the sheet centered on the wall.

"Let me help," Jisun said quickly. "I'll give you a hand with these tonight. Think how much quicker it will go with two people."

"Not interested."

Jisun could see that with the number of bulletins in his stash, it would take him hours. No wonder he started barely after curfew. It would take him until morning to get them up all over campus.

"If you let me help, I'll take your place for as long as you want. A month, six months, whatever. You don't have to tell anyone. I swear I'll say you did it all."

He still had his back to her, but she saw his shoulders registering the offer. "A year, even," she said. "You can take all the credit. I won't say a word."

He turned to face her. "How do I know I can trust you?"

"Look. I'm desperate enough to camp out in a smelly bathroom all night. Isn't that some kind of proof?" She met his eyes and delivered her best shot. "Of course, if you can't get me in, I understand."

"Hand me the tape," he said curtly. Jisun smiled. She cut off six pieces and lined them up on her arm, handing them over at the precise moment he needed them. When she gathered up her things and followed him to the next location, he ignored her but also didn't tell her to get lost. Without any small talk to slow them down, they were a brisk team and finished before three A.M. Before they parted ways, he gave her a brief nod. "Tomorrow night, ten fifteen. Gray Basket," he said, naming a drinking hole she'd heard of but never been to. Jisun waited until he had turned the corner before celebrating. She felt a glow of triumph, dampened only by the fact that it had not been more of a challenge.

The boy lasted only a few more weeks in Apple, evidently disillusioned by the mundane work of lower-rank activism. Jisun, too, quit a few weeks later. But not because she was frustrated with posting flyers and running meaningless errands. It turned out that the members

of Apple, as brilliant and incisive as she had hoped, were also chauvin-
istic, power hungry, and vain. They loved the trappings of activism
as much as—or more than—the ideas they supported. They pre-
tentiously wore Lenin hats and *gomushin,* the rubber shoes worn by
farmers, as if they had just stepped off a Bolshevik rice paddy. They
wasted whole afternoons interrogating new recruits on their reading
histories—not to discern their interests, but to prove their own superiority. Lenin's *What Is to Be Done?* was a prerequisite, along with
Gorky, Marx, and Sinclair.

The second group she tried, Mayday, cultivated a belligerent and
hawkish reputation, pulling fire alarms and conducting what they
called "kamikaze operations"—actions that could be completed within
five minutes before the authorities intervened. They sometimes created more theater than social action, but after the verbal pretensions of
Apple, it was a relief to *do* something. To create a noise that anyone
could understand. And Mayday held close contacts with undercircles
at Yonsei and other universities, where protests had begun to spill off
campus into the streets, disrupting traffic and resulting in the deploy-
ment of riot police.

At her first Mayday meetings, Jisun came prepared with a mental
list of questions. Foremost in her mind was learning the ropes for
street protests. She wanted to know how to prepare for tear gas, what
to do if she was arrested, how to handle interrogations. The main
leader, Yosan, was a senior majoring in German lit. He had a streak of
white hair at the nape of his neck and planned to work as a journalist
after graduation. He was passionate about censorship issues, with an
encyclopedic knowledge of authors whose names Jisun did not even
know how to pronounce. But he was contemptuous of females, especially ones who might be considered attractive. Despite Jisun's numerous questions, Yosan ignored her completely. She had to doggedly
repeat herself before he'd even look at her. When he did, it was only
to articulate what his attitude had been projecting all along. "You're
just a first-year. Paint some signs. Prove yourself. We'll move you up
to leaflets."

She persisted. What weapons could they use? Rocks? Pipes? At what point could they justify using violence? And what would the police come with? She asked if anyone had any experience making Molotov cocktails.

The boy slowly raked his eyes over her, as if she had arrived at the meeting naked. "They get one photo of you anywhere near a Molotov, you'll be in prison swinging from your toes. Be happy you don't have a dick to hang by." His disciples twittered dutifully, but Jisun was undeterred. She had been raised by a man who had slowly killed his wife with nothing but the grinding edge of sarcasm. This undergraduate version barely registered on her scale.

She returned his stare and asked again.

"Look. If you're worried about the gas," he said, "stay home. We don't need another scared-shitless girl to drag back, anyway."

When the gas deployed at her first street protest, Jisun was close enough to see it coming. It enveloped her and everything around her like a tunnel, flooding her eyes and nose with searing liquid. She could feel her own tears burning as if her face were on fire. All around her was noise, and no one knew which way to run. It felt impossible to keep moving with the suffocating smoke filling her chest. Only the terror of being trampled kept her from collapsing on the street, because everyone was running and no one could stop to help her even if they wanted to try.

Afterward, she was more livid about her lack of preparation than the brutality of the police response. The more experienced student activists, she'd noticed, had come with wet towels, bandannas, even goggles, the obvious solution of which particularly galled her. The seniors had chosen to keep her in the dark, using the police tear gas as some kind of substitute for hazing.

She cornered Yosan. "I *asked* you about the gas."

"And I told you to stay back." He had a sheaf of leaflets in his hand rolled up tight like a baton. As he talked, he flicked up the edges so the pages snapped back on the roll. She wanted to snatch it from his hand

and slam it across his nose. He lifted his lips in a humorless smile. "But now you know what it's like. Congratulations. You've been to your first big-girl protest."

"Why bother protesting the government—so *you* can be the tyrant?"

"That's how the rest of us learned. Me, him. All of us. What makes you so special?" He reached out and tapped her forehead with the paper baton. Two taps, square between the eyes. Not enough to hurt, only to prove he was in charge. When the baton came down again, Jisun knocked it from his hand, scattering the sheets across the floor.

"What makes me special is that I actually care," she snapped.

Instantly his face was so close, she could see a piece of black seaweed lodged between his teeth. She could smell the oil on his nose clogging his pores in a mosaic of grease. "Worry less about the cops and more about your attitude," he snarled. "You want tips? Keep your mouth shut and do as you're told. Or else get out. Bitches like you never last, anyway."

Jisun held her ground. "Thanks. I'm not going anywhere."

AT THE NEXT protest, Jisun was ready with a bag of bandannas soaked in vinegar, which she'd heard helped against the gas. She hesitated over goggles, which she could have easily swiped from her family's stash and even shared with others. She had enough equipment for a dozen people. Swim goggles in clear, dark, and prescription lenses. Even better were the ski goggles, large enough to provide full peripheral vision. But she remembered how they had caused a division of haves and have-nots within the ranks. Worried that someone else could feel similarly betrayed, she left the goggles at home.

Knowing what people would say about her when they found out who her father was, Jisun worked harder than anyone, volunteering to do the grunt work everyone else avoided. She hauled five-gallon kettles of water to boil for tea and late-night ramen. After everyone else had left for the night, she picked up empty bottles and scraped gum and washed cigarette ash off the floor. They might criticize and reject her anyway, but at least she'd have done everything she could to argue her case.

"YOU FINALLY FOUND what you've always wanted," Namin said.

Jisun had been trying to explain the different undercircle groups, what each had meant to her, why it was so important for her to be involved. She hadn't expected Namin to share her enthusiasm, but she didn't expect to be treated like a freak, either. The way Namin reacted, Jisun felt like one of those cases in abnormal psychology texts. Those people who went around searching for lost messages or misplaced clues for decades following a trauma. War survivors. Or jilted lovers.

"So are you finally happy?" Namin said. "Can we expect an era of peace and tranquillity now?"

"Maybe I'm properly miserable," Jisun said. "Having your consciousness raised isn't a picnic, you know. I can see why you Circle types avoid it. You wouldn't want to accidentally change your mind."

Namin laughed. "Well, misery becomes you. You look like you've come out of a milk bath."

"Yes, that's what we do. Protests and milk baths."

But she couldn't manage a real edge. Namin was right. She might not have known what she always wanted—unlike Namin, who always knew what she always wanted. What she'd do after college, Jisun genuinely had no idea.

But she was happy. Happier than she'd been in a long time.

2

. . . .

t was through S4—the most extreme of all the undercircles—that
Jisun learned of UIM, the Urban Industrial Mission, from the United
States. UIM had originated in the late 1950s as a faith and counseling
ministry for factory workers, but by the 1970s it had shifted focus to
social issues. It educated workers about labor laws and the need for
trade unions. Because it was an American organization, the Urban Industrial Mission was granted greater leniency to make public state-
ments in support of workers' rights and hold demonstrations and
sit-ins despite laws that might have prohibited local people from doing
the same. The authorities, well aware of the power of the American
Christian lobby and already sensitized by criticisms of human rights
abuses from the Carter administration, were wary of creating additional friction between Seoul and their most important ally, the United
States.

In the second semester of her freshman year, Jisun heard murmurs
of UIM staff looking for English translators who could help them
communicate better with workers. Jisun was fluent and might have
been perfect for the job, but she didn't think twice about it. Translation
was a desk job and she wanted to be out where the action was. She
might never have considered it if the S4 leaders hadn't pushed her into
the role. By that time, it was obvious that Jisun was running out of options in the SNU underground network.

S4 was the radical group, many of whose members eventually went
into garment factories, steel mills, and shipbuilding docks posing as
ordinary workers. This was the most extreme decision a student activ-

ist could make, tantamount to renouncing the good life and a stable future, not only for themselves but also for their families, who had collectively sacrificed every resource to see them through the grueling years of college preparation. She watched fellow activists make heart-wrenching decisions to leave the university, knowing it was bringing crushing disappointment and disapproval from their families.

Although it did not mean nearly the same level of sacrifice for her in terms of either future or family, Jisun wondered if she would ever be able to make such a decision. Factory work promised only mental and physical drudgery, social alienation, and a long, painful period of adjustment. It was not easy for former college students to fit in with the customs and speech of factory workers, but it was imperative for them to keep their identities hidden—or risk serious consequences. Last year, a male activist had gone missing after leaving the university to work in a steel mill. After his disappearance, his mother seemed to have a nervous breakdown and made daily visits to campus, begging anyone who would listen for information about her son.

Stories like this only fueled greater fervor among the activists, who regarded each arrest and horror story as an additional casualty to be avenged on the political battlefield.

Commit suicide as a class and be reborn as revolutionary workers.

The men and women of S4 did not ask Jisun if she had read Lenin. They did not expect her to pass initiation rites or bow ninety degrees, as if they were brothers in some street gang. They valued work and sacrifice, a language Jisun trusted. She admired their ceaseless sincerity as much as she sometimes chafed against it. Was there any rule against cracking a smile every once in a while? Did it hurt to have a little fun? Among the undercircles, S4 occupied hallowed ground, and Jisun was genuinely awed by their resolve to live out their convictions with total action. But she sometimes missed the humor, however vainglorious, of Apple and the reckless spirit of self-expression among the other, less serious groups. The members of S4 scrutinized Jisun's every word, every gesture, with an eye so severe that she felt like an ant being burned under a magnifying glass.

Any small personal extravagance could become a point of contention. Clothing with English-letter logos. Going to the movies. Majoring in something as decadent as art history, which glorified aristocratic excesses.

In Jisun's case, it was a pair of round oversize sunglasses, inexpensive but overtly fashionable in the "maxi style" that was everywhere on campus and the streets. Jisun had bought them at the outdoor *Namdaemun* markets: a cheap plastic frame and flimsy lenses that wildly distorted her vision and gave her a headache. She would have discarded them sooner had she not seen how the girls of S4 reacted. They seemed visibly pained by them and refused to address her until she took off the glasses and hid them away in her backpack. "Thank you," they'd say with exaggerated decorum, waiting a beat longer than necessary before speaking.

Finally, one of the girls took a public stance. Kana was a tall girl with wide-set eyes and the short, blunt haircut everyone else grew out as soon as they were released from high school. The die-hard female activists cut their hair short in this unflattering style as a symbol of asceticism, believing that fashion was an elite privilege that needed to be disavowed until everyone could access it equally.

"Personally I prefer a much simpler attitude without these bourgeois trappings. Clothing should be about honesty and utility. Anyway, do these even help you see? They certainly don't help us see *you*."

"The factory girls are all wearing this style," Jisun pointed out. "They're wearing the whole ensemble: skirt, boots, hat, everything. The other day I passed a girl who looked just like Ali MacGraw. She had the entire look from head to toe. What do sunglasses have to do with honesty, anyway?"

"We don't call them 'factory girls' anymore," Kana said. "They are workers who deserve respect."

"Of course I respect them. But that doesn't mean we all have to dress like janitors and farmers. They don't want to dress in their uniforms either, you know," Jisun said, thinking of Namin's sister. "Haven't you noticed how they change into street clothes as soon as they have a chance? If you want to respect them, don't treat them like 'workers.' They're people, like everyone else."

"They change because they don't want people to look down on them for being 'factory girls.' If we respected their occupation, they wouldn't have to be ashamed."

"But that doesn't change the fact that the uniforms are ugly. And some people actually care how they look."

Jisun knew she had hit her target. Kana said stiffly, "I guess you would know. I care about more *important* things."

"That's very clear, Kana," Jisun said. And even though they were inside, she flipped the glasses back on her face. Later she regretted it—was she a child that she had to act on every impulse, alienating everyone she met? But it was done.

In less than a year, Jisun burned through the entire underground network, trailing a reputation as firebrand and liability. In the fall of 1977, she was arrested twice, and again in January 1978. Each time, she was immediately released after the police were alerted by someone in her father's camp. Jisun always went straight back to activism, but these unusual episodes created rifts between her and her peers. A single arrest and long detainment would have raised her to martyr status, but this ongoing hide-and-seek with the police made the student leaders nervous. She was too visible.

That winter, S4 leadership passed her off to UIM, praising her with the overabundant generosity of people newly relieved of a problem. UIM needed interpreters, and Jisun's English, the product of years of foreign tutors, was confident, if idiomatically haphazard—littered with overly obsequious phrases such as "Don't mention it" and "Cheers," which would later make the American aid workers smile at her strangely. But at this first meeting, the missionaries kept pumping her hands and calling her a "lifesaver." The more she spoke in her fluent English, the more overjoyed they became.

"You cannot *imagine* the trouble we've had," they kept saying. Interrupting one another in their eagerness to be understood. "You see, none of us speak any Korean—"

"Or *enough* Korean."

"And the culture is so difficult—"

"Lovely, of course, but yes, quite difficult."

And wiping their brows as if they were stranded in a desert, streaming sweat. In fact the weather was raw and freezing. That day, Jisun met a couple from Ohio named Bob and Julie Anne. A portly older woman in a gray dress and white shoes who had the unpronounceable name of Beverly. And a young man her own age, who turned out to be Peter. He shook her hand warmly but did not gush like the others.

Jisun understood that her former comrades had given the Americans rave reviews of her talents and reliability as both devoted worker and translator. She understood this because it was clear they did not want her back. *We understand if your new duties keep you too busy to come to any more meetings. We understand completely.*

Falling headlong into that space between desperate people—the workers, local but disenfranchised from their rights; and the UIM staff, foreigners who had come to help but could not communicate the basic facts of their message—Jisun surprised herself. She discovered she had a talent for translation, which she had previously considered the domain of diplomats and stuffy tutors. In practice, she was exhilarated by the power of translated language to transcend boundaries of race and culture. All it required was her willingness to become silent in the conversation, letting other people's words pass through her as through a sieve. Jisun was touched by the ways in which both groups gave themselves over to her, allowing her entry into their questions, answers, barbs, and jokes. She had never expected it to be so intimate.

Within two weeks of working with UIM, she had moved out of her father's house into factory housing with the workers who ran the textile machinery. Twelve to a room lined with bunk beds. No windows, no baths. Just cold water in the sink and toilets that had to be emptied every week for the number of people who used them. The machines covered the girls with fine fiber dust the color of unmixed cement, marking everything they touched. Sometimes two girls rented the same bed, since one could sleep while the other worked. As long as they stayed on opposite shifts, they could share and save money.

Although she shared sleeping and eating areas with the factory workers, Jisun's days as a translator were quite different. Some days she trailed the UIM staff, touring factories and meeting with union leaders. Mostly she worked with Peter. They had a shared desk at the tiny unheated office where she translated the labor laws from Korean to English. She also translated his speeches and notes, which he planned to use during small group factory meetings, from English to Korean. When they met, he had been in the country only three weeks and his Korean was limited to basic body functions referring to eating, sleeping, or using the toilet. They spoke English, but he tried to use as many Korean words as he knew—a short but growing list that he kept in a battered notebook small enough to fit into his back pocket.

"It's about earning trust," he said about his commitment to learning the language. Jisun wondered whose trust he meant. Was it that he wanted to earn her trust—?

"The people, the trust of the people," he said. She pretended that's what she'd thought all along.

Although Jisun was always with him to interpret, Peter insisted on giving at least a portion of his talks in Korean wherever he spoke. He organized lunchtime meetings at the steel mill, night classes at local churches, anywhere they were willing to have him. And when he had delivered the Korean part of his presentation, the workers broke out into applause as if they'd witnessed a wondrous circus trick.

Jisun never officially dropped her classes at SNU—she had not gone to many classes in her pre-UIM days anyway, occupied as she was with her seminars and protest work. But she assumed eventually she would be withdrawn from the registrar and her status as a student rescinded. The prospect did not upset her in the least. Now that she understood what was possible for her in the world beyond the campus gate, there was no future for her at SNU. All her heady readings of theories, manifestos, treatises, declarations; all those nights spent in impassioned seminar debates that seemed to go round and round in an ever-tightening circle—all of it had been training for what she was experiencing now. Among her own people, in her own time, not re-enacted from books written a hundred years ago.

Jisun felt that she had finally joined the ranks of *useful* people, doing something that mattered. She had transcended the expected path that had been carved out for her, forging her own surprising fate.

Once a week, then once a month, Jisun called the house when she knew her father would be out. By the end of each short call, *ajumma* always lost her temper and hissed into the receiver—*This is enough*—as if there were anyone listening in that endless, vacant house to even warrant lowering her voice.

She always told *ajumma* to take care and hung up the phone. Her old life had receded so far into the distance that nothing could reach her. The house would never change. She could picture everything precisely. The sharp arrow points on the gate shutting out the world. The billowing camphor trees: mature specimens imported from some miraculous countryside that had managed to keep them safe first from Japanese colonial deforestation, then from the bombs of the Korean War. The lemon-eucalyptus scent of furniture oil, rubbed diligently into antique armoires and étagères. The heavy silk drapes that pooled at the floor like frozen waterfalls. All these things were as intact in her mind as if she were standing there herself.

But Jisun was not there anymore. She had finally excised herself from the immaculate picture. And like a painting coming alive, she felt the discovery of the world rushing with fresh meaning into her veins. She was free.

3

. . . .

S NU was shut down all week following a student demonstration
that had turned violent. For two days, there had been tanks parked
at the gates and no telling when classes would resume. Namin briefly
worried about how much work she would miss and how long it would
take to catch up—just because their campus was closed didn't mean
the rest of the country did not go on with their studies. But between
the full flush of spring and seeing Sunam nearly every day, it was hard
to stay too concerned. Mostly they took long walks in the area around
campus and in his neighborhood in central Seoul, which was lined with
wide avenues perfect for strolling. They sat on park benches and
snacked on street food. Mealtimes, they ate at casual noodle shops frequented by students. These were inexpensive treats that Namin felt
comfortable letting Sunam pay for.

That day, Sunam had suggested they meet at the fancy tearoom by
Ewha University, a women's college situated on a lush hillside. This
time of year, the cherry trees were the main event and everyone made
giddy plans to go "see the trees." Namin was inclined to make fun of
the breathless frenzy—every year people made a fuss, and every year
she ignored them. But coming up on the hill and seeing the display
transcended expectation. It was like peering over the edge of the mundane earth into a flowering paradise. Huge clouds of blossoms lined
the avenues like heaps of organza thrown about by a giant seamstress.
Couples posed under the branches, sniffing the boughs and miming
raptures.

She arrived fifteen minutes early, but Sunam was already waiting. A small bouquet of yellow tulips dangled from his hand, and he thrust them at her. "Here." The plastic wrapping snapped and crinkled like tiny electric shocks.

"I've never actually seen a man give a girl flowers before," she said. "Only in the movies." She tried to imagine him going in the shop and asking for flowers. "Were you embarrassed?"

The corners of his mouth twitched. "A little," he admitted.

It was too glorious outside to go in for tea, but Sunam seemed disappointed when she suggested they just walk instead. Perhaps he had an idea of the proper date they'd have at the teahouse. It was the sort of place people went to prove they were truly a couple: girls wearing shiny lipstick and stacked boots. Boys with hair hovering in that perfect length between conservative and hippie—long enough to periodically fall over the eyes, but not too long to draw dirty looks on the bus. It was strange and wonderful to think of herself as half of a couple in a place like that. But it was also nerve-racking, sitting there as if on display for passersby to scrutinize through the window.

"It's still a date even if we don't drink tea." She rustled the bouquet at him like a shaman shaking sticks. "Look! I have this to prove it."

He took her hand in his and shook their joined hands, mimicking her action with the bouquet. "I have this to prove it too," he said.

Namin didn't have a camera and Sunam hadn't brought his, so they simply admired the trees without the pressure of posing. Twice, couples stopped them and asked if they wouldn't mind taking a shot. Sunam complied, waiting for them to arrange themselves under the prettiest branch, giving them enough time to smile. *One-two-three.* For Namin, there was something deeply satisfying about watching Sunam from a distance, knowing he would return to her momentarily. Even with his back to her, they were connected. She knew he was thinking of her, that in some small way she was on his mind even as he focused on another task. These were ephemeral moments, insignificant and possibly meaningless. Namin would have laughed if someone else had described the feelings she was having. But she felt instinctively reassured by Sunam. By his boyish bravado hiding the outlines of seriousness, which she suspected frightened and exhilarated him just as her own ambitions filled her with jittery purpose. These were intangible hunches, impossible to explain or to prove. But Namin trusted them like stones in a river, each of which she could use to cross closer to the other side, the future she imagined with Sunam.

Strolling hand in hand under the pink cotton-candy blossoms, she told Sunam about Hyun. Starting from the beginning, the second birthday, followed by the trip when he didn't return. The dolls on the floor. The guilt. She described the village where her grandparents lived. How they used to carry him into the fields on their backs when he was small and how he loved to bask in the sun like a cat, wearing the hated hat that cast a shadow over his lap. As she talked, Namin almost forgot where she was, even whom she was speaking to. She was barely aware of herself and the slowly passing scenery while her memories rose up, one after another. Sunam listened quietly without interrupting. When she finally ran out of words, she felt as if she'd woken up in a warm but totally unfamiliar place. Telling Sunam about Hyun, she'd shed the protective layer that hardened her against outside opinions. Now she was totally vulnerable.

"I don't usually talk this much," she said a bit sheepishly.

"I don't see how that can possibly be true," he said—but he was smiling. "Every time I see you, it's an Olympic event. I think you won all the medals this time. Gold, silver, and bronze. I didn't even stand a chance."

"It's your fault. You should have stopped me." Namin tried to match his lighthearted tone, which seemed to say that nothing had changed between them—that her family troubles were not a mark against her. But she wondered if this was his way of avoiding the topic, speeding past it as quickly as possible. In some ways, Namin thought that would be worse than outright rejection. "Maybe I said too much," she said.

"I would have listened if you talked for ten times as long," Sunam said. "It was an important thing to say. I'm glad you told me."

Those few words, that was all she needed. She felt the years of loneliness and private struggle evaporate off her chest, weightless as a cloud. She wanted to hold and preserve that moment forever.

She must have been staring at him too intensely because he laughed and said, "Anyway, I'm too scared of you. I wouldn't dare interrupt any of your stories."

It was a joke, but a sly one, referencing a genuine qualm.

"Scared? Still?"

"You're scarier every day," he said, elbowing her gently in the ribs.

He had taken off his jacket and she could smell the fresh laundry scent of his shirt. Someone had carefully ironed the points of his collar. She felt the urge to lean into his shirt and take a deep whiff. "That's very flattering," she said. "But now I'm afraid I won't live up to it."

"Something tells me you live up to whatever you set your mind on."

"You make me sound like such a dragon lady."

"It was a compliment," he said. "I admire it."

"You think Juno would consider me a shark?" she said, teasing. He had told her what Juno had said about their generation, their country. Frog pond, shark pond. As if there were only two species in the world. "You think I could earn that honor?"

Sunam said, "You're the king of the sharks."

THAT DAY, THEY walked until blisters rose on both Namin's heels and then broke, the skin tearing and the lymph seeping into her socks. Sunam insisted they take a break and sit on a bench for a while. She took off her shoes and laid them on the bench next to them. Holding her bare feet off the pavement to keep them clean, she felt as if she were sitting on a pier, the concrete a body of water that she would eventually jump into. The broken skin alternated between hot and cold.

"It hurts more because you're paying attention," she said. "If you weren't here, it wouldn't hurt at all. I would just get up and go."

"Knowing you, you'd probably march home with a broken foot," he said. "Doesn't mean you should. Stay here, I'll go find a pharmacy."

Namin leaned back on the sun-warmed bench. She arched her toes, testing the swelling in her joints. It was like stretching after a twenty-four-hour sleep, returning to her body after floating in dreams. She thought of the night she'd met him. Not in that horrible room with the hostess game, but outside, dark enough to fear stumbling. He had been wearing a leather jacket zipped close to the neck, a scarf thrown carelessly around his shoulders. He was so slim and tall, his silhouette perfectly suited to shadows. It was the *feel* of him, blended into that velvety darkness, that had seemed to her both familiar and electric. She sensed how he was always fighting himself, pushing for more, the anxiety pulsing at his jaw. The word *fragile* came to mind, the word *brittle*. Only when Jisun taunted him—*New Guy, he's so* impressed *with everything*—and he had been caught speechless and unable to deny it, had Namin allowed herself to acknowledge what she was already feeling. Kinship.

WHEN SUNAM CAME back with bandages and ointment, he seemed determined to do everything himself. "Let me," he said. "Maybe I'll discover a hidden talent for medicine. It could be a life-changing moment for me."

Namin hesitated. It was a surprisingly intimate request, letting him touch her bare feet and dress her torn, bloody skin. Mistaking her shyness, he said, "I won't hurt you, I promise." He pulled her calf across his lap and uncapped the tiny bottle of Mercurochrome. The glass dropper full of bright, viscous medicine, the color of cherry candy, glistened in the sun. "Ready?" Namin nodded, wondering if he would blow or wave his hand over the cut. He let the liquid fall onto the blisters, three tiny drops that stayed beaded and did not run. He blew gently over the sting, his mouth poised over her skin. His breath was steady and cool.

"Did that hurt?"

She shook her head.

"Okay, next." Carefully, Sunam unwrapped the gauze and wound it around her heel and over the ankle. His hands were warm and confident, flexing her foot to make sure she could still move her ankle as he pulled the bandage tight. He tied the ends over the low, round bone that resembled a peach pit on the inside of her ankle. He had made each side perfectly symmetrical, the lines of gauze tight and parallel.

"I think that was my very best work," he said. "How does that feel?" He was holding her instep, his thumb pressing the arch.

"Impressive." She could barely hear herself over the adrenaline pounding in her ears. Her foot was tingling under his fingers. "I think you might have a future."

"If you think so, then I'm happy."

THAT NIGHT IN her bedroom, Namin sat in front of the mirror with a brand-new tube of lipstick. It was the first color she'd intentionally owned, not a castoff from Kyungmin. The thing was entirely hers, a flat and untempered burgundy shade encased in white plastic, the number 084 stamped on the bottom indicating a secret company code. Namin had thought it a friendly number, even and divisible.

The light wasn't good enough to see the color properly, but she applied the formula carefully, following the contours of her mouth. The wax tugged at her lips. When she pressed her lips together, the brief drag of flesh on flesh was its own thrill, deeply satisfying. She loved that this instinctual gesture of femininity could feel as good as it looked. She could watch herself blot in the mirror for days.

She fell asleep that way, the lipstick ablaze on her mouth, replaying how carefully Sunam had wrapped the gauze over her feet. It had felt like a moment she could trust, a window into the future. No one ever said how to fall in love, what signs to look for, but she felt certain that she was not making a mistake.

All night she seemed to dream of Hyun. He was walking with clean white bandages wrapped around his feet. He was *walking*.

"I never realized how tall you are," she said. He had a cane of smooth blond wood. The top was carved like a river stone, fitted to his palm. He was so tall that she had to look up into his face.

"I'm saving my energy," he was saying. "I want to see how far I can go."

"You'll make it," she said.

Then he was swimming in a river. "There are creatures in the river that live to five thousand years. Come in and see them, they're not afraid. I asked them myself."

In the morning, her mother shook her awake. "You're a sight," she said, dragging a rough thumb over Namin's lips. "What is this?"

Namin drew her sore feet up against herself and rolled closer to the wall. "Nothing. I'm sleeping."

"With lipstick on, like a whore?"

Namin squeezed her eyes shut and waited to hear her leave.

When she was gone, Namin swiped the heel of her hand across her lips. The color was almost brown now, like old dried blood. She sat up and massaged the balls of her feet. The bandages were still tight. Sunam's bows had held.

Carefully, she undid the gauze, wrapping it around three of her fingers to make it stay together. She wound the end of it around itself and tied it off like a *jeogori*. From her desk, she took out the box that had once held a dictionary, a gift from her high school for ranking second at graduation. Exhausted after college exams, she had missed first by eight-tenths of a point. Despite this, people continued to think she had placed first, and Namin never corrected them.

The dictionary sat in the parlor, but the box was her private domain, full of things she'd outgrown but could not bear to lose: paper dolls she'd drawn and colored as a child; special notes from favorite teachers; an empty perfume bottle that was missing its cap but still contained echoes of its famous scent. Most important: river stones from visiting Hyun. She had started with large, palm-sized stones at first, tempted by the wide streaks and colors. The smooth flatness stayed warm in her hand during difficult exams and even seemed to smell like the country, the river, her brother. Now she chose smaller pebbles. The box was getting tight, and it was crucial that the stones stay together.

The folded gauze fit neatly in a corner. Namin patted it down and closed the lid. Soon she would have to tell Sunam about Kyungmin, who had been gone a month already without a word. In her wildest, most undisciplined dreams, her sister came back home and resumed work at the factory before Namin was forced to tell anyone, especially him, the truth.

But lies were for people who didn't believe in the future. Who saw only an endless stretch of present without consequences or change. The closer she got, the more determined Namin was to have all the things she dreamed of.

Not just for herself, but for Hyun as well.

4

. . . .

Sunam's father insisted that the entire household eat breakfast together each morning. A formal affair involving soup and rice and
fish. A meal that required the maid—if not the maid, then Sunam's
mother—to arrive in the kitchen before daybreak to start the rice. Sunam's father might miss the evening meal several times a week, eating
and drinking with his subordinates after work. But he was not, lest his
sons mistake the point, *just* eating and drinking. He was building spirit.
Educating. Instilling that all-important *ownership mentality*. To work
not just with diligence but with passion, as if by doing so the gains of
the company would fall directly into one's own pockets.

On these occasions, he might come home too drunk to properly
remove his own shoes. He might appear with strange stains on his
clothing that the maid would have to discreetly scrub with bleach in the
morning. But no matter how he had behaved the night before, Sunam's
father appeared at the breakfast table at the same time each morning,
marking each family member in a silent roll call. He had the bearing of
a former naval officer: broad shoulders, muscular neck. Abundant silver hair neatly combed and oiled, gleaming like the belly of a giant
tuna.

"Sunam," he said one morning. "Bring her for dinner. Bring her
tonight."

Sunam dared not feign ignorance about whom his father meant.
Later he'd pummel each one of his brothers in turn to find out who
had been the one to squeal, but lying now would only cast Namin in a
less flattering light, as if he had something to hide. "Couldn't we wait

a bit longer?" he asked carefully. "I've only known her a couple of months."

His father pushed back his chair from the table. "All the more reason for us to meet her now. Before it's too late."

"BUT WHAT DOES he want to see me for?" Namin asked when he told her. "What did you say about me?"

"Nothing," Sunam said. She gave him a sharp look. "There wasn't any time," he said quickly. "It was the first he's ever mentioned it. I didn't even know that he knew."

"And now that he knows, you're upset?" she said.

He had expected her to be alarmed, if not actually frightened. He had prepared to take on a protective role, to reassure her that he would stand up for her even if his parents disapproved of her background. Instead Namin seemed miffed that he had not already mentioned her to his family. Far from worrying what his parents might think, she wanted Sunam to have *bragged* about her. He could not gauge whether this was an indication of her ego or her staggering faith in their relationship, new as it was.

He decided to believe it was the latter. "How could I be upset?" he said. "I want everybody to know about us. I'd walk around chained hip to hip if you'd let me. I would wear a sign around my neck."

"Be serious," she said.

"I am serious. I'd do it."

She narrowed her eyes. "You'd wear a sign tonight when we have dinner with your parents?"

"Sure, but you have to wear one too."

"I think I'm wearing enough signs," she said. "Whether I want to or not."

It was the only indication she gave of understanding what she might be facing at dinner. He now realized that Namin wanted to know what he'd said about her not because she expected him to brag, but because she hoped he had laid some groundwork. In her own way, she was afraid.

"Don't expect me to act all bridal and demure. I won't do it," she warned. "It'll only make me feel worse if I have to put on an act."

"Do you even know *how* to act demure?" Sunam asked, teasing. He tried to picture Namin behaving the way women did in books and movies when they wanted to impress potential in-laws. Bringing gifts of delicacies and health potions. Cosmetics for the mother. Department store long johns for the winter, packed in gold boxes as if they contained jewelry. Could he ever imagine Namin bringing his parents thermal underwear? He laughed. "That's something I'd like to see."

SUNAM ARRANGED TO meet Namin at the bus stop near his house so they could walk back together. He arrived just as she was stepping onto the curb, wearing a soft gray skirt that covered her knees and matching jacket with a Peter Pan collar: the picture of demure. "My sister made it a long time ago," she said slightly defensively, as if to say the outfit did not contradict her earlier claims.

"You look lovely." He wished they were not standing at a busy intersection, otherwise he would have twirled her around and admired her from every angle.

She had even brought a box of sweets. Soft pink taffies and bite-sized rice cakes studded with black sesame seeds. Sunam was surprised by how grateful he felt for the effort she had made. Surely his parents would see it, too, and not denigrate her, at least not in her presence.

When they arrived at his door, he squeezed her hand tightly. "Whatever happens, it won't change anything between us," he said.

"Don't make it so obvious," she said.

"What, obvious?"

She shook her head.

IN RETROSPECT, IT seemed so inevitable that Namin would win the admiration of his parents, but at the time Sunam had been sure the meeting would be a disaster. His mind had even flashed forward to the ways he could comfort her in the aftermath, the things he might say and do to prove his unaltered devotion. His plans proved unnecessary.

That evening, everyone with the exception of Sunam's father was overdressed for this unprecedented spectacle. A dinner guest would normally elicit bored good manners from his brothers. Now they buzzed with hormonal electricity. A girl at the table! An interrogation! Swift judgment! His mother flitted between instinctual hospitality and frosty caution—running into the kitchen to fetch new dishes, laying them down with casual indifference far from Namin's reach.

His father, not one to bother with preambles, began firing questions right away.

"I hear you scored perfectly on the entrance exam. How did you do it?"

"I studied, of course," Namin said, unperturbed by the many eyes tracking her responses. "I imagined the rest of my life if I didn't succeed."

"And that was . . . ?"

"Selling *odeng* skewers with my parents," she said simply. "It wasn't a mystery."

There was a brief pause as Sunam's father absorbed this answer, taking in her characteristic frankness.

"I take it your parents never had to push you." He glanced at Sunam, who had been pushed all his life. Without his father saying so, he knew he lacked the drive to have made it this far on his own.

"They were pushing themselves." Namin smiled, as if to acknowledge the joke. Her parents, their whole life set on wheels, transient in every way. "We all have our jobs."

Sunam's father fixed his gaze on each of his sons in turn, lingering on his eldest. "Did you hear that? Pay attention," he said. "All of you could learn a thing or two."

FROM THE START, it was obvious that Sunam's father and Namin were charmed by each other. They seemed to understand each other implicitly, as if they were old friends or possibly compatriots in a past life. Though a generation apart, they were built for the same purpose: both engines for success. His father, with his great bulk and straightforward energy, was a locomotive. And Namin, something new. Sleeker, quieter, but more powerful.

After dinner, the family gathered at the door to see Namin off. "You keep him on track, Namin," Sunam's father said. He patted her shoulder with all the warmth and affection of a mentor blessing his true disciple. He was as pleased with her as if he'd dreamed her into being. They had lingered an hour after dinner, eating fruit and cookies and tea. Everything that could possibly be taken out had been offered to Namin, and still his father seemed reluctant to let her go. "You keep my boy on track," he said again. "I'm trusting him to you."

Outside, Namin was elated. "Did you hear what they said? They loved me."

No one had actually used the word *love*. A small part of him wanted to contradict her. *No one said love.* But vocabulary aside, it was true. They had loved her.

It was full dark now as they made their way back to the bus stop. They walked slowly, gazing at the sky, their faces upturned to the warm night air. Namin held his arm and leaned into him, heavy with victory.

"And now you are free to reform me," Sunam said. "Remold and remake me. You have my father's blessing."

"That was just a joke," she said. "He was only being nice."

"But are you going to do it?" He pulled her close to him, wrapping his arms around her. They breathed in unison, great inhalations and exhalations that pressed them even closer together. Her head nestled against his chest. He could feel the release of her breath, her whole body relaxing.

"They loved me." Her voice held the joy of marvel, turning the evening's events over and over in her mind like a jewel held to the light.

He kissed the soft crown of her head. "They loved you."

5

. . . .

One month.

For one month after the arrest at the textile factory, Jisun obeyed. She stayed in the house like a captive princess, silent and submissive, following the rules drummed into her since childhood. She ate at the right times, went to bed early, rose early, exercised in the garden, read in the solarium. *A productive schedule is what separates humans from animals.* Putting away the simple layers she preferred, she chose clothes her father approved of—blouses with multiple closures, navy knee-length skirts, and pearl-button cardigans. When she needed to go out, she notified Ko. She followed a strict regimen that anyone could remember, then forget. She wanted to numb the household to her presence.

Campus five days a week. A movie every Tuesday. Saturday, shopping. Late nights at the library each Wednesday and Thursday. She added the extracurricular outings, even though she had no desire to watch films or shop. A rhythm was important. Since actually going to the library and sitting among her gossipy classmates was not an option—a snake pit was preferable to that—she locked herself into an empty classroom and sat with the lights off for the appropriate length of time. Those nights, she took to packing her satchel with a blanket and alarm clock in order to sleep more comfortably on the cold floor.

Jisun rarely saw her father. But whether or not he was personally watching, she knew she was being observed by Ko and *ajumma*, who reported every detail according to his instructions.

"Sure you're not going overboard with the outfits?" *ajumma* asked archly. They were having breakfast at the enormous rosewood table in the kitchen. It had seating for eight, as if they were one of those large, active families who ate together each morning. Jisun thought how it must have been for *ajumma,* eating alone here day after day. The table was polished to such a high sheen, it would throw her solitary reflection back at her.

"Just dressing the part," Jisun said.

It was six in the morning, early enough that the food seemed to stick in her throat. She had eaten at a similar time at the factory cafeteria, but it had seemed less early then and the food hardly a burden with so many hours of work ahead.

"No need to dress for me," *ajumma* said. "Make yourself comfortable."

"Why, don't I look comfortable to you?"

Jisun sipped her tea. *Ajumma* knew better than anyone how much she hated fussy clothing. Even as a girl, Jisun used to cut the embellishments off her skirts and blouses—any unnecessary bows and ribbons, buttons that didn't hold anything together, ruffles that added bulk and made her feel like a cushioned crystal goblet. To appease the boss, *ajumma* would try to sew them back on, but most were beyond rescue. He always noticed the mangled garments. *Just like her mother.*

As much as she despised the clothes, there was a small, satisfying buzz in being ostentatious, in throwing the rules in his face by following them to the point of theater. Jisun was working on a bigger plan than just ruffles and cardigans, but it would help in the long run if they were distracted by her compliance, if they believed this was her rebellion. In the meantime, she would follow the rules impeccably and win the ultimate prize.

Freedom.

One month.

At first, Jisun thought she would hear from Peter. At the very least, she expected an apology. She considered the ways in which he might frame such a note. *Having had time to consider my behavior, I realize . . .* Or maybe he would be more direct, in his fashion. *Jisun, I was wrong.*

Please forgive me. But as the weeks passed and she heard nothing, she realized there would be no apology. No communication at all. It bitterly humiliated her now to think she had expected even more than that. Not just an apology but a declaration of love. A blossoming of their relationship. She had been so certain.

Everything he'd said had been devastating, unfair—she would remember each of his accusations as if they were branded on her skin.

You're the real saint. Topless and all. Congratulations, Jisun.

But you see, going forward I need a partner who shares my values.

Who understands the expectations of a missionary's wife.

When they were working as equals, side by side, Jisun had considered him a man for whom it would never be important to control a woman, body or mind. She had thought him a man who wanted the people he loved to be free.

So how had she been so wrong?

She could console herself that she had not been mistaken about his feelings. In his own way, Peter had loved her, too. But there was no joy in the information, which had come at such a price. For all his self-righteous talk, Peter was as parochial and possessive as any man who wanted to tame the woman he loved.

CAMPUS FIVE DAYS a week. A movie every Tuesday. Saturday, shopping. Late nights at the library each Wednesday and Thursday.

Jisun waited. She planned. And when she was ready, she made an appointment to see her father. To make it official, she had called the office and spoken to his secretary the week before. "A meeting with your father?" Having met the secretary once, she could picture him in her mind. He had striking eyes, eyelashes that seemed to poke straight out at whomever he addressed, and a voice that demanded exact details. Although young, he used the power of his office to behave as if each request presented the most irritating burden of his life. "Surely you can speak to him at home."

"This is a business matter," she said. "We don't conduct business at home."

There was a conspicuous pause clocking his displeasure, but he was smart enough to leave it at that. "Fine. Thursday. Two o'clock. Don't be late." He hung up as crisply as he dared.

Thursday, Jisun had to insist three times before Ko consented to believe she actually had an appointment with her father. Ko hated Jisun's dependence on him almost as much as she did. She would have been happy to tell him it would be over soon, but knowing him, she was sure he would have rolled his eyes in disbelief. Ko treated her as the greatest simpleton who couldn't negotiate her way out of a bus fare, much less handle the boss. But he hadn't been drilled as she had. *Never underestimate those you despise. They have caught your attention for a reason.*

Ko would see. Jisun knew what was most valuable to her father, the one thing he dearly wanted that he could not buy or compel into being. She had been trained by the master, and she knew how to strike a deal.

When they arrived at the office, she told Ko, "No need to wait. I'll see myself home."

Ko killed the engine with a decisive click. "How long will you be? Do I have time for a nap?" His hand was already on the lighter, preparing his usual cigarette.

"Sleep at home," she said. "If I'm wrong, I'll handle the consequences. You know the rules. Then you won't have to drive me anywhere."

Ko considered her words, rolling the lighter's spark mechanism with his thumb, scraping his fingernail along the grooved wheel.

"It's up to you," she said. "Wait if you want. It's your time you're wasting, not mine."

She knew he would not give her the satisfaction of an answer. She got out and slammed the door. Instantly the engine roared to life. She smiled.

Jisun stood at the curb and watched him drive away.

THE SECRETARY'S NAMEPLATE on his desk read KIM TAEYOO. He showed her into her father's office without asking what she would like to drink, as he should have. She would have declined, but since he didn't offer, Jisun requested a hot tea. "And some fruit." He'd tell everyone about the boss's daughter who'd come around ordering him about like a serf—but he might have done that anyway.

"Did you know I was coming?" Jisun asked her father.

"I did."

"I won't waste your time. I don't know how long you plan to continue with our current arrangement, but it is not sustainable for me. I'm willing to negotiate a new deal."

"I'm very happy with the current circumstances," her father said. "I have no wish to change them."

"The offer I had in mind concerns the future, which I believe you are interested in." Although he gave no outward indication, Jisun knew she had his full attention. He had raised his company from a bicycle shed on a dirt yard to a national conglomerate personally praised by the president. He was the envy of his peers. A miracle. Every year, his company grew exponentially larger and more valuable. And—here was Jisun's opportunity—the greater his success, the more pressing it became for him to secure its future. Assuming his good health continued, he could run the company for a long time still. But even if he could work for another century, he needed an eventual successor. He could have his choice among a nation of eager men and women, but Jisun knew he wanted blood. His son. His daughter. Otherwise he could never close his eyes in peace. Many times he had spoken those words exactly. *Everything I've made with my hands must stay in the family. I will never close my eyes in peace.*

Although Min was the firstborn and the son, Jisun knew in her heart that her father preferred her to be his successor over her brother. She, more than him, had inherited his drive and single-mindedness. Though their interests and political inclinations ran in opposite directions, Jisun was her father's natural heir, their fiery temperaments cast from the same mold.

"I will trade you four years for four years," she said. "Give me my freedom now. If you don't interfere for the next four years, the four years after that are yours."

"Four years is hardly the future," he said. "What use do I have for four years?"

"But you have nothing now. You have a prisoner. I can walk away anytime, disappear, and that's the future. In that case you can gamble on Min. Perhaps he won't disappoint you."

"I repeat my question. *What use do I have for four years?*"

"You have my full cooperation for four years. I will train in what you want here or study anywhere in the world, the discipline of your choice. After four years I will be free to do again as I choose. Perhaps you will have succeeded in changing my mind, in which case you will have gotten what you want. It's a risk for me and a risk for you."

"It's a unique proposition," her father said. Jisun heard the faint glow of praise in his voice. She had impressed him, and now she knew he would agree. "If I agree, how do I know you will keep your side of the bargain? I notice you receive your prize first."

"You know because I'm your daughter."

ON THE BUS, Jisun took off her constricting jacket and loosened the bow at her throat.

"Must feel better," said the woman next to her. She was carrying a net sack full of vegetables, and her lap was littered with scraps of onion skin, pearly white against her dark green pants. "Too nice a day for so many layers."

"Yes," Jisun said. Her father had bet on the future, but she had chosen the present. She could have disappeared. She could have taken herself anywhere in the world and started a different life. Perhaps that would have been the smarter choice. But this was her home and she was not ready to leave it, not yet.

"How will I know you will keep *your* end of the bargain?" she'd asked him. Jisun knew there were ways he could act without her knowledge. Arranging and obstructing her life without lifting a finger himself. In fact, she expected it.

"I agree you're getting the better end of the bargain."

"That isn't what I said." In truth, Jisun felt he had gotten the advantage since she was giving him what he didn't have, while he was only returning what was rightfully hers.

"In business you must sometimes trust people you don't like," he said. "Otherwise no one would prosper, only shaking hands with friends and neighbors who are in the same condition."

"Well, we are family."

He stood up and offered his hand. "But there's a reason you came to my office."

She took his hand and shook it.

V

1

. . . .

J isun stood outside churches listening to the voices joined in song. She imagined the Christ dangling on a fluorescent cross, his pierced drooping head pelted with the congregation's four-part harmony, the pianist's good shoes heavy on the damper pedal. She imagined herself opening the door and walking up the red-carpeted aisle, flinging off her clothing, lying naked on the silk-laid altar.

You're the real saint. Topless and all.

At home, she shivered under the summer quilt. She had won her freedom, but it did not change what she had lost with Peter. No one told her that heartbreak would feel so much like an endless flu, which only got worse as time passed. Or was she actually sick? Jisun was so rarely ill that she never recognized the symptoms, mistaking them for depression or some kind of existential crisis. As a child, she had been so wretchedly healthy that she had held the embarrassing distinction of winning her school's perfect attendance award for twelve straight years. Her father gloated over the strength of her immune system, which perfectly mirrored his. He had never been sick a day in Jisun's memory. She could not recall ever seeing her father lie down.

Nowadays, all she did was lie around, listless and heavy with rage. Weird, half-formed thoughts swirled in her head. Her body was simultaneously overly present and disconnected from her mind.

God was a cloud in the shape of a fox. A fox formed of cypress branches, gnarled and heavy as iron. God was an ox yoked to the sea. A white dog in a stream bloated with maggots. A cliff.

God was a man she loved who said, *But you should have known bet-ter. I expected more.*

But *how* should she have known better? How could she have done or given more?

She became fixated on the idea of disproving Peter. She hung around churches, hoping to capture some insight, some argument she could use against him. She wished God were a senator or president she could write a letter to, complaining of her ill-treatment by one of his emissaries. Jisun had a mental map of the local churches in alliance with the labor movement—the ones that worked with UIM or with union leaders and student activists willing to tutor workers at night. She avoided the churches where Peter had organized classes and lec-tures, as well as the ones they had planned to approach next, not know-ing if he had already succeeded. She had a good idea of which churches stuck to teaching the "safe" classes on religion, literacy, and current events and which others became radicalized and went underground with their meetings, moving from church basements into unlit attics and abandoned warehouses after curfew.

Like a moth hovering at the edge of a window, she tracked this lat-ter group, searching for a way into the secret meetings. She was as uncertain of her motives as she was drawn to push forward. She went from church to church in remote areas of Seoul, on the eastern and western peripheries where she hoped no one would know or recognize her. Out there, the churches all had a makeshift appearance. They were former restaurant spaces, bathhouses, automobile repair shops con-verted into rooms of worship, and all seemed to have the same frosted-glass door painted with a cheap black logo—usually a cross with a flame wrapping around it, or a dove alighting on a glowing hand.

But inside, the atmosphere of hushed reverence reminded her of Peter. There was a visceral sense of him, as if he might walk in any minute. She could conjure his voice, his smile, in her mind as easily as she could smell the musty carpet under her feet or hear the sound of pigeons scuttling against the cracked cement windowsills. In this strange half trance, Jisun found herself sitting in the back pew of half a dozen tiny sanctuaries, watching the light travel across the rows. Killing time because time was all she had.

Sometimes a church secretary or deacon spoke to her. "Can I help you? Are you waiting for someone?"

Most of the time she said no and hoped they would assume she was just praying or meditating or whatever people did when they came to churches alone. But sometimes she asked for the schedule of evening classes.

"Bible study?" the deacon might ask, as if they were rehearsing for a play.

"Yes, of course, but also the other classes," Jisun would say. "Perhaps something more . . . practical. For working people?"

And they would name a time and day when Jisun could come and inquire further. Wednesday at nine o'clock, newspaper literacy. Thursday at eight thirty, personal finance. It was a matter of reading between the lines, choosing the right class and, once there, the right person who might lead to more information.

2

. . . .

The meetings took place in a burned-out yarn factory, now serving as a warehouse for rubber slippers and cheap athletic shoes. The smell of acrylic and new rubber made the space feel tight and claustrophobic. But soon close to forty men and women would form a loose circle on the floor, and the room would seem to expand around the warm fellowship of kindred people. The candles would be lit, the dim light flattening the usual hierarchies of age and gender, encouraging a mood of whispering. Claiming a spot by the door, Jisun felt suffused with expectancy and ease, as if she'd come to witness a performance she knew by heart.

Sometimes the arguments rose and fell around her like the crackle of a large bonfire, jagged and lulling. People spoke with hushed urgency, knowing the concrete walls would echo and amplify sound. Without the aid of volume for emphasis, they used their bodies. Pointing, jabbing. Crawling into the circle on hands and knees to get closer to an argument, an opponent. At certain angles, the light caught and illuminated an eye like a polished onyx. Sometimes Jisun fought an inexplicable upwelling of tears. *This must be how it is in a family.*

Content to just listen and observe, she never spoke during these meetings. Sitting with her legs pulled under her like a proper student, she absorbed the familiar rhythms of debate and discussion, the rough accents and idioms of the factory floor, which she had not known she could miss so much. Merely being part of the scene soothed her, giving her back the part of her identity she had been separated from and craved all these months.

She was careful not to attract too much attention to herself but also not to appear overly withdrawn or aloof, which might mark her as a suspicious figure. She answered any questions posed to her as honestly as she could, explaining how she had found out about this meeting location and that she had formerly worked with women in a textile factory. She purposely kept the details of her work history vague and dropped hints to indicate that she was a student activist whose identity must not be pressed. The story passed easily. As it was, people seemed to know she was a student even before she hinted at it. There was no hiding her urbane Seoul accent and aura of education. Jisun would have never passed for a true worker, and it seemed they did not require her to be. Because she had inquired at four churches before finding someone willing to disclose the location, they assumed she was a Methodist. Peter was a Methodist. A particular irony, which both comforted and stung.

"They used to spare the churches," a woman was saying. "But they're targeting us now. Turning the workers against us." Her big hands hacked the air as she spoke. Solid, square palms that projected competence and leadership.

For weeks, this group had been discussing the government crackdown on church groups, an unusual and worrisome turn of events because the churches had historically enjoyed a level of protection. Korean churches, with their American missionary roots, still had strong contacts in the West. And while their American allies might turn a blind eye to the president's oppressive political tactics, they would not ignore violence against the church or persecution of Christians, which hit closer to home even if it was on Korean soil. Jisun had discussed this paradox with Peter many times while they were working together.

"The West won't act if they hear of violence against workers and students. But Christians are not to be touched? Why? What's the difference?" she'd asked.

"Americans understand Christianity. They don't really understand you. Koreans, I mean. I guess maybe they figure violence is just a part of your culture, but they don't want to see it happen to Christians."

"But a Korean who is a Christian is still a Korean like anybody else. Does being a Christian suddenly make them more valuable?"

"I never said it made sense, Jisun. I'm just telling you how it is."

And now, instead of going the way they had hoped—a loosening of government interference, a decrease in persecution and abuse—the country was moving backward in history, the Park government flexing its muscle in increasingly flagrant postures of aggression.

Jisun listened intently, inching closer to the circle, not wanting to miss a single word.

"The workers were always against us. What's new? They think we're just out to make them soft and take their money."

"You know that's untrue. We were making progress with the study cells. We had to add another class last week to accommodate the growth. Even the ones who hate the religion want to learn about their rights. They don't want to be left behind."

"Fine, but we're not talking about whether or not the classes are successful. We're talking about the risk. You heard about the arrests. Three pastors and I don't know who else. They're calling them subversives this time, and it's serious. They don't even care that they're foreigners."

"Foreigners?" Jisun interjected forcefully. "Americans? Do you know who they are?"

The woman who had been speaking dragged a tired finger across her brow, an expression of profound exhaustion compressed into a single gesture. "They are English," she said. "And as I was saying, they've charged them with subversion under the National Security Law—"

"Please, wait. Are you sure?" Jisun's voice thumped in her ears as if it were coming at her, not from her. She was aware that she was speaking too loudly, but she could not bring her voice down or control the quaver. "Not American?"

The woman gave her a long look and resumed speaking in a way that indicated Jisun should not interrupt again. "They've been here since '62. Practically Korean by now, I'd say. But originally from England."

"I'm sorry. It's just—"

"We all have friends." Pupils glittering in candlelight made the woman seem almost omniscient, peering into Jisun's selfish motives. "You're not the only one."

"Of course," Jisun stammered. "Thank you."

The door was so close. The temptation to flee churned in her stomach, swirling with the vast relief that, anyway, it wasn't him. Peter was safe. Someone, a sympathetic voice, murmured, "Don't be so hard on her, she's obviously suffering." But relief overrode everything, canceling embarrassment, canceling shame. Jisun exhaled loudly, expelling the air that had been trapped in her lungs.

The young woman sitting beside her tapped her hand. "You know, you look so familiar." She had a thick braid over one shoulder. Shy, steady eyes. Jisun smiled vaguely, still thinking about Peter. But the girl was studying her carefully. Her eyes widened with delayed recognition.

"You were at the Mun-A strike, weren't you? I was there too." She grasped Jisun by the arm as if expecting to embrace her as a sister. "I can't believe I didn't recognize you sooner!"

Panicked, Jisun shook her off. "No, it wasn't me. You must be thinking about someone else."

"No, I'm sure of it. You were at the front line. So brave. You were one of the first, weren't you? I saw they took you away in a van." The young woman turned to the group. "Everyone. This is someone special. A great worker, very strong for our cause."

Jisun stood up. All eyes trained on her, ready to bring her into the fold. All she had to say was yes. But if they knew she was at the strike, if they knew she had been arrested, it would only be a matter of time before they would also find out that she had been released—and why. And wouldn't they judge her as harshly as Peter had? How could she expect these strangers to understand, when the person she had trusted most had rejected her without a second look?

"Don't be so modest," the girl was saying. "We're safe here. You don't need to be so cautious. Come, introduce yourself. I'm sorry I never knew your name—"

"Safe, you say?" Jisun said. "How can we be safe if you don't even know who I am? I'm not one of you. I'm not even who you think I am." There was a fire in her chest. She barely recognized her own voice; the acid tone burned her throat. Who was speaking? She would never have allowed these words, denouncing the people she wanted so much to be a part of. It was fear that was making her speak so harshly, rejecting them first so they could not come any closer to knowing who she was. "Instead of telling me what *I* should do, how *I* should be," she heard herself say, "I advise *you* to be more cautious. Use your head, sister. It's this kind of thoughtless stupidity that puts us all at risk."

Quivering, Jisun waited for the next thing, but nothing came. Not tears or apologies, recriminations. The woman who might have embraced her earlier had turned her back, and the circle tightened around her, closing Jisun out. She felt as terrified as a child abandoned in a strange city, the people all turned to stone.

She wanted to take it all back. She was willing to suffer whatever punishment they might mete out, whatever rejection might come, if only she could be forgiven for these terrible words. They were the opposite of everything she truly believed.

"I'm sorry," she whispered.

It could be that no one heard. It could be that everyone heard. Hot tears threw light in every direction, multiplying and magnifying dread. Jisun groped for her shoes where she had left them by the door. She paused for the briefest moment, hoping for a final word or gesture of kindness. But the circle was locked in silence, unwilling to utter even one more word in her presence. Waiting, as if with eyes in their backs, for her to leave.

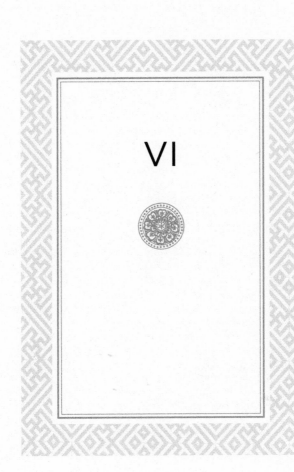

VI

Sunam had heard rumors of the Circle taking its members to a nightclub before the summer break, but it had seemed the kind of easy, outrageous claim people made when they were protected by the veil of secrecy. The nightclubs at the foreigner hotels were exclusive domains reserved for entertaining international investors, who might be persuaded to see the future of Korea in the chandelier-laden lobbies and red-carpet entrances. Exempt from city curfew, these tourist establishments stayed open until four A.M., constituting a parallel country more daring and rich than the one locals knew. With names like Koreana, Chosun, Savoy, and President that projected a jumble of local and Western promises, these hotel nightclubs were beyond the reach of normal citizens.

But there were exceptions. And where Min's Circle was concerned, Sunam found it was unwise to discount rumors.

"Did you know," Namin said excitedly, "this is only the third year we're going to the club? Min set it up before he graduated and now it's become a tradition. Aren't we so lucky?"

"We?" said Sunam. "I don't remember being invited."

"Of course you're invited. Juno put together the list and I'm sure it's fine. Everyone knows you're my boyfriend." He chafed against Namin's glib, reassuring tone, which irritated him more than the insult of being excluded. *Everyone knows you're my boyfriend.* If he went to the event, it would be only as a tagalong, the accessory. On his own, he was nobody. From the beginning of his relationship with Namin, he had suspected he would become eclipsed by her success. He told himself he would not mind, that it would be enough just to bask in her affection. But barely a couple of months had passed before he found himself struggling with the indignity of being overlooked.

Sunam knew how much Juno loved to flaunt his ability to write lists and cross people off them. His non-invitation had not been an oversight. No other non-Circle member had been invited. The only exception was Jisun, whom Juno had specifically dispatched Namin to invite, knowing Jisun would never consider it otherwise. Sunam was surprised that even Namin had been able to persuade her.

"You know he only invited Jisun to show off," Sunam said.

Namin gave a quick, irritated laugh. "Well, that's where you're wrong. You know this sort of thing would never impress her."

"But you know what I mean."

"Why do you care what he does?" she asked.

"Don't you care? She's your friend."

"Trust me, Jisun can take care of herself. We of all people don't need to worry about her."

The prospect of visiting the fancy hotel and the out-of-bounds disco had made Namin so giddy with anticipation that nothing was worth worrying about in her estimation. Sunam was surprised it didn't bother her more, the similarities between the nightclub and Itaewon, where her sister had ended up.

It was nearly July before Namin had finally told him about her sister, who was living with a GI in Itaewon. Living with him and pregnant. *She says they're getting married*, Namin had said dubiously. *She says they're moving to America*. He tried to be understanding, but this new development seemed to weigh them down more than any of their other differences. Namin's sister became a specter in their relationship, embodying Namin's worst fears about the future and providing a living reminder of the horrible consequences of sex.

So it surprised him that she had no qualms about going to the nightclub, which felt to Sunam like a glitzier version of America Town. The foreigners were businessmen, not soldiers, and landing a job there as a waitress or hostess was likely harder than working in Itaewon, but the trade-off was the same. No respectable girl would do it. Everyone would naturally assume she was selling her body for money or the promise of a visa—and probably she was.

SUNAM ALWAYS REMEMBERED that it was Namin who had kissed him first that night at the party, Namin who had lain down on the bed when he was a stranger whose intentions she could not surmise. But their physical relationship had stalled since those early days.

"Did you know sperm can live up to *five days* inside the body? It just stays in there, swimming around causing trouble," Namin said. "Five days!"

He offered to wear two condoms. He would wear two condoms and pull out.

"I can't take the chance," she said. "Think of everything I've worked for. Wiped out. Just look at my sister. How stupid do I have to be to make that same mistake. You understand, don't you?"

Sunam said he understood—and he did in theory. But it was like buying a car and losing the key. A car always in park. In recent weeks, the topic had become so tense that he and Namin barely breached arm's length with each other. She seemed to fidget even when he tried to hold her hand, as if always anticipating the next move and marking out her defense. Maybe he was being petty and unreasonable. Sunam could no longer judge one way or the other. Probably there were just as many couples having sweet, chaste relationships like him and Namin. Couples who saved sex—and its consequences—for the proper confines of marriage. But on campus, all he ever seemed to see and hear about were the girlfriends who weren't so cautious, who found ways to plan weekend trips with their boyfriends. Who laughed and played along with dirty innuendos, relishing their new sexual experience. Sunam envied those relationships and the guys in them, even the ones who never flaunted their newfound prowess. Perhaps he envied these men more for their quiet satisfaction. He suspected the bigmouths, the ones who went around bragging about how many girls they'd slept with, were probably just as frustrated as he was. He loathed to feel he had anything in common with them.

As if to compensate for their receding physical intimacy, Namin became more verbal, affirming their relationship through words if not by touch. *Everyone knows you're my boyfriend.* But Sunam didn't like the way she kept telling him what to do, how to feel. How she decided what was and was not worth worrying about. She should worry a little more about Juno, he thought. She should feel defensive against *him* rather than against Sunam, who was actually on her side. Hadn't she learned anything from the way Sunam had been treated?

But he had had the same blind spot when he was in her position. That sense of being placed on a straight track to success, being so close to what everyone else wanted but could not have. If not invincible, he had thought himself protected, chosen. And Namin had so much more reason to believe it than he had. Without question, she was special. The one everyone wanted. He hated to think it, but she probably thought he deserved to be cut. She must, because the people who had judged him unfit had given her all the attention she deserved.

"I think you should wear that blue and brown check shirt I like," Namin was saying. "You think there'll be a lot of foreigners there?"

Sunam stopped listening. He was thinking about Juno, who believed he was entitled to Jisun purely because he wanted her, because he had planned for it as if for a difficult career move. Angling to get closer to her was so blatant an attempt to curry favor with her father that he thought anyone would be able to see right through it. Yet Sunam found himself feeling inexplicably furious, as if he'd caught a player rearranging stones on the *baduk* board, cheating at the most juvenile level. The difference was that Juno wasn't cheating—he was free to pursue Jisun, free to make a fool of himself trying—so why should Sunam care? Jisun would never fall for something so obvious.

"So how did you do it?" he asked Namin.

"How did I do what?"

"Get her to come. Jisun, I mean."

"Are you still worrying about that? Should I be jealous?"

In fact a little jealousy wouldn't have hurt. But by the wry twist of her smile, Namin implied that it was incomprehensible that she should envy Jisun. "I just told her it would be fun. We haven't had fun in ages," she said. "I told her there'll be plenty of businessmen there, she could sell away her father's company secrets. That made her laugh."

"Does she actually know anything worth selling?"

"She would if she paid the slightest attention. She ignores anything to do with money just to spite him. If I were in her position, I would try to learn everything I could about his affairs. How can you spite someone when you have no information about them?"

"Maybe it's not spite, then. Maybe she's just not interested."

"It takes a lot of energy to be that uninterested. That kind of effort requires spite."

"So you guys have fun, then. Why do I have to go?"

"Because I want you to come," she said. "If you're worried about Juno, you should know you belong there just as much as I do. You don't even have to talk to him—you'll be too busy talking to me. Besides, I won't go if you don't."

Sunam knew Namin was only trying to be loyal, including him in her fancy outing so he wouldn't feel left out. As much as it annoyed him to be her guest, he understood that she had done something genuinely nice by making sure they could go together. But with this last comment, she had overplayed her hand. "You really won't go if I don't?" he said. He was willing to give her credit for having been generous—but not for being a saint.

Namin paused, her good mood finally disrupted. "Are you saying you're not coming? Or is this some kind of stupid test?"

"I need to know your answer first." In truth Sunam had already decided to go, but she should know he was doing her a favor, not the other way around. This fancy after-curfew experience might excite Namin, but he had no special wish to be at Juno's mercy, drinking on his bill, expected to fawn over him with gratitude.

"In that case I'm going," Namin said. "Does that answer your question?"

So they were both bluffing.

"Actually it does."

Sunam supposed he should feel flattered she wanted him there at all, insisting he was required when it was clearly untrue. Her confidence was at times overbearing, making him feel irresolute and small, but he had never experienced anything like being the recipient of her devotion. She hurled herself at the project of loyalty and love with the same persistence with which she tackled life. Full force. No doubts, no questions. More than loved, Sunam felt lucky. Many days it was a kind of uncomfortable luck, like finding a precious thing and realizing the rest of his life was shabby and common in comparison. It made him restless and discontent, but what did a person do in a case like this? Only a fool would allow himself to lose the most valuable thing he'd ever held.

"And you won't sulk about it?" she said. "You won't blame me for the things Juno says?"

"So you admit he's going to be a jerk about it."

"I'm just covering the possibilities. But yes, there is a chance he will be difficult."

"I won't blame you if you don't blame me for what I might do in retaliation. Deal?"

She sighed. "Deal."

WHEN THE WEEKEND arrived, Sunam chose a different shirt from the one Namin had mentioned. He had already had the right one cleaned and pressed, but looking at it, perfectly starched and crisp on its hanger, he suddenly grew disgusted with the idea of himself as an accessory to her. Instead he put on the oldest shirt he owned, a wrinkled red oxford with sleeves that pulled at his wrists and an uneven, shrunken hem. He felt more comfortable thinking of himself as a disgruntled interloper than Namin's loser boyfriend rescued from the heap of rejection. People would be expecting him to be tucked in and acquiescent, yessing everything to death. He had expected it himself. Pulling on the awful shirt made him feel that he was in control.

When he arrived to pick her up, Namin was wearing a belted dress with a pink and brown pattern and alarmingly high white heels that made her unsteady on her feet. Her hair was curled back in huge wings away from her face. She kept pressing her lips together to check that her lipstick was still there.

"Too much?" she said, apparently catching something in his face.

"Certainly not," he said, taking her hand. She must have prepared for hours. Everything in her appearance projected how much she intended to enjoy the evening. He could tell that nothing would deter her, not even him. He could have arrived naked or in an ancient clanging suit of armor and she would have asked for his arm in the same preoccupied way, to keep from falling in the uneven streets.

It was like that all night, and not just from Namin. Sunam was universally invisible as everyone else was focused on grooming his own image, establishing his own position. No one bothered directing any energy his way, the social and practical nonentity.

Early on in the evening, Juno acknowledged him once. *Are you here, too?* But he didn't wait to hear the answer. He was haunting the door with his eyes. Waiting, Sunam knew, for Jisun, who had not shown yet.

"Is she coming?" Sunam asked Namin, if only to snatch her attention for a second. She was pulled into one conversation after another with people who pretended not to recognize Sunam. He felt like a toddler grabbing at apron strings. *Is she coming?* She could ignore him only so many times before turning puzzled, surprised eyes his way, saying, "Is *who* coming?"

Sunam drifted away.

The bar was packed with foreign men in white shirts and ties, loosened and crooked around their necks. Sunam recognized the clipped lilt of Japanese, blocky gusts of German. Of course the Americans and some of their women were there, too, flaunting curly yellow hair and blue eye shadow. An army of hostesses sauntered throughout, wearing bright, heavy platform heels—slips of women strapped to their shoes like ballasts without which they might float to the ceiling like helium balloons.

Alone in the dark, crowded place, Sunam felt a sense of freedom and surrender. He ordered drinks with a flick of the wrist. They arrived one after the other like the next turn on the disco ball. Time passed in long waves of amplified sound. Songs he knew. Songs that sounded instantly familiar, although he had never heard them before. He had not forgotten about Namin, but she was far away, ensconced within layers of popularity and social greed. Sunam felt clear-eyed and insulated within himself.

When the strobe of a disco light caught the face of his watch, he saw that it was nearly three o'clock in the morning and he felt exhausted by the whole scene. There had been a gyrating Tom Jones impersonator in lurid purple, his belt buckle flashing in obscene rhythm as he danced. There had been neon yellow drinks and tiny paper umbrellas anchored with maraschino cherries. Pale, fleshy breasts quivering on the verge of full exposure. Glasses smashed, swept up, and replaced. Curses and cheers rising in half a dozen languages. Throughout it all, waitresses slithered through the constantly shifting human maze, wielding mirrored trays as wide as shields.

He saw Namin sitting at a table crowded with empty bottles. She noticed him, too, sending a dazzling satisfied smile as if to say he— *they*—should be congratulated for their success. When he sat down next to her, she rested her head on his shoulder and snaked an arm around his waist. She said, "I had such a good time. Did you hear Juno got us hotel rooms?"

He looked at her. Was she implying—?

"Not *us* specifically," she said hastily. "I meant for everyone. To rest until morning."

The opening bars of "Unchained Melody" quavered from the loudspeakers, soaking the room with plaintive lust. Newly formed couples rocked under the spinning strobe light, explorative hands flashing from shoulder to hair to rump. The *sunbae* he recognized as H.G., who had bragged about the oil in Saudi Arabia, swayed pelvis to pelvis with a diminutive coed, their bodies locked in private pendulum.

"You mean so he can 'rest' with Jisun." Sunam hadn't noticed when she came in, but he had caught glimpses of Jisun in the last hour. She was at the bar, Juno by her side.

"This again? Why are you so interested in what she does?" Namin asked. "You've been talking about her all night."

"I haven't seen you all night. How can you know what I've been talking about?"

"Well, Juno's been tethered to her since she got here. She doesn't seem miserable about it. Maybe she's finally giving him a chance."

"Give her a little more credit," he muttered.

"Just because you can't stand him doesn't mean everyone else needs to hate him too. You don't know Jisun like I do—maybe it's what she needs, someone like him. He's liked her since they were kids, you know, and all she's ever done is treat him like dirt. But he's steady, isn't he, never gives up. Doesn't that count for something? Anyway, I don't see her doing any better on her own."

"Why would he give up?" Sunam said. "This is just a long job interview for him, that's all. He's a sleazy jerk trying to jump ahead—" They were shouting over the music. *A long, lonely time . . .*

"Don't be naive, Sunam. Someone will end up with her money. Why shouldn't it be someone who actually worked for it? Besides, who's to say that kind of dedication and purpose isn't really love?" She paused, as if waiting for his counterpoint so she could retort. When he didn't fire back, she said with somewhat deflated intensity, "This isn't a morality contest, you know. It's just life."

"Since when do you think life is 'just life'?"

Her eyes glittered with resentment. "Is your point that I'm crass? And Jisun needs to be protected from predators like Juno, preying on her future? In case you haven't noticed, she isn't exactly helpless."

Are you still mine? The melody howled. *I neeeeeeeed . . .* They gave up, pretending to be defeated by the music. They sat, side by side like stones, ignoring each other.

There was a commotion rising on the dance floor as couples jolted apart, stumbling to give way. It was Jisun. She sliced through the crowd and marched toward their table, Juno close on her heels. It was obvious that he was trying to make her stop and listen to whatever he needed to say, but she was ignoring him in as blatant a manner as possible. At one point Juno had a grip on her blouse, and she continued walking forward with such force that he would have torn off her sleeve if he didn't let go when he did.

Jisun arrived at the table. "There you are," she said as if they had kept her waiting, as if they were only just beginning the evening together instead of ending it. She sank into the seat next to Namin and threw back someone's abandoned glass of whiskey. "What a night of endless delight," she said with a grimace. "Am I in hell?"

"He's coming," Namin said drily.

"Can we talk?" Juno said to Jisun without acknowledging anyone else at the table. "I think you misunderstood what I meant."

"Listen, man. If I 'misunderstand' you any more clearly, I might be sick," Jisun said. "I plan to forget about it. Can we forget about it? Sit if you want. Have a drink. Have five drinks. You'll be happier in the morning if you don't remember what an ass you made of yourself tonight."

Juno sat down and glowered at the wall. His fingers were laced together so tightly that they appeared purple with throttled pressure. His face was a mess of failed masks—disbelief, anger, forced indifference, humiliation—flickering one after the other. Sunam poured shots, which no one except Jisun drank. Couples gradually melted off the dance floor into the darkness of the bar as the music sank into melancholy. Matt Monro. Elvis Presley. Jim Reeves, crooning the perfection of lost or misplaced love.

Jisun closed her eyes and swayed in her seat. "Why do you think it feels so good, music and alcohol? Is it just the alcohol? Or the lights—it could be that. Spinning lights and alcohol." Whatever had happened between her and Juno, she seemed to have put it behind her. "Did you know . . . they used to worry more about giving the soldiers liquor than supplies. Boots and bullets are not as important as alcohol. You can do anything when you're drunk, you know. Do you think we could go to war, right now? Are we drunk enough? What about you, Sunam? You feeling patriotic?"

"Too late for me. Just want to lie down."

"Well, it's not a simple science. The right balance is absolutely essential. Too far, and you want to lie down. Too little, and you want to run away. Our scientists should study it," she said. "War and alcohol, very important."

Juno looked at her, his eyes expressionless and flat. "You are such shit. All you talk is shit."

Jisun opened her eyes. "We all talk shit. So what?"

"The difference is you believe your shit."

"Hey. It's not easy. Another rare science, believing your own shit."

"You don't fool me." Juno's face was dark and bloated, his features exaggerated in shadow. "You don't fool anyone."

"Who says I'm trying to fool anyone? Relax, you don't have to believe anything about me. Actually I suggest you think as little about me as possible. We'll both be more comfortable that way."

"That's another one of your myths you'd love us to believe. You want to be invisible, you want to be left alone. How can anyone believe that? Everything you do is meant for attention."

"You're doing it again. You're thinking."

"It's late. Both of you," said Sunam. "Let's just get some rest."

"He used to be terrified. Of you, of me. Now look at him telling us to get some rest," Juno said.

"It's love making him fearless," said Jisun. Sloppily she patted at Sunam's head, mostly missing the mark. "Namin must be taking good care of him."

"Leave me out of it," said Namin.

"She doesn't approve of me anymore," Jisun said. "What she wants is life, straight as an arrow. The brilliant future. I'm afraid I drag her down. Or maybe she's afraid I drag her down."

Sunam could no longer tell if she was joking. "Leave it alone," he said. "It doesn't matter."

"Isn't this what I just said," Juno said. "She loves it, so full of shit. She loves the idea of herself dragging someone down, doesn't she? And look where she is. In a nightclub! With all of us! You think you're such a rebel, but you're nothing but a spoiled brat playing activist dress-up." He looked at her with hatred in his eyes. "I give you five—no, *three*—years. You'll fall right in line. Three years, you'll be working for your dad and marry someone just like me. No one will be a bit surprised."

Jisun cackled. "How can anyone say the things you say without dying of embarrassment? Drink more," she said. "You're making poor Sunam miserable and giving me a headache. Is this why you dragged us all here? So you can yell at us under strobe lights? It's terrible. And costing you a fortune. I hope you don't do this often. It must be a drain on our national resources, feeding your ego."

"'Poor Sunam'? Why does he get the special treatment?" Juno said. "Just because we didn't let him in, he's not as bad as we are? He'd come back in a second if we let him. Why do you think he's hanging around Namin? He may not be smart, but he's not stupid."

"I *said* leave me out of it," Namin said, but she was glaring at Jisun as if she were the problem.

"Hey," Jisun said sharply. "I had nothing to do with this. Remember, *you* made me come."

"My mistake, then," Namin said.

Sunam stood up, thinking this must be it—what else could anyone say?—but no one else was standing. Awkwardly, he sat back down. Everything felt so unreal, it was hard to tell what was serious and what was a horrible overextended joke. The room seemed to tunnel around them, the world wrapped around the four of them arguing over . . . what? It was either nothing or everything.

"We should get back on topic," Juno resumed with mock pleasantness. "Let's see. Who else shall we consider for Jisun's future, her three-year plan? Maybe you fancy one of those yellow hairs over there? Unfortunately I see suits. Not your style, I know." He paused to make sure he really had their attention. "But listen, foreign isn't quite far enough, is it? Our princess needs them poor and pure of heart to get Daddy really furious. A foreign do-gooder type, then. Do you know anyone like that, Jisun? Anyone?"

She froze. Purple lights dragged across her face, briefly illuminating the whites of her eyes. The strobe passed, but it was as if her face were permanently marked, streaks of panic giving her skin a strange gray light.

"You're following me," she said so softly that Sunam could barely hear it across the table. "I should have known. He's having you follow me."

She stood up. Incoherently, Sunam thought, *She is the only woman wearing pants in this room*. They watched her walk purposefully, even sedately, away from the table through the bar area, disappearing through the velvet curtain marking the exit. *Someone should go after her*, he thought. *Namin should go after her*. But Namin stayed in her seat, bisecting the stem of a candied cherry with a thumbnail, dragging it through the length of the stem until she had two thin fibers. She picked the thicker of the two and started again.

"Namin? Can I talk to you?" Juno said. "Privately."

She looked at him. "Now?"

"Don't worry, I'm leaving," Sunam said. Someone should have gone after Jisun, and he realized now it would have to be him.

THE LOBBY WAS deserted save for the massive chandeliers dripping light. He glimpsed Jisun just as she was flinging open the heavy oak door of the ladies' room. She went inside and the door swung silently shut behind her, sealing her in as securely as if she'd passed into another dimension. Sunam paused at the door, wrestling with what he should do next. The door was hung with a wide brass *W* over a symbol of a figure wearing a triangle for a dress. A symbol so forbidding, he'd never crossed it even as a child.

"Jisun?" He touched a knuckle to the door, a nearly inaudible tap.

He waited. Nothing.

Opening the door, he stepped inside.

The bathroom was cold and white and mirrored, so brightly lit that he didn't register Jisun at first. She was bent over the sink, crying.

So many moments that night held a murky, underwater quality— the dancing, the bright, sweaty cocktails that left a sticky aftertaste in the back of his throat, the darkness sluiced through with disco light. These were moments that would come back to him over his middle decades, clearer in memory than in real time. But the hours in the bathroom, flooded with the surgical brightness of white hot lights, were microscopic in detail from the start.

He sank down on the cold tile. His body felt light with exhaustion, as if he could get up and walk from one end of the country to the other, back and forth forever, never needing sleep or food. Jisun was weeping, a low, steady sound, and he was on the floor of this women's bathroom. There were four toilets separated by ivory-toned stalls. The doors came down to just a handsbreadth off the floor. Each door hung at a slightly different altitude and angle, forcing him to catalog their discrepancies. The grout in the tile, which had seemed immaculate at first glance, was in fact pitted with mildew. The time in which he should have said something, profound or banal, had passed, and it was now all right for him to be sitting on the floor, a helpless witness.

Finally, Jisun turned on the tap. She let water collect in her hands and buried her face in it, a gesture like drinking after a long drought. She, too, slumped onto the floor. The bank of sinks stood between them, and when she started talking her voice was far away, hollow, and disembodied. The room was windowless, vaultlike in its enclosed sufficiency—the perfect acoustic for confessions.

"You probably think I'm stupid for even being surprised," she said quietly. "You'd think I'd learn."

"You're probably entitled to be surprised."

"Well, you and I always seem to disagree."

There was nothing he could say about that. He couldn't contradict her, as that would only prove her point, and he couldn't agree since he had already dissented. He let the bright sterility of the room swallow them up. For a long time he thought she wouldn't say anything else, that he had offended her and she was simply waiting for him to leave. He wondered how long he was supposed to wait before he said anything else or if he should leave her alone. He was just about to get up when Jisun started talking.

"Last winter, I was sitting in the house and I saw my dad come in," she said slowly. "He was wrapped up in his coat and scarf. He always wears those hats, I don't know what they're called. The flat ones that snap in the front. I looked up and saw him coming in from the cold. He hadn't seen me yet. He was wiping his feet on the mat, looking down. I could only see his coat, and the hat. And I thought, Who is this old man? He's gotten so old."

She was speaking about a man everyone knew, but not the way she knew him. Sunam realized then, with a flash of pity and insight, that Jisun, in her private way, still loved her father. Despite her harsh criticism of him, despite the identity she had built for herself in direct opposition to his life, his values, his accomplishments, Jisun was still vulnerable to him, still capable of feeling bitter betrayal.

"And I realized, one day he'll die. He'll be gone," Jisun said. "All that power, that energy, *vitality*—you know, he can fill a room just by sitting there, just by looking at it. It won't last. I suppose that sounds childish. Maybe I *am* childish. I don't know what I'm supposed to know, I never have. I really thought he could go on forever, same as always. And then I suddenly *saw*. He's old—and one day he'll die."

"I guess we're all worried about our parents dying," Sunam said.

"But I'm not really worried about him dying. Not how you mean," she said. "It just never seemed possible before. Not truly. It sounds like a joke—but I was surprised. I was actually genuinely surprised. And when he's gone, that's it. I'll still be here."

She peered across the row of sink pipes and he finally caught her face. It was as swollen as if she'd been beaten. Purplish half-moons outlined her eyes. "Does that make sense?"

He nodded. Not because he shared her sense of epiphany. His own parents had always seemed old to him; they had never inspired that threat of immortality Jisun attributed to her father. But he understood the end of things. Of premonitions that carried equal measures of dread and comfort.

Sunam knew it was time to add his own confession. Perhaps she had already guessed.

"I was there at the Mun-A strike," he said tentatively, each word a step on untested ground. "But I didn't know why I was there. It was before I met you and I didn't even know what I was supposed to be looking at. But I was there with him. Juno, I mean. I was there the morning you were arrested."

"Did you see me?"

"No. I didn't know who you were."

"You didn't know who I was until I told you."

"That night at the party. Outside."

"You thought I was lying. I had to have Namin say so. Why did you believe her and not me?"

"She wasn't lying on the ground, swimming in gravel."

"Was I doing that?"

"You don't even remember. You see why I didn't believe you."

"But I remember you didn't believe me."

"You'd probably wake up from the dead and remember being indignant."

"It's true." As if testing herself, she laughed. He could tell by the strain around her eyes that it hurt to laugh.

"That was the only time," Sunam said. "And that was before I met you. I wanted to tell you before you heard it from someone else. Are you angry?"

"It wouldn't have been the only time if he had given you the chance," she said. "And you should have told me earlier. So I should be angry."

"But you're not."

"I don't remember," she said. She lay down on the floor, her legs curled into her stomach, her arm pillowing her head. She closed her eyes. "I guess I'll remember tomorrow."

. . .

JISUN FELL ASLEEP, shoulders jerking at intervals as if she were being poked with invisible rods. He took off his jacket and tried to cover her, but it didn't stop the shivering. "You'd better sit up. It's too cold on the floor, you'll get sick." Her eyelids flickered, but her breathing stayed deep. He shook her a little and repeated what he'd said, but there was no waking her. Finally he sat next to her so that his thighs lay against her back, sharing warmth.

He kept watch, pricking his palm with the prong of his belt buckle to stay awake. They were under curfew for another hour.

Jisun slept with her lips slightly parted, her breathing a low rumble at the back of her throat. Her back became warm against his leg. Eventually the unnatural colors drained from her face. He let her sleep.

Around five, he started hearing activity in the lobby. "Jisun," he hissed. "Wake up." On leaden legs he crawled to the sink, turned on the tap, and cupped a generous well in his palm, which he let drop over Jisun's face. Not all at once. A slow trickle that ran down her cheeks and into her blouse. Her eyes opened with blazing indignation. She scrambled to sit up, sputtering, "What are you doing?"

"We have to go," he said. "It's time."

She gaped at her watch with a bewildered expression. "Did I sleep? Were you awake the whole time?"

"Hurry," he said. "I need you to check if it's clear."

"Wait." She stopped him with a hand on his arm. Sleep and grief were etched into her face, one indistinguishable from the other. "What we talked about? I'm not angry."

Sunam looked at her. He was so far past exhaustion, his eyes no longer blinked involuntarily. He had to remember to do it. Shut the eyes. Open the eyes. His stomach burned with acid hunger. He could not remember if he was still drunk or if he always felt like this. He remembered another morning when she should have been angry, when she'd said, *You don't have to say hello.*

"*Jisun,* hello," he said. "Get me out of here."

2

. . . .

August.

It was the third week of *jangma*, the monsoon season, and the twelfth consecutive day of rain. Everything, everywhere, was wet or dripping. Roofs leaked. Basements flooded. Wallpaper that had withstood years of *jangma* finally capitulated in dramatic fashion, falling limp and yellow on the floor like old elastic pants. People hurried in out of the rain, wringing out handkerchiefs and towels that never completely dried. On the windows, condensation ran like tears.

As usual, Namin was in the library studying, but neither Sunam nor Jisun had the heart to keep her company anymore. Far from being a sanctuary from the elements, the library felt like the belly of a ship packed with stale respiration. On the rare occasions that Sunam made up his mind to study, he preferred to do it at home in bare feet and boxer shorts. If he fell asleep, he would wake up feeling virtuous and improved, whereas dozing in the library made him feel like a degenerate.

After the night in the hotel bathroom, he and Jisun had formed a sort of auxiliary friendship. Since they had nothing in common other than Namin, she became the center of their conversations, a kind of scaffold to their own fledgling friendship. It had the effect of making her seem less real, as if she existed only in their imaginations.

"Our Namin is not the sort of girl who requires a constant escort," Jisun told Sunam. She always used that moniker, "our Namin," with a special look in her eye—as if they were the proud parents and Namin their crowning achievement. *Now don't you crowd her,* she would say.

Our Namin is far too intelligent and independent, and original, and modern to act like the typical lovesick coed.

Sunam thought that actually Namin had looked a little hesitant about sending him off with Jisun to the movies. He had lingered, hoping she'd change her mind and join them. It was the summer, after all, and even the other diehards were taking it easy. But Namin had it in her mind to skip a year to make it easier on her parents. It would mean one less year of school fees. She worried constantly about keeping up. Even when she allowed herself an afternoon or evening off, Sunam knew she was secretly preoccupied with how many pages she had to read the next day, how many problem sets to complete. He tried not to hound her, but he seemed to lose track of his own feelings, especially with Jisun's voice in his ear. He knew she was only teasing, making a show of possessiveness over Namin to put him in his place. But her words hit a nerve. Sunam couldn't help thinking that Namin was simply neglecting him with her "intelligence and independence and originality," not—as he at other times understood and admired—trying to make the best of a difficult situation.

"It doesn't matter what we watch. Actually, I prefer the bad ones, so I don't get distracted. . . ." Jisun was always talking, regardless of his attention. "What I like to do is . . ." They were approaching the theater, walking close under a single umbrella since she had shown up—in this weather—without one. Namin would've had a quick, biting comment about that: Jisun's incurable rich-girl ways. Clearly, she was so used to being driven around that she couldn't even remember to bring an umbrella during *jangma*. But Sunam kept quiet, thinking they were not friendly enough for such jabs. Instead he stored the detail in his mind, something he would tell Namin later if she seemed in a good mood, ready for jokes.

Jisun had a way of hopping puddles that ended up splashing him or left him stranded outside the radius of their shared umbrella. "I get in early and watch the last fifteen minutes. Then, before it starts again, I try to guess what the film's about. I make a bet with myself. I make it something really specific, so I can't cheat. The wager has to be really clever too. It's no fun if you cheat."

"But you can't exactly pay yourself."

"Of course not—what would be the point? So I wager something I want or don't want. I make it really exciting. One time, I wagered cutting my hair *this* short—it looked absolutely awful, but every time I looked at myself I knew why I had done it, and it was kind of interesting. Like hiding a secret in plain sight, you know? Another time I wagered five sugar doughnuts in five minutes. They used to be my favorite food. Of course now I can't touch the stuff. Another time I wagered stealing something from the housekeeper. That kind of thing. Nothing earth-shattering."

"But what's the point of it?" he said. "If you lose, something terrible happens. If you win, nothing changes."

"I didn't tell you everything," she said meaningfully. "There were good things too."

There was a pause while they both wondered if he would take the obvious bait and ask. But Sunam felt uneasy about having left Namin alone to have fun with another girl. It felt too intimate to nudge Jisun to reveal the good things she had wagered and won against herself.

"So," he said, looking at his watch. "If we hurry, we can see the last fifteen minutes of the two forty-five."

"*Don't* tell me the title," she said. "I always try to avoid looking at the title."

"But I already know. It's not fair if you don't know and I do."

"Fine. So I'll give you another game," she said impatiently. "A variation. I have tons."

"Can't we just watch the movie?" It was an irritating business, this need of Jisun's to make everything into a game, as if ordinary pleasures were not enough for her. He just wanted to disappear into the theater, fold into those rickety seats, and forget about life for a while.

"You're just saying that because you've never tried this," she said. "You'll never want to watch a movie the normal way again."

They hurried to the Daehan, where Sunam bought two tickets

while Jisun stood far enough away under a dripping awning so she wouldn't accidentally hear anything. She carefully avoided looking anywhere beyond the circle of the umbrella.

"I didn't see *one* poster," she bragged as they pushed into the dark theater. They found two empty seats in the very last row with their backs against the wall. The air was as suffocating as a steam room, the vapor clearly visible in the projector's beam. Jisun sat down, hugging her handbag to her chest in a surprisingly childlike posture. Surveying the packed theater with a blissful expression, she seemed to forget him completely.

On the screen was a night scene: a watery overlay of a woman's crying face over an onward-rushing train. The actress was sitting on an overpass above the train. The close-up on her face filled the screen's right side, the train filled the left. The wind whipped her hair around tearful cheekbones, the train cut through nighttime fog. Fade-out.

The next scene seemed to open many years later. Two men chatted at a dry-cleaning shop and one mentioned that he had seen a woman named Young Ja. "Young Ja?" the second man said, visibly taken aback.

"Must be an old lover," Jisun whispered to Sunam.

"Who?" Sunam said.

"That guy!"

Sunam shook his head.

"Just watch," she said.

It turned out Jisun was right. Young Ja was the woman who had been crying on the overpass. The man was her former lover. She was married now, with a young daughter. Her new husband had a lame leg. Young Ja had a prosthetic hook for a hand.

"What's with the *hook*?" Sunam whispered.

"Oh, this is going to be good," Jisun said.

The film closed with the two men—new husband and former lover—introducing themselves and making plans to share a meal together sometime.

Appreciative sighs rose from the audience. Throats cleared expressively across the rows. Then the lights went up and a hundred people hurled themselves into the aisle, talking and laughing, melding into the fresh audience arriving for the next showing. Even after the crowds intermixed, you could tell by the set of the shoulders and the body language who was leaving the show satisfied and who was settling in with anticipation.

"Would you ever miss this?" Jisun said raptly. She was standing on her seat to study the scene with shining eyes. "This is almost my favorite part. I always watch where people are shoving in opposite directions and see who gets out the fastest. You can't always judge by size. The big ones do okay, but you have to keep an eye on the ones with the really aggressive perms. You know, the ramen-hair ladies? Those mamas really move. . . .

"Come on, try it," she insisted. "Stand up, you'll see."

Sunam stayed put. "I'm exhausted just thinking about it," he said. "Anyway, I'm getting shoved good enough right here."

Jisun looked down at him with a pitying expression. "Are you like this with Namin too? You're no fun at all. What does she see in you, anyway?"

"Whatever it is, I guess she likes it," he snapped without thinking.

"Confident guy," she murmured. *She* always sounded casual, the way he'd intended and failed. She laughed, showing perfectly even teeth. "Let's have our little wager, then," she said. "The plot is too obvious. So we need to make it more interesting."

"Obvious?" he said. "We saw a train and a couple of people talking. How is that obvious?"

"Oh, come on. They practically gave us the script. The hook hand?" she said. "Really, Sunam. Use your imagination."

"Exactly, the hook hand!" he said.

"Fine. Here's what happens. That girl Young Ja and that guy Changsoo were in love, but something went wrong. She's considering jumping in front of a train. But we have that full redemption ending," Jisun mused. "So it must have been a pretty tragic past for poor Young Ja. Maybe she was forced into prostitution, maybe someone cut off her arm. So there it is, there's our story."

Sunam shook his head in amazement, but Jisun plowed on. "Now for our objective," she said. "We have to guess how many sex scenes there are in this movie. We already know there are none in the last fifteen minutes. But that doesn't mean anything. There could be tons of sex in the beginning." She paused as if solving a difficult equation in her head, then nodded in quick confirmation. "I call seven sex scenes. You pick too. Closest one wins."

He had already collected a bundle of objections. About the "plot summary," which was so full of holes that he could only hope she was joking. And the suggestion about tallying sex scenes was absurd. The sheer bravado of the number seven seemed to him outrageous. Unless this movie was about a brothel and she counted every time a woman entered a room with a man, there were not going to be *seven* sex scenes.

Sunam had all these objections at hand, but he didn't say a word. Something wasn't right; it was too obvious. It seemed that Jisun *expected* him to raise these challenges, to disapprove in just this way. She was watching him carefully, a playful set to her mouth. A splotch of red no larger than a thumbprint rose on her throat. And finally Sunam realized the true nature of this test, which was to see if he would keep up with her games, however childish or nonsensical her rules. It was his choice. Play or forfeit.

"Define sex scene," he said.

"What?"

"Obviously, there's not going to be actual sex," he said. "So where do we draw the line?"

"When the director wants to imply they're having sex . . . you know."

"Like a kiss and fade-out—you call that a sex scene? Because the director wants me to think so?"

"Maybe."

"That's crap. A kiss is not a sex scene."

"Fine, so that's out. Groping and fade-out counts."

"Only if someone takes off some clothing."

"Fine. Groping with at least one article of removed clothing counts."

"The article of clothing cannot be a jacket or coat."

"Fine!"

"It's starting," he said. "Do you want to adjust your wager since kisses are out?"

"Why should I?" she said. "I said seven and my intuition is always right."

He shook his head. She was crazy. "Fine. I pick four," he said. "Four and under, I win. Five and over, you win. What are you doing?"

"Here," she said, handing him a pen from her purse. She ripped out a sheet of notepaper and waved it in his face. "Since we're being so proper, you better keep a close count. Use your watch if you have to," she said. "Mark the exact times so we can compare notes."

He made a show of smoothing the paper on his thigh. He licked the tip of the pen. "Ready," he said.

THE OPENING SCENE was a police raid on a brothel. Women fled into dark alleys, pursued by uniformed men wielding clubs. Sunam gripped his pen, even though there was nothing to record. He refused to glance at Jisun, who was presumably waiting for him to look so she could gloat: the opening scene and already three prostitutes! He refused to give her the satisfaction. Jisun finally dug the end of her pen into his thigh. He backhanded her wrist, saying, "Watch the movie, will you?"

"Rookie," she said.

The first sex scene was between Changsoo and Young Ja, who was a prostitute after all. But Changsoo had been in love with her from the time she was a wholesome housemaid in his foreman's house. Visiting her at her brothel, he wanted to know what happened to her arm, but she wouldn't tell. She was wearing a loose red dress like a smock, hiding her missing arm. She put out her palm for money, simpering: "Well, are we doing this or aren't we?"

Changsoo threw the money on the ground and dragged Young Ja onto pink and yellow quilted pillows. He fell on top of her, his face twisted with grief. Young Ja smiled and grabbed his crotch. End scene.

Jisun scribbled busily on her notepaper.

"What, that doesn't count," he whispered. "No one took anything off. It looked like he might change his mind."

"Don't be such a baby," she said. "He gave her the money, didn't he? Anyway, she's barely wearing anything to begin with."

The next sex scene undeniably involved the act, but it was a rape. The foreman's son, with his hippie haircut and loutish whistling, forced himself on virginal housemaid Young Ja in a flashback just as she'd finished reading one of Changsoo's letters from the war in Vietnam.

Jisun's pencil scratched on paper.

This time he didn't argue, even though he'd raise the point later if necessary. He wouldn't have counted rape as a sex scene. Of course it was sex, but they had clearly meant romantic sex. Love sex. If it became the decisive point, he would fight. But heartless to wrangle over technicalities now.

Three and four were customers.

Five was a scene that actually involved romantic sex, between Changsoo and Young Ja in a bathhouse.

The pen again in his thigh. "You lost," Jisun whispered.

"But we didn't bet anything." Sunam had realized this around the time Jisun started taking notes. They had entered this elaborate game with rules and points, but no penalties, no rewards. He tried to feel amused, really savor the stupidity. But instead he felt cheated, as if they'd both lost.

"Of course we did," she said.

"What?"

"If I win, you do whatever I want. If you win, I do whatever you want."

"Liar," he whispered. "We never said that."

"It's written right here," she said. She tapped a line at the top of her page, which he couldn't read in the dark. But he believed if the lights went up right now, it would be there. Not that it proved any-thing.

"I won," Jisun said as the credits rolled. She presented her sheet as if it were a winning lottery ticket.

"You won," he conceded. In another mood, he would have con-tested the rape scene, but he was tired of the charade.

They walked out of the theater and saw the rain had stopped, at least for the moment. Stepping out from under the awning without struggling with an umbrella felt like miraculous, implausible freedom. The purest luxury not to do battle with the sky.

"Let's go somewhere and drink seven bottles of *soju*," Jisun said. "In honor of Young Ja."

He burst out laughing. "You must be crazy."

"Don't be such a sore loser," she said. "I'll take four. You can man-age the others, can't you?"

Ignoring the implied insult, Sunam briefly considered suggesting they pick up Namin. She hated *soju* and would never trade precious study time to indulge one of Jisun's whims, but it felt disloyal not to at least consider it.

As if reading his mind, Jisun said, "We could get Namin if you want."

But they both knew what that would entail. Taking the bus back to the library, finding Namin, explaining the proposition, heckling her to join them, absorbing the inevitable rejection—all of it would kill the mood. They would need a drink just to remember why they had wanted to drink in the first place. But for Namin's sake, he pretended to dwell on it. "She really needs to study," he said.

Jisun shrugged, as if that's what she'd expected to hear. "Anyway, she hates *soju*. She wouldn't come even if she had nothing else to do. She'd rather count lice on rats." She laughed at his surprise. "Listen, I know everything about her. You've only known her, what, a few months? Namin hating *soju* is basic. Wait till you find out the really juicy stuff. You'd be surprised. Or maybe you wouldn't be." She looked askance at him. "How much do you know about her family?"

Sunam cleared his throat. "I know enough to change the subject."

Jisun nodded. "Good man. Respect."

They walked in silence for a while, and Sunam began to wonder if he'd made a mistake. Maybe he should go back to the library, at least give Namin a chance.

He was about to suggest they turn back when Jisun asked, "So. What is this virginal relationship you and Namin are having? Aren't you two ever going to do it? How can you, if you never even see each other?"

She looked so delighted with herself, Sunam didn't bother being embarrassed. Calmly he said, "Hey, let's worry less about me and more about you. Aren't you interested in anyone?"

"Not interested," she said. "But back to you and Namin—"

"Not interested in anyone or not interested in love?" he asked.

"I don't believe in love—who said anything about love? I only believe in sex."

"Come on."

"Really. Sex is direct, it's useful. Love mucks everything up."

"Sounds like someone's in love," he said.

She stopped in front of a dingy little bar half below street level. The people drinking inside seemed to peer up at the passersby like ghouls in the underworld. From the looks of it, they were all poor students and laborers drinking from unmarked bottles, stuff his father would be ashamed to see in his hand. "Last chance to go pick up Namin," Jisun said. "Once we start drinking for Young Ja, we don't stop for anyone."

All day it seemed she had been daring him to stop her from doing something rash, crossing some dire line. And now she stood with her hand on the door, waiting. He could almost hear himself say the expected reasonable thing; he could see them walk away, maybe see another movie, maybe go sit with Namin in the library after all.

But life these days had felt too close, the August humidity like something personal under his skin. Before he had fully decided to do it, Sunam was already pushing past Jisun through the narrow doorway down the short, steep stairs. Even those few steps down achieved the full basement atmosphere. The damp hit his lungs like an alcoholic steam. He turned around. "After this we're even."

"I'm impressed, New Guy," she said. She hadn't called him that since the night of the party. "But we're not even yet. Seven bottles."

3
. . . .

"But love is so *bourgeois,*" Jisun slurred. "It's just ever-last-ingly stupid, Sunam. You know that, don't you? Say you know. Tell me they haven't gotten you too."

"No, no," he agreed. "They haven't gotten me."

They drank another shot, clinking their glasses sloppily. Jisun wiped her mouth with the back of her hand. "Liar," she said. "You're in deep. You don't even know how deep you're in." She looked at him sadly. "My intuition is never wrong."

"Why do you demo types always say everything is bourgeois, any-way?" He refilled their glasses, steadying the bottle with his other hand. He found the drunker he got, the more attention he paid to his enunciation. His voice echoed, overly correct, in his ears. "What is so bourgeois about love, anyway? Love has always been around, hasn't it? No political party can claim love or denounce it. It's just *biology . . .* comrade."

Jisun threw a hand over his mouth. Her hand was cool and soft. "Shhhhhhhh," she said loudly so that half a dozen people turned to look at her. "We must be careful, comrade," she said. "You can't just throw that word around in public."

"What word—"

"*Comrade,* comrade!" Sunam grabbed her chair to keep it from up-ending as she collapsed in laughter. She laid her head down on the sticky table, her hair falling into a puddle of spilled booze.

"I was in love recently, Sunam," she said.

"In love with an idea," he said, feeling clever. "Yes, I know. Democracy and all that."

"It was more than an idea," she said. "It was a real person, Sunam. A real man."

He realized she was crying. He tried to pat her shoulder, but his hand felt like a useless implement, clumsy and ill suited for the job. "Come on, don't cry," he said. "I'm sorry, it was just a stupid joke."

"I'm not crying about you, you idiot," she said. "And why do people always tell you not to cry when you're crying? When you're crying people should stand up and applaud. Bravo! they should say. Good for you, cry your heart out. They should be envious and jealous."

"Maybe that's why they tell you to stop, because they're jealous."

"Is that why you're doing it?"

He shook his head. "No. . . .

"So were you really in love?" he asked. He wondered what kind of guy was capable of making Jisun cry. She seemed like the kind of person who would laugh at anyone who dared reject her. "You must still love him if you're crying."

"You know what he said to me?" Her voice echoed in his ear. He wondered if she was actually speaking louder or if it was just the alcohol thumping in his eardrums. "He said I wasn't good enough for him. I know he had feelings for me. It wasn't just me suffering over unrequited love. He loved me too. But he changed his mind. He said I *embarrassed* him."

"Someone actually said that? To your face?"

"I'm *summarizing*, Sunam." She tapped herself heavily on the forehead with an index finger, as if to say, *Think, Sunam.* "What he actually said was even worse," she said. "The point is, I trusted him. I thought he was the best guy in the world. And it turns out, he thinks I'm worthless."

"Then he isn't worth your time," Sunam said gallantly, offering her another shot. "Forget about him."

She drank the shot and wiped her mouth.

"If it were that easy, why would I be drinking seven *sojus* for Young

Ja? With you, of all people?" She jabbed a finger at his shoulder, hard. It hurt more than he wanted to admit. "I know you think I'm crazy. You're not so good at hiding your feelings."

"So after all that, you still love the guy?" Sunam said, to change the subject.

"I must, since I really hate myself. That's how you know it must be love." She burst out laughing again. "Too serious? Don't look so shocked. I told you love mucks things up. It'll happen to you too and you'll think—Jisun tried to warn me and I went ahead anyway."

"Have we drunk enough for Young Ja now?" he said.

"Not even close. Two more."

"Five is good enough. We should stop." He peered at his watch, but the numbers seemed to swim on his dial. "Isn't it time to go home?"

She grabbed his arm. Her eyes were still glistening with tears. "No! We have to get to seven, we promised. Anyway, I want to show you something. One thing. Please?"

SUNAM WATCHED THE revolving door, the gleaming brass poles reflecting chandelier light from the lobby. A sodden red carpet lined the sidewalk in front of the entrance. At the curb a black limousine idled; a uniformed driver dozed behind the wheel. The granite facade rose into the night, the name INTERCONTINENTAL glowing high above the city like another moon.

"I'm not going in there," he said.

"Just follow my lead." Before he could react, she had his wallet in her hand. She brandished it overhead. "Besides, you'll need this to get home. Come on."

She pulled him through the revolving doors, across the empty lobby, and into the elevator, where she pressed PH. "Penthouse," she said. "Top floor."

The elevator carried them slowly upward while he tried not to look at their reflections. Everything seemed mirrored and brass plated, giving him back their red eyes, his flushed and puffy complexion. Jisun's skin had gone pale. Her pupils, wide and glassy, stared at the numbers changing above the doors. She looked so serious, her lips colorless. It occurred to him that he should be frightened, not of this hotel, but of her. She seemed capable of anything.

"Isn't anyone going to stop us?" he asked.

The elevator let them out into a short hallway. Jisun turned the corner into a long blind hall. There was a single door at the end. Roof exit.

The door opened easily and Jisun turned with a big smile. "I was afraid they might have locked this. It's been a while."

They climbed a short flight of stairs, Jisun in the lead, swaying slightly. She flung open the heavy door and stepped out into the warm, thick air.

Sunam walked to the high edge of the roof. The city sprawled in dark panorama below, the river to the west heavy with the recent rain. The water lay slick and black, a mirror to the sky. It was a deceptively deadly expanse, studded with low-slung bridges. He knew each bridge was packed with enough explosives to cut off invading tanks from the North.

"Feel that," she said, lifting her nose. "Wind."

His ears were full with the sudden miraculous air and the whirring of the massive roof turbines. The steady drone wiped his mind blank. He felt part of the sky, of its elements: dark and wind and height.

When he joined her on the other side of the roof, Jisun was drinking from one of the bottles she'd smuggled up in her bag. They sat on the roof with their backs to the wall. "We used to come here on Sundays," she said dreamily. "Kind of like our church. We would eat early at the restaurant and my father would take these meetings and leave me with one of the hotel maids. They were always so terrified of me, afraid I'd get them in trouble somehow. Or else they'd be mean as spit—like they'd love to tie me up and slap me around for a while." She looked at him with a strange little laugh. "Don't worry. No one ever did.

"I found out about this place on my own. Lost the maid, got her good and worried. When they brought me down, I said, I'll stay up here from now on. You have your meetings, I'll have mine. Wasn't that a funny thing to say as a kid? I was seven years old. Of course he agreed. You think he'd be worried I'd fall off or something. Or jump.

"I used to think sometimes I would," she said. "The only reason I didn't was because I didn't want people to feel sorry for him. They'd say, Oh, poor man. Losing his wife and his daughter. They would have made him some kind of bereaved saint—ha!"

"Here, give me some of that," he said.

She handed him the other bottle and watched him take a long shot.

"We're friends, aren't we?" she said. "We understand each other?"

He handed back the bottle. "You don't really want to be understood, do you? I don't know what you really want, but not—"

"See, you do understand."

She climbed on his lap, and her weight was loose and warm. "We're doing really good for Young Ja." She kissed him hard on the mouth, putting her hands under his shirt. Her mouth was warm and wet, her tongue so natural in his mouth, tasting like himself and the alcohol they had both drunk, but also something else, complex and bracing. He grabbed her hips and pulled her closer to him. She rocked over his groin, fitting herself to him expertly. Even through clothing, he could feel her heat. She was unbuckling his belt, undoing his pants. He began to dread what was happening, knowing he wouldn't stop it.

She flung off her shirt. He dimly remembered this as if it had already happened. She was wearing a white cotton bra with a bow at her cleavage. The cotton was sheer, and he could see the dark outline of her nipples. He pulled away and wiped his mouth with the heel of his hand.

"Believe me, I want to, but . . ." He hesitated to say her name. With the taste of Jisun's mouth still on his lips, and her body, her breasts warm on his hands, Sunam couldn't bring himself to say Namin's name. He averted his eyes. "It's not right," he said instead, and knew he had already betrayed her by not saying her name.

"Not *you*," Jisun said. Her face was unreadable—he might have expected her to look angry or guilty. Even if she had laughed in his face, mocking his belated loyalty, he would not have been surprised. But what he saw in her face was something else—a combustion of outrage, disbelief, and pain—that he could not adequately attribute to himself. *He* had not caused this; he knew instinctively it had nothing to do with him.

"Not you," she said again.

"Not me what?"

"I can't believe you're going to be virtuous about this," Jisun said. Her face was stunning with bitterness. "I really bring out the best in you righteous types, don't I? He was the same way, you know. With all his feelings—*but*. Who does he think he's fooling? Not me," she said. "And you're not fooling me either."

"*He?*" Sunam said. "Who are you talking about?"

And suddenly he knew. It was not him, Sunam, she was thinking about, but the other guy. The one she loved so much, she hated herself.

He groped for something else to say, something else to talk about, but Jisun, as always, was ahead of him. Her eyes were still fiery with rage, but the corners of her lips twisted down in an expression of sadness that was worse than her anger. "*She* won't do this," Jisun said. "You think she'd risk all that for you? Her big future?"

Sunam didn't have to ask, this time, who *she* was. He knew instantly, and there was nothing left to argue.

Jisun stood up and took off her bra. She pulled off her skirt and panties. Naked, she stood over him, letting him look at her. Her body seemed wrapped with shadows, another layer of the night. Leaning back to look at her, he put his hand down on something sharp, a pebble that dug into his palm. He ached to touch her skin.

Jisun lowered herself on top of him.

Pride and shame. Relief and regret. It was all the same. He held on to her as if he were drowning.

"Whenever you want me to stop, tell me," she whispered in his ear. "I can stop whenever you want."

. . .

AFTERWARD, THEY LAY on their backs staring at the sky, an arm's length of roof spanned between them. Wearing just their underwear, they had piled the rest of their clothes under themselves for padding. He was grateful for the haze of alcohol dulling the discomfort of the concrete roof and the shock of what they'd done. He suspected both sensations would seem far worse in the morning.

Sunam said, "What are we going to tell Namin?" His mouth was so dry, he could feel the bumps on his tongue. He could taste the residue of every guilty word.

Jisun rolled over on her side so he couldn't see her face. "You'll tell her something."

"Don't you feel anything? She's *your* friend," he said as if Namin were a stranger to him. "You told me yourself, how much you love her."

"Don't you ever do terrible things to people you love?" Jisun said. "Or maybe I don't know what love means. I always thought I knew."

Sunam felt the weight of the sky pushing him down and swallowing him up. It was the closest he'd been to the stars, but instead of any great transcendence or grandeur, he felt inescapably pinned to himself. This flawed and limited body.

"Between sky and land, I'd always choose land," Jisun murmured. "Up there, it seems so *crowded*." She curled herself under his arm. Pressing her back against his ribs, she seemed to fall asleep. Her slow, soft breathing vibrated through her spine into his side. He kept absolutely still, afraid even to flick a strand of her hair from his face.

Already he felt how the guilt would become his intimate shadow, beside him when he opened his eyes in the morning, putting him to bed each night. He tried to match his breathing to Jisun's, desperate to sleep just to escape himself. He succeeded in catching moments, bare preludes of subconsciousness, before jerking awake, dehydrated, disoriented. He dreamed he was drinking rain but woke up with his molars clenched.

4
. . . .

The bus roared onto the highway, scattering traffic, achieving more noise than acceleration. The axle clanged and vibrated, bouncing him against Namin. Sunam shifted closer to the window, his eye on a red hatchback stuffed with an entire household packed and dressed for the Chuseok harvest holiday. Three generations, the kids deposited on women's laps like handbags. The smallest child smeared the contents of his nose on the window. His mother talked while applying lipstick.

Namin said, "It's not as bad as you think, where my sister lives."

The child licked his finger to the second knuckle and drew lopsided stars on the glass.

Already Sunam regretted the moment of generosity that had culminated in this reality. It was only because he felt guilty—he owed Namin this, at least—but he was not really interested in knowing more about her sister or becoming further implicated in her family's troubles. Secretly he had made himself a deal. Go to Itaewon, do this thing she wants. Then he could end it with an appeased, if not clear, conscience. ·

Across the aisle, two GIs in fatigues occupied four seats. The smaller of the two had his elbow propped against the window, supporting his head like a loose bracket. His body jerked and realigned with every bump in the road. He stared out the window as if cursing everything he saw. His companion dozed, cap pulled down over his eyes.

"You ever talk to an American before?" Namin asked, as if the question had just occurred to her.

"Don't be stupid. Of course I have." He had decided to be nice, but deciding and doing were two different things. Under the veneer of Namin's usual composure, he could sense her anxiety, her desire to interpret these moments for him ahead of time. It made him snappish and unreasonable, determined to foil her even at his own expense. It made far more sense to let her prep him—what did he know about Americans? The only ones he had ever spoken to were teacher types, who probably talked in the simplest baby English in order to be understood. There had been that chaplain at his high school, Reverend Ellerton, who sang with a womanlike vibrato and cried during the Lord's Prayer. Also, his English-language teacher, a young Korean woman who wore high heels in the classroom, had once hosted a photographer from New York. They sat in the darkened room while the foreigner showed slides of Gyeongbokgung Palace and the Seokguram Buddha, as familiar and uninteresting to them as pictures of their own mother and father.

Namin said doubtfully, "Well, Hal doesn't speak a lot of Korean."

"I'll be fine."

He had no reason to speak to this Hal or even to know him at all, and it peeved him to think Namin presumed otherwise. As far as he was concerned, he was just the man who had gotten her sister pregnant, who would likely disappear before the baby was born. They were living now in some army housing, supposedly married, although no one had been invited to any ceremony. Namin herself admitted doubts. "Maybe she meant they're *going* to get married?" He couldn't tell if she was actively obscuring the truth or if the vagueness was second-hand, carried over from her sister. Either way, there was no reason she should act as if he and this Hal should have anything to talk about. *They* were not relations, quasi or otherwise.

But he had decided to be nice. If only for the future, for Namin to look back and concede, *Well, at least he did this for me. He wasn't a total jerk.*

He softened his expression. "Then how do they speak to each other?"

"She just talks. In Korean—what else is she gonna do? She says he understands anyway."

"You think he does?"

She shrugged and gave a little smile. "Maybe it's better he doesn't."

"But she knows we're coming." It was a statement rather than a question. It seemed to him a visit like this should be prearranged, all parties in agreement. He was a little squeamish, too, of bursting in unannounced. Would she be lolling around in a red smock like the one Young Ja wore in the movie? Would she laugh in that fake open-mouthed way, showing all her teeth and flicking her tongue? He stopped short of imagining how Hal might be. In his mind, American men were all movie stars or soldiers. Best and worst. To imagine one at home, boots off, pretending to understand his Korean-speaking girl-friend, was like trying to peer beyond the frame of a Hollywood set. He preferred the mirage.

"Of course. She asked for you specifically."

"Me—why?"

"Guess she wants to check you out, see what the fuss is all about. She is my sister."

Again Sunam, rather than feeling flattered by the implied compliment, bristled at the presumption. She wanted to check *him* out? Not once since agreeing to come to Itaewon had it crossed his mind that he should be the subject of scrutiny or judgment. Why should he worry about making a good impression?

The bus stopped to pick up a group of factory workers wearing light blue polo shirts and tan pants. The women didn't bother to cover their mouths when they laughed. A soft-faced man, bespectacled, with a shaving cut near his lip, was the loudest, calling everyone *"yah!"* regardless of age, as if they were all schoolchildren on the playground. Sunam had never heard a grown man talk to a woman that way, but no one seemed offended. One of the ladies, vigorously poking at her incisor with a toothpick, said happily, "I love that place. Worth every bit of the bus fare."

"These stinking people," growled the soldier. The women flicked their eyes at the sound of his voice. "Can't stand this country, this whatchacallit shit they eat. I'm suffocating, man."

His friend adjusted his cap lower on his face. "You know what it's called," he muttered. "I've seen you eat it and like it."

"Could say the same about you." The GI sneered and spit between his feet. "How many times you gonna pay for that little girl? What is she now, twelve? She's a child, man." The dozing soldier lifted the cap off his face. He peered with a bloodshot eye, the other eye squinted against the sun.

"She's eighteen."

"If she's eighteen, I'm Santa Claus."

Namin gripped his elbow. "Don't listen, it's filthy."

Sunam shook her off, his blood thumping in his ears. "I thought you were worried about my English," he muttered.

The factory woman behind Namin tugged her shoulder, whispering, "What's that they're saying, student?"

"Nothing, *ajumma*." Namin smiled brightly. "I just meant the spit."

"Never seen such dirty people. Do they act like this at home?" Sunam shifted away from the woman's breath. She must have eaten raw onions at lunch, but even that didn't mask four decades of smoking. "Still, I guess we should be grateful. Think where we'd be," she said. She folded her rough brown hands in a surprisingly prim position over the back of the seat. When neither of them responded, she gave them a sharp look. "Don't you think we should be grateful?"

"Certainly," Namin murmured.

"To think we need foreigners to protect us from our own people," she said. "Don't get me wrong, I'm grateful, I'll be grateful until the day I die, but"—she grimaced at the GIs slumped in their seats—"some of them don't act right. You have to be careful, student. A young good-looking girl like you, especially. You have to watch yourself. Now if only we could convince those Reds to come to their senses. What a shame, the same people—brothers—needing a foreign army between us. We need to remember who we are, we need to—"

Sunam sensed that she would continue to lecture for the foreseeable future if he didn't intervene. She was a living embodiment of those patriotic essays assigned to them in school. Inevitably, she would start listing the achievements of their shared history. She would catalog the natural resources found in the North versus those found in the South, how joining them was the key to gaining first-world status. There would be a sure mention of Kumgangsan, the peninsula's tallest peak immortalized in paintings, poems, and songs—it, too, lost to the North. And a greedy eye toward the long boundary with China. A particularly fervent classmate of his had won the high school essay contest three years in a row using his trademark mention of the Chinese border. Sunam even recalled his finer points verbatim: "Though we are bitter enemies now—one day following a victorious reunification led by the South, anything is possible, even the reinstatement of the great Goguryeo border." The boy, a son of a local government officer, always used the cash prize to pay other students to do his homework for the rest of the year. Sunam had been happily in his pay until he was supplanted by another classmate, who tucked such idiosyncratic errors in the copied work that no one could ever trace them back to the cheater.

"Surely it's a matter of time before reunification," Sunam said smoothly. "Sometimes a little competition is beneficial. It forces both sides to push harder to excel." And because he saw that the *ajumma* would interject and launch into a detailed rebuttal, he quickly added, "And think how one day when we're able to bring them back into the fold, we'll have both superpowers as allies. The U.S. *and* China—an unthinkable position. Unique in the world."

She nodded, pleased with his logic. "And when the North develops the bomb, we'll have everything we need when we are reunited. Even nuclear weapons! We won't be so little anymore, eh?"

"I doubt they're truly close to developing the bomb," Sunam said. Even though the two Koreas were brothers with shared blood, culture, and history, the North had the greater natural resources and had suffered less wartime damage. It had taken the South much longer to recover, and progress would have been slower still without President

Park's aggressive economic measures dragging the country toward development. It wasn't until 1974 that the South had managed to eke out a higher GDP than the North, and while Sunam might look forward to a unified Korea like everyone else, the two sides remained fierce rivals. This *ajumma*, old enough to remember predivided Korea, might consider North Korea's nuclear arsenal "half theirs" if they succeeded in developing it first, but Sunam was not ready to feel so neighborly. What was to stop Pyongyang from turning such weapons against Seoul if they had them? Reunification or not, he would be happier if the North never developed the bomb. "I'm sure they're nowhere close," Sunam said. This time he was more emphatic.

"Surely it's a matter of time," she said, repeating his earlier phrase. He decided to leave it alone. He was weary of these speculations and the people who spent their lives indulging in them—as if there weren't enough to concern them in the present time.

"Anyway, we're going to Itaewon to meet her sister," he said.

There was a flinch behind Namin's eyes—perhaps he imagined it—but she stayed composed otherwise. He could see the *ajumma*'s forehead creasing, the mental effort of reorganizing information around this unexpected news. "Her sister?" *They seemed like such nice young people.*

Namin said simply, "She's having a baby."

"I see."

For long minutes, Namin stared straight ahead and said nothing while the *ajumma* resumed chatting with her group. They were talking about a new night class advertised around their factory. "Union or Jesus?" said another lady, not the *ajumma* they'd been speaking with.

"Probably both," said the soft-faced man.

"No, no, this one's strictly union. College students. Talking about workers' rights and the 'class consciousness.'"

"The Jesus ones came with the same thing. Class consciousness. Labor unity, industry cooperation, that kind of thing. Actually it's not so bad."

"They must think we're unconscious, eh?"

"What factory did Jesus work at, anyway?"

They were still laughing when the bus arrived at Itaewon. Namin was still quiet, but not in a way that felt directed against him. She had either forgiven him for telling the *ajumma* where they were going or decided it was just a mistake, not intentional. By the time they'd climbed off the bus, he'd convinced himself it was fine, a normal thing to say to a stranger. They would never see her again. Anyway, Namin had never said it was a secret—and she had volunteered the part about the baby herself.

Sunam made her wait until the soldiers trudged wordlessly around the corner, their shadows darkening the width of the sidewalk. "You didn't have to tell her about the baby," he said. He had meant to sound apologetic, but it came out sounding as though he were blaming her.

"If you're not ashamed, neither am I," she said. "It's a baby. Not something you can exactly hide, anyway."

"People hide babies all the time," he said.

She looked at him. "People you know?"

He didn't reply. He wanted to ask what they were doing there, really doing. By bringing him there, she was making him half sidekick, half future fiancé, when he was properly neither of those things. Neither someone who could disinterestedly accompany her from point A to B nor someone who could shoulder the burden of her future. Maybe it was some survivalist instinct pushing Namin to gauge his commitment to her. Desperately, he wanted to come clean about Jisun. He craved the end of this relationship, which he was already cataloging as memories in his mind. But he owed Namin this. At least this. Today, he had to be nice.

Across the street, a lanky teenager was watching them, one foot propped against the building behind him like a stork. He had dark skin and tight, curly hair, but Korean features. The boy slowly closed his hand into a fist and raised his longest finger. His eyes flashed at Sunam. He did the same with the other hand. Clenched fist, longest finger up. He danced the fists in front of his face.

"What does that mean?" Sunam demanded. Laughing, the kid disappeared into the building.

Namin shook her head. "He's just a kid," she said. "You shouldn't have stared at him like that."

Sunam shoved his hands into his pockets. "Why don't you tell me how I should act. From now on," he said, "don't leave anything out. I'll do exactly as you say."

"For starters—"

"For instance, how should I walk?" he continued. "How should I breathe?"

"No one forced you to come. I know I asked, but you agreed. No one kidnapped you."

"But do we really need to do this?" he asked. It was cowardly to make her say it again—why this was so important to her, why it was necessary for him to meet her sister. All things she had made clear so many times. Almost from the instant they'd met, before they were even romantically involved, Namin had been obsessed with the notion that there would be no secrets between them. *I don't want anyone saying I tried to trick you.* He had been flattered, this stunning girl laying out her life to him. Giving him the power to judge, yes or no, good or bad. Sunam had wanted only to be worthy of that gift. He had wanted to be worthy of *her.* But now, he was desperate to be released from her trust. "It doesn't seem right for me to be here when your parents won't even acknowledge her or the baby," he said. "Who am I? I'm nobody to her—why do I have to come?"

"You're my boyfriend, that's why," Namin said. "You're somebody to *me.*" She didn't have to say anything else. The rest, which they both knew so well, was written in her eyes.

He should have told her the truth weeks ago. He should never have come. "All right. Let's go," he said. Today, it was too late.

5

. . . .

Namin's sister lived in a concrete apartment block, painted flamingo pink like a cheap cocktail. But it was clean and modern, more prosperous looking than many of his friends' homes. It came to him like a photo in sharp focus, this building and this life, side by side with the life that Kyungmin had recently left. He sensed that she must love the pink building, the freshly paved parking lot with the numbers painted in white between the lines.

Namin punched the number 5 on the elevator panel. It was really the fourth floor, but the builders had skipped that number, considered unlucky because it sounded like the Chinese character for death. He wondered if the Americans knew that or if they thought it was a mistake, something else to make them feel superior. He felt faintly ashamed stepping out into the hallway marked with the number 5, as if he were participating in that lie.

The units were packed close together, doors lining an outer corridor that overlooked a playground. The halls had been recently swept. A single brown leaf scuttered in their wake. When they rang at the unit, he noticed two packed army bags marked *H. Jackson*. Duffel bags large enough to contain the full extent of a soldier's belongings. Namin surely noticed it, too, but said nothing.

Kyungmin opened the door, and Namin gave a little cry.

"I cut it," Kyungmin said calmly. Her hair circled her face in a feathery halo. Her lips were painted a deep red and seemed to take up half her face. Between the makeup and her immense pregnant belly,

Sunam felt as if he were looking at a naked woman. He didn't know where to put his eyes.

She shuffled back into the apartment, leaving her guests in the narrow space inside the door to take off their shoes. The area held a tumbled disarray of combat boots and brightly colored slippers, which Namin automatically started matching and shoving into a low cabinet. Sunam stood by and tried not to look past his immediate surroundings. He had put off meeting Namin's sister for as long as he could, but now he realized it would have been better to come earlier, when Kyungmin wasn't so hugely and unavoidably big. Everything about the place seemed pregnant to him, as if the apartment itself were pregnant with the consequences of Kyungmin's actions.

"Are you coming?" Namin said. She had turned a corner into the apartment where he could no longer see her. He trailed after her voice. The narrow foyer dead-ended into a bedroom. The kitchen and living room were to the right. Adjoining the living room was a small balcony dominated by a drying rack hung with laundry. Women's laundry. Pink and yellow things with multiple straps and narrow lacy bits. On the wall was a framed photo of an American family in an outdoor setting: graying parents and a young man with a crew cut, his arms around two women who seemed to be his sisters. Sunam assumed the young man must be Hal. He was extremely tall, standing at least a head above his mother and sisters. He had brown hair and a long, bony face with sleepy, downturned eyes.

Sunam wedged himself into a chair at the kitchen table, trying not to touch anything. The table looked sticky and was piled high with several meals' worth of dirty dishes: A fried egg yolk that had calcified into golden resin on the plate. A bowl littered with the last curlicues of instant ramen. Three overripe persimmons resting fatly in their own leaked juices. The fruit gave off a sickly-sweet scent like fermented syrup.

Namin stood several paces away with her back to the refrigerator, arms crossed. He knew it was probably killing her not to tackle this mess, but once she started they'd be here for hours. At least he could be grateful for her restraint. He might have expected Kyungmin to offer them something to eat or drink, but she didn't seem troubled. She picked up what appeared to be a stack of mail and went through it with a bored expression on her face, as if he and Namin weren't there, waiting for her to say something. Since there was nothing else to do or look at, Sunam stared at the television set in the living room. Boys and girls were singing on the steps of a carpeted stage. Automated puppets in the shape of flowers nodded to the beat, or what he assumed was the beat. The sound was muted.

"Well," Namin said to her sister finally. "Where is he? You said he'd be here."

"As you can see, he's not."

"Do you expect him anytime soon? We weren't planning on waiting all day."

"You and your plans," Kyungmin said curtly. "Not everybody lives according to your schedule." She put down the mail and settled herself in front of the TV. Now the children were doing calisthenics, turning out one foot and then the other. A grown woman with exaggerated pigtails and smears of freckles led the group, beaming at the camera.

"The bags outside," Namin said. "What does that mean? Are you going somewhere?"

"Use your brain, Namin. Does it look like I'm going anywhere?"

Namin enunciated every word, as if she were talking to a child. "Then why are there bags packed outside?"

"Furlough," said Kyungmin. "The man says he has *furlough.* I put the bags outside because I don't want them here. I suppose he'll come get them before he leaves."

They listened to the buzz of the electric clock. When Sunam glanced at Namin, she was biting her lip, apparently having reached the same conclusions that he had. Furlough—at a time like this? Anyone could see the baby was due any minute.

Namin crossed the room and snapped off the TV. They watched the screen suck itself into blackness, punctuated by a small, static click.

"Well, what are you going to do, then, where will you go? Don't you think we'd better talk about this?"

"There's nothing to talk about," Kyungmin said. "You're always getting worked up over nothing."

"Nothing? Look at your belly. Is that nothing?"

"It's a baby." Kyungmin said the word *baby* as if it really were nothing. "Am I the only woman in the world ever to have a baby? I'll be fine."

"But what if he doesn't come back? What if it's not just a furlough—"

"*If?*" Kyungmin said with a strange little snarl, a smile that had dangerously changed course. "Who said he's not coming back?"

"Yes, *if*," Namin repeated. "What's your plan? What will you do?"

Kyungmin stood up, her hands supporting her back, her stomach pushed to its limit. "You're always trying to act so smart, like no one else ever had a wise thought except for you. Did you forget who sent you to school and paid for all those fancy books? Do you think I couldn't have gone to college and been just like you—so special, so smart? There's nothing you did that I couldn't have done, little sister. I just let you have it."

Namin made a sound from the back of her throat that was half sob, half hysterical laughter. "So. You did this instead—is that it?"

Kyungmin started clearing the table, moving around the small kitchen as if Sunam were not there. He had to stumble over the chairs to get out of her way, and even then he was always in the wrong place—she seemed to make sure of it.

"What part of this bothers you more," Kyungmin murmured, squeezing soap on the sponge, then dropping it unused into the sink. "The fact that you think I'm ruining my life—or that I'm ruining yours? I know why you're here. You thought you'd come out here and put on a nice show for your precious new boyfriend. Practice a little truth telling, check that off your list, so you can continue your perfect courtship with a clear conscience? If that's the case, you have a long way to go. A lot of checks to clear, little sister. We come from the same place, you and me, we're just the same. I see no reason to put on any airs. Not for any college boy."

Sunam watched the color drain from Namin's face. Her complexion turned nearly white with rage, her hands and neck a dangerous shade of maroon. But when she spoke, her voice was firm and controlled. "We are not the same. We will *never* be the same." She said it with such ferocity that Sunam knew the conversation was over.

Kyungmin narrowed her eyes. "College boy, get your coat," she said. "I've got things to say to you privately."

"Ignore her," Namin snapped in a low voice. "You don't have to go."

As if he couldn't make his own decisions. As if he needed her permission to do what he wanted.

"It's fine, I'll be back in a minute," he told her. "We'll leave right after."

OUTSIDE, THE SOUND of children playing bounced off the concrete walls of the facing buildings. The happy shrieking felt like a balm after the tension inside. Kyungmin leaned her elbows on the open hallway partition, gazing down at the kids below.

As they watched, it was clear the children had organized a war of mud pies. Under a low slide, three girls and a younger boy squatted, stacking a pyramid of snowball-sized clumps. They passed them off to the older boys, who ran from swing to jungle gym like a SWAT squad, celebrating silently when they made a hit. The other side had no cover and a sporadic stockpile, but they were bigger boys and had more intimidating throwing stances.

Kyungmin pointed out the ones she knew.

"That one, her father is American. She has a half sister, full Korean. Doesn't talk even though she's three years old. That boy lives downstairs. His father died of TB in the spring. That one came begging for salt after wetting her bed. I gave her a chocolate and now she calls me auntie. Her mother hates me."

Sunam looked where she pointed but said nothing.

"Feel like taking a pregnant lady for a walk?" Without waiting for an answer, Kyungmin took his arm and started down the hall. Sunam assumed they would just take a lap around the complex. Instead he found himself being led out into the neighborhood. He thought about demanding to go back but kept going, propelled by curiosity.

They walked through alleys where trash was heaped in the gutters and young women hung out windows, smoking. One of them called out, "Sister, who's the handsome stranger?" and Kyungmin laughed and kept walking. At the next corner, the scent of roasted sweet potatoes filled the air, reminding Sunam how long it had been since he'd eaten. He bought a bag from the grandmother vendor, but Kyungmin insisted on paying. She offered the change to the woman's granddaughter, who had been busy stacking gingko leaves into tight yellow fans.

"Thank you," the little girl said solemnly, carefully switching the leaves to her left hand so she could accept the coins.

The grandmother tried to make her give it back, saying, "She'll buy candy. Rot her teeth."

Kyungmin gently pushed the money back at the child. "She'll get new teeth, grandmother."

So this was Itaewon. Signs in a hodgepodge of Korean and English advertising beer and girls. Huge awnings hung over entries and windows like Venus flytraps, both beckoning toward and hooding the activities within. Sunam feared someone—one of the miniskirted girls yawning in the doorway—would recognize Kyungmin and embarrass him as the other woman had, but they passed on without incident.

She led them off the main street to a row of bars all named in English. Rodeo. Starlight. My Fair Lady. "We should really get back to Namin," Sunam said.

"Relax, college boy, I'm just thirsty."

They ducked through a double row of beaded curtains at a place called Tennessee. Inside, the words *Memphis Girl* glowed in blue neon over the bar, and a disco ball wobbled over an empty dance floor. In the far corner, a woman mechanically counted a roll of cash, then turned it around and counted it again. She nodded at Kyungmin but did not say hello.

Kyungmin deposited him at a booth lined with red vinyl and helped herself at the bar, bringing back a can of 7UP and two shots of whiskey. For a moment Sunam thought she planned to drink one of the shots herself, but they were both for him. "Drink them quickly before she sees," she said, nodding at the lady with the cash. He gulped them both, but the liquor was so watered down that it could have been anything. Noticing his expression, Kyungmin laughed. "Yeah, I know. She's cheap about her booze." Sunam nodded.

"You wanted to say something to me?" he asked, just as Kyungmin said, "Let's just get to it." Now that they were sitting face-to-face, she seemed less outlandish. Her bright lipstick had worn off, and he could even detect the resemblances between her and Namin. He realized their features were quite similar, but Kyungmin had a way of squinting askance at him, completely different from Namin's straightforward gaze.

"I want to talk to you about my sister," she said. "I want to know if you've told her the truth."

His heart dropped at the word *truth*—but how could she possibly know? "The truth about what?"

"I'm sure you know what I mean. This relationship is not what she thinks, is it?" Kyungmin dropped her voice. "When Namin said she was going to that fancy school of yours, I knew it would be trouble for her. What kind of people would she meet there? Boys from good families. Rich girls. Huge clothes allowances. Fancy shoes, handbags. How can you compete with that? I said. I told her she's better off where she belongs. Save herself the heartache."

He laughed with relief. Was this what she wanted to talk to him about? Namin's supposed inferiority, her inability to compete? "She's doing just fine," he said. "Actually she does better than everybody—including me."

"But that's not what I mean," she said. "Boys like you, they end up

marrying a certain kind of young lady. They're not just interested in
test scores—she puts so much faith in them. Her personal savior, those
test scores. But they're not nearly enough for a future, are they? You
don't have to lie to me, I already know. But does she know?"

"She's very ambitious," Sunam said stupidly, as if he were Namin's
teacher, not boyfriend, giving an evaluation.

"She wants the things that everybody wants."

"What's wrong with that?"

"Nothing. Of course, nothing. But other girls already have the
things she wants. They don't have to be so ambitious. Everything—
the good family, the right clothes, the fancy education—they have it
already. They don't have to start so far behind."

He wanted to disagree on principle. He wanted to declare his love
for Namin, to disprove this thesis, which Kyungmin was laying out so
calmly, as if they were discussing some movement in history that had
happened twenty centuries ago. But she was right. Perhaps it was not
true universally, but it was true in his case and there was no point in
denying it.

Nodding, Kyungmin said, "You and I barely know each other and
I doubt we'd get along even if we did—but we're both practical people. There's a way the world works and we understand. Not like
Namin. You think she's hard, pragmatic. But she's a dreamer. Idealis-
tic. She thinks telling the truth makes things better—isn't that why she
brought you here? Thinking you'd respect her and love her more for
being honest? You and I know—she should have never told you a
thing."

"And what about you?" he asked, starting to weary of her lecture.
"What will you do?"

"About Hal, you mean."

"And the . . ." He couldn't quite bring himself to say the word.
Baby.

"Do you think he's telling the truth?" she asked.

"About leaving?"

"About coming back."

There was no point saying things neither of them believed. She would find out soon enough, and what he said would make no difference.

"No," he answered.

She twisted her upper lip under her teeth. Outside, a young Korean couple loudly debated whether they should come inside or go someplace else. The proprietor lady called out, "We're open, come in," but the couple decided to move on. Grumbling, she turned up her radio. The three of them sat in the otherwise empty bar, listening to the confident tenor of the radio host inviting listeners to call in for real estate advice.

"If Hal doesn't come back, this baby isn't mine," Kyungmin said finally.

Sunam stared. "I don't understand. Then whose?"

"No one's." She looked away, ripping the paper sheath of a plastic straw to shreds. "If it has no father, why should it have a mother?"

6

. . . .

Classes resumed after the Chuseok break, and while Sunam had abstractly looked forward to the return of routine to offset the chaos he felt inside, coming back to campus only highlighted how small his world had become. Just six months ago, walking the quad of SNU had felt like traversing secret passageways. There had been a sense of countless doors, so many that he could not possibly know what lay behind them all. Now the whole of campus had become swallowed by people and places all too uncomfortably familiar.

A thousand times in the weeks since that night on the roof he'd resolved to break things off with Namin, to do the honorable thing, at least in retrospect. A thousand and one times he'd reversed himself. There was always a good reason to put it off. She was studying for an important exam. She was having a terrible time with her family. She was having a rare good day, postexam, and celebrating her success. There were too many people around. They were alone, without any distractions to limit the damage of confessing. At first Sunam genuinely believed he was protecting her feelings, looking for the right time to tell her. Then he knew it was his own fear.

And not just fear, but also his unwillingness and greed to let go of what, even now after everything that had happened, made him feel that he was someone important and special. Because Namin had chosen him—him!—people gave him a second look, wondering if he were not as ordinary as he appeared. Sunam knew eventually, inevitably, they would dismiss him as unremarkable after all. But for those moments when he was the mystery element that Namin the genius, the

Machine, had chosen over everyone else, the recognition he craved was still within reach.

And finally—foremost among all the selfish, cowardly reasons, there was something worse than fear. It was a paralyzing misery, leagues beyond guilt. Sunam could not bear to think how it would hurt Namin to know what he had done, betraying her with Jisun. Of all the sins—unfaithfulness, cravenness, deceit—this was the greatest. That it had been Jisun who had supplanted her.

When he calculated how many days, weeks, had passed, he could not recognize himself as the person who had allowed it to go on so long. And when it happened again with Jisun, and when it became so frequent that he counted not the infractions but the times he had somehow resisted, Sunam knew it was too late to tell Namin the truth.

The way I see it, you have two choices. Jisun reiterated these points as if she were merely teaching a logic lesson, not in fact an active partner in their current disaster. *Stay with her or break it off. But either way, confessing won't help. You see that, don't you?*

The problem was that Sunam did see. If he wanted to stay with Namin, he could not possibly tell what he'd done. She'd never accept a betrayal of this magnitude. Even if she did, Sunam could never bring himself to face her after admitting such a thing. Lying and keeping secrets were hard enough, but moving forward after telling the truth was impossible.

And on the other hand, what was the point of telling if the decision was to break it off? It would only heap more pain on the situation, like bombing an already burning house.

Stay with her or break it off.

It seemed he had chosen the first option. The default option. Jisun never included herself in the world of choices he had to make, but she was there, as present as all the other questions to which he had no answer. *Stay with her or break it off.*

THE FIRST SEVERAL times Sunam visited the house, he brought along a heavy bag packed with textbooks and kept several paces between them even behind closed doors. Jisun lay on the bed, reading and laughing at him while he maintained his position on the opposite side of her bedroom. He fiddled with her record collection and spoke loudly about mundane things so as to broadcast his platonic intentions to anyone who might be within earshot.

"No one is listening," she said. And it was true. The house was like an empty museum, heavy with the collected silence of artifacts. Only her suite of rooms with the balcony overlooking the garden felt like a living, breathing oasis.

"But they must know I'm here?"

"Maybe. It doesn't matter."

"Doesn't matter to you or them?"

"Doesn't matter means doesn't matter. How many times are you going to look through the same records?"

Sunam didn't understand it but eventually accepted that he could come and go as he pleased and never see anyone other than Jisun. They would lie naked in her bed, sometimes not even having sex, just lying there, her head propped on his shoulder. Whole afternoons would melt away, one into the next. They'd have something classical and repetitive on the stereo, Bach or Handel, and make loose, disjointed conversation until one of them felt sweaty and moved to open a window.

They talked about nothing important: where to eat *mandoo*, swimming at the beach, body hair. She showed off her knowledge of penis trivia.

"Did you know, the gangsters constantly cut the tip to make it scar?"

"What? No."

"The women at the factory told me, they've seen it. They keep at it to make more scar tissue. They make them look like flowers on a stalk."

"To scare off their rivals? Come on, why would they do that? Some kind of macho mutilation? Don't tell me it's just for show."

"Not just for show. Better for the ladies."

More quickly than he liked to admit, Sunam grew comfortable and then brazen, staying long stretches of the afternoon into evening.

Laughing at the irreverent jokes Jisun made at her father's expense. As long as he was wrapped in her world, he felt insulated from reality. No past or future, only a buried and distorted present in which he was invincible and free.

Didn't I tell you—love mucks everything up.

7

. . . .

Sunam hurried to his bus stop, trying to lose Tae, whom he'd unfortunately run into after his economics lecture.

"Seems like you've been keeping yourself busy these days," Tae was saying. "Hard to see your face around here."

To tune him out, Sunam counted steps in his head, resetting to zero each time he reached the twelfth step.

"Guess you've been busy with that genius girlfriend of yours. Must not be easy keeping up with her."

Seven eight nine ten.

"You know, of course, about her sister. I'm sorry to tell you I saw her myself. Last weekend. I mean, not *that way*, of course. I saw her at the bar. Looks like she's just pouring drinks now—she having triplets or what?"

Two three four five six.

"Must be tough on the family. Well. At least you got the good one."

Sunam said, "This is my stop."

"What about the car?"

"What car?"

Tae indicated the corner, where a long black car was idling, the dark tinted window cracked a sliver on the driver's side.

"That's not for me," Sunam said, but the driver had come out of the car and was walking toward them with unmistakable purpose. He had a limp and an exaggerated side part in his hair, slick with grease. It was like watching something happen to him in a dream. He felt the urge to run, but his feet stayed rooted to the sidewalk.

The driver stopped in front of them. "I'm here to take you to your meeting."

"I don't have a meeting." Sunam glanced at the car. He had heard of student activists being picked up by black cars and never seen again, but he had never been remotely involved in a protest or underground group. It was probably just a mistake, a mix-up—someone saying the wrong name or thinking he looked approximately familiar. He squared his shoulders and forced himself to stay calm. As long as he didn't get in the car, he would be fine. "You must have me confused with someone else," he said. "I have nothing to do with you." He started to walk away, but the man stopped him with a firm grip on his arm.

"You have a meeting with Mr. Ahn," he said. "You know who he is?"

Mr. Ahn. *Jisun's father.*

Satisfied, the driver turned and walked back to the car without waiting to see if Sunam was following. Tae let out a low whistle. "Fancy friends," he said.

Sunam knew the story would find its way around campus, the narrative framed as Tae saw fit. With this in mind, he tried to act undaunted, the hero of his story instead of the frightened victim. He tipped his head toward the car. "When the boss calls, you answer," he said with as much bravado as he could muster. It must have been enough. When the car pulled away from the curb, Tae was still standing there. As they passed, he saluted Sunam with a mixture of amusement and envy.

"What is this about? I didn't know about any appointment." The plush luxury of the car, which would have impressed him under different circumstances, now filled him with dread. They were heading toward the river, and he wondered if he would be taken to the house and ambushed with some kind of forced confession involving Jisun. His mind instantly supplied the appropriate scenes stolen from movies: Jisun thrown to the ground to grovel for forgiveness, only to be hauled out by her hair. And what would happen to him? A beating in the rain while he maintained undying devotion?

In fact the sky was cloudless. And Jisun was more likely to laugh in her father's face than fall to her knees weeping. Nor would Sunam voluntarily endure a beating for love or any other reason.

"Driver, can you tell me anything? Stop the car."

The driver ignored him.

THE OFFICE WAS a study in navy and light wood, polished to a high sheen. The grain of the wood was wavy and irregular, reminding Sunam of sunlight refracted through a clear lake. He could sense the richness of it, almost smell its vitality. Yet compared with the grandeur of the rooms in Ahn's house, his office was human-sized, designed for utility.

On the low table between their armchairs were two steaming cups of tea and a plate of sliced pears, each glistening sliver garnished with a bamboo toothpick. The tea was too hot, but Sunam gulped it anyway, scalding his tongue and sending a searing pain through his mouth. From everything he had heard about the great Ahn Kiyu, he had developed a certain mental picture: a man whose physical presence evoked words such as *executive* and *tycoon*. In reality, Ahn, wearing a white buttoned shirt and loose brown trousers, reminded Sunam of a senior mathematics professor. He stood at average height, with slender neck and shoulders, trim waist, and long, wiry limbs. His face, on the brief occasions that he smiled, erupted into a series of vertical wrinkles from cheekbone to chin.

"I hope I haven't disrupted your schedule today," he said in a cordial voice, as if they were business associates conducting the prelude to an important deal.

"That's all right," Sunam said. He had planned to see Jisun today. It struck him that Ahn might know that as well. He cleared his throat and said, "I was just planning to study with my girlfriend in the library. She's always there, but I'm . . . not nearly so disciplined. I'll join her after this."

"You mean Namin," said Ahn.

"Yes, I forgot you must know her well."

"An extremely bright young woman. Very determined. I'm sure she will go far."

"Yes."

"You say you're not as disciplined?" said Ahn. "Are you less interested in your future than she is in hers?"

"Less interested? No. Just not as talented."

"Not as motivated, perhaps."

It was uncomfortable chatting like this when he still had no idea why he had been summoned. When he'd arrived he was almost certain that Ahn must know about him and Jisun, but the more time passed in small talk, the less likely it seemed. Surely he would have said something by now, or at least given some signal of displeasure. Instead, Ahn seemed . . . if not exactly jovial, then friendly. His manner of conversation seemed to say he understood more about Sunam than he might have thought. Such as: His girlfriend was leagues more motivated and brilliant than he was. And: He did not deserve such an extraordinary young woman's affections. And: He needed to try harder to keep up with her. But these were gentle, almost sympathetic, criticisms. Despite his formidable reputation, Ahn did not seem to know what was happening under his own roof.

Ahn helped himself to a piece of fruit, carefully removing the toothpick and popping the morsel into his mouth with his fingers instead. His white teeth flashed as he chewed. He wiped his fingers on a handkerchief before reaching for another slice, once again removing the toothpick and grabbing with his fingers—a strange ritual mixing fastidiousness and blunt appetite.

"Eat," said Ahn, pushing the plate in Sunam's direction. Sunam hastily grabbed the piece closest to him by the toothpick—then removed it and ate with his fingers as Ahn had done. The juice was not sticky, but he did not have anything to wipe his hands on. With a sly look, the old man passed him the handkerchief he had been using and watched as Sunam uncomfortably blotted his hands.

"You must be wondering why I've asked you to come," Ahn said. "Or do you already know?"

"I'm sorry, I don't."

Ahn studied him for a long moment. "I'm not surprised to hear you say that, but I am disappointed. Then I'll be clear. It's about my daughter, Jisun. I believe you two know each other quite well."

A large muscle in Sunam's eye spasmed, and for a horrifying second, he worried that it had appeared as a *wink*. Quickly he scrubbed his eye with the heel of his hand. If the old man noticed, his expression did not change. "As you know, I have two children. The elder, my son, has returned to his studies in Germany."

"The former president of the Circle," Sunam said, eager to show his knowledge of Min and steer the conversation away from Jisun. It dawned on him that perhaps Ahn needed him in the same capacity that he might be using Juno. An informant. Perhaps it had come to his attention that he and Jisun were *friends* and he wanted a closer observer than Juno, who was certainly not her friend. If that was the case, if Ahn wanted another spy, then the matter was simple. He would refuse. Unequivocally. It was sheer relief to have figured it out, to know that he was prepared to do the right thing in the face of pressure.

"Yes. President of the Circle," repeated Ahn with thick condescension. "He would like to be president of every circle he stumbles over. Every circle, every square. The triangles, too, why not?"

"You disapprove of the Circle?"

"The Circle is not the problem," he said. "I'm talking about my son. No vision, no discipline, but popular everywhere he goes. Beloved. He lives to be beloved. If I leave my company to him, he will run it competently. And when he feels he has done enough, he will sell it to one of his new foreign friends. Someone as foolish as he, with deep enough pockets.

"One day I must choose an heir who will not sell my legacy, who will protect what I've built and grow it," Ahn said. "Between my son and daughter, I have one adequate option, and one wild. But I prefer the girl. Even as children, she had the stronger mind. She knew her own will completely. So you see why you must not interfere."

Interfere? Sunam had been listening as if hypnotized by Ahn's voice, stunned by the revelations the old man was sharing. He could not imagine a father who would feel dissatisfied by a son of Min's capacity and who would perversely bet on the daughter, who despised and opposed him.

"She may be the stronger, but she will never see it your way." Sunam didn't know where he was getting the courage to speak like this, but he had nothing to lose.

"Have you ever noticed, Sunam, how someone like my daughter, who is so headstrong, so decisive, can change one hundred eighty degrees when she sets her mind to changing? With the right circumstances, the right influences. She is still young and I have time to wait. And watch. So you see."

"I don't understand what you mean," Sunam said.

"I believe I have been exceedingly candid with you, more than the situation required," Ahn said coldly. "I expect the same courtesy in return. I was notified several weeks ago by a hotel employee. You were at the Intercontinental with my daughter. You were there overnight. These last weeks, you have been in my home a dozen times. I have no need for the details of your relationship, but I will make myself clear. There's a long way ahead before Jisun finds her proper path. She resists it now, but there is time, as I said, for change. In the meantime I see numerous obstacles which may prove costly for her future."

"I have no intention of obstructing her future," Sunam said. He hoped to match Ahn's icy tone, but he knew he sounded anything but calm. Ahn knew everything and yet he had conducted this meeting as if his interests were purely abstract. The emotional aspects of his daughter's entanglements did not factor at all. Sunam understood the facts, but he struggled to catch up to the implications of Ahn's knowledge. His mind buzzed stupidly. He was a cartoon character after a decisive knockout, his bruised and battered cranium surrounded by whirling stars.

"You were not the obstacle I had in mind, but let's begin with you. I'm not an unreasonable man, Sunam, and I remember what it is to be young. To be young is to be passionate and full of unmade mistakes.

At this age it is easy to make big swings. Everything is potential. You form attachments that feel life changing, momentous. And suddenly a relationship that should have lasted mere weeks or months becomes a lifetime—and both people are ruined.

"I know *you* are not the one to ruin her," he said, answering Sunam's question before it had fully formed in his mind. "The American missionary—Peter, was it?—was a concern. Fortunately they have been separated for the time being. But I would prefer to have more security.

"Let me speak to you frankly, as men. It would have been smarter to stay where you were with Namin. But now you are mixed up. A girl like her, Namin, who is already on her path, will not tolerate this kind of betrayal. You've made it difficult for yourself. No doubt you must see that."

Sunam squirmed silently, unable to defend himself. This was a narrative of his present circumstances in the most efficient, factual manner possible. And yet there was the unspoken hint of threat. Sunam had made it difficult for himself, Ahn seemed to say, but it could easily be worse. Was it exposure he was threatening? It would take only a tap for Sunam to tumble the long way down.

He saw now that the conversation was building to this—the enumeration of his many failures so that Ahn could provide the solution, which he would likely have no choice but to take. Some ruthless answer that would either slay or save him. His adrenaline ratcheted between fear and anticipation, wondering how the boss would play the next step and how he would respond.

Ahn stood up and walked back to his desk. He opened a drawer and retrieved a black lacquered box. The box was the size of two encyclopedias, stacked atop each other. Its cover was inlaid with fiery bursts of abalone and mother-of-pearl, its brass hinges etched with roses. He placed it on the table. It breathed between them like a living thing, daring Sunam to touch it.

Ahn lifted the lid to reveal ten-thousand-won notes, neatly cordoned with red bands. As casually as choosing cigarettes from a pack, he selected two bundles and slid them in front of Sunam. The impact of that simple action wiped his mind blank, and he stared at the bills without understanding. He had never seen money so pristine, so utterly divorced from the concept of commerce. These were brand-new bills so stiff and clean they looked as edible as the fruit on the plate. Sunam could pick one up and lick it.

"This is a payment in good faith," Ahn said. "A million won. Just a taste of the future if you agree to meet my conditions."

Sunam stared at Ahn in alarm. He was so staggered by the easy mention of this amount—as if they were speaking of a simple lunch bill and not the equivalent of a college graduate's annual salary—that the notion of payment and the accompanying questions—to whom? for what?—came as an aftershock. He could not imagine that Ahn was actually offering him the money stacked so neatly in front of him, nor could he fathom the possible meaning of such a gesture.

Ahn continued calmly, ignoring Sunam's stupefaction. "My conditions are simple. You will continue to see my daughter. It is my preference that you see her for four years—the remaining years of your education and the year following. You will keep her occupied, away from the American or anyone else who might disrupt my plans for her future. After that she will go abroad to study like her brother. At that time, you will release her without any encumbrances. I call these my preferences, as of course I cannot force you to continue the relationship, as you cannot force her. But if you can manage until graduation, there will be another payment, far more sizable. Furthermore, you may expect a long career of your choice in one of my companies. I never forget a favor—or a job well done."

The arrogance and foresight of the plan cut off Sunam's breath. Now he understood. Ahn had merely been biding his time, calculating the ways in which he might use Sunam to his advantage, devising the perfect solution. And who was he? A placeholder, someone who could safely occupy Jisun's time until the critical phase of her life could be activated abroad. He was being offered a princely reward for the privilege of distracting Ahn's daughter. The prize represented the total fulfillment of his wildest ambitions. In his heart, Sunam knew this was the closest he might ever get to achieving them. It should have been an exhilarating prospect, akin to being shown a dazzling future all within his reach. And yet the insult of being considered a voiceless pawn in Ahn's plan gnawed at his pride.

Far from being considered a threat, Ahn had cast him as the collaborator, docile and trouble-free. More than anything, it was this realization that humiliated Sunam.

I know you are not the one to ruin her.

"Without encumbrances?" he said bitterly, recklessly. "Do you expect people to just turn a switch according to a date on a calendar? And what happens if it doesn't end in four years, if your schedule is violated?"

Ahn replaced the lid and it shut with a soft click. A subtle sound of closure that struck Sunam as supreme luxury, confidence that did not require a double check.

"There's no point discussing things that will never happen. The timeline is four years. I find that very generous.

"I will leave you now. When you have made your decision, you may see yourself out. If you have taken the money, I will consider my terms accepted."

Ahn left the room. Sunam sat for what felt like a long time, staring at his hands, the money on the table, the box gleaming where Ahn had left it, so confident that it would not be disturbed. He noticed his shirt was dotted with sweat and he could not think a complete thought through, could not link from one consequence to another. It was money he had not earned. It was money that didn't matter. Whether he took it or not, whom would it hurt? It was not a contract, not really. He could stop seeing Jisun tomorrow. Conversely, she could refuse to see him anytime, today even, and the money would still be his. *In good faith.* And if she refused to see him—today, tomorrow, a month from now—and he had walked away, leaving that fortune on the table, it would have been the most foolish decision of his life, a moment to regret for the ages. Jisun might even be pleased if he took the money, any loss of her father's being her gain. Jisun was a surprising girl. Perhaps if she were sitting here with him now, she would laugh at his indecision and goad him to take it. The truth was he didn't know her well enough to know for sure what she'd think.

Sunam picked up the bills and hefted the soft, solid weight in his hands. The corners were so taut and sharp, he could run his thumb along its edge and feel the nick.

He tucked the stacks in his satchel, first one and then the other. Thinking it was not yet decided. He was still testing it out.

He slung the satchel over his shoulder and strode out of the office, down a clanging metal staircase, into the street. At the corner he hailed the first taxicab he saw, but when the driver asked where he was going, Sunam could not recall his own address, where he had lived all his life.

"Where you going?" the driver asked again, the surly kind who would kick him out in a second if he did not speak up.

Sunam started to laugh, a rumbling rising from deep within his gut. "Driver, the strangest thing just happened to me. You'll never guess."

"Get out." The driver threw the car into gear. He would speed off the minute Sunam opened the door. He looked at Sunam's packed leather satchel, disgusted. Another privileged college kid, not knowing the value of real work. "Meter's running. Get out now before I charge you for my time."

Sunam opened his bag and peeled off the top note in his stash. "For your time." He put the money in the driver's hand and stumbled out of the car. Sweat ran freely down his back, emitting a green metallic smell like river mud, like iron. The car sped away. He was still laughing, his body convulsing as if in tears.

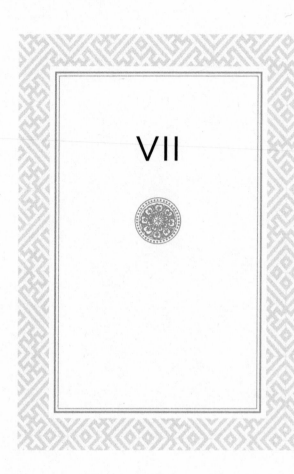

VII

1

....

Jisun was ten years old when her father presented her with her own bank account.

"This is your future, which you must nurture and protect," he said. "Open that book, what does it say?"

She opened the ledger, a palm-sized booklet bound in flannel-soft cardboard. It had a soft green cover stitched with white.

"At the top," he prompted.

"It says my name," she said.

"Which means you must know everything in this booklet as if it is your own face. Remember—this *is* your face to the world," he said. "I will test you. I expect you to pay attention."

Every month that first year, her father asked the closing balance on her account. The interest she had accrued. The rate.

It was meaningless to her, this column of numbers. Up. Down. Red. Black. Even when she made a genuine effort, the numbers seemed to fall from her like water through a sieve.

"February balance."

"Around twenty thousand won."

"*Two three three six four.* You just lost over three thousand won. Three thousand three hundred sixty-four, to be exact. That's what happens when you don't know. You get cheated and robbed."

It took Jisun months to realize there were deposits and withdrawals from her account that she had not made. Her father, simulating thefts and windfalls, had engineered these fluctuations as a teaching tool. He had expected her to catch them right away, but she had not noticed until he pointed them out in anger.

"Three thousand three hundred sixty-four," he said, enumerating the extent of his disappointment in her. "By tomorrow you will produce a list of one hundred separate things you can buy with that money. *One hundred things.*"

Where did one find out how much a hundred different things cost? The next morning after breakfast, Jisun asked *ajumma* how much it cost to buy the breakfast they had just eaten.

Ajumma looked at her, eyes narrowed. "It cost enough."

"But each thing separately," Jisun said. "How much do those fried fish cost?"

"They don't sell them fried, young lady. Didn't you see them sizzling at the table? I fried them myself."

"Raw, then," Jisun insisted.

"Those are *jogi*. Four hundred won apiece."

"How about the spinach."

"Ten won."

"Only ten?"

"Would you like them to cost more?"

"How about that apron, the one you're wearing?" she asked. "What does it cost?"

"Are you planning to become a cook?" *ajumma* said, exasperated. "You don't need to know how much these things cost."

"*Abba* says I do," she said. "He says I need a list."

"The apron was fifty-five won last spring."

"So little?" Jisun asked, thinking of the fish. "But surely an apron must cost more than a silly fish."

"That fish is a king's meal. I used to dream of them as a girl."

"Do you eat them all the time now that you're a grown-up?"

"When young ladies don't finish their portions," *ajumma* said archly.

"I wouldn't eat mine at all if I knew how much you liked it. I don't like fish anyway."

Jisun looked at *ajumma*. Every day she wore the same kind of apron, and a predictably shapeless dress in brown, gray, or green, and white slippers that shuffled on the brightly polished floor. "*Ajumma*, do you earn a lot of money?" she asked.

"Your father knows how much I earn, you don't need to write it on his list."

"But *I* don't know," she said. "The list is supposed to teach me, not him. I'm sure he knows how much a *jogi* costs, and spinach."

"Surely he knows," said *ajumma* with an unreadable expression, a mixture of fatigue, admiration, and something else—possessive fear. "Your father knows the price of spinach before I do."

"But what does he pay you?" Jisun asked.

"Six thousand won a month."

"Six thousand." Jisun thought of the number in her account and the number she had theoretically misplaced by not paying attention. "Is that a lot?"

Ajumma folded the flowered cloth she was using to clean the table, efficiently halving the rag once, twice, before wiping the surface clean a final time. "If it isn't, I wouldn't know. Now go upstairs, I'm busy."

1. Eight *jogi* fish, raw
2. Three hundred sixty-four sides of spinach
3. Sixty-one aprons
4. More than half of *ajumma*'s monthly salary
5. Fifty pounds of rice
6. Twenty-nine school notebooks
7. A leather-bound English–Korean dictionary
8. Monthly salary, pesticide-spray truck driver
9. Seven pairs of indoor rubber slippers
10. Six hundred thirty-two aspirin pills

It was supposed to teach her the value of money, but Jisun learned instead that money was the least reliable measure, sliding from great value to worthlessness depending on the spender. With the same amount of money, you could feed a family for a month or a single person one extravagant meal. You could pay a man's wages or unlock two thousand pages of vocabulary, an entire universe of words. You could clothe a soccer team. You could save someone's life.

"You did well," her father said. To prove her ease with his purported punishment, she had far exceeded one hundred items, squeezing in calculations in the margins to check her arithmetic. The last line she scribbled before handing him the page was: *137. The amount of money someone could have taken from me without my knowledge.* Whether he interpreted the line as an apology or forgave it as mild impertinence, Jisun had the satisfaction of knowing she had added her signature to the punishment. A proper flourish.

"This is your inheritance," he said. "Not only the money, but the knowledge"—he ruffled the page—"the discipline, to protect it as you would a member of your family. Inheritance *is* family."

Despite earning her father's approval, the list did not make her pay closer attention to her account. The following month, her guesses were further off the mark than ever. Assuming she would be watching, her father had made even more numerous, significant changes. Jisun, making the opposite assumption—that he would leave her alone now that she had passed his test—never saw them.

Over time, the monthly questioning stretched to bimonthly. Then became more infrequent still. Jisun could see her father's expectations, his stock in her, waning. She did not need a ledger to see that.

The last test she remembered—she was thirteen, it was the spring she had been reprimanded at school for letting her hair grow half a centimeter beyond the compulsory length—her father closed the account book and left it on the table between them. Again she had failed. And this time, his disappointment boiled over into anger.

"Go outside," he said. It was after dinner, the windows opaque against the night. Outside, the air was chilly and damp with impending rain. "I want you to stay out there and don't come in until—no, don't take a jacket. I paid for that jacket with money. Money you don't care about." He picked up the account book and slapped it hard against the edge of the table as if confirming a prior agreement, a deal gone sour. "Inside doesn't exist without money. You know what buys this roof? These walls? What does it cost to buy a roof, Jisun? What does it cost to buy a jacket?" he said. "Go outside and think about it. See if you don't care when you're cold and miserable. Don't come in until you do."

"Until I what—die?"

"I assume you'll be smarter than that. Let's not make this an unnecessary contest of wills."

Jisun was tempted to go outside and stand in the middle of the garden like a tree. Or to start walking and not stop at the gate but continue on into the city, into the world beyond the reach of her father.

But it was raining and cold. And she realized her father *expected* her to make a spectacle of her defiance. He expected her to suffer to make her point. He assumed that much about her character.

They both knew exactly how it would go. She would go outside, fuming. She would vow to stay out there until she died, frozen like a shrimp curled against the foundation, seeking whatever vestigial warmth might seep through stone and brick. *Ajumma* would come with a blanket and contraband jacket and whisper harshly that she must apologize and get into a hot bath immediately. And her father would pretend not to know what was happening, though there was nothing he did not know that went on under his roof.

And what would any of it prove other than that Jisun was willing to inflict pain on herself in order to spite her father? He had already won his point.

So she got up, walked briskly to the door, and opened it, letting in a gust of wind. With one hand still on the doorknob, she stepped outside. She counted one beat, then came back inside, letting the door slam.

"Good enough?" she asked. She could not tell if she was trembling from frustration or cold.

"'Good enough' is why anyone can steal your money. You haven't learned anything."

"It's not my money, it's yours," she said. "And they can have it."

The baby had no name, first or last. The birth record, when Namin tracked it down, simply listed the infant as "Baby Boy." The mother: Kyungmin Kang. The father: Hal Jackson. He was born, also according to the record, on the morning of October 16, weighing 2.4 kg. Until Kyungmin showed up at their door—feverish, her milk dried up, the baby wrapped in her coat and wearing just a soiled diaper drooped to his knees—they hadn't even known he was born. They focused on the immediate crisis. Put the sick girl to bed. Check the baby for fever. Is he hungry? Will he drink? He suckled their littlest finger with desperate focus. Namin ran out for diapers, formula, bleach. Although the items were urgent, she walked to a different neighborhood where she would not be recognized. Waiting for her change, she felt the shopkeeper's assessing curiosity: a girl too old to have an infant sibling, too young and obviously unmarried for a child of her own. Namin fought the urge to protest. *It isn't me.* But who? *My sister came home with a baby.* That was no better. She pushed down her pride and clamped her mouth shut.

Of Hal, Namin could make out from Kyungmin only that he was tied up in America. That he was coming.

"So he came back, then, from furlough? He saw the baby?" Namin asked, surprised and relieved.

"On his way," Kyungmin muttered. "On his way." She closed her eyes, falling into the kind of sleep that barely seemed to breathe.

They had never seen an infant so dirty. His pale skin had a sickly blue cast and was stained with watery feces and yellowed spit-up.

Weeping rashes bloomed behind his knees. There was a constellation of blisters, adult sized, under his chin, where Kyungmin's thin milk had become trapped and gone rancid.

Namin and her mother bathed him, handling his limbs as if he were a damaged bird. He lay still in the tepid water, watching them with slow, blinking eyes. Namin held his head and upper back while her mother washed around his neck, in the hollows under his arms, and around his wrinkled, swollen testicles, as purple as August plums. Namin didn't say it, but he had his father's long, skinny limbs. There was a slant to his chin that perfectly reflected Kyungmin, her sharp obstinacy and intelligence. Namin's mother swirled the short hairs on his head, cupping water over his soft hairline. Pulling him dripping out of the bath, she said, "Well, he looks like us, anyway."

That day, Kyungmin slept for nineteen hours straight. When she woke up the following afternoon, she went out claiming she was in the mood for an ice cream.

Namin, watching her leave, said, "At least put on a pair of socks. It's freezing." After a golden summer that seemed to linger well into October, the weather had recently turned bitter. Overnight, white silvery frost gathered on the windowsills and blackened the last of the pepper plants, which had produced for months as if they would never stop. The peppers left on the vine became shriveled and surprisingly sweet, their natural sugars crystallized by the cold.

Kyungmin replied she was only going around the block; she just needed a bit of air. She left in the same outfit she had arrived in, dragging her shoes with the crushed heels through the November slush, her ankles white under a long knitted dress. They let her go without a fuss, thinking ice cream was a positive symbol of homecoming, signaling a return of normal appetites.

When there was still no sign of her by the second morning, Namin took the bus to Itaewon, to the apartment she had visited with Sunam. At 5U, there was a yellow and blue tricycle parked in front of the door. She could plainly hear the children's voices inside—the yodeling prattle of a little girl and a younger child of indeterminate sex, shrieking.

She rang the bell anyway. A young blond woman came to the door, huge pink rollers attached to the ends of her hair. "Oh," she said. Her blue eyes jumped at Namin as if they'd met before. The children stared from the mouth of the hallway, the exact spot where Namin had once examined a photograph of Hal with his family. "Yes?"

"Nothing," Namin blurted. It was the only word that came to mind. The lady started to close the door, her lips drawn tight against her teeth.

"Wait," Namin said. "Where is the owner?"

"We live here now."

"I meant owner of the building."

"Rental office is on the first floor. Ask them there." The lady shut the door. The children resumed yelling. After a few seconds, as if the pink-roller lady were on the other side listening for her footsteps, Namin heard the dead bolt turn.

She walked down to the ground floor, trying to postpone the inevitable conclusion. Her sister was gone. This apartment was the only place she knew for sure Kyungmin had lived, but it was clear she hadn't lived there for some time. She had been gone long enough for a new family to move in and unpack, for the children to leave toys outside the door.

The rental office was staffed by a dark-haired American man, wearing a short-sleeved khaki shirt despite the frigid weather. "Hal Jackson? Hasn't lived here in a coupla months. Can't say where he might be now. Girlfriend of his"—he made a gesture over his belly, indicating her pregnancy—"she probably went back to her folks. . . . You a relation?"

"Yes, her sister."

"Well, then you probably know better than me where she is."

"Thank you."

Namin went home. She tried to convince herself that her sister would be there. With no money, she couldn't have gone far. She had probably gone to pick up her things and the baby's clothes. Maybe she had gone to find out about Hal. Maybe he had been transferred somewhere south that required a long bus ride. Kyungmin had been so delirious, maybe she had meant to tell them but forgot. She would get in touch soon.

In her heart, Namin knew none of these scenarios were likely. What was the point of inventing stories and lying to herself? It doubled the work of dealing with the obvious reality. She stopped pretending. Her sister was gone.

At home, her mother was boiling the new diaper cloths in bleach. They took turns stirring the pot with a long wooden paddle. Huge plumes of chemical-smelling steam rolled into their faces. Namin told her what she could: how she knew where to go, the new family living there, Hal's vacancy as of two months ago. Her mother asked no questions. She fished out a diaper as if she did it every day, examining it to see if it was white enough. She waited until Namin stopped talking and said briskly, "I wouldn't bother yourself. Either she'll turn up or she won't. She knew what she was doing when she left."

There was a permanent ridge between her mother's brows that hadn't been there before Kyungmin first left home, a slump to her back that made her seem like somebody's ancient grandmother instead of her own recently vigorous mother. Despite these obvious signs of grief, she spoke about Kyungmin as if discussing someone else's daughter. *What's done is done,* she seemed to say. *What's spilt is spilt.* It was Namin who felt newly rattled each time she saw the baby, as if he had only ever been an idea, a symbol of her sister's rebellion that would eventually vanish. Even though she had seen her sister's pregnant belly and, indirectly, in a photo at his apartment, the father of the child— she found she was still unprepared for the reality of his existence. And now Kyungmin was gone, leaving him in her place like a conjuring trick. One for one. An unequal exchange.

"She's made her decision," her mother said. "Can't force someone to be a mother."

"She made her decision, but what about us?" Namin asked. "What are we supposed to do with him?" Already she had a sinking feeling about who would end up caring for him in Kyungmin's absence. Her parents had to work—and who else was there?

Her mother looked critically at the child. "He's weaker than a day-old hatchling. I imagine we'd better get some weight on him."

Namin waited to hear the end of that sentence, but there wasn't anything else. *We'd better get some weight on him*—and then what? Would they keep him? If not, what difference did it make how much he weighed?

"And then?"

"And then the next thing," her mother snapped. Her eyes flashed, daring Namin to ask another question. She shut her mouth.

Namin wrung out the boiled diapers to hang on the line in the courtyard. The steaming cloths quickly cooled to cold, heavy lumps. Wringing the excess water felt like trying to squeeze barely thawed meat. Her hands turned bright red, then fell numb. By the morning, the fabric would have dried to planks on the line, rough on the baby's skin.

Sterilizing cloth, dissolving formula, they were already making decisions. The baby, as small as he was, seemed wise to his predicament. Whether they wrapped him in Namin's undershirts—the smallest clothing they had available—or rags, whether they fed him cold, lumpy milk or neglected to change him for hours, he made small mewing noises like a kitten but did not cry. He took his bottle with single-minded determination, as if he had been given his work order. Gain weight. Thrive.

He was building his case, becoming a person his family could not deny.

The case for kin.

METHODICALLY, NAMIN WENT to every bar in Itaewon. She took a photo of her sister. She described Hal. *Have you seen them? Have they been here?* The hostesses and bar owners treated her as if she were some kind of door-to-door evangelist, oozing that same naive high-mindedness that embarrassed and bored them. They glanced at the photo. Namin hadn't been able to find a recent one, so it was Kyungmin in her black-and-white high school uniform, her hair cut severely to the ear. *Nope, not here. Try down the street.* They were tired of family members coming with photos of girls who had once been predictable and good, girls who had disappeared into the night.

Namin went into a bar called Starlight, where the proprietor plainly did not believe she was looking for her sister.

"Your sister?" He cocked his head and seemed to peer around her, as if considering how she might look in a different dress. "What did you say her name was?" When Namin repeated her name, she knew he wasn't listening.

"How old are you? You'll do all right. I can offer you Thursday and Friday nights to start." He smiled broadly, a man happy with his decision. "You'll be making good money in no time. With your looks?" He winked. "No time at all."

Namin thought, *This must be the place.* This must be where her sister had started. Not because Kyungmin wouldn't have seen through him, but because she must have been desperate enough to agree.

"If my sister comes here"—she enunciated coldly, carefully—"tell her we need her at home. Tell her to get in touch. It's important. Please—"

"Thursdays and Fridays." He wet his finger and smoothed out an air bubble in the black vinyl covering the windows. Namin imagined all the smears of spit layered on that window, all the air bubbles flattened and folded into slits. "You think about it," he said.

3
. . . .

Kyungmin's son came to be called Dori, which was not a proper name but a nonsense baby word. *Dori-dori-dori,* something you said while tickling an infant to make him gurgle and smile. When Kyungmin had arrived with the baby in such scandalous shape, they hadn't stopped to ask what she'd named him. Thinking there was plenty of time later, thinking it was the least of their concerns. They were preoccupied with rash ointments and cheap formula that, rather than dissolve, gathered in gray clumps inside the bottle. If they were honest, they knew they were punishing her by not asking his name. Not fully acknowledging her right to be a mother. Kyungmin had matched that expectation by walking away.

That first week Namin stared at the child, peering into his eyes, willing him to tell her what Kyungmin had called him. She realized he would never be able to say, not even when he was older and able to speak. It would be buried so far in his nascent consciousness—if a name had ever existed at all. It was possible that her sister had never called him anything. Sunam had told her what Kyungmin had said at the bar in Itaewon. *If it has no father, why should it have a mother?*

It was this fact that made Namin pity him more than anything else: that he would never know what his own mother had imagined for his identity. The elemental gift of a name.

No one said the family words: grandson, grandmother, nephew. No one counted the days to plan his *baekil,* his one-hundredth-day celebration. Everything surrounding his existence was suspended in uncertainty. Who was he? Did he belong to them or to his other family in America? Would they keep him and, if so, for how long? If they didn't, what reason would they ultimately give themselves for letting him go? Would they justify abandoning the baby as they had justified leaving Hyun? *He'll be more comfortable there. . . .*

Until then, Dori was a permanent visitor, a burden, a future, a past. A homeless orphan with a startlingly familiar face.

To help with expenses, they found a boarder to rent Namin's room. Namin was relocated to the living room and the baby placed under her care. Her parents, the only income earners, needed to sleep if they were to survive sixteen-hour days on their feet in the cold, with only a plastic tent to protect them from the elements. To clear room for her sleeping mat, all the living room furniture was shoved against the wall. When she could find the time to study, she had to climb over the sofa and wedge herself into her desk like a puzzle piece, shimmying sideways into the chair since there wasn't enough room to pull it out. It was like being suspended in the eye of a tornado, living and sleeping with all the artifacts of her life crowded around as if ready to tumble down.

In a few days, the Kang household regained a semblance of its pre-Dori rhythm. Her parents went to work. Kyungmin was still missing. Only Namin's life was completely upturned. The baby colonized huge portions of her day that she should have spent studying. Instead she was washing his diapers, feeding him, changing him, walking him around when he was fussy, begging him to sleep.

The first weeks passed this way in a black haze of panic. Namin was so exhausted, she fell asleep as soon as she sat down. The bitter taste of bile was constant in the back of her throat, threatening to spill over. Everything she ate turned to lead in her stomach.

The neighborhood seemed to come alive with advice flung at her door, as if she had suddenly become an underdog fighter facing a fierce opponent. *Don't pick him up the minute he starts crying, he'll become a terror. Don't mention his mother, they hear everything even at this age, you know. Better watch he doesn't eat you out of house and home, must take after his father.* They were no longer fans wishing her well, but a nosy mob jeering her rough odds. Namin became jittery about leaving the house. She wanted to hide out in her room and not see or speak to anyone until she had regained what she remembered of her composure. Only she no longer had a room to hide in, and she could not be alone in her house. She had an infant and a boarder—both strangers, both intruders. And even if she tried to hide away, people came to her door. People who never listened when she told them to go away.

"What you should have done is taken in a female boarder," Jisun said. Namin had said nothing about the baby, and here she was, playing with Dori on the floor; Sunam must have told her. Just thinking about him talking about her problems, especially to Jisun, enraged her. But Namin didn't have the energy to fight anyone other than herself. Herself and this creature, who as the days wore on discovered his voice. Who wailed with full-throated agony, making up for lost time. Jisun was bent over Dori, letting him grab her little finger, pulling it back and forth as if he were a fish on a line. "Look at him. He's so *serious*," she said. "I guess he really is related to you guys after all.

"Anyway, back to what I was saying. A female boarder, someone with experience with babies. She could take care of the baby and pay you a little less for the room. Or pay no rent. Whatever makes sense."

Whatever makes sense. Nothing made sense. She hated how Jisun's glib suggestions implied that they had overlooked an obvious solution, as if they only needed guidance from someone like her to haul themselves out of their troubles.

"Just the room wouldn't be enough—whoever it was would want to be paid." It was like explaining physics to a child. "Anyway, why would a woman like that board all the way out here? She could make a lot more working for a richer family." *Or even the factory*, she was going to say, but she didn't want to incite another one of Jisun's speeches. "Like your *ajumma*," Namin said instead.

"You know I wasn't a baby when she came. She didn't raise me."

"The point is, she was a young woman once when she hired herself out to live with another family. Can you imagine someone like your *ajumma* living here? As it is, we pay the neighbor when I have to go to campus. We couldn't afford to pay for more than that."

"Maybe I could help," Jisun said.

Namin looked at her. "You want to watch the baby?"

"Well, no. Not that. But I can help you find someone to watch him—"

"I already told you, we can't afford it."

"But couldn't you let me pay for it? I'm sure I have the money. Let me, Namin. It would be so much easier for you," Jisun said in a rush, as if heaping on more words would prevent Namin from turning her down. "You wouldn't have to do a thing. I'll take care of everything. You don't even have to think about it."

Namin felt the blood rush to her face, darts of heat and pain as if she were being attacked from the inside. She ached to say yes, to finally surrender to the reality between them. It would be so easy for Jisun; the money made no difference to her. But for Namin, it would be life-saving. Like being lifted from a scene moments before a catastrophic explosion and taken away to safety, as if she had never been in danger.

But she couldn't say yes. She couldn't agree that she was powerless and Jisun so carelessly powerful. *I'm sure I have the money.* She had to give it away to remember she even had it.

"People *want* to think about their own lives. At least I do," Namin said. "I can't accept."

"But wouldn't it be better if you didn't have to think about certain things? Like rushing back to pick up the kid. Or how long it's been since his last bottle. You're already so busy, Namin. This can't be what you want to think about right now."

It was so absurd that she almost laughed. Of course it wasn't what she wanted to think about. But it didn't mean she would take Jisun's money. Was that what she would do, have Jisun and her money solve all her problems going forward? First, Hyun. Now Dori. The laughter died in her throat.

"We all have things we have to think about. Even if we don't want to."

"What difference does it make who pays for it? It isn't even my money, you know that."

"And yet you get to give it away," Namin said. "Seems like your money to me."

Jisun didn't leave immediately after that. She lingered, as if aware of the fact that the door to their relationship was closing for good. This would be one of the last times they were alone together. One of the last times they would remember being young. Though they didn't feel it at the moment, in retrospect they would see. They were still young then.

"Do you remember when we visited Hyun, how he thought we were both his sisters?" Jisun asked before leaving. Namin nodded. She remembered how long it had taken her brother to fix her in his mind. *So* you're *my sister?*

"I always wished we were," Jisun said. "Sisters, I mean." She seemed to pause, to give Namin a chance to echo the sentiment. When Namin didn't, Jisun busied herself tickling the baby, arranging his hair over his soft, bumpy skull, waving his arms in jerky approximations of dancing.

"She'll come back," Jisun said. They both knew she didn't mean it. It was another form of charity, a small kindness Namin could accept without debt.

"Sure," Namin said. "Maybe."

4
. . . .

t was not true that you could not force someone to be a mother. You could easily make it happen. Namin knew because it was happening to her.

Every moment Dori was awake, she was longing for the moment when he would close his eyes and sleep.

She could tie him to her back and walk the length of the small courtyard with a book in her hand. If she kept moving, he was more likely to let her read in peace. But trying to study with an infant on her back was like being hunted, constantly looking over her shoulder and jumping at the smallest sounds. She told herself she would get used to it. She would emulate those women in the market, walking with a platoon of children variously wrapped and hanging from their bodies. *But not too used to it.* Namin had never felt overly keen about babies to begin with, but now she was certain she would not want any of her own. In one month, she had already paid the penalty of a lifetime.

She read the same phrases in her texts over and over, her eyes clearly going over the print but her mind shuttered against the meaning. It seemed so long ago that she had been able to read for hours uninterrupted, soaking up oceans of information, limited only by the parameters of her patience and wakefulness. Now every mundane task required a dedicated strategy, combined with dexterities of hand and mind she had not previously considered possible.

And instead of learning her organic chemistry, her infectious diseases, her general anatomy—Namin learned about babies.

Why they went naked in the summer. Why they were ever present on a woman's back. One minute of inattention—he could drown in bathwater too shallow to properly wash a grown man's foot. He could suffocate from the weight of his own head. Everything was a threat against his life. Everything, including himself.

Every day, Namin boiled diapers in the same basin she washed him in. First she scraped the soiled muslin with a flat gray stone, washing the mess off her hands afterward. Then she scrubbed it with a hard brush, raising a dun-specked lather more disgusting than the original mess. Then rinse. Boil. Hang dry. Postponing the wash for another day only made it worse—the mess caked into the fabric, becoming harder to scour. The boiling took longer, the stirring and inspecting seemingly endless, while the baby cried and cried. Namin trained herself to do the wash in the afternoon, midway between lunch and dinner, but even the briefest thought of the task ruined whatever she was eating. Sometimes she bolted awake in the middle of the night, gagging.

A thick rubber cord tied with an overhand knot held the diaper at Dori's waist. The cord was hollow and soft, more like tubing than a band. As the baby grew, Namin let out the knot. If she forgot and the cord grew tight, it left a red welt around his belly. He grew plump while Namin lost weight. Her shirts billowed around her waist. Pants legs swished at her ankles, slapping like sails in the wind.

She dreamed constantly about Hyun. He was showing her the house they had built together, the floors glistening with polish. The halls wide enough for his chair. The rooms glided past, every color and texture and smell. *See, we did it, we really did it.* Inside the house there was a courtyard lined with potted trees. Mature figs and dwarf laceleaf maples and a leaning juniper tree, buffeted by invisible wind. The tree roots grew over the rims of the pots as if at any minute they could crawl up and out. A blue jay screamed from the topmost eave of the roof.

They need bigger pots, she said. *Look, the clay is cracking. They'll topple.*

Hyun shrugged. *But let me show you this other room*—the rooms were endless. On and on. You could live in this house for a lifetime and never see the same room twice.

See what we did, Hyun said. *It's even better than we ever said it would be. Why are you crying?*

She woke up with tears on her face, gasping. The smell of that juniper was still in her nostrils—as if it were planted right outside the door.

The baby was sleeping on his back, one arm raised to his ear. A frown wrinkled his brow. She could no longer pretend he looked just like Kyungmin. He was becoming a stranger, his foreign genes swallowing up whatever might have been familiar. Namin could already see how he'd look in a year. Three years. Ten. A kid she'd raised. A kid who had nothing to do with her.

5

. . . .

Busan Mother had six children of her own, the eldest twelve and the youngest three. She had arrived in Seoul as a bride more than a decade prior, when her young face, round like a silk cushion, belied the shrewd mannerisms of a woman four times her age. Her regional accent and dialect were so colorful that people in Miari collected her phrases like souvenirs. In the market, the vendors remarked how she always knew when they were fibbing a price or saving a better product for someone else. *Like a little devil,* they said, affectionately at first but with increasing wariness as the years passed. She had the honeyed tongue of a snake charmer, they said, but the bite of a cobra.

She claimed she had raised eleven younger siblings while her parents worked at the port of Busan. She had stood at the stove since she was five years old and pounded laundry and hauled *yeontan* coal bricks for fuel and done everything a mother did—aside from nursing them at her own breast. Her stories were mostly unverifiable, but people believed her. She *would* have raised eleven younger siblings, they said. How else did she know the price of everything from needles to eels?

Busan Mother was willing to keep an eye on the baby when Namin was on campus. "An eye? More like half an eye," Namin told Sunam later, explaining the arrangement. "An *eyelash.*" For this, Namin's mother negotiated a price, heavily padded with her cooking.

But the extra outings when Sunam wanted to take Namin on a date, a real date, when he was tired of seeing her at home—the two of them plus Dori, as if they were playing some terribly realistic game of house—were separate negotiations. Ever canny, Busan Mother made it pay.

"Seems like I saw some nice beef at the market," she'd say.

She eyed Sunam and then Namin, keen to judge who would be the weaker of the two. She always seemed to prey on him first, as if sensing his willingness to play the hero. "It's been a long time since my little ones had a treat like that. You gotta eat meat to grow up tall like this young man." She squeezed his arm, the soft flesh just under the biceps. "Not just rice and vegetables. Protein! Your mother must have fed you well, young man. Beef every week, eh? Twice a week?"

Sunam knew Namin would not have the money to buy the meat Busan Mother wanted. Namin complained about how much formula cost, even the cheapest kind, which she suspected must be cut with powdered rice or flour. There was absolutely no extra money, especially not for extravagances like beef. The Kang family never went hungry—her parents ran a *pojangmacha*, after all—but they ate the day's leftovers. Noodles and fish cakes, *tteokbokki, mandoo, jjigae*, and tofu. Cheap, tasty dishes anyone could afford. At the cart, they served the kind of meat that went well with *soju*. Blood sausage, pork skewers, whole dried squid charred over the fire. Chewy bits best served under dim lighting and doused in hot orange sauce.

The kind of meat Busan Mother wanted—*kalbi*—would cause a ruckus in her family. The kids would fight over it and talk about it for days, and the neighbors would sniff the air and wonder, *Who . . . ?* It was an unreasonable, exorbitant request, but Busan Mother had the power of gossip on her side. She telegraphed this without having to say a word. Who else would agree to bring a bastard child into her house? And not just a bastard, a GI baby, with his pale skin and unmistakable wide-eyed look. Lanky as a weed—*his daddy must have been a tall one*. She had kept quiet about him, hadn't she? She hadn't stirred the pot the way some other people would have. She hadn't asked if the kid would grow up next door, mixing with *her* children all day. *Such a confusing influence for them*. Really, she had been quite understanding.

Her gaze lingered over the SNU badge on Sunam's coat. An SNU couple. The two of them must have *such* a bright future ahead. How lovely.

"So the beef," Busan Mother said, her eyes hardening. "I can rely on it for dinner?"

And of course, Sunam had the money. Ahn's money. He could feel the bills practically rising from his wallet into his hands like a magic trick. He could pay Busan Mother's bribe twice a week for the rest of the semester, the rest of the year, and not feel a thing. Maybe this was how he would make it up to Namin, since he still had not figured a way out of his predicament. It occurred to him that the money would far outlive their relationship, yet on days like this when it felt almost normal between them, Sunam wondered if he could somehow make it right. It was a dilemma he could not unravel. But the *kalbi* was easy, a quick solution among all the other unsolvable problems. Although he knew he shouldn't dig himself deeper into her life, forcing gifts that would make her feel indebted to him in just the way she'd hate, he couldn't resist the temptation to be the big man for once.

"Is it *kalbi* you wanted, Busan Mother? If that's what you're in the mood for, we can buy some on our way home. Sure thing."

Namin had shot him a look he wished he could have captured in a photo. Incredulousness mixed with horror mixed with . . . gratitude? Admiration? He also savored Busan Mother's reaction: the surprise of a cat that had accidentally caught a fly out of midair. A big fat fly now buzzing between her teeth, rendering her speechless. All around, it had been a satisfying moment.

The minute they closed Busan Mother's gate behind them, Namin grabbed his arm. Whatever positive feelings she'd had had evaporated, and now she appeared on the verge of tears. "Don't you know we'll have to bring it every time after this?"

"Don't worry about it," he said.

"You should have talked to me first."

"It's a gift," he said. "You don't talk about gifts, you just give them."

"I don't see how I'm going to be able to keep this up. I told you how she is."

"Listen to me. It's not a problem," he said. "I'll take care of it."

BUT NAMIN WAS right about Busan Mother. She might have been surprised the first time, but after that she bargained as boldly as if they were at a real market. The rate of inflation was high throughout Seoul, but at Busan Mother's house it was astronomical.

"You know, this is the most difficult age. He doesn't sleep as much and cries like a blue chickadee. For attention, of course, not that he ever goes wanting." Her clever words tightened like a coil fastening around her goal, the money in Sunam's pocket. "You know how my little ones treat him like a precious doll. Watching everything he does! Hounding me like little devils the minute he's wet. You'd think he was a little lord, the way they fight to feed him. You never saw a baby eat so much! He's getting so spoiled at my house."

Sunam knew how the little ones dragged the baby into their street games and dropped him in the dirt when they grew tired of him. The youngest, Namin said, had once tried to feed Dori a "*kimbab* roll," a leaf stuffed with dog droppings.

"I saw some nice fish at the market today, Busan Mother," Namin said.

"Oh, but the children had their hearts set on beef. You know how children are when they're disappointed. They go on for days, begging and whining, giving a person such a headache."

"Of course, Busan Mother."

Having settled her dinner menu, Busan Mother bared her teeth jubilantly. "Have yourselves a nice long date. Don't worry a bit about this baby. He's like a little prince in Busan Mama's house. Our sad little Western prince."

Energetically, she shimmied Namin's waist with strong brown fingers, a broadly suggestive gesture apparently for Sunam's benefit. Someone else must have done the same to her once, six children ago.

She winked to make her meaning doubly clear. "You have a nice time now. Handsome young men like this don't turn up every day, eh?"

"I HATE HOW she does that," Namin said as soon as they were out of earshot. "Holding you over my head like a punishment."

"More like a prize." Sunam winked. "A handsome young man like me."

He looked at her. She was not smiling. "Come on," he said. "In a few years you'll never have to think about her again. Her or her six thousand children or what she eats for dinner. And you can buy me three *kalbi* dinners for each of the ones I bought. By that time, it won't even be hard for you. It'll be like buying a cup of coffee." He poked her mouth and pushed up the corners with his fingers. She batted his hand away, but he persisted.

"Come on, it's done. What's the point of being miserable about it?" There it was. A smile. "Just remember," he said. He slung an arm around her shoulders and held her tight, even though she tried to duck away. They were still in her neighborhood, and she liked to pretend they were not a couple, just friends, to keep the gossiping *ajummas* at bay. "I plan to charge you interest. Heaps and heaps of interest. You'll think Busan Mother was a saint compared to me."

"I'll remember that," she said. It was a real smile this time. "I doubt it, though. I don't think you have it in you to be so mean."

6

....

"Do you know about that guy Jisun is seeing?" Sunam asked her one day. They were sitting on a park bench, so cold that he was shivering even as he smoked. When he exhaled, the wind instantly whipped the smoke over their heads. Namin could almost get as much vapor from her breath as he could from the cigarette.

"Sure," she lied. She couldn't remember the last time she and Jisun had talked without arguing. Didn't Sunam know that? Or was the gossip such common knowledge that he expected her to have heard about it anyway? She was too tired to parse it out. "They getting serious?"

He was looking at her so strangely. "Seems like it could be. Or maybe she's just sleeping around," he said after a minute. "If that's what you mean by serious."

Sleeping around. It was odd how he said it so casually, as if people they knew did things like that. Or maybe Sunam wanted to make it seem that everyone else was doing it to make her feel guilty for being so stingy with him. Namin did feel guilty. But—she thought about Hyun and she thought about her sister, and she knew it would never be worth the risk. She had to be different. She had to make sure what happened to Kyungmin would never happen to her.

She yawned and leaned her head on his shoulder. "You know Jisun. She probably wants people to think she's having wild affairs, but you'd be surprised how chaste she really is. She's quite old-fashioned about love. Really, she's the type to obsess over just one guy privately for years."

"You're probably right," he said. He threw away his cigarette without putting it out. It rolled away from them, the burning end still glowing in the fierce wind.

"And what about you? Are you the type to moon over a guy for years?" he said, smiling too brightly. His face became a series of muscles in movement, lacking true warmth. Namin braced herself for the conversation she feared was coming. She couldn't believe he would bring it up at a time like this. Now? Right before meeting him today, she'd had to scrape shit from under her fingernails where it had gotten lodged doing the wash. She needed to buy some new rubber gloves. Gloves were what she needed. Not sex.

"Depends on the guy," she said. She still remembered how hard he had tried to impress her in the beginning, how grateful and surprised he'd seemed that she liked him, too.

"How about a guy like me?" he said. Again she could not decipher his tone. In the past he would have said it flirtatiously, probing for affirmation. But now his voice was flat.

"A guy like you would know without asking," she said, to buy herself more time.

"You think a guy like me is worth the trouble?"

Namin thought of her sister, who had gambled on that question, hoping the "trouble" would land her a husband and ticket to America. Was that the kind of trouble he meant? She looked at him and tried to wipe those reckless thoughts from her mind. Of course not. Sunam wasn't crazy and neither was she. They both knew no one was worth that kind of trouble. She tried to keep her voice light. "Hey, you're no trouble. I'm just trying not to break your heart."

"Right," he said. "I'll be watching out for you."

She hugged his arm tighter, turned her face into his coat. It should have been an affectionate, cuddly gesture, a cozy winter couple braving the elements just to spend time together. But it was more like hiding, swallowing the things she wanted to say. They sat like this for a long time, neither one of them speaking. She wished she could pitch them forward in time, intact, just like this. If only they could catapult past these obstacles, if only he could just have more faith in the future.

"It's going to be worth it." Her voice was muffled against the thick blue wool of his overcoat. "You'll see."

This was all she could say, hoping he understood.

He looked at his watch. "We'd better get going. Busan Mother will be waiting."

"This wasn't much of a date," she said apologetically. "For how expensive it was."

"Don't worry about it," he said. He got up first, brushing the errant bits of tobacco from his lap. She wished he wouldn't say that, *Don't worry about it,* as if it were remotely possible. How could anyone not worry, with so much money flying out of his pocket every week? She should have stopped it the first time. But she had been desperate to get away. More important, she had sensed his pride in being able to pay. She saw how necessary it was to accept this gift, which made up for the times he might have felt flattened by her, by Juno, by all the others who didn't matter to her.

But the actual cost of his pride, the money changing hands at the butcher to bring home the prize to Busan Mother, who did not deserve it, sent spasms of anxiety down her back. She had considered it a one-off—surely no one could afford it more than once—but Sunam continued to insist. He made it a weekly occurrence. It seemed the two of them, he and Busan Mother, were matched in a perverse partnership against her. Haggling in such a way that Namin felt she was a hostage held for ransom. How much this week? Too much. The more he paid, the more distant he seemed. Although she would never be able to pay him back, she kept a mental record of how much he had spent. An outrageous figure that grew in tandem with the baby. Both in leaps and bounds. Where did he get the money? She wished she had no idea, but she suspected Jisun must have something to do with it. Was she funneling the money through Sunam since Namin had refused to take it herself? Were they discussing her problems behind her back? Every time she thought about confronting him, she thought how humiliated he'd be at the suggestion that he wasn't capable of doing something like this on his own.

"Next week I'm busy with exams," she said. *Think of all the money you'll save.* "So I'd better stay in and study. Dori and I will be wearing matching sweatbands. I wonder if he's any good at memorizing equations."

"You sure?"

"Without you to extort, Busan Mother will be feeling lean," she said. "She'll have to eat gruel. That's satisfaction enough, isn't it?"

"She'll find a way to charge double next time," he said. "New rates for skipping a week."

She wrinkled her nose. "Let her dare."

Sunam laughed. She realized it was the first time she'd heard him laugh in a long time. Hearing the familiar sound loosened the tightness in her chest. Maybe she had been too quick to worry, too quick to succumb to the doubts and uncertainties tangled up with exhaustion. Maybe she was the one losing faith too soon.

He took her hand. "Let her dare," he said.

7
. . . .

In the beginning, Jisun thought about Peter every day.

Although she never went anywhere he was likely to be, she prepared herself to run into him, dreading and hoping in equal measure. Seoul was not an infinite city, even for two people avoiding each other with assiduous diligence. Each day she imagined facing him on the sidewalk, in a bus, at a lunch shop. The simple thought brought icy sweat to her palms, a painful pleasure like sucking blood from a cut.

Alternatively, she tortured herself with the possibility that she would never see him again, that their last encounter was already behind them at the UIM office the morning after her arrest. That, too, was unlikely. Her despair was formed on this unique paradox—that two opposite fates were equally bound to happen and that she could not be ready for either case.

For months she followed a series of superstitions, which might variously determine her future. Riding on the right side of buses. Walking with her eyes straight ahead, resisting the urge to look for him. She counted steps as she walked from corner to corner, feeling irrational bursts of triumph if she arrived at the curb on an even-number step. She believed there must be a balance of scales, some spectral reckoning to tally the marks for and against her. To give her what she deserved. Which was—what? Their relationship was irreversibly broken, yet she could not help hoping for some measure of redemption.

The idea that she could simply get on a bus and ride to the UIM annex or the steel mill where Peter met with the workers or the union office—simply *choose* to see him again—seemed inconceivable, as far-fetched as streaming to the moon.

Instead Jisun developed her own system of faith, of divining signs and symbols.

A bright red leaf planted like a hand on the sidewalk.

Three consecutive nights of dreams about the same abalone-inlaid box, which opened the first night but not in the subsequent two.

A child with a mouthful of candy crying on the street.

A bus driver who demanded absolute silence in his vehicle. A commuter crowd who miraculously obeyed.

Collecting these events, Jisun sometimes felt a flush of unity and texture in the world. A sense of possibility, if not of hope.

What did she want?

WHEN IT HAPPENED, there was Peter Lowell, waiting for her in her neighborhood. It was windy and his coat was pulled up over his ears, his long body hunched in a manner of exhausted perseverance. His hay-colored hair glowed in the streetlight. Having feared and imagined this moment for so long, Jisun expected to feel a rush of emotions—anger, relief, nervousness, joy. She braced herself for it, expecting to be wholly upended. Instead there was only a brief inward jolt, a recognition she might feel for anyone she hadn't seen in a long time.

She knew him. And yet she didn't.

Peter turned around. He opened his arms, an uncharacteristic gesture that she did not question. It didn't matter what it meant. She stepped into them instinctively.

She buried her face in the smooth weft of his coat. The smells absorbed in the wool recalled vivid memories: kerosene fires, newsprint stacked on concrete floors, garlic chopped by a blunt-edged knife. But there was also an unwashed smell she had never associated with him. Peter, who was so fastidious in his American way, who had once joked that the pleasure of the public bath was the real reason he had decided to come to Korea.

"Can we go somewhere quiet to talk?" His voice, too, sounded different from the way she remembered it, nervous and hollowed out. "Somewhere private. The topic is sensitive."

Snagging on the word *private,* Jisun examined his face. It looked puffy, the skin around his eyes heavy and bloated as if he had gained weight. But he was as thin as ever. She could see his sharply outlined shoulders, his knees pointy in slacks. Hugging him, she had sensed the angularity of his ribs, the ridges defined like bumps on a topographical map.

She said, "There's nowhere out here unless we go to my house—" And forestalling his objection: "No need to go inside as long as you don't mind the cold. It's not far."

He nodded and she blurted out, "Just like that? No lecture?" She allowed herself to smile. She should have restrained herself, but she was distracted by the changes in his demeanor. The simple fact that he was agreeing to step onto her father's property, which he would never have permitted in the past—even the fact that he had hugged her, though technically he had only opened his arms and she had hugged him first. It all suggested that catastrophic events had occurred since she'd last seen him. Changes far more seismic than their broken relationship.

She led him quickly to the house, through the high iron gate at street level and the smaller inner gate leading to the grounds. He followed without comment, allowing her to open and shut the doors as he stood by, careful not to be in the way. He must have been uncomfortable, but he walked steadily over the gravel, not attempting to mask his footfalls. That was Peter. In the past Jisun might have called it arrogance, but she saw now that it was only his nature to fight unease with a cover of certainty.

They sat under the boughs of a large fir tree. There was a bench there, granite, which felt like sitting on a slab of ice. The chill of the stone seeped through her clothing with shocking efficiency. Within a minute, she felt as exposed as if she were naked to the elements.

"Here." He motioned for them to move to the ground, which was at least insulated with years of fallen needles. They sat like this among the detritus of the fir tree, their backs against its rough bark.

Something told her Peter had not come to discuss their relationship, but she wondered if he would skirt around it. Or would he move straight to business as if they had no shared past at all?

The silence became strained. She gritted her teeth to keep them from chattering.

"They have the agents on the churches now," Peter said without preamble. "They're watching us closely."

Jisun let out her breath. Business. It was a relief to focus on the things they still had in common.

"I know," she said. He paused as if surprised but didn't ask how she knew.

"We had to suspend the meetings at the steel mill after a few of our men got a visit. Agents picked them up right in front of the building. Questioned them overnight and dropped them off in front of their homes in the morning. Timed it so their kids going to school saw their fathers kicked out on the curb like dogs.

"The bosses wanted an end to the meetings immediately," Peter went on. "So we complied. We don't force people to be responsible for us. We moved the meetings to another location. Of course only a few came. Everyone saw the black cars. They didn't want to risk being the next ones to be made examples of."

"But what did the agents say? What did they want?"

"The same things they always say," Peter said. "The same threats, the same questions. Are we communists, do we have plans to subvert the government, who are we working with? Bullying nonsense. The point is, they want the workers to be silent and uninformed. They want us to leave."

"But why now?" Jisun asked. "What's changed that they're suddenly focused on UIM? Were you doing anything different that might attract their attention?"

Peter shook his head. "The same thing we always do," he said in a weary voice. "We were working to build a coalition of workers and union leaders across industries, but that's not new. If anything we were focusing on the soft values—nothing that should raise any new alarms."

Jisun could hear the frustration mounting in his voice. Peter was knitting his fingers together so tightly, she could see the white bones of his knuckles straining against the skin. She could hear the rasp in his throat dragging at every word he spoke.

"When I came to Korea, I had no idea what to expect," he said. "Here I was halfway around the world from anything I know—and even where I'm from, I don't know much. In my high school, they took a vote. Most likely to succeed. Class clown. Most beautiful, most handsome. Do you know what they voted me for?" He didn't give Jisun a chance to answer, as if she could never guess anyway. Why— because she didn't know him well enough? Because she couldn't fathom such a thing as high school nicknames?

"Class do-gooder," he said. "Do you know what that means?"

She shook her head. "Tell me."

"It's just how it sounds. Going around doing good things, like it's my job."

She asked—was this a compliment or a joke?

"So that's the question I ask myself. Was this a compliment or a joke? The longer I stay here, the more I think the joke's on me. The more I think it was a curse. But that was such a long time ago, I think. No one can say I'm the same person I was back then. Eighteen years old, I was a baby. No one can say I came here just to be a do-gooder."

He turned to face her, his eyes enormous in the moonlight. "You used to ask me all the time, why I came here."

"I was only curious—"

"I took it as an accusation."

"Peter, we were partners. Why would I accuse you? I wasn't questioning your mission. I only meant why here? Why not closer to home? I was only curious—" She realized she was repeating herself, babbling because she could not reveal the real reason she had asked this question so often. It had been a secret idea of hers—embarrassing then and truly mortifying now—that he had unknowingly traveled across the world to meet her. A fantasy of fate bringing them together across geography and culture. It hurt to even think about it now.

"But you had the right to accuse," he says bitterly. "Because I didn't know. I *don't* know why I came here."

"Do you . . . regret coming?"

"Of course not. It's the only thing I've ever really *done* in my life."

"So you did good after all. Your classmates were right."

"You say that because you don't know what happened."

"I'd like to think I know some things, even if I haven't been—"

"You don't know," he said.

Though Peter had not raised his voice, the effect was as if he had shouted at her. Jisun forgot what she had intended to say, the rest of her sentence swallowed by his ferocious insistence.

"Is that why you came here tonight? To bully me with what I don't know?" Her hands were already icy fists in her pockets. The nails dug deeper into the meat of her palms.

He picked up a handful of needles and crushed them with a single snap. They were so dry that she could hear them crackling between his fingers. He crushed pile after pile. Needles, twigs, gravel. Crushing it all as if he wished to grind them to sand. Jisun pried open his hands and felt the smear of blood on his palms.

"We need money," he said. For a moment he looked at her almost defiantly, challenging her to say what she thought of him. After all these months of silence, to ask a thing like that. But he would not mitigate with weakness or apologies. Then he looked away, the mask slipping off. "I didn't know who else to ask."

8

The movie was a horror film Sunam had already seen, full of knives and oversize needles and a memorable climax involving a severed pig's head. Namin fell asleep within fifteen minutes, chin on her chest, oblivious to the screams both on- and offscreen. He didn't wake her. He watched the movie. The fake blood, phony the first time around, was even less convincing now. It looked shiny and plastic, as if they'd painted it on the film. The soundtrack hammered on the speakers. He and Jisun had been out late drinking the night before—not enough for a true hangover, just enough for the macabre colors and sound effects to grate on his nerves.

When the houselights finally came on, Namin jerked awake and seemed not to realize where she was. "Is it over?" People were swarming the aisles. The screen was blank. She looked at her wrist as if to check the time and laughed ruefully when she realized she wasn't wearing a watch. "What time is it?"

"You missed the whole thing."

"Was it good?"

He shrugged. "Skippable."

"Guess it's good I slept."

The movie had been her idea. She wanted to see something really gory and violent—"to get the blood moving." Now she was happy she'd slept. Maybe it was silly to let such a small thing annoy him, but Sunam struggled to contain his temper. It seemed so obvious to him that their relationship was on its last strings, but Namin seemed determined, as usual, to stay the course.

She threw her arms overhead, stretching. "Actually, it's relaxing, sleeping in a huge room full of strangers. Try it next time." She looked at him. "Don't be mad. I was so tired."

"You should have just slept at home if you're so tired."

"But I couldn't. I can't."

"Why? Busan Mother took the kid. You could have slept. You need to pull yourself together."

She stifled another yawn, then let it spread over her face, succumbing to the total pleasure of it. Tears formed at the edges of her eyes and she wiped them away, smiling. "But I wouldn't have seen you."

"But you didn't see me anyway."

While they were arguing, the theater had filled up again for the next showing. They had been alone in the theater only briefly, a sensation like being adrift at sea. Now they were surrounded again, the crowd pushing in from all sides.

"Let's just go," he said. "If we stop at the market now, you can go home and sleep for a couple more hours before you have to pick up the kid. You might as well, it's already paid for."

"No, I've slept enough," she said. "I'm fine now. I have plenty of energy. We can do something else."

"Forget it. I'm tired. I should have stayed in and studied last night. Now I'm behind."

"You never study until the last minute anyway. You always do fine. Let's go to that Chinese place you like. Or hey, I'm in the mood for a drink. Feel like getting drunk with me tonight?"

Sunam remembered the night Jisun had made a similar suggestion after a movie. *We should get good and drunk for Young Ja.* It seemed so long ago, a lifetime. He had set himself an unofficial rule: Never think about Jisun while he was with Namin. He had broken his own rule a few times, even asking Namin if she had heard anything about Jisun. In retrospect, a huge risk. The kind of bravado undertaken by fools. But otherwise he had succeeded in keeping them separate: The public Jisun, who was Namin's friend. The other Jisun, who did not exist. But today, for a reason he could not name, the edges of his life seemed to bleed together. Maybe it was the alcohol that was still in his system from the night before. Maybe the movie, though *Young Ja* had played at a different theater, in a different season. Maybe the money, which had previously seemed so fantastic that it was a thrill even to waste it. Now he felt spasms of remorse when he considered how easily he had been bought.

"Sleep, Namin," he said.

"I want to drink," she said. They were outside now, where it was already dark enough for the streetlamps even though it wasn't yet five o'clock. There was a desperate, dangerous gleam in her eyes. "Let's forget about Busan Mother and everything else and stay out all night. I know what you think—you think I'm no fun. You, Jisun, everyone. I know what people say when I'm not there, like it's funny that I have to live my life like a robot. It's not because I want to live like that. I never get to do what I want."

"Don't worry, you'll be laughing at all of us in ten years."

"It's not a joke, Sunam. I'm serious. Who were you out with yesterday?"

The sharp turn caught him off guard completely. "Yesterday? What do you mean?"

"You said you went out. Who were you with?" Suspicion flashed in her eyes. "It was Jisun, wasn't it? I know you think I don't know, but I'm not stupid. I know what the two of you are up to. Were you even trying to hide it?"

He stared at her dumbly, too stunned to speak.

The street lighting cast deep shadows under her eyes and illuminated the rough, angry patches on her skin. She was wearing the same red coat she'd been wearing when they met, and the color seemed to flare into her cheeks. Everything was just under the surface, like a terrible fire threatening to blaze up.

"I guess you were hoping I wouldn't figure it out. Well, it wasn't hard." Namin seemed angry but willing to talk, to listen. It seemed possible that it might still be all right, though he did not understand how this could be. She seemed to have captured the entire situation and accepted it as an inevitable consequence . . . of what?

"Well. Say something," she said. "I know it was her idea, but how could you go along with it?"

As if he had no part, as if he were only *going along with it*.

Even in this moment when he knew he should feel only shame and remorse, Sunam felt stung to know that Namin thought him only an accomplice. *It was me*, he wanted to say. *I did it*.

He expected apologies to fly out of his mouth. Justifications. Pleas. Denials. Instead, he heard his own voice like a distant mediator, calm and steady, explaining the situation as if all she needed was to see it from a different perspective. "It's not what you think. It's not like we're in love, it's not a relationship, Namin. She's in love with someone else, you were right about that. You were so busy and we were always talking about you. It was like we were trying to be with you, only we couldn't." He listened to himself with a kind of two-part fascination, simultaneously impressed and repulsed. A virtuoso performance, dismantling the catastrophe one point at a time.

"In love?" she said with a sharp shake of her head. Her voice teetered between confusion and clarity. "What is this? Are you saying you two are in love?"

"No. *Not* in love. Not. What we're doing, me and her, it's, it's just—" Here he stumbled because there was no way to say it without actually saying it. "It's just sex."

The wind whipped her hair across her eyes and she tore at it roughly, trying to free herself. "You're *sleeping* with her?"

"No," he said reflexively.

"*Just sex*. You just said it."

It must have been shock, Sunam thought later. They stayed rooted to their spots, facing each other like blank statues. Neither of them able to comprehend what had happened and what should happen next. He truly did not understand how it had unfurled so quickly.

"You said you knew," he said, a quiver of blame in his voice. As if somehow she had tricked him into telling the truth.

"Money," she spit out. "I thought she was giving you the money for the baby since I wouldn't take it from her myself. Where did you get it, then? All that cash?"

The money. It was only the money she had suspected. Never him, trusting him despite all the ways he'd tried to shake her faith. Sunam had never felt so unworthy.

"It wasn't from Jisun," he said helplessly. Even now when the damage was done, he could not bear to tell Namin the truth about Ahn. "That's all I can tell you, Namin. But I promise you, it was my money and she had nothing to do with it. Please, I hope you can believe me."

She stared at him for a long time, waiting for him to say more. But there was nothing more he could say. An apology was so clearly required, but it was impossible to utter the words. How could *I'm sorry* possibly mean anything to her now? The words were too cheap, absurdly inadequate. It seemed better to say nothing and simply absorb the misery of the situation than to offer the additional insult of an apology.

When she started walking back toward her bus stop, he followed because it could not end like this. She marched forward, ignoring him. They rode the bus in silence and got off together at her usual stop. They walked through the market and stopped at the butcher, where she asked for the cheapest cut of beef in a toneless voice, which the butcher strove to misunderstand. "Eh?" he said, reaching greedily for the *kalbi*, an even bigger piece than the one they had purchased last time.

"The *cheapest*," Namin said again, gripping the counter. She pointed to a thin, ropy cut. It had an unhealthy gray cast, more ligament than meat.

The butcher poked at it with his tongs, frowning. "That one? No. Not much good."

"Yes, that one. Quickly."

Sunam took out his wallet.

Namin hissed, *"Don't you dare."* She paid for the meat herself, muttering, "She wanted beef, let her have it."

He stopped near the corner where they usually turned onto her block. It seemed their entire relationship had been conducted in the street, the idea of privacy a constantly deferred future luxury. His hand brushed her elbow, the most he could manage in the way of apology. He could feel her rejecting even that tiny gesture. She did not move or say anything, but he could feel the invisible buttressing of resolve, the layers closing against him. She would despise him for the rest of her life. Worse, she would forget him as soon as she turned the corner.

"The kid needs you," he said. "I'm just getting in the way."

"Getting in the way of *what?*" Namin said with a terrible smile, white teeth dragging on the cracked flesh of her upper lip. "Spit it out, Sunam. Accuracy is important at a time like this."

"Do you want me to walk you home?"

She shook her head. "You're a coward," she said. Her eyes were dry and her voice clear. Tiny wrinkles gathered in the corners of her eyes as she sneered at his weakness. Sunam caught a glimpse of how she would look in twenty, thirty years' time. The same, he thought. She would always be the same. Unassailable and taut with infinite potential. "In my worst estimation of you," she said, "I never expected you to stoop this low."

Sunam nodded. He let her go.

With a sense of obligation, he watched her walk away, watching as long as he could. The bag for Busan Mother hung slack from her hand. When she reached the corner, she dropped it in the trash. A single swift motion, the way she always did things. Efficient. Decisive. She never looked back.

9

The money Peter needed was for the families of workers he was educating, four men accused of antigovernment activities and now awaiting trial at West Gate Prison. Charged with violating the National Security Law, each faced execution by hanging. The wives had poured their last pennies into hiring a lawyer, and every day the lawyer's changing projections whipped them between despair and hope. In the neighborhood, people were already acting as if the men were dead. Whatever their true feelings, they shut their doors, afraid the authorities would be watching for sympathizers. The children were going hungry, ostracized at school. And now the lawyer was hinting he would require further payment if the men were so lucky to have a long trial.

"And if they were so unlucky to need an appeal," Peter said, "further payment still."

Jisun said, "Did he actually say that?"

"As often as he could."

"And will the extra money make him more eloquent?"

"It will give the families courage." Peter looked at her. He seemed almost translucent with grief. "We will try—I will try—but you know it is unlikely we can ever pay you back."

"And if you did, it would be like your father paying my father, wouldn't it." She wondered if Peter had even considered asking his family for help. Or was she more convenient, someone he did not have to see again if he chose not to. And was that what he had done to them already, disappeared from his family the way he had disappeared from her?

"Is that fair?" he asked.

"I think it is. Yes," she said. "It is exactly fair."

SHE HAD TWO stipulations:

1. She would not look at any details of the account. She would sign for whatever he needed, but what he took—all or none—was up to him. He was not to tell her.
2. He would stay away from Seoul until the trial had concluded.

Peter tried to protest on the second point. "I can't abandon those men. I'm the reason their lives are at stake."

"If I give you the money, those are my conditions," Jisun said. "We both know you're not safe here. And what good will it do anyone if you're arrested too? Take the money, Peter, and come back when it's safe."

She saw him wrestling with the implications. Was it a show of control—or protection?

Love or vengeance?

Her feelings for him might have changed, but Jisun would never forget the strength of her love or the hurt of his rejection. Those residues would linger in her memory for years. *Now you know how it feels. Now you see how we're all forced to compromise.* Peter would take the money because it was the only way he could help save those families. But now he'd know what it meant to be trapped between his conscience and his pride. It was never as black and white as he thought, the decisions of love and duty.

"And that's the only way?" he asked, and Jisun knew he understood.

"That's the only way."

AT THE BANK, the teller eyed Jisun's disheveled collar and the plastic bag she clutched instead of a proper purse. He helped three other customers from adjacent lines, taking a long time with each one—a grandmother, a young housewife who daintily licked her finger before counting her money, and a taxicab driver who had the bleary, bloodshot eyes of a night-shift worker. Peter waited outside.

It was her account, which her father had once called her face to the world, but she could not remember when she had last even looked at her ledger. It was long lost; she'd have to have a new one made. It was possible that in these years of neglect the account had been emptied or closed. But Jisun wagered that being a man of unerring habit, her father had continued his practice of adding money every year on her birthday. Birthdays. Graduations. Holidays. Celebrations bypassed in favor of placing money directly into her account, like dropping gold pieces into a well.

And now she was dredging it up, an eerie feeling like stealing from a ghost, a fictional character with her name and identification number. Was it possible to steal from yourself? A police car sped past, sirens screaming. Startled, Jisun caught the inside of her cheek between her molars. Thinking they were coming for her, the thief. She poked the ragged flesh with her tongue and tasted blood.

On the other side of this transaction was freedom. Grief, sorrow, guilt, on one side. Freedom on the other.

And the cost?

With this money Peter would be connected to her forever, not as a friend or compatriot in a cause, but as her counterpart in a great debt—with all the unwilling obligation and forced decency that that relationship entailed. After this week, it was unlikely they would see each other again. But the debt would stretch between them like a lifelong tether.

Only money could do this, binding them together past the usual limits of time and distance. Persisting, whether they acknowledged it or not. As strong as blood.

Finally, the teller gestured that it was her turn. Jisun forced her legs to approach the window. No more than a dozen steps, but a huge distance, spiraling her back in time. Her mind flooded with the numbers of her childhood. The interest rate in July 1970. The spring of '71, when her father deposited and withdrew the same amount four times, testing her attention. The number 732: no other details, but the *sense* of it, recalled in her throat like a phantom fish bone.

With shaking hands, she slid her identification card and stamp through the slot. Her signature stamp, a gift from her mother, was carved from luminous jade more blue than green and shot through with white veins like sunlight over water. It was as slender as her pinky finger, but heavy like gold. Everyone, even children, had a signature stamp to mark official documents. For most children it was merely a plaything, given to them to mimic the business of adults. But Jisun's stamp was the single extravagance her mother had bestowed, an object of beauty by any measure. The actual signature had been designed by a famous calligrapher. Jisun remembered her mother had been upset that it was not more abstract and stylish, the only time she had wished for fanciness and received plainness instead.

"I lost my account book," she said.

The teller examined the jade with myopic concentration, rubbing it appraisingly with his thumb. "Real?"

"Probably just resin." Her voice sounded robotic. "Cheap."

He nodded as if to say he thought so, too. "Wait here, I have to get it approved."

As he stepped away, Jisun suddenly remembered where her old account book must be. Stashed in the cover of her high school yearbook, crammed into her bottommost drawer with the other useless mementos of childhood she had been happy to leave behind. The money—or the idea of money—had not propelled her into the future, as her father had hoped.

The same teller returned with a new book and an entirely different demeanor. A new voice. A pronounced sniffing tic, as if he thought that constituted an aristocratic manner.

"If only you would have made a sign, I would have helped you right away."

She stared. "What kind of sign?"

"Or—said something."

He slipped her stamp and ledger through the slot with a cunning, obsequious bow, using both hands to push the small objects forward. "I hope everything is entirely in order. If there is anything else——"

"Thanks."

Outside, she handed Peter the account. She watched the blood drain from his face, the transmogrification of numbers turned to money.

He dragged his eyes over her face. "You didn't look?"

"No."

"You really don't know."

"I really don't know."

"Jisun. Is this truly what you've decided? Are you sure you don't want . . . any of it?"

She shrugged. A world lifted off her shoulders. Now it was his burden. His to carry, measure, explain. She was free.

"You once said the difference between you and me—what was it? That I was willing to be rescued and you weren't? I remember, Peter. *I'm out here on my own*, you said. *I'm not looking for an almighty hand to save me if I get in trouble.* You made yourself so superior. You broke my heart.

"Take it all," she said. Because he was still waiting for permission. Still wanting an answer to his question, mistrusting her. "Does that make it clear? I've said it a hundred times and still you don't understand. That money has nothing to do with me. Take it all."

10

. . . .

Namin dragged herself to the end of the semester like a combat soldier trapped behind enemy lines, inching toward home. Exhausted beyond tears, she had no use for anything except sleep, even food a waste of time and energy better spent lying down, unconscious. She had lost so much weight that none of her clothes could be worn without the use of multiple safety pins cinching the bands at her waist. When she managed to wash her hair, she came away with clumps that wrapped around her fingers. Dreams crowded the edge of her waking mind.

The long respite of winter break would give her a chance to collect herself, to rest rather than simply survive. She scraped by the final days of exams and collapsed for nearly twenty-four hours when it was over, sleeping so soundly that she did not hear the baby wailing at her side. Busan Mother came and took him while she was sleeping. "He was choking on his tears, the poor thing," she said later when she dropped him off. "Screaming like a devil. You were dead to the world. I thought no one was home." Namin had not, in fact, noticed he was missing. Instead she had woken up in a panic, realizing that she had forgotten to attend her German final days before. She had been so consumed with her major prerequisites that she had completely overlooked the language exam. She tore out of the house wearing the clothes she had fallen asleep in the day before, not even pausing to grab a coat against the frigid weather. On the bus to campus, tears streamed down her face and dropped into her lap. Tears of terror, like a child lost in an endless dark city. Like a child, she had no plan, only hoping for rescue.

When she arrived on campus, the professor was not in her office and there was nothing to do but leave a letter begging to reschedule the test.

That night her mother called Namin into her bedroom and suggested she take a semester off. "We could use you home. We could save a little money."

For weeks she had had no tears—not even that afternoon when Sunam said *Just sex* in the street. That day she had stumbled home and waited for the tears. Waited and waited, her face completely dry. She had buried herself in quilts, her cheeks incandescent with rage. Her heart pumped to the size of a volleyball, set to explode. No tears. She had not cried for Sunam once. And now twice in one day, enormous drops fell from her eyes.

"What difference does a semester make?" Namin said. "He'll still be here in three months—it'll only be worse when he starts crawling and walking around. You'll have me staying back another semester. 'Until he's walking.' 'Until he's out of diapers.' 'Until' when?" She looked at her mother. "He's not my responsibility. Finishing college is. Our future is. That's enough for one person."

"Since you know everything, what should I do, fling him out into the street?"

"Fling him somewhere," Namin said bitterly. "Just don't fling him at me."

IN THE MORNING, her mother had deep shadows under her eyes as if she had not slept at all. Silently she watched as Namin brushed her teeth and washed her face. She handed Namin her towel, heated by the *ondol* floor in her room. Burying her face in the warm cloth, Namin wished they would all go away and leave her. She didn't need much. The minimum in food and water. A roof. Just a little quiet, so she could fix her life.

If her mother thought a warm towel would begin to change her mind—

"I heard about the Chang girl," her mother said in a low voice.

Namin didn't look up, though she understood the significance of her comment immediately. The Chang girl had gotten pregnant last year when she was only fifteen and refused to name the father despite vicious beatings from her parents. The ongoing ordeal—the secret pregnancy, the public beatings, the neighbors becoming reluctantly involved, and the bitter altercations that ensued—had captured the attention of the village for the better part of a year. Everyone heard about the Chang girl. Eventually they heard about her baby, too, the child who was so dark-skinned that the mother would not allow her daughter to breast-feed the infant for fear the color would somehow transfer. The infant was given up to an orphanage in a matter of days.

"The Chang girl" quickly became code for a certain situation. And Namin understood what her mother meant by it as clearly as if she'd spelled it out.

"Do you need me to come with you?" her mother asked, taking back the towel. It was no longer warm, hanging limply from Namin's hand.

"No, I can do it."

Her mother did not ask when she planned to go. She could do it tomorrow or she could drag it out for months.

Namin remembered that day long ago when she had played on the floor with her dolls while her mother said goodbye. Was her mother thinking of that now? And Kyungmin—wherever she was, did she ever think about that day? Another boy. Another ghost. Life was not long enough to redeem all the things you lost, and yet it would leave her stranded at the start if she did not keep up with the necessary decisions.

"I'll go next week," Namin told her mother.

"I can get more formula. If it's only a week."

IN THE WAITING room, Namin read from a textbook on viral infections. There were other pairs of adults with children, but no one spoke except when necessary to a child. Namin read about meningitis. She let a little girl, a toddler wearing yellow corduroy pants and a floppy hat, crawl over her shoes. A very old man, wearing a traditional *hanbok* and horsehair hat, held the hand of a boy who had to be at least seven years old. Too old. The boy chewed gum with a mixed expression of anxiety and pleasure.

Lunchtime passed and Dori grew restless, but no one called Namin's name. She read about influenza. She had packed a tin of rice in water, which she spooned into Dori's mouth. The utensil was too big, but he managed in his way, never having known any better. The old man and the gum-chewing boy had been called through the blue swinging door. The boy pushed the door with both hands, fingers widespread. Reveling in the novelty of a swinging door. She now saw that the grandfather, seemingly hale enough while sitting, had a painfully bowlegged, tottering gait. His skin, the color of tanned cowhide, was slick with perspiration.

A long while later, he came out alone, somehow even older and smaller without the boy at his side. Namin buried her attention in her book, erasing herself as witness. She made herself block out everyone else in the waiting room, the people who came and went through that blue door, which swallowed up children and spit out adults.

At three o'clock, when the assistant called her name, Namin had waited nearly five hours. She had long ceased trying to soothe the child and let him cry and whimper in her lap while voiceless admonitions looped in her mind. *Try. You want them to like you, don't you? Pull yourself together.* To whom these warnings applied, her or Dori, was unclear. At least he had ignorance to shield him. No culpability other than being born.

The assistant wore white rubber shoes that squeaked on the linoleum. She was dressed like a nurse even though it was not a hospital. Not much older than Namin, she had a strict, streamlined movement that made her seem far more mature and in possession of great authority. She waited while Namin gathered her things and met her at the door. Before they went any farther, she set alarmed, disapproving eyes on Dori's bottom. Her nostrils flared. "Just a minute. You can't go in like that."

So much time had passed that Namin no longer discerned his smell. Although she was grateful, this intervention was yet another humiliation, pointing out how unacceptable they were already. Namin felt as if she, too, not just Dori, were smeared with shit.

She was directed into a tiny room furnished with a cot and metal table, where she could clean him. Immediately her eyes snapped to the stack of fresh diapers. *Disposable* diapers, each one's stretchy backside stamped with a parade of lilac-toned elephants and periwinkle hearts. If the elephants had started speaking, she could not have been more astonished. Decorations on a thing designed to be filled with excrement and thrown out. She laid Dori down and changed him with deliberate slowness, savoring the pleasure of the immaculate, padded plastic. She looked at him, lying there dressed in his American diaper. Already he looked so much more valuable.

Before leaving, she ran her finger down the remaining stack, admiring its perfect white folds, counting and calculating how many days they would last if she used only one a day. One a week. She dropped Dori's soiled cloth diaper in the trash, too ashamed to bring it out with her. She would not need it after today, but it still felt wrong to leave it behind. A permanent property, traded for a disposable convenience. Such a waste.

"He must feel better now." The assistant didn't smile or touch him the way most people did with babies. She didn't direct any affection to Dori at all.

"I didn't realize we would wait so long."

"Mr. Lee will see you now."

The office smelled strongly of stewed kimchi, as if the man had finished eating it minutes before. In fact the dirty dishes were stacked by the open window, the white bowls stained with a rim of bright orange. Mr. Lee himself was a slight man swathed in an enormous shirt and brown-patterned tie that seemed to drag at his neck. He had smoky, square-rimmed glasses and thin, obedient hair that swooped over his forehead in a perfect parabolic curve.

"Birth certificate?"

Namin unfolded all the paperwork she'd brought and smoothed the pages on his desk.

"Kang Kyungmin—that's you?"

"My sister," she said quickly.

"Deceased?"

"No, of course not."

"Then?"

"Gone. In America, I think."

Mr. Lee looked at her squarely for the first time. He put down his pen, clasped his hands, and leaned slightly forward, as if to let the furniture absorb some of his great fatigue. Afternoon light flashed off his glasses and hid the shape of his eyes. Without curiosity, he said, "But you don't know."

"No."

After gathering up the papers, he handed them back to her. "Miss. This is not a babysitting service. If this is your sister's child and she is not deceased, there must be consent. I don't know how many times relatives bring in these children claiming they've been abandoned and the mothers show up a month later, a year later, demanding them back. Many times it's too late. A filthy business for everyone. Not to mention an unfortunate waste of our time and resources."

The agency man was clearly in the right, at least officially, but Namin felt as enraged as if she were the victim of targeted injustice. She had made the mistake of telling the truth about her sister, and now he was behaving as if she were the one to blame, as if he lived in a perfect world where children were never abandoned by their mothers. He had said so himself—relatives surrendered children all the time. Why, then, should he not take this child as he had the others?

"You won't be seeing his mother," she said, remembering what Kyungmin had said. "This child has no parents."

Mr. Lee licked his thumb, leaving damp prints as he flipped between pages. *"Here."* He scratched tight X marks as he talked. "And *here.* This is where we need signatures releasing the child." He squinted through his thick glasses. "You read these? They're right outside."

Namin had read about dengue fever, tuberculosis, Japanese encephalitis. She had avoided the gray brochures explaining protocols of overseas adoption. In a different context, they might have looked like travel brochures. The cover showed a flattened globe with certain countries highlighted in yellow. United States and Canada. Sweden. Germany. Netherlands. France. An icon of a *taegukki,* the Korean flag, waved jauntily within each country's border. As if by sending orphans, their country had somehow colonized these luckier parts of the world.

Namin turned Dori's face so the man could get a good look. "As you can see, he's American," she said. "Hal Jackson, that's his father's name. You could find him. Or someone who knows him. His relatives probably don't even know this child exists—and don't they have a right to know? To have a chance to claim him?" She didn't care that she was babbling. "Look at his hair," she said. "It's getting lighter every day. Maybe another GI couple, an American father and Asian mother—he's a wonderful baby. He would be the perfect child for people like that."

The man fixed his gaze on her. "You say this is your sister's child? This isn't perhaps *your* son? He looks like you. The resemblance—it's quite strong."

It was like a nightmare, one of those never-ending terrors where she was being tried for a crime she did not commit. Except this was real and she could smell the ripe vinegar scent of old kimchi from the man's lunch. She was bathed in the animal stench of her own sweat.

Namin clamped her hand around the baby's shoulder, lodging her thumb under his armpit for leverage. She swung down to grab her coat, which had fallen on the floor. On the lapel was pinned her university badge and nameplate. She raised it for the man to see. "Do you see that? Kang Namin. That's me," she said. "This child is not mine."

Did she expect him to stand up and applaud? To simper and bow and suddenly remember special policies reserved for people like her, future-heavy aunts of inconvenient babies? She had come, sacrificing the last of her pride. She might not have expected moral fanfare, but was she not entitled to a sliver of recognition for her suffering? For the injustice of having to bear the consequences of her sister's thought-lessness when *she* had tried so hard to do everything right?

She was so upset that she was nearly panting for breath, still holding up her SNU pin like a talisman against failure. But the agency man's unmoved expression was a door slammed in her face.

"Congratulations," he said mildly. "In that case I'll be straightforward. The Americans don't want mixed; we haven't placed a mixed-race child in three years. They want a Korean baby that looks like a Korean baby. Black hair. Oriental eyes. He'll be here for years waiting, watching the other ones go. You can imagine how that makes a child sullen, unattractive. Take my advice. Go home. He's better off with you."

11

There were dregs beyond dregs. At the bottom, a trapdoor revealing further depths.

Ajumma answered the door and would not let her go through to the sunroom, where she said Jisun was, without foisting on her milk in a cut crystal glass, a slice of Swiss roll cake filled with cream and strawberry jelly. "Take another one for Jisun," she insisted. "You girls have been such strangers lately."

Jisun was sitting under the leaves of an enormous potted plant, reading a paperback. She was wearing a waffle-knitted sweater, ivory, and a circle skirt the same shade of green as the glossy leaves overhead. Her hair, as usual, was wild and frizzy. She looked like a heroine in a British novel, the kind who succeeded at the end while lesser characters succumbed to disease or heartache. Normally Namin would have said as much, knowing how it would annoy Jisun. Today it seemed a barb against herself. Setting the plate on the table, she said, "*Ajumma* wants us to eat cake."

"I guess you didn't set her straight," Jisun said with a shadow of her usual smirk. Quickly, as if correcting herself: "I didn't expect to see you here."

"No, I expect you didn't. I can't stay long," she said. She had taken days to prepare the words she was going to say and weeks to convince herself to say them. She would do it quickly, like running a knife across tautly held flesh. Hesitating would only bungle it and make it worse.

Jisun's face held a mixture of apprehension and defiance. Sunam must have told her—of course he had—and if Namin did not hurry, if she gave Jisun even half a chance, she would have to say something about it. Quickly, quickly. Namin took a long, shuddering breath. It was on the tip of her tongue, already wanting to be taken back and swallowed forever. She must say it before time ran out.

"You offered to help me hire a girl for the baby and I said no. But I was wrong about it. I want to change my answer. I'd like to take the money. Soon, before the semester starts."

That was everything. What she needed. When, so there was no confusion. And since she was begging: a brief clear acknowledgment of error, a bowing down. Surely Jisun would not demand more than that.

She knew immediately.

"Oh, Namin," Jisun said. Her face was stricken, as if she were the one on the verge of being denied and humiliated. Namin wanted to turn around and flee, save herself from what was coming.

"The money's gone," Jisun said. "I don't have it."

Namin saw her as if from far away: Jisun, standing in a glass room surrounded by plants of rare, outrageous value. Wearing a skirt in the dead of winter. In a mansion dug into the same mountain that also housed the president. And she didn't have the money.

Namin could not stop the hot tears slipping down her cheeks. They were on her chin before she realized she was crying.

Jisun stood up to come to her.

She put up a hand. "No, don't."

"Couldn't you have come sooner?" Jisun said, standing the safe distance away. She had let the book fall to the ground.

"Sooner?" Namin said, bewildered. "I came as soon as I could."

SHE WOULD HAVE let herself out through the glass door, to the terrace and around the garden to the gate, which she knew how to operate. It was the easiest and most direct exit, saving her the route back through the house, through the long hallways lined with vases, the intricate parquet floor undulating with its ceaseless pattern.

Only she couldn't. It would have seemed too natural, too familiar.

As if they were friends possessing the details of each other's lives and homes. No. She was a solicitor, and solicitors used the front door.

Namin retraced her steps. She was so tired. She carefully closed every door behind her and walked the dead center of each hallway, favoring neither the left nor right displays of precious objects. She did not run. She said goodbye to *ajumma*, who, seeing her leave so soon, raised both eyebrows like a startled scarecrow and tried to feed her another slice of cake, a cup of tea.

She had left Dori with Busan Mother with the promise that she would not be more than two hours. She was vaguely, laboriously, aware of the fact that someone else in her position might not go back so promptly. What might that person do? That person who was not her, but who was in her exact position? Namin didn't know. Perhaps that person would walk and walk until she was emptied of every thought. Perhaps she would drink herself into a stupor. Or collapse on a prominent intersection and wait to be rescued. Perhaps that girl would take up playing banjo or read Tolstoy on the lawn of the quad or throw herself in the river.

Namin, numb to possibilities, did none of these things. She rode the bus to her neighborhood. She arrived at Busan Mother's door. Exactly ninety-six minutes had passed since she had dropped him off.

"Back so soon?" In the past, Busan Mother always made sure to come to the door holding Dori, as if she had not put him down for a second for all the hours she was away. Now, as there was no *kalbi*, she did not bother to flatter her with charades. The baby was probably at the bottom of a heap of her youngest daughter's dolls. The child had lately discovered the miracle of stacking, and Dori was always the first layer underneath it all: dolls and doll clothes. Regular clothes. Pillows. Last time the child had buried him and gone out to play, forgetting all about her earlier game. Dori was so quiet at the bottom of that mound, it was half an hour before Busan Mother thought to unearth him there.

"Another test?" Busan Mother asked. Last time, Namin had left him to take her rescheduled German final. She had been gone four hours and Busan Mother had hinted that the food from her parents' cart, however nice, was a disappointing trade. "Considering our earlier arrangements," she'd said, "this seems somewhat . . . lacking.

"I suppose you'll be a doctor soon enough. Making big money, eh? Hope you remember your old neighbor Busan Mother. Hope you don't grow too important to say hello to her in the street. Oh, I suppose you'll be living somewhere much fancier by then."

It was not just idle banter, and Namin knew Busan Mother expected to be paid. If not now, then later. In that later future, when Namin was someone worth knowing.

"So I wonder, do we have a deal?"

"What kind of deal, Busan Mother?"

"Oh, we don't have to be so official. Don't be so alarmed, child. Just a little joke between neighbors."

So it was an open-ended deal, this little joke between neighbors. Unbounded and liable to drag into her future as far as Busan Mother could sink her pointed nails. But what else did she have with which to barter? Her future was the only valuable thing Namin owned.

"No test today, Busan Mother," Namin said. "Just—an appointment."

"A date?" The thick skin of her nostrils flared with eager anticipation. Another *kalbi* suitor? Or the same? No matter, she would take what came.

"No."

One of the children appeared with Dori, and Busan Mother plucked him up before Namin could do it herself. She cradled the baby possessively, her hips turned away from the door.

"Too bad. Haven't seen that nice boyfriend of yours lately. I thought he was quite the keeper. Go catch that handsome boy before someone else snatches him up," she said. She switched Dori to the opposite hip as if to add punctuation to her advice. "Remember, I can watch this one for you anytime. He's no trouble. No trouble at all."

. . .

NAMIN NO LONGER seemed to sleep. Her eyes were perpetually open. Her mind was a solitary machine, whirring with great effort in an empty room. The product was survival. Was she surviving?

It was the year of the sheep, that dull-faced creature whose gray wool was always bunched with dung. A zodiac year seemingly designated for suffering. A year to endure, not live. In the Kang household there was no special food or celebration for the New Year, which seemed a grotesque expenditure of energy no one wished to spare. Namin's father went alone to the family's grave site to pay respect to his parents, as if by leaving the rest of the family behind, he could trick the ancestors into overlooking the missing daughter and orphaned grandchild. He returned before dark with *soju* on his breath, the trip made so quickly that Namin dimly wondered if he had even gone at all.

They were sheep, driven back by the tiny being eating, sleeping, pulsing, at the center of their house. Rooms became closed doors, cells. Namin learned to read in the courtyard with a flashlight, dressed in all her warm layers and her quilt lashed around her shoulders like an Everest explorer. The cold froze her eyes wide open and kept her from falling asleep, which was how she would die if she was not mindful. Every night she survived was a feat against nature, against herself. In the morning icicles variously dripped or broke, grew longer and twisted or wider and smooth. The child stubbornly expanded. He grew hair that curled up from his skull. He was a striver for things just beyond his reach, his fists grabbing air with misplaced certainty.

For the sake of survival, they were all suffering. The flashlight batteries died out and she switched to an oil lamp, which had the benefit of heat but created new hazards. Freezing to death. Death by burning. She imagined a scenario in which she first froze, then burned. She could not remember when she'd last slept more than two hours at a time. All the hours the baby slept was sacred time for studying. All the hours he was awake was time she had to bargain and steal, shutting her ears to his demands, shutting her eyes to his needs. A child could grow, she realized, with such minimal encouragement. You never knew how indestructible an infant was until you held his life in your hands.

In the night sometimes he sputtered and coughed. Namin heard him vaguely as she studied on her Everest perch. He sputtered and coughed and righted himself again, resuming that silent slumber that still held a pitch, inaudible to everyone except the one who was listening, dreading the interruption. Her jagged mind braced against the wail, which was always ringing in her ears even when there was nothing to hear.

In their future house, she and Hyun would build a movie room lined with aisles, each seat convenient to come and go. They would line all four walls with screens, each playing a different film.

Choose, he'd say.

I'll watch this one for a while.

Then I'll watch it with you.

She had once seen a young woman seated at the back of the theater, directly below the projector's window. A young man stood by her wheelchair through the entire film. When it was over, he carried her in his arms like a bride while someone else brought the folded wheelchair the half flight down to street level. She had been wearing a skirt the color of marigolds that gathered below her knees as he held her. A dazzling skirt, like something out of an Audrey Hepburn film. On her wrist was a thin gold chain that glinted in the light. Namin remembered that touch of embellishment, a humble luxury that seemed the embodiment of all her aspirations.

Wouldn't it be enough? A normal theater with one screen, where they could watch the film together at the back. She would not mind standing for the entire movie. A theater with no stairs and double-wide doors. Namin remembered there must have been a car waiting to pick up the marigold bride. A bus had steps and would not endure the delay of a handicapped procession.

They, too, must have a car, she and Hyun. At least money for the taxi, both ways. And it must not seem so costly as to distract from the enjoyment of the movie.

A gold chain. A car.

She was like Dori grasping at air.

In the night, the oil lamp flickered and showed her everything she did not know. The endless pages to slip into the exhausted caves of her brain. The long road left to go.

Epilogue

At graduation, someone set off a smoke bomb during the valedictorian's speech, and the poor guy—Sunam never knew him—screamed and crouched behind the podium as if he believed himself the target of an assassination attempt. It had been over a year since President Park's assassination by his chief of intelligence, but in the audience the gist of the boy's panic was immediately clear to the graduates. They snickered loudly at his reaction. Sunam, too, laughed at the comments, circulating thicker than the smoke. "Who does he think he is?" "That's what happens when your head gets so big, you think every shot and bang has your name on it." "Must be pretty nice to feel so important."

The bomb put up a good show at first, but it was small and homemade, emitting just a single column of dirty gray smoke that dissipated quickly into the clear sky. Only the smell—powdery, damp, and faintly sulfuric—lingered and blew back into the stands. Behind Sunam, someone joked that the lasting feature of his university education would be the ability to differentiate among various explosions by scent. "Better leave it off your résumé" was the wry response.

The university president had taken over the podium and commanded everyone to return to their seats. He gripped the microphone with a white-gloved hand and seemed to wish he had a gavel to pound. His satin fist gleamed ineffectually, bouncing on the podium. Still, order was quickly restored. Only the students in the front rows had had time to scramble from their seats, and they gamely complied, straightening upset mortarboards and mimicking the speaker's frantic response. (*Ahhhh! I'm hit! Am I bleeding?*) Someone said, "If only we had known he had such quick reflexes, we would have made him short-stop." In the commotion, the three bomb setters had loped off, shedding their robes like black shrouds. Two of them managed to slip away, unimpeded. Uniformed guards tackled the last and dragged him away.

The president made the humiliated valedictorian start his speech again. He rushed through it in breathless, high-pitched agony and spent the rest of the ceremony onstage staring glumly into the crowd, flinching at any sudden noise.

Namin had been the previous year's valedictorian, graduating a year early just as she'd planned. Sunam hadn't heard her speech. By that time, they hadn't seen each other in over a year. Recently he had run into a mutual friend, Yumee, a pretty dance major who had married a commercial pilot. She now dressed like a stewardess in navy skirt suits and bouffant hairdos—too bad, because she had been sexier before in her wrap skirts and loose hair. She mentioned Namin was in medical school, then gave a frightened little gasp, apparently believing herself the perpetrator of a tremendous social blunder. "I forgot—you two used to date, didn't you?"

"It's all right," he said. "It was a long time ago."

"But *still*," the other girl said reproachfully.

Sunam laughed. "Still—what?"

She didn't answer, but the implication was that he must be heartbroken—*still*—after all this time. He wasn't offended at Yumee's assumption that Namin had thrown him over. Everyone thought that, which was better than the truth.

Many decades later, Sunam would open the newspaper in a foreign country and read that Namin had been appointed the minister of health under the new populist president. The first female cabinet member of the Republic of Korea.

At expat reunions and alumni functions, people he had barely known even when they were classmates would suddenly recall—after a few beers and in the service of cheap nostalgia—the flimsy trivia of Sunam having once dated the current minister of health. *I'm sure it's a terrible life, public service,* they'd say, extravagantly patting his back. Meaning, of course, the opposite. It was just a joke—the hilarity of having passed up on such a life. *Imagine, if things had been just a little bit different,* they seemed to say. *Imagine.*

According to the newspaper bio, Namin had married a fellow doctor. A pediatric oncologist, who donated twenty-five percent of his time to pro bono cases. The couple lived with her younger brother, who had become something of an icon for the rights of disabled people. The article mentioned no children.

Not every day. Not even once a year anymore. But sometimes, he'd catch a glimpse of a young woman with a certain silhouette—a red coat and a brisk, wistful set to her mouth—and there would be that dip of vertigo. The calcified edge of regret.

Guilt, for Sunam, was never that full-bodied tragedy that could derail a life. Just a silent companion. A brief weight dragging at his heels sometimes. A ghost.

HE SAW JISUN briefly at graduation. The ceremony had ended and he had just pinned the corsage on his mother's lapel. His brothers, looking solemn and itchy in their best clothes, had passed around the mortarboard so frequently between them—half mocking the novelty of it and half in awe of the honor it represented—that the inner cardboard was no longer stiff, but clammy with sweat. Jisun had stepped out of the crowd and offered to take their photo. He had nodded as if they had no reason to be awkward with each other. The whole family—his parents, his brothers, his aunts and uncles and grandmother—had clustered tightly around him, each holding someone's elbow or hand or leaning over a shoulder. His mother had treasured that photo. He still had it, framed, in a drawer somewhere, the color faded and blotchy now. Sometimes he took it out and looked at it. The picture memorialized the fact that he had given his mother a corsage of yellow roses tied with a glaring pink ribbon. In his memory, the roses had been pink and the ribbon ivory white.

After taking the photo, Jisun had returned the camera to his uncle and they had stood apart from the family and congratulated each other like children being made to apologize after a fight. "You should write. I'm a good pen pal," she had said, because he was beginning his military service in the fall. He had probably agreed and never done it. Then, with nothing else to say, they had talked about Namin, skating around what had happened and trying to behave as if any discomfort were long behind them.

"Have you seen her recently?"

"Maybe if I went to the library more often," he'd joked. But actually he had avoided the library, convinced he would run into her if he so much as crossed the threshold.

"Not after . . . what happened?" she'd said.

He shook his head.

It was painful to speak of those months. He and Jisun had continued to see each other through the end of the semester and once or twice around the New Year. It was Jisun who first received the terrible news about Dori. He, in turn, had heard it from her.

That winter had been brutally cold, the streets treacherous with black ice. Everyone complained of the skyrocketing cost of coal; radio programs covered the plight of poorer families who could not afford to heat their homes. Sunam realized that Namin's family would have been among those struggling. And the baby had gotten sick.

"They did everything they could for him," Jisun had said. "Nine days in the hospital. I don't know how they paid for it."

Sunam would never forget the stricken look on Jisun's face, which mirrored his own shock and sorrow. Inexplicably, he felt tied to Dori's death, as if he had been somehow complicit in this tragedy. He had not done enough to help. He had let the child down. He had let so many people down. He knew without question that Jisun felt this same guilt. This mixed-up grief.

"Have you seen her? How is she?" Sunam had asked. It would be a long time before either of them could say Namin's name to each other. "She" was more than enough to signal whom they were talking about.

"I went to see her, but she wouldn't let me in. The neighbor told me what happened. You know her? They call her Busan Mother?"

"Yeah," he'd said. "I know her."

They must have left it at that. He couldn't remember ever speaking of it again.

When Jisun had cut it off shortly after that, Sunam was more relieved than disappointed. If she knew about the meeting in her father's office, the money that had so easily found its way from the black lacquered box into his hands, she never gave any indication. The way information seemed to leak strategically between father and daughter, he would not have been surprised if she knew. Perhaps it had benefited Ahn to tell her, perhaps not. Sunam never asked.

He packed the remainder of the money in a battered old sock at the bottom of his dresser, where it stayed when he left home for his military service. A part of him hoped it would be gone when he returned, accidentally thrown out by the maid. But it was still there when he got home, less crisp than he remembered, softened by humidity and the passing of several rainy seasons.

In that first listless year after military service, when his life sputtered and stalled with the lingering remnants of overgrown adolescence, Sunam asked after Jisun and heard she had gone abroad. She was studying economics and German literature at the University of Chicago.

"It snows in April here," she wrote from America on blue airmail stationery. A single sheet folded in thirds to form an envelope she could simply affix with a stamp and mail. "There is a deep lake that looks bluer than our ocean."

He applied to half a dozen graduate programs in the United States and three in Europe. He was accepted at just one, the master's of business administration at Notre Dame, which turned out to be less than two hours' drive from Chicago.

It took him four years to complete the MBA with a concentration in international finance. He saw Jisun a handful of times during that period, and it occurred to him that they might rekindle their former relationship. But she had changed since their university days. She was quieter now and more serious, absorbed in her studies and running a local chapter of a national charity that distributed laundry and public transportation vouchers to the poor and homeless. In time, she moved in with a philosophy lecturer, a bearded Australian who called her "love." They invited Sunam over for dinner, where they ate improvised kimchi and toasted with *soju* that the Australian had hunted down for Jisun.

"Are you really going back to Seoul? You won't regret it now that you've had a taste of the 'foreign' world?" she asked him, smiling. He heard a glimmer of her former SNU voice, when it was never clear where the joke ended and the knife edge of truth began.

It was Sunam's last semester at Notre Dame and he had already accepted a position back in Seoul with a British bank eager to expand its holdings in the Asian market. They would start him at the Gangnam office but hinted at opportunities for a Hong Kong transfer, where he might rise more quickly through the ranks. While he was not comfortable here in the States, so far from everything he understood, Sunam found himself attracted to the idea of Hong Kong, of living just beyond the periphery of his home country, close enough to peer over its shoulder if he wished.

"I haven't adapted here as well as you," he told Jisun, partly to flatter her but mostly because it was true. There were things he loved about America—the broad public spaces, the avenues effortlessly lined with trees that had never seen war, the way drivers waved each other through intersections rather than trying to ram their vehicles into traffic if there was even an inch of room to spare. He was awed by the brightly lit supermarkets, the seemingly endless aisles of mystery food. The young mothers who seemed in constant dialogue with their children, even the ones too young to reply.

But these were details he collected in order to report to his family back home, a kind of prerecorded memory in anticipation of leaving. He would never relax here the way Jisun seemed to, soothed by the diversity of neighborhoods and people. She was content to mingle and sometimes disappear, a drop in the giant pot. For him, America was too big, too boundaryless. He was acutely aware of his own lack of history here, his existence as rootless as the leaves that fell in fiery, mountainous heaps each November.

"And you—will you stay?" he asked Jisun. He could not bear to use his broken English with her, always addressing her in Korean even when there were only other English speakers present. She answered in English, for the Australian's benefit.

"I don't know if I'll stay here forever, but I won't return to Seoul," she said.

"Won't your father be disappointed?"

She smiled. "I've done my degree. He is contractually forbidden to be disappointed."

He nodded, not quite sure what she meant by that comment but unwilling to pursue it. When it came to Ahn, there were secrets he had no wish to uncover.

Sunam returned to Seoul in the summer of 1988—to a country drunk with Olympic fervor and high on the limelight of international attention. He put in his hours at the office, taking lunch with everyone else, each meal a great migration of dark-suited men trailing fumes of garlic, cigarettes, and chili. Meals followed by compulsory after-work drinks, followed by promotions, followed by more hours at the office. More meals, more drinks.

He allowed himself to be introduced to a suitable wife. He had a son. Was it enough?

At some point, he ceased asking himself the question.

HE PLAYED THREE times a week now, an old-timer at the *baduk* club in Central, Hong Kong, where the young guys played with music blaring into one ear. The little white earbuds broadcast the tinny bass line of whatever American or Korean pop they were listening to these days. After the first few weeks, Sunam gave up making small talk and motioned for them to put in both buds if they wanted.

"Sure?" they asked in English. He nodded, sure, sure. More than the music, he was annoyed by the automatic judgment on his Cantonese, which was not so bad, he thought. Better, in fact, than his English.

He won most games easily. They were beginners, drawn to *baduk* by some idea of sharpening their business skills, honing the killer instinct. Maybe some boss of theirs, a big-shot managing director, had shamed them into thinking more in terms of risk. He knew the words that activated this bunch, words that had suddenly lit up their corner of the world with unforeseeable success. *Capital. Leverage. Outsize returns in volatile emerging markets.* They came into the club dissecting the latest trades they'd put on, talking in single-digit numbers that really meant millions or billions. None of them were even thirty. They wore Hermès belts and custom suits with the dry cleaner's tag still stapled to the inner label. They read *The Art of War* and the biography of Steve Jobs, quoting from both as if success were only a matter of gaining a critical mass of ego.

This was a new generation that would have pleased his old *sunbae*, Juno. And like Juno, they saw their careers spike early and flame out just as quickly, the rest of their lives left murky and blank ahead of them. The 1980s had been loud with talk about Juno heading up massive construction contracts for Ahn in Saudi Arabia, Kuwait, and Libya, where a generation of Korean laborers worked through the night in continuous shifts while their Western competitors slept or demanded costly safety precautions. Newspapers speculated as to Juno's future in Ahn Kiyu's *chaebol*, printing his photo next to Min's, the playboy heir apparent. But before long, new faces replaced Juno's, a revolving door of bright young men Ahn used to keep his empire fresh.

"How long you been in Hong Kong?" the young men asked Sunam. They didn't know not to tap the board with their finger, not to shuffle the stones in their cupped fists as if they were preparing to throw dice. *This is not Macau*, he wanted to say. *Not Las Vegas.* But there wasn't a still-sitting one among them, not in this under-thirty crowd. They were all amped up: finger-tapping, leg-shaking, gum-chewing, mobile-phone-checking machines. Their lean, efficient bodies generated a constant excess of energy, conditioned as they were for prosperity. How long had he been in Hong Kong?

"Sixteen. No, seventeen years."

"Like it here?"

His wife had stuck it out for three years, the contract of his original transfer, then returned to Seoul with their boy when he reneged on his promise. The boy was fifteen now, halfway through high school, and his mother fasted and prayed at every temple in Seoul, asking Buddha for a second-generation legacy at SNU. Separated fourteen years, they had never divorced. She was a farsighted woman, spartan in her own needs but willing to use any resource toward the boy's future. She treated their son as if he were a burgeoning economy requiring heavy interference: tutors, special programs, trips abroad, and a wardrobe worthy of Prince William.

Did he like it here? The fiddle-footed young men were waiting for his answer. "Like? It's business."

They nodded, replacing their earbuds. Familiar story.

He walked home after a game or two, stopping to have a drink if he felt too alert and pessimistic about sleep. His wife allowed the boy to spend summer and winter vacations here with him, emphasizing—as if some other benefit were required—the advantage of his hearing and learning Chinese in its proper elocution. "Speak it at home. *No Korean*," she instructed. "And make sure he does his work. No slacking." As if Sunam were just another tutor, those ungodly extortionists charging mortgage rates by the month. Of course, he and the boy disregarded her completely: they spoke Korean, and sloppily. They watched kung fu movies (with the subtitles on). He allowed beer within reason, but not cigarettes. The boy was lazy—as Sunam had been at his age—but bright and easy, somehow unfettered by his mother's claustrophobic ambition. He would get into SNU if that's where he wanted to go.

Certain days, when the sky was clear, Sunam crept up to the roof exit in his high-rise apartment and climbed the stairs marked clearly with forbidding signs. The ledge was high, not dangerous, unless someone wanted it to be. He rarely looked out over the city, though the view at this height was panoramic, a galaxy of human achievement. Instead, he lay on his back with his face turned north, instinctively searching out Ursa Major and Minor. A long time ago on an important day, someone had pointed it out. *Let's look for that bear-y thing.* He never remembered if they had seen it.

Acknowledgments

Thank you to my agent, Suzanne Gluck, for some of the most exciting, unforgettable days of my life. Thank you, Clio Seraphim, for your guidance throughout this process. The amazing folks at Random House have been a dream to work with. Thank you, Andy Ward, for the brilliant suggestion of the title. Thank you, Rachel Ake, for the gorgeous cover design. My endless gratitude to Avideh Bashirrad, Jessica Bonet, Susan Kamil, Leigh Marchant, Sally Marvin, Shona McCarthy, Kaela Myers, Melissa Sanford, Lucy Silag, Sona Vogel, and Alaina Waagner for their enthusiasm and hard work. Enormous thanks to my editor, Andrea Walker, who is a superhero and made this book immeasurably better.

I am indebted to many books for historical research, but two in particular were essential: *The Making of Minjung: Democracy and the Politics of Representation in South Korea*, by Namhee Lee, and *Korean Workers: The Culture and Politics of Class Formation*, by Hagen Koo.

Thank you to the writers, faculty, staff, and director of the NYU MFA program. Particular thanks to Emily Barton and Susan Choi, who are inspiring, generous humans in addition to being brilliant writers and teachers. Thank you, David Lipsky, for such relentlessly careful readings of my work—I still debate whether to use "the" or "a" (not to mention all the other word choice dilemmas) in certain sentences because of you. Thank you, Aleksandar Hemon, for your class on editing, which changed how I think about writing.

Thank you to my first writing teacher, Anya Ulinich. Your humor and encouragement gave me so much courage. Thank you to fellow

"Anya's Kids," Jason Merrell and Lori Azim, who are the closest people I have to office mates with our online shenanigans. I would be much less cheerful without your wacky loveliness.

Thank you, Geoff Sledge and Alex Demille, for including me in your writing group when I was too shy and afraid to actually share anything. Thank you for reading early drafts: Patty Pryor Skinner, Brigette Roth Smith, Connie Shulman, and Margaret O'Connor. Thank you, Lisa Mecham, for your generous friendship and Skype chats. Thank you, JiYeon Kim, for our shared childhoods of compulsive book reading and intrigue-heavy letter writing.

I might have been in danger of spending my life obsessively reading in a dark room if not for my family, who are the funniest, most ingenious and life-loving group of people. All my love to the Kim/ Hwang family: Yookeun, Soo Jin, Yena, and Gideon. Big hugs to Allison Wuertz and the Portsmore family: Lauren, Matthew, Madelyn, and Alexa. Love and gratitude to Christine and Frank Wuertz, truly the best, most supportive and generous parents-in-law on the planet. I am incredibly lucky to be your daughter-in-law. Thank you to my *immo* and *immobu,* Juwon Koo and Mansup Chun, for the stories. This book would have been far less fun (to write and read) without your detailed memories of the 1970s. Giant thanks to my parents, Young Il and Jaseup Kim, who are the most intrepid people I know. Thank you for raising me with so much love, courage, and faith. This book is my heart for you.

None of this would have happened without the crazy love and endless support of my husband, Rob. Thank you for believing this could happen, and for giving me every opportunity to carry it through. All the best, most fun and delicious things in my life are because of you and us, and I don't know how I got so lucky.

Hello, beautiful Emmett! Thank you for being born. You've made me incredibly happy.

About the Author

Yoojin Grace Wuertz was born in Seoul, South Korea, and immigrated to the United States at age six. She holds a BA from Yale University and an MFA from New York University. She lives in northern New Jersey with her husband, son, dogs, and chickens.

yoojingracewuertz.com
@gracewuertz

About the Type

This book was set in Fournier, a typeface named for Pierre-Simon Fournier (1712–68), the youngest son of a French printing family. He started out engraving woodblocks and large capitals, then moved on to fonts of type. In 1736 he began his own foundry and made several important contributions in the field of type design; he is said to have cut 147 alphabets of his own creation. Fournier is probably best remembered as the designer of St. Augustine Ordinaire, a face that served as the model for the Monotype Corporation's Fournier, which was released in 1925.